The Last Time I Saw Alice

A Novel By
Richard Kirschenbaum

The Last Time I Saw Alice
By Richard Kirschenbaum

Published by
TEXAS MULESHOE PRESS™
An imprint of
THE OLD WEST COMPANY™
5118 Village Trail Drive
San Antonio, Texas 78218

Tradepaper (ISBN-13): 978-1-7320072-9-1
Tradecloth (ISBN-13): 978-1-7320073-6-9
Printed and bound in the United States of America

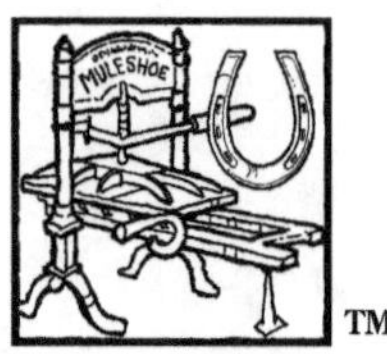

TEXAS MULESHOE PRESS™
SAN ANTONIO, TEXAS

THE LAST TIME
I SAW ALICE

By Richard Kirschenbaum

For that glorious time of WASP Goddesses,

fast convertibles,

endless summer twilights,

and incredible women like my wife Danielle

who can still keep a straight face

when their pathetic husbands swear

that it all really happened.

Not an hour goes by, I don't stare at the sky,

while I sit and compose silly rhyme.

With dreams torn asunder, I'll wistfully wonder,

where you are at that moment in time.

—B .B. Taylor: Gloriann

TABLE OF CONTENTS

TABLE OF CONTENTS

I.
YES,
YOU CAN GO HOME AGAIN

1. ELEVENTH STREET 1980

The white frame house where we once lived still stands on Eleventh Street in Michigan City, Indiana. It's on that mile-long stretch where wide pavement is cut clean down the middle by tracks of the Chicago, South Shore, and South Bend Railroad, and where front lawns are compressed slivers of brownish green.

It wasn't unusual once, to have your own personal railroad instead of a real front lawn to mow, but by the time we lived there, it was. There might have been one or two other streets like the Eleventh then, where several hundred tons of train trundled through your life two-dozen times a day, but there's not one such phenomenon anywhere else in all of America now.

Days there still start at four in the morning with a six-coach Westbound to Chicago. Sleep through it is a province of the deaf or the dead.

Among other things, it makes for cheap real estate with a helping of magic thrown in for those of us who knew what we were getting, and I have no doubt that anyone who's ever lived there did. We were, and for life, remain the track people.

There are three traffic lights on that stretch of street where unlucky trains must still halt for a red.

The station, where I first saw Alice, is still there too, on the north face of Eleventh just a quarter block east of the stoplight at Franklin. It's boarded up now, for sale I'm told, its tasks given over to a glass shack with three sides that's quite useless in winter.

But it was all a long way from that the evening in April 1980 when I returned to Eleventh Street from Texas to discover that indeed you can go home again.

There's little to it really.

It's like nothing so much as square dancing on a minefield that's been lying under clover for a couple of decades. You need only be dumb enough to do it and the rest happens all by itself.

2. THE GLASS DRAGONFLY

Usk had descended on Eleventh Street when I stepped off my own personal railroad by the Franklin Street Station. It was a bad choice for a man on the lam since it likely be on a list of places to watch. But the call to Max, my lawyer that I'd made from Chicago had convinced me that a window of two or three days existed before any serious hunt for me began. I'd have time for the stiff ones I'd been thinking about since long before the call to Max.

I'd come "home" for the express purpose of getting the money to disappear or "go fugitive" as Max had put it. I had but a single prospect: my stepmother Lola, someone with far more reasons than not to say "no." But I couldn't remember the last time Lola had said "no" to me.

My approach required little rehearsal.

"Mom," I would say to her, "I'm out on bail pending a new trial but on the advice of Max my lawyer, I'm headed for parts unknown and a new identity. I can't risk a trial and going back to prison. I wouldn't last a month there. I need money and if you give it to me you will likely never see it or me again but you will save my life." And Lola would help me, Lola would.

That could wait, the drinks couldn't. Probably it was unreasonable to expect the bar on the West side of Franklin, just south of Eleventh, to be where I'd last seen it twenty years before, but there it was, and open at that.

I couldn't remember what it was called then and it might have had a dozen names since. But on that night in April a large red neon insect, wings fluttering and green two foot high letters over the entrance announced it was now *The Glass Dragonfly*.

It was not twenty, but twenty-two years since the first and only time

I'd been inside, too young to either drink or buy cigarettes, my mission then. I had been promptly ejected. I'd remember nothing about what it looked like inside, but that night in 1980 a soft green neon fog fell on an assortment of mirrors, plastic laminate counters, booths, and stools, all of them trimmed in leatherette and chrome. At least a dozen Lexan dragonflies hung from wires twirled slowly about in a draft from ceiling fans. The place offered a kind of warm intimacy despite the fact that there wasn't a scrap of wood to be seen anywhere.

My thirst included none for droplets of the past, when I noticed the bartender who'd thrown me out so many years before and aborted my cigarette habit at sixteen, was working that night.

His tattoo, a large Marine corps eagle, now more of a red green blur in a forest of hair and the thing my eyes had locked on to when he pushed a very young me none too gently through the door, was the tip off. Other vague features, the ape like forearms and oversized nostrils cinched the image. He may well have saved me from nicotine enslavement though I doubt it was anything but the by-product of his fondness for kicking smaller people around. And my alcohol budget had no allocation for tips. I meant to drink up every last cent of it. Wordless, he asked for my order with an index finger pointed obliquely.

"Rye whiskey," I replied, "you know, American Pie?" He whistled the first bars of the then nine-year-old hit.

"I hear that number forty times a month," he offered, pointing at a Wurlitzer jukebox replete with moving bubbles in glass tubes.

"Would not playing it pass for a tip?" I smiled having no intention of playing it or as I said before, tipping him. He read that like the flashing neon of the sign outside. His face hardened.

"I didn't say I was tired of it, and nothing but cash money passes for a tip here, Mr. Shitheel."

Great, I could leave now, find another bar, or expect slow service and weak drinks. There are things you don't trifle with.

He returned with my drink after enough time to mix five of them. There are things you don't trifle with.

"Addison July," he said, setting it down in front of me. I stared straight ahead making no acknowledgment. It hadn't been phrased like a question.

"Are you Addison July?"

"Why?" For someone who wished to disappear, I'd already left a trail of gasoline awaiting a spark.

"Because if you are, this drink is paid for—if not, it's $2.75."

I nodded, expecting him to demand identification. Instead he turned in the direction of a man my age at one o'clock, taking twelve as straight ahead of me, and signified my "yes" with a nod of his own to the one o'clock man who offered a wave that I returned. He was sitting almost directly below one of the Lexan dragonflies. His wave melted into one of those "come-here" orbits for which he was smart enough not to employ a crocked finger, a gesture near the top of my hate list. I walked toward him in a gait intended to signal he was being a bother and should consider coughing up the price of at least one more drink.

Recognition came at about ten feet from the buyer of my rye whiskey.

His face was one of those that were puffy and bony at the same time, although the last time I'd seen it, it had only been bony. Now it offered up both in a somewhat juxtaposed conflict. The hair, curly once, was curly still, though it had receded to about two thirds of its original acreage, and approaching from the side, I noticed a fleshy hubcap peeking through the back. I remembered that he'd once been about my own height, five foot-nine. But because he was sitting and slightly heavier, I couldn't tell his present height for certain. He might have a few inches on me or I on him. He wore some kind of light denim apparel that I pegged as sailing gear by the yachtsman cap parked on the bar in front of him.

His name was Ralph Falonhurst. Since his name was anglicized from Falstein before he was born, I suppose you could have called Falonhurst his real one.

There was one additional item. He reeked of cologne that had once been sprayed on me in a department store without being asked by a salesgirl who must have figured her looks could sell anything. It was called *Eternal* and was well named because it couldn't have better aped the scent of decomposition.

"Long time, no see," said Mr. Rye Whiskey. I remembered that among other things, Ralph could summon up the tritest bromide to suit any occasion. The talent hadn't abandoned him.

"I guess luck's run out for us both," I countered, deciding that my cliché was a less worn one than his.

"No one told me you were in town," Ralph countered.

"You're the first to know. And I'd like you to be the last."

"Felix was the first," said Ralph," gesturing to the bartender. He was right. All of La Porte County might as well know now.

"Of course, you're here for the reunion, Addison."

"Of course," I replied, "what reunion is that, by the way?"

"Willkie High, the class of '60—you know the twentieth."

I didn't graduate with that class, at least not here, not from Willkie."

"You were part of it."

"A small part."

"They're all the same size."

"Are you some kind of a communist, Ralph?"

"I'm too rich for that Addison," he replied.

I'd known Ralph was rich having been born so. I recalled hearing he was a psychiatrist.

"A psychiatrist," I said.

"A psychiatrist," he repeated, "and you're an architect."

"Like I said, both our luck's run out, mine left quite a while ago. When did yours?"

"Who said it has?" He snapped icily, and realizing he'd revealed something he hadn't meant to, forced a smile while his speech defaulted to the controlled cadence I was beginning to recall as his.

"It surprised a lot of people," said Dr. Rye Whiskey, "hearing that you'd become an architect, but not me. You always talked about doing something that would live on after you. You had an artistical bent. I could see it in the way you worked on that car of yours. When you set your tools down you arranged them in a pattern. Most of the time, you didn't even know you were doing it."

Had Ralph been aware of my memory, he would never have floated these two fabrications. I'd never mentioned nor cared about what lived beyond me, nor had I ever set my tools down any manor but random. Often, I'd thrown them. But there wasn't any point calling him on it much less telling him that there was no such word as "artistical." Best to let him think I was buying his line of crap, especially if I hoped to score any more free drinks.

"You remember that about my tools, eh? You shrinks have a name for that, don't you?"

"Yes."

"Well?"

"We call it putting your tools down in a pattern without knowing you're doing it." The smile on his face highlighted the boniness by forcing fatty flesh into small islands and peninsulas.

"And you still have that car of yours, don't you?"

"No."

"Yes you do, you'd never sell the Lincoln Zephyr."

"Are you calling me a liar, Ralph?"

"No, of course not."

"Well you should, and you're right, I'd never sell it." But I hadn't seen it in twenty years either.

The perfect follow up question to Ralph's would have been if he still had his ride: a '50 Nash Airflite Ambassador, a bathtub shaped beast he'd named the *Mulholland Rocket*.

But I didn't ask about it just then. It would have reminded Ralph that he owed me, and I wasn't ready to do that yet. I would of course, but after a buildup. Ralph owed me. Fate had placed him in my path. The debt might be twenty years old, but I meant to collect on it in full.

3. ENTER THE ROCKET

In the spring of '58, when the age of the Willkie High juniors struck the magic two digits that made driving a car legal, there was hatched among the class of '60, an unofficial, but quite real, race to be the first with your own wheels—or more specifically, to get laid in the back seat. I should have won that race hands down, but didn't, one: because the car I'd gotten, a Lincoln Zephyr, didn't run, and two: it had no back seat. No matter that, owning the Lincoln Zephyr by itself made everything else irrelevant.

The great hurdle in acquiring one's own car was the parental one, the great "absolutely not!" My solution had been to not ask the question in the first place, but simply to buy a car as if it were any other purchase and deposit it in our driveway.

This was how I handled the matter of the Lincoln Zephyr. We'd met—the Zephyr and I—on the first warm day of 1958, a Thursday. It was proper I should meet her on the day that winter died. Like the Zephyr, the first warm day was that harbinger of great things to come. She was the first thing I'd ever really, *really,* wanted. Dear old Lola called the Zephyr the first girl I'd ever married. My wife was the second.

We might have missed each other had she not been towed from the rear by a truck with a non-existent muffler. When I turned toward the shrill blast of exhaust and saw her for the first time, I knew I had to own her. I left my books on the street and after a short sprint, jumped aboard her front bumper and rode it the two miles to her destination: Al's Auto Graveyard, where I learned that she was an hour from the crusher. Inside that hour, I owned her instead, and she stood in our driveway where my father normally parked his Chevy. Tattered, rusted, and with no small number of dents, I believed then, and do still, that she was among the great works of men, a metal goddess, no less alive than if she performed stripteases or blow jobs. I cut classes for the rest of the day and spent it dancing rapturous circles around my Lincoln Zephyr.

The Great Frog, a.k.a. my father—he was French—had the predictable reaction. One look told dear old Dad what was afoot and he wasted no time by asking stupid questions such as what it was, who's it was, or how long it would be there, or could it possibly belong to somebody else? He knew better and probably had prepared the tirade—the only one he ever unleashed on me—several months or years in advance, anticipating that day, long before I ever imagined there would be one. The French throw a peculiar kind of tantrum. It is, well, laughable. There is just no way of trying to intimidate somebody or force an issue in that language without a weapon. But I had to make some concession to his pride and mimicked a hint of fear while pretending to take in every word of his sermon. Of course I listened to none of it. I was too busy rehearsing what I'd say when he was done, which—also in French—was roughly:

The car stayed. Any attempt to move or molest it would end with the molester's remains being discovered in some remote corner of the state after being feasted on by whatever wildlife inhabited the region. I also mentioned having read that they'd eat the eyes first. I love you papa, I said, but in all fairness, this must include you. Parents, like any spirited animal, must be at some point, broken if they are to be useful. I then invited dear old Dad to toast the new arrival with a liter of his favorite cognac I'd lifted because the store wouldn't sell it to me.

Ralph faced a different problem. He'd asked permission and got the great, "*absolutely not.*"

And then Ralph did something that must have amazed even himself. He withdrew his Bar Mitzvah haul from the bank and bought a car with it.

If "resistance to tyrants is obedience to God," you might call Ralph's act divinely inspired. Knowing his father, there's no other describing it.

Ralph selected a Nash, a make young people rarely would have looked at once, but for the attribute that made their owners—so they thought—a force to be reckoned with. Their seats converted into king-size beds. That fact, and all it implied, was known to none better than the car dealers onto whose lots the Nashes lured teen-age males like Ralph on that April morning in Crown Point. Ralph never told me exactly what transpired. He didn't have to. I've scripted it.

It went like this:

Dealer: "What can we do for you this mornin'?"

He'd already spotted the conspicuous bulge from a wad of bills screaming "take me!"

Ralph: "Just looking."

Dealer: "Well look all you like, we're no pressure place. Been anywhere else?"

Ralph: "No."

Dealer: "Saved yourself some trouble. And I ain't gonna tell you that I ain't got all day, 'cause I got all day and Lord will'n, all of tomorrow too."

Ralph: "Well…"

Dealer: "And some of the next day too, Lord will'n and the crick don't rise, but this here car you're look'n' at ain't got but two hours or so 'fore some feller from Chicago owns her."

Ralph: "There are other cars."

Dealer: "Ah yeah, there are other cars, but unless they're like this here Nash, they got no bed in the back. But that's something I don't need to be telling you, is it boy?"

Ralph: "No sir."

Dealer: "And one Nash is all I got just now. And come sundown that there feller from Chicago and some young thing are going to be fornicating their brains out in that Nash that should'a been yours. But that part you know. You know that boy, and so do I. (Ralph nods) Just one thing though. I don't like the son of a bitch much. He's a jock. Don't like jocks. Where you go to school, boy?"

Ralph: "Willkie."

Dealer: "I went to Whitcomb-Riley, class of '41. They say it's a different world out there today, Sputniks and such. Everything's changed, but there's one thing that ain't changed and ain't gonna, and that's pussy and them what gets it; them, of course bein' the jocks.

You're no jock are you?"

Ralph: "No." (as if it wasn't obvious.)

Dealer: "And like I was saying, if it weren't for him gonna give me fourteen hundred dollars for her, part o' which I already got, I'd just as soon see him poke his stick into a one-ten socket."

Ralph: "Fourteen hundred dollars!"

Dealer: "That number shock you boy? Expect me to give it away? You see some sign that says 'FREE CARS'?"

Ralph: "No sir, but…"

Dealer: "Okay, sorry. What do you want to give me for this here car that comes with a bed?"

Ralph: "You said it was sold."

Dealer: "Ain't a deal been made yet couldn't be undone. I'll tell the jock that it throw'd a rod and it's in the shop. Besides, I like you; you remind me of a cousin got killed in Korea. Nice boy, hope he didn't die without getting some o' that yella meat. Truth is, I just want to help you get laid—been laid yet?"

Ralph: "Sure" (Suuurrrre!)

Dealer: "How much you got on you?"

Ralph: "Twelve Fifty." (Jesus Ralph Falonhurst, if you're going to lie once in your life, lie to this son of a bitch.)

Dealer: "Done."

I was the first person Ralph showed the Nash to, and as it turned out, the only one who'd know about it for a while. There was, by the time he'd driven his acquisition the twenty miles to Michigan City, a good reason for that. I had a job at one of the gas stations that did serious repair at the east end of Eleventh Street, in an area known as "auto row." A city of any size has one. Ralph rolled the Nash into the driveway honking its horn and calling out my name. There was a tone of panic in his voice. The Nash was being followed by a thick white cloud the size of the Goodyear blimp. From deep beneath the hood, came a noise in synch with the engine pulses. I can only describe it as something like a ping-pong ball being struck hard five times or so a second. It's called a rod rap. For a lad with a neutral complexion, Ralph might have, just then, been mistaken for an albino. His face darkened slightly at my approach. I later learned that his father forbade him to have anything to do with me under threats that would have brought small countries to their knees.

"Hi, Addison," he forced out the words, slurring a little. We'd barely spoken in years. He smiled as the rapping got louder.

"Hello, Ralph, I shouted over the clatter, "Fill her up?"

"I was wondering…" he blurted out and pointed toward the hood.

"Ralph," I said, "shut her off before we're both killed by shrapnel." He did.

"Yours?"

He nodded.

"Just buy her?"

Another nod.

"Where?"

"Jessup Motors, Crown Point, know them?"

"They're the stuff of legends, Ralph." A sudden hissing sound came from beneath the hood and white smoke started to gush from the seam where it met the body.

"How bad is it, Addison?" asked Ralph, now no less white than the smoke.

"Bad, Ralph, *bad.*"

"You don't suppose?"

"What? That they'd take her back?"

He nodded.

"I can hook her up to the wrecker and we can find out. She'll never make it back there on her own, but we'll need something else."

"What?"

"A gun, Ralph, we'll need a gun. Don't happen to have one do you?"

"My father does."

"Just kidding, which one of the Jessups took you?"

"I can get the gun, Addison. I can be back here in an hour; I know where he keeps it."

"Forget it, Ralph," I said, "I was kidding. The Jessups have enough guns in their office to fight a small war."

"I'm going to kill them, Addison," he said, shaking so that the words came out wave like. And I'd thought he was as white as he could get. His face was a sheet of paper.

"Do you want to lose your money and your life in the same day

Ralph? Forget it."

"I've got to get my money back, Addison!"

I realized that there was something Ralph feared far more than the Jessups: his father, Henry J. Falonhurst.

Like so many gallant acts of defiance, this one had turned into a disaster. And the irony was that whatever Ralph had paid, or probably overpaid for the Nash, it was chump change to H. J.

"Ralph," I said, and realized I had no advice to offer him. He wouldn't have heard me if I did. He started to bury his face on the steering wheel. The horn went off. He bolted back with a guttural scream before shoving said face into the passenger seat. His left fist pounded at the dash and a radio knob went airborne. I didn't see the face again for the better part of a minute. When I did, I might not have guessed to whom it belonged. It was a twisted mask of terror, tears, and snot.

How could anybody be so frightened of a parent, especially a runt like H. J. Falonhurst? But Ralph couldn't be any more scared. Had I sensed—and I usually can—that the terror was anything but genuine, I wouldn't have offered him what I did.

"Ralph," I said, "it's not as bad as all that."

"I've got to get my money back, Addison,"—I made out through the sobs—"my father…" He halted at the word "father" which seemed to have slashed his tongue on the way out, and now hung in the air in front of him threatening to smash every bone in his face.

"Is going to what, Ralph? Kill you? It's unlikely." It was just unbelievable that he could be so afraid of his own kin, but there was no convincing Ralph of that. Had H.J. been my father, he would have had an "accident" around the time of my twelfth birthday.

"Will you fix it for me, Addison?" he almost croaked out. His sentence traversed the whole of the tone scale and ended oddly with a hiccup.

I nodded.

"How much will it cost?"

"About four hundred dollars, how much you got?"

"One fifty."

"You're lying," I snapped, and then recognized he wasn't. I had really hurt him. He must have been wrongly accused before and it wasn't hard to guess by whom.

"One fifty will buy the parts, Ralph, and I don't work free, especially not for the sons of malpractice lawyers."

"Can I pay it out? Say, ten dollars a week?"

"The answer is 'no'," Ralph. It adds up to too many weeks and that's if you don't stiff me."

"I'm a dead man, Addison."

"But not if you show up with it running?"

Ralph's nod said he thought so. H. J. might actually let Ralph off easy should he show up in a working car with a bed in the back, even if he'd paid twice what it was worth.

If the son of H. J. Falonhurst were the first in his class to Christen the back seat of his car with the stain of fornicants, H. J. might just have the sort bragging rights that would allow Ralph off with a reprimand that was no reprimand at all because of the vicarious element. One look at H.J. told you that he would have never gotten sex without marrying it first, and still had to pay cash up front for it.

But were Ralph to show up with a Nash having a blown engine, tell old H. J. that his son had been snookered, and Ralph would roll down a dark road of tirades and brow beatings that would cease only with the ground closing over either him or his father. For too many people, H. J. Falonhusrt, a borderline dwarf, was the face of terror. As a malpractice lawyer, he'd ruined more than a few lives swiping their savings as if it were sport, which to him, it was.

"I'm not going to fix her, Ralph," I said, "You are."

"What?"

"Ray—my boss—asked me to find us a gas jockey and someone to clean the washrooms so we can do our work uninterrupted. You're it. In exchange, you'll have a place to work while you fix this thing. After hours I'll show you how, and I'll show it only once, so you better pay attention when I talk. Oh yes, and you'll call me Professor Addison."

Ralph had watched me pull "Ds" in every class we shared at Willkie. He started to raise a hand in protest.

"Overruled, Ralph," I snapped. "And one more thing: Ray, being one of the truly decent people still walking around, will pay you $1.20

an hour. The first fifty of that money you'll give to me." There was no need to ask Ralph if he agreed; he had no choice.

"How long do you think it will take, Addison?"

"Professor," I corrected, and then realized that I'd rubbed his nose in it enough. People will hate you for lesser reasons.

"How long do you think it will take, Professor?"

"Not long at all, Ralph, I said. Considering that the sooner you finish, the sooner you can quit and call me every name in the book. But to answer your question, about two weeks."

"Addison," he said, "I never hated you—my fath…"

"Yeah Ralph," I said, "your father."

There was a real reason his father hated me. The Great Frog—a physician I might mention here—had been a defense witness on a case old H.J. had figured he'd all but won. When Frogie gave his most gentile French-accented testimony, the mostly female jury swooned, H.J.'s case fell apart, and his client was ordered to pay the defendant's court costs plus punitive damages to the tune of fifty-five grand.

The next day, Ralph began work on his Nash, and he showed a natural bent for mechanical logic that amazed me. I needed to explain to him only once how to do a specific task and he would ask a question that rendered the rest of the sermon unnecessary.

At the outset, I explained what we'd probably find when we opened up the Nash's engine—and why. When Ralph had bought the car in Crown Point, it likely had no more wrong with it than a blown head gasket. To replace it would have taken say, an afternoon between gas fill-ups; and at that by a novice mechanic. But about ten miles out of Crown Point things started to get serious.

Among the jobs assigned the head gasket of a car's engine is that of sealing off the cooling system from the rest of the engines functions, namely combustion and lubrication. The telltale sign of a blown head gasket is an enormous white cloud trailing behind the car signaling that the engine is attempting to burn its coolant along with the gasoline because said coolant has made its way past the head gasket and into the combustion chamber. Shut down immediately and there's probably no appreciable harm done.

Ralph hadn't done that.

So the coolant that had made it into the combustion chamber soon found its way past the screaming pistons and into the oil sump settling to the bottom where the oil pickup resides. And the engine which is going round and round at say forty or fifty times a second, and is prevented from burning up by a micron thick film of oil between its moving surfaces, now replaces that oil with a greenish cocktail of water and ethylene glycol that has been sucked into the oil pickup and sent where the oil was supposed to go. With no oil film to protect it, said engine promptly beats itself into lump scrap like the one Ralph had under the hood of the thing that he'd believed would pluck him from the hated halls of virginity and place him on the golden road of sexual glory.

Ralph had probably never seen the inside of an engine when I explained this to him, but when something in his nods told me he understood. I wasn't wrong. He amazed me. I hardly had to oversee him; we worked different tasks simultaneously.

Ralph began his employment that afternoon, cutting classes for the rest of that day, cleaning the station's washrooms and pumping gas.

I had cut all classes too, my usual Friday custom when the first warm days broke. At 8:00 that evening, we started on the Nash.

And by 4:30 AM Saturday morning, we had its engine out and sitting on a configuration of 4x4s arranged to accept it. We slept three-and-one-half hours with heads propped against the car's tires until we were awakened by my boss, Ray, and told between curses, to get our butts to work. Ray's attempts at hard ass were, of course, a joke. I learned later that he had offered to advance Ralph any money he needed for parts an hour after being introduced to him.

Ray had been born in December of 1903, in the same hour—so he claimed—that the first airplane had flown at Kitty Hawk. He had, over the years, settled on the belief that the world had been going to hell in a hand basket and was salvageable only by a race of mechanics and inventors such as the Wright brothers—and himself—the ranks of which had been thinned to the point of extinction; a myopic view, but I shared it then, and do to this day. Among Ray's missions in life was to replenish those ranks. How many teenagers—who had shown up at his garage with a ruined collection of parts, once a car—asked for help, and had been promptly offered employment, I will never know. I was one, and Ralph another.

The rain we awoke to that Saturday cleared by ten. And Saturday was a warm day too, the warmest one yet that year. Michigan City has a Great Lakes climate, meaning its winters are a hellish march through the better part of five months. Whoever wrote *Winter Wonderland* should be pelted with rocks and garbage.

For me, winter is a beast with a black soul, a meteorological malignancy that lays siege to your life and closes over you like an arctic cataract.

So days like that Saturday bore sacredness beyond the highest holiday of any religion yet invented. The laziness that so often accompanies the first warm days we quickly replaced by a kind of kinetic sizzle that saw Ralph, and me, tear into the innards of the Nash's engine with the ferocity of and Indy pit crew.

Those Nash engines are solid, under stressed, overhead valve inline jobs lacking a single quirky feature to make trouble for the dullest of mechanics. Ralph's engine was apart, its basic components separated out in almost parade ground alignment and ready for the machine shop that Saturday afternoon.

Since the machine shop would not open until seven the following Monday morning, Ralph and I spent the whole of Sunday polishing and cleaning his engineless car. I was not exactly without things of my own to do, but Ralph had a way, even then, of getting you to extend a helping hand, and before you knew it, swallowing your whole arm between thank yous.

About four in the afternoon, he announced to me that he'd decided on a name for his car. Ralph said he would call it the *Mulholland Rocket*. He started to explain his choice, but I told him that it wasn't necessary because I too, had seen the picture.

There was a soft drink ad circulating that spring that showed five automobiles parked on a precipice overlooking what could only be the city of Los Angles. It was a night scene, and three of those cars were convertibles occupied by the luckiest people on this earth. From their perch on this warm night—since L.A. has no other kind—the half dozen young people—and L.A. had no other kind—stared at lights spread out a thousand feet below. For them there could be nothing but happy endings, bright tomorrows, and orgasmic glory. The picture was titled "Midnight on Mulholland Drive." I believed then, and do now, that the young males who saw that picture swore that they would one night be among the people in it. I'd made such a pledge, apparently so had Ralph.

At six Monday morning, we pulled up to Blake's Auto Machine Works in the station's pick up, its back springs squashed flat under the weight of the *Rocket's* dismantled mill.

There should have been an hour's wait. There was none. Blake's, which had opened at seven, and not one minute earlier, opened that Monday at six—and hadn't before or since as far as I knew. By six-thirty, Ralph's engine was being boiled out, squared, and measured for the boring, grinding and polishing operations it would take to resurrect it. We were told we'd get its components back three days later.

Dutifully we arrived at four-thirty Thursday to pick up the hundred or so freshly machined or new parts of the *Rocket's* engine. There were no hundred parts to be picked up. There was instead, just one. I still don't know whether it was bad communication or instructions Ralph made unknown to me, but Blake's had machined and completely assembled the engine for the Nash. There was nothing left to do but re-unite it with the car with the bed in the back seat. Had it been my engine I might have been mad. There is a certain pride in driving something with a power plant you've put together yourself. Ralph might be denied this, but it meant his rolling bedroom would see the road that coming weekend.

It almost didn't. We were hit with a battery of standardized tests at Willkie that week designed to measure what God alone knew. The threats of what would happen should we cut class and miss any of them were the usual ones: detentions, expulsions, and inclusion on various dishonor rolls, all with which I'd had great familiarity. That, and a backup of work at Ray's meant that the engineless Nash would remain so until late Saturday night. Sunday morning then was a virtual mirror image of that Saturday the previous week since everything we did was the reverse of taking out the *Rocket's* mill.

At ten thirty Sunday Morning we were done. At 10:05, engine started, at 10:06, back and forth a few times, then a few more, at 10:10, a drive around the block, then the neighborhood.

No glitches, the Nash's performance was as predictably dull as on the day it was made.

Ecstatic Ralph declared, while jumping an invisible rope, that his virginity would end in the next twenty-four hours. He named the four best-looking girls at Willkie, none of whom he'd yet to exchange a hundred words with.

At 10:15, Ralph quit his job telling Ray thanks. He had yet to thank me, a fact I ignored then, but never forgot. Ralph explained to us that he must now concentrate on schoolwork so he might one day be equipped to singlehandedly save the free world from communism. Ray, barely able to keep a straight face, shook his hand and wished him the best.

Done, but not quite. There remained the matter of telling H.J. Falonhurst about the Nash. For that, Ralph needed me, or so he thought. "Would I come with?" Would I! It was the one dividend for me in this whole mess. I never did get the fifty dollars.

The Fallonhurst house was almost new but designed to look a remnant of some previous century. It offered tastelessness and opulence in equally huge helpings. Not a detail of its facade failed to quarrel with adjoining ones; a tour de force in visual doubletalk, a lawyer's house.

Standing at the head of the front stairway, beneath an oversized portico, was the rather undersized father of Ralph. But for the short pegs he had for arms and legs, H.J. was an oval from the front or the back and a series of oddly projecting bulges when viewed sideways. You might have called him troll like, but if so, he was a groomed, well attired troll with every feature of his face locked into expressionless arrest by a torus of crimson fat. In his right hand he held what I first thought a pamphlet. I was wrong. It was Ralph's bankbook. H.J. had obviously made periodic (probably weekly) audits. I was just in time for the festivities. Where, oh where, was the money Ralph had bought the rocket with?

H.J. strutted down the stairs brandishing the bankbook as if it were some kind of weapon, a bullwhip or a revolver. Reaching the car, he pointed it at me as if it were the revolver. His nostrils flared open wide enough to dwarf his eyes and make it possible to see an inch or so inside them, wherein resided a forest of hair and dried debris. His breath wasn't as bad as I might have expected, but he was a sprayer.

"Tracksider!" He snarled out the epithet for anyone who lived along the South Shore tracks. "Trackside trash. You…"—he pointed at me with the bankbook— "did this!" Ralph started to say something but either arrested the words, or never found the air or guts to make them with. I smiled.

"Of course, I did, Piggmyhurst," I said, "and guess what: there isn't a Goddamn thing you can do about it."

There was of course. Had I sold Ralph the Nash, the whole deal could be undone since we were both minors. And the deal with the Jessups could have too. But I'd done to H.J. what I'd hoped: provoke him into hitting me. He swatted me across the face with Ralph's bankbook. Probably he hadn't meant to connect, and the blow wouldn't have killed a mosquito. But he'd hit me just the same. And that was enough to make anything I did now, self-defense. I am a great legal mind. Ralph had one final lesson to be taught from all of this.

For a couple of seconds, I studied H. J. Some lawyers, him obviously included, must have thought personal violence so remote a possibility, that they made no effort to avoid what he should have seen coming. His face was no more than a foot from mine and his tongue darted in and out of his mouth like a small fleshy animal testing the daylight while he delivered a storm of threats and curses. His right fist orbited in elliptical jerks, while his left just shook. When I'd synchronized his rhythm, I let fly an uppercut through the open window that lifted him what seemed like six whole inches off the ground.

And it did more than that: about a half-inch of fleshy animal was caught between his teeth. For an instant after he landed, H.J. stood staring at me trying to decide what new threat to hurl. He started to speak, but quit after the first word came amid a half-severed tongue… and a whole lot of blood. A second later, the pain struck, along with the realization of what had happened. The tongue limped back behind H.J.'s teeth, and blood began to ooze from the spaces between them. He swallowed some of it, before coughing it back up on the freshly waxed door of the *Mulholland Rocket*. Ralph bolted from the car, and a second or so later reached his father. He opened the passenger door, motioned me to exit. When I did, Ralph ushered H.J. into the passenger seat of the car with the bedroom in the back.

So the *Rocket's* first passenger was not to be the sweet young thing Ralph envisioned, but instead, this enraged pigmy-esque weasel of an old man. I can't describe exactly the sight of H.J. staring at me as they drove off to an emergency room, but I'll try: The face reminded me of nothing so much as a monkey's stenciled on a big red balloon. It seemed to get larger rather than smaller as did the rest of the car moving away. H.J. must have been afraid to open his mouth for fear of losing a section of tongue, so he allowed the blood to drizzle through clenched teeth, past a pair of puckered lips, and run down his porky chin. You had to have been there.

4. YESTERDAY'S RAINBOW

Noting that the better part of my drink was well on its way, Ralph signaled Felix for another.

"So why haven't you asked me?" His tone fell just short of accusation.

"About what, Ralph?" I asked, fairly sure he meant the *Mulholland Rocket*.

"The *Mulholland Rocket*," said Ralph.

"What about it?" I asked.

"Do I still have it? Don't you want to ask me that?" he coached, almost smiling, but his voice had picked up an edge.

"Is it important?"

"What do you think?"

"That's the question shrinks get—what is it—eighty dollars an hour to ask?"

"Shall I send you a bill?" Ralph was smiling now, but the voice hadn't lost its edge.

I breathed hard and hoped that asking the question Ralph wanted asked might yield yet another round. Felix, whom it could be surmised by the purposeful snap of his motions, was at least part owner of *The Glass Dragonfly*—set down a shot glass of rye in front of me.

"Do you still have the *Mulholland Rocket*, Ralph?" Ralph's tone lightened, but it was obvious he'd forced it.

"No Addison, I don't, it was stolen."

"Long ago?"

"Twenty years, around the last time I'd seen you."

"Well, I didn't take it," I said almost laughing.

"I know that."

I hadn't imagined Ralph getting attached to a car the way I could. He went on as if I were showing more interest than I was.

"After it was stolen, father bought me a new Corvette, my reward for being valedictorian. It was his selection, not mine, and it being that it was his, he didn't care what it cost. His kid had a Corvette. I would have rather had another Nash. I took Cassy Rapaport to the senior prom with the Vette. The *Rocket* would have been more useful, much more. With all the motels full, we ended up on the grass; it ruined her dress and my rented tux. I wound up paying for both. It made for an expensive evening."

"It's supposed to be expensive, Ralph."

"I would have much preferred the *Rocket*."

"Do you still have the Vette?"

"Stolen too," Ralph replied. "If I were offered either of the two back, I'd take the *Rocket*."

I smiled.

"Physician, heal thyself."

"I mean it."

"I do too, Ralph. By the way, how is your father?"

"ALS, Addison," he replied, and after pausing added, "Lou Gehrig's Disease," as if an explanation were necessary. I guess a lot of people got their wish.

"It wasn't mine."

"Did I ever tell you that after the incident with the *Rocket*, he told me to cultivate you as a friend, that some of your *chutspa* might rub off on me?"

"No, if you had, I would have remembered, and called you a liar then, by the way."

"It's true."

"I don't believe you, Ralph."

"As you wish."

"If I had a wish, it wouldn't be wasted on that."

"What would you waste it on?"

"Money, Ralph, what did you think?"

He weighed this for a moment and surprised me with, "I might be able to help you there, Addison."

"Now you're talking, Ralph."

"By the way, where are you staying tonight?"

"My mother's place if she's home, a bench in the South Shore station if she's not."

It was not common knowledge that Lola, my mother's twin, was in fact my aunt as well as my stepmother, and I doubted that Ralph knew. Lola had no idea I was in town as I hadn't called ahead imagining that her phone might be tapped.

"Addison, the Station's closed after ten," he said.

"A park bench then, Ralph, I need the money."

"To do what, if I might ask?"

"Vanish."

He shook his head slightly, and gestured toward the bartender with an almost imperceptible nod. "Felix reads lips, and sells what he reads, not to mention what he hears."

"Should we go to a booth?"

"They're bugged," he said in a way that left no doubt that he wasn't kidding.

"They're what? Why the hell do you drink here?"

"Didn't you hear me? Felix sells what hears. Sometimes I make a purchase." He said this as if no explanation were necessary. Ralph continued at one third his previous volume barely moving his lips.

"An Eastbound comes through in about ten minutes. Look at your watch and make like you mean to catch it. I'll meet you opposite the station on this side of the track. Leave now. Probably it won't fool Felix, but we should try anyway. You can stay with me tonight." Ralph didn't have to offer me that twice.

It was a number of degrees warmer when I stepped outside where a slight breeze had brought a fog with it. I'd always liked that combination. It usually meant a warm front was on its way. And, but for the moving automobiles, the landscape's features were blunted to near timeless anonymity by the mist. Eleventh Street could have been a scene twenty years earlier or even further back than that, a place in time I'd like to have been just then.

The approach of a four car South Shore Eastbound out of the fog made for a photograph I would like to have taken. The orange and brown coaches, the last three of them empty and unlit, ground to a halt abreast of the Station just as they had done in the decades before, and those since I'd lived in Michigan City.

They rocked in place for some seconds and then were still. Air compressors, strapped to their undercarriages, kicked in to replenish what had been used up for the stop. A wisp of that electric perfume, called ozone, teased me while the train's headlights drilled yellow shafts into the mist.

Those things will take you back if you'll allow them to. I would have loved to walk up to that train shimmering in the dampness, caress its faded paint, and drag my hand along a wet film of dirt when it rolled east. Instead, I remained on the sidewalk, facing away from the train, lest a debarking passenger recognize me, though I couldn't have given myself better exposure at the bar.

Ralph drove up. His choice of car surprised me. Ralph drove a gold Citröen SM, a French/Italian collaboration that mated Maserati power with French lines sensual enough to be called automotive porn. I'd read in more than one place that Citröen lost money on every SM they made.

I got inside.

Traction motors wined as the train began its roll eastward on Eleventh. We kept abreast of it for three blocks before making an abrupt right turn. Ralph smiled.

"Remember?" Ralph asked, then:

"She rolls, she rumbles, she buckets, she bolts,
To the crack and the pulse of fifteen hundred volts.
Now we're rolling so fast that with wings we would soar..."

He nodded to me.

"No there's nothing like riding the mighty South Shore," I said, finishing the verse of a poem we'd learned in grade school. There were about fifty verses to it.

"Nice," I said as I patted a dashboard that spanned the car's interior in one sculpted sweep.

We accelerated.

"I would have guessed you'd pick a Benz."

Ralph gave me a disdainful look.

"A Citröen Maserati is twice the car when it's not in the shop. Besides, Krautmobiles have our blood on them."

"True," I allowed.

"People who think they're drivers," he said with a wry smile, "go to France, drive Citröens, get used to what they can do, come home, try the same tricks with a Benz...and get hurt."

I doubted that, it sounded like Ralph might be playing up to my being half-French. I remembered now: he also had a talent for backhanded complements that didn't sound patronizing but couldn't be more so. I waited until we hit the feeder to Route 70 (the main East-West highway) to ask where we were going.

"New Buffalo," Ralph replied.

There was a much more direct, but slower route. East on 20, but it was obvious that Ralph was in no particular hurry to get there and meant to stretch the Citröen's legs, possibly for my benefit.

"Live there, New Buffalo I mean?"

"As much as I can for the next six months: I've got a sailboat in Snug Harbor. Do you know the place?"

I did know it, an artificial inlet with a hilly backdrop complete with a railroad that peeks through breaks in the trees, something you'd expect to find on the New England coast, missing only the craggy rocks. It's about as far south in Michigan as you can go before crossing into Indiana.

Ralph accelerated to seventy-five—far too fast, I thought, for this much fog—and held the Citröen there. The posted speed limit was sixty.

"They won't stop you for seventy-five," he explained. "But do anything over eighty, and they throw the book at you complete with punctuation."

"What will she do?" I asked, having read one-forty somewhere.

"One-forty is what they're supposed to do. This one can do it with a fresh tune up."

We cruised eastward for several miles and were finally out of the fog. Route 70 was all but empty and Ralph inched the car up to well past eighty ignoring his own caveat.

"So why haven't you asked me?" Ralph said for the second time that evening.

"About what?" This time I didn't try to guess.

"Her."

There was no need to guess who he'd meant by "her," as we both well knew, but I decided to play dumb anyway.

"Her?"

"Her," Ralph repeated, his tone one that he probably used on patients he'd checkmated into some admission.

"Okay," I said.

"Okay, what?" His voice was assuming an arrogance that was more than a little irksome. I decided to give him what I was sure he wanted, an acknowledgement that he was the kind of genius shrinks see themselves as. And he *had* said something about money.

"Have you seen her, Ralph? Did she mention me, and when was it?"

"Yes, yes, and yesterday," Ralph replied.

"And what did she say about me, Ralph?"

"Not much, you were mentioned in passing."

"With regard to what, Ralph, the reunion?"

He nodded.

"She wondered if you'd be there. I told her I didn't know where to send an invite so I doubted it."

"And did she seem relieved, Ralph?"

He nodded again.

"Say anything else?"

"No."

"Spit it out, Doctor!" I said, "I'm past being hurt." A colossal lie.

He shrugged. "She said you were a narcissistic crybaby that believes he's the handsomest man alive. I told her she was wrong."

"You're right, Ralph," I said. "I don't just think it, I...I'm just kidding."

"No you're not...kidding that is."

"No, I am the handsomest man alive. I would know, wouldn't I?"

"Does what she told me...hurt?"

With a shrug, I tried to indicate that "yes" it did, but not let on how much by adding: "I should know better than to ever imagine I'd get over her."

"You've got company, Addison."

"I doubt it. I'm in a class by myself about Alice." Alice! The name I meant to avoid was front and center, glaring at me like a pair of high beams.

"She never meant to hurt any of you, men get obsessed over women, hurt themselves, and very often others. It happens all the time."

"Not much consolation in that."

"All I'm saying is don't blame her," clarified Ralph.

"I don't blame Alice, I said." That much was true, I'd never blamed her.

"I did the best I could at the time." I went on. "It wasn't what she was looking for and she was kind enough, and fair enough, to say so." I didn't believe the second part for a minute.

"That sounds rehearsed."

It had been. I didn't intend to say any more, but the name Alice, and all it stood for, had been uncorked like a mischievous genie.

"It's just that I wasn't taking no for an answer."

"Yes," said Ralph. "That's when the trouble usually starts."

"And did it ever," I affirmed. I shook my head, this time vowing to say nothing else. But a question that I couldn't arrest was clawing its way out of me.

"Does she think I killed Collin Walker?"

There was a pause, Ralph drew a deep breath, and followed it with a short silence. Then: "No, for a time she might have, but the facts were the facts. You were in Texas when it happened. She gave up that idea if she ever had it in the first place."

"If I know her," I said, "she probably hated it to.

"Sounds like you had quite a discussion with her—about me that is."

"On other occasions," Ralph replied, "but not yesterday."

Yesterday! He'd seen Alice the day before! I hadn't for twenty years, three months, and what was it? Fourteen…no eighteen days. The time that had passed was easy to figure, since I'd last seen her on December 31, 1959. I simply counted from the first day of 1960.

"How does she look Ralph?"

"How do you think?"

In a reflection from the windshield I could see the smile I offered was one of resignation.

"As ever," I said, "sensational of course," as if there had been any need to ask.

"You are correct, of course," Ralph replied. "Goddamnit!" he suddenly barked," realizing he'd taken the wrong exit off 70. We were heading South instead of toward the Lake. For the about-face, Ralph used the ramp of an abandoned Gulf station I remembered from when it was still in business. Ray's station had sold Gulf gas too. Farther down the road, another landmark I'd remembered, a huge Pepsi sign was alive and flashing.

We were in the parking lot of the marina minutes later. The harbor had been dredged out to twice the size of what it had been when I'd last seen it. There was mooring for perhaps a hundred boats. The enlargement could not help but diminish the intimacy the place once offered, but those who hadn't known it then might still surmise that it was all the name *Snug Harbor* implied. Just then Ralph's boat and eight others were its only occupants.

"We're not supposed to be in the water until this weekend, but to avoid a log jam at the ramp they've been launching boats since Monday. Mine was the first." He pointed to an off-white sloop with cabins fore and aft of the cockpit that were connected by a pass through. It looked to be about forty feet long.

"Had her long?" I asked.

"Four years, but she was in storage for two. I can just about handle her alone now. She was a divorce thing, a patient whose wife kept accusing him of loving the boat more than her."

"Was it true?"

"He had more affection for the appliances in their house than her. I advised him to get a divorce ASAP at the end of our first session, but he waited four years, and only after being nailed with a sweet young thing in a Motel 6 by the same gumshoe that he'd once hired to follow his wife, did he do what he should have in the first place. It's common enough."

"Was the boat to settle his bill?"

Ralph nodded. "Yes, and to keep his wife from getting it, she got all the rest, and I do mean all. Funny, I think she was the first one to cheat."

"Do I know them?"

"I can't tell you that."

"Then I guess I do."

Like the other eight, Ralph's boat was moored bow first. I clanked my way to the end of a two-foot wide aluminum dock suddenly curious about the name he'd selected for her. I was pretty sure it wasn't the *Mulholland Rocket*. The name on the transom read "YESTERDAY'S RAINBOW." The letters, which formed a semi-circle, and the colors— orange and pale blue—that tried to suggest a rainbow, were sharply defined, but fell short of conveying the intended image.

"Like it?" Ralph asked as I stepped aboard. I was pretty sure he meant the name since he saw me look at it, but he could have meant the boat itself. I did my best, but tact had never been my strong suit.

"It's got a ring to it. Does it mean something?"

"It's an observation. Sit down and I'll explain it; it's brilliant, if I do say so myself, even though I'm probably the only one who thinks so. And it is *my* boat and you are *my* guest," he reminded me, chuckling.

Boarding the sloop, I seated myself in her cockpit. Ralph went down a short ladder into the forward cabin, emerging a moment later with a Styrofoam chest that held a cache of iced PBR (Pabst Blue Ribbon) in the stubby bottles I remembered liking better than tall necked ones. A chill had crept up on us. Maybe that front I'd figured on had taken a right turn around Louisville and gone on up the Ohio River valley to warm Cincinnati and not us after all.

I reminded myself that in a Midwest April we could easily wake up on a boat covered with snow, assuming, as I now did, that this was where he meant for us to spend the night. I wanted to bring up the money he'd mentioned in the bar, but I decided that listening to the origin of the boat's name first, might serve me better.

We each opened a bottle.

He began with: "Going to the reunion?" apparently forgetting the boat's name, at least for the moment.

"When is it?"

"Friday night, in the Willkie gymnasim."

"Did it have to be there?" I asked.

The most memorable thing about Wendell Willkie Secondary School was that it was so forgettable, a fitting tribute to its namesake: one of four Republicans who ran against Franklin Roosevelt and needn't have bothered. Big Frank had even trounced Willkie in his own hometown, though Willkie did carry Indiana. The reunion's ambiance was going to be the chlorine stink of the natatorium next door to the gym. I wondered how much nostalgia that would serve up.

"Having it in the school gym," said Ralph, "was one way to keep the admission down to twenty dollars, and have decent food besides. Also, there will be skinny-dipping in the pool. No attire will be allowed there, you've got to go native."

"You expect takers, Ralph?"

"I've got a bet that there will be at least fifty, including myself. They did it last year and the first thing I was asked—the phone rang off the hook by the way—once the invites were out, was about having it again. I guaranteed it."

"All for twenty bucks. With the tickets we sold, I could afford the extra security I wanted for gate crashers who might want to get into the pool party action."

"It's amazing," he went on, "for how many the line between coming and not is twenty dollars and not twenty-five, even for people coming from California."

"I doubt that, Ralph."

"Doubt it if you like, it's true."

"So you planned the reunion?"

"I chaired the committee."

"Anyone else I know on this committee?"

Ralph smiled. "Bobby Dardinelle, Clifford Fitch…and Randy, uh Alice."

"Randy" was what everybody besides me called Alice Miranda Jones.

"How is Clifford?" I asked, trying to divert the impact of her name. Clifford Fitch was the one real friend I'd had at Willkie. But the thought of Alice overpowered everything. I couldn't care about or focus on anything else. I'd spilled all I was going to spill about her. Jesus! He'd also been on the committee with Alice.

"Cliff's bitter," replied Ralph, "but not as much as he has a right to be."

"About what?" I asked, forgetting that it was Clifford I'd asked about just seconds before.

"He lost an arm in Vietnam. He's a deputy for the sheriff's office in LaPorte County, a charity job, he knows it too, probably hates himself and the world."

"Who could blame him?"

Ralph paused, "As you remember, Cliff was no movie star, but having the most marauding case of acne, one that invades your eyelids, earlobes, and probably your scrotum doesn't make you any less horny at twenty-one."

"You're familiar with his scrotum, Ralph?" I said trying to keep a straight face. Ralph ignored the barb and continued.

"Anyway, one night about three years after we graduated, Cassy Rapaport had a fight with her jock boyfriend, got drunk, and let Cliff have her. The next day she patched things up with the jock and left Cliff to twist in the wind. The only reason I got to take her to the prom, by the way, was that she was between jocks. When she is, she's pretty easy."

"Not hard on the eyes either, I would say." I could recall Cassy well enough; she was the daughter of the Rabbi who'd Bar Mitzvah'd me. A brunette with wide set eyes on a nicely proportioned face set atop tight curves that she learned to use better than any of the other cheerleaders on the Willkie squad, something for which I held zero esteem. I'd seen Cassy perform at the pep rallies they forced on us but had never gone to a game.

"No, not hard at all. And Cliff," continued Ralph, "having never previously so much as touched a girl in Cassy's league, gets this marvelous night of passion. Then the next day the postman, so to speak, comes back to tell him it was all a big mistake, the package wasn't for him. So, for a week, Cliff wonders how he can prove to Cassy that he's some kind of superman that's worthy of her. She'd forgotten all about their night together, or at least, was trying to."

"And he enlisted?"

Ralph nodded, "You wouldn't believe how common that is. I know because I spent two years in the army counseling the maimed. Right out of medical school they made me a captain, a rank men spend careers struggling to reach. My basic training was a two-hour movie. I never got nearer to Vietnam than Fort Ord in California. I was supposed to make sense out of the madness that had sent healthy nineteen-year olds to the other side of the planet so as to have slugs or shrapnel rip through their organs at twice the speed of sound leaving them paralyzed, blind, armless, legless, or all of the above. That's not even mentioning the burn jobs. I couldn't make myself look at half of those while I was supposed to tell them that I knew how *they* felt. How the hell could anyone begin to imagine how they felt? I never heard a shot fired in anger and these kids had to call me "sir." Let me tell you something else: the most common thread that ran through them? They were trying to prove something to some stupid bitch that had rejected them. I swear to God that was the reason." Ralph stood up and stared out at the harbor looking like he was going to throw up.

"I've often wondered" he continued after a moment, "how many of the dead in any war are lads who thought that coming home with a chest full of medals might change the minds of the girls who jilted them. But the medals they got were posthumous ones received after the metal that killed them. Most of the time, the girls never heard about it and those that did were well into the next phase of their lives and didn't want to know, especially the ones that connected the jilting with the poor kids dying in battle."

Ralph raised his beer high, as if performing some kind of salutation and took in a long hit and after swallowing said: "I was glad to be long gone from that duty by the time Saigon fell in '75. I sure as hell didn't want to be around those kids when they heard about that. Were you in the army, Addison?"

"No," I replied matter-of-factly, "I was a draft dodger; want an explanation?" I stood up trying not to sound embarrassed.

"No, not necessary," he replied, "actually, I thought I just gave you one."

"Okay, but for the record, there's only one reason, and that's that I didn't want to die." I set down the fat, now empty bottle, and got up and snatched another from the chest. "I'm not proud of what I did, I'm not sorry either and…"

"And what?"

"And I didn't want to come back in a box with a shipment of metal in me." I said this while almost tearing the cap off the fresh bottle with the opener and hurling it into the harbor. I loved Alice, but suicide wasn't in my arsenal of things I would do to win her over.

"And?"

"And have her not know or not care." I took a hit of PBR.

"Her," declared Ralph.

"Her," I affirmed. Dumb as I was, I couldn't imagine that having a slug rip through me was going to make any difference to Alice.

"And you wanted one more time at the plate?"

"I wanted as many as it took," I snapped, annoyed at the sports analogy. I'd always regarded spectator sports, except the motor kind, as stupid and irrelevant.

"Which brings me back to the name of this boat," said Ralph.

"*Yesterday's Rainbow*," I said sitting down.

"Right, it's something we're all chasing to a greater or lesser degree, you, me, Clifford, Bobby Dardinelle...even Randy."

"That son of a bitch!" I barked at the mention of Bobby.

"You broke his jaw."

"I did that? Great!" That made me feel a little better. Up until now, I thought I might have broken his jaw, but had never been sure.

"Be glad he wasn't a lawyer then."

"Perfect line of work for a creep like that."

"And so," added Ralph, "is Randy."

"No!"

"Yes."

"Randy Jones is a lawyer?" Now *I* was calling Alice "Randy" too.

"It's Randy Walker now."

"Since when is it Walker?" I guessed she'd married some other Walker, she was too young to have married Collin before he died and besides...

"Since quite a while before you pissed on her husband's corpse twenty years ago." Ralph peered over the gunwale as if looking for fish. "She and Collin were married. And all you thought, all you did, was piss on her dead boyfriend at his funeral. Now why should that so upset her?" The sarcasm in his voice was thick enough to distort the pronunciation.

I might have known that talking anymore about Alice (Randy) might serve up some new disaster or revelation, or disastrous revelation, but this one ran off the charts. What I'd done was ten times as bad as I'd thought. The task of winning her over was going to be much harder than I'd imagined. I was reaching for another thought and the first one to hit me was: *if her name was still Walker, Randy had probably not married anyone else.*

"She's still single then, Ralph?"

"Yes, Addison, she never married again."

"Alright, Ralph," I said, afraid to say any more on this subject, "what about all of us chasing yesterday's rainbow?"

"Oh, now you want to talk about it." He turned back, sat down, parked his beer on the deck and crossed his arms over his chest.

"Sure." *What I wanted was to talk about the goddamn money.*

"Of course you don't, but we're going to anyway. This is my boat after all, but let's goes inside, I'm freezing."

When we were seated in the cabin, Ralph turned the transceiver to a weather broadcast that predicted a high of seventy-seven the next day. I told him I doubted that.

"It does seem unlikely," Ralph replied, "but they're rarely wrong; we can go out tomorrow if they're right."

"*Yesterday's rainbow,*" I repeated, hoping we dispose of the subject and talk about the money. Ralph turned on wall sconces with a single switch and the cabin glowed in warm yellow light.

"Okay," said Ralph, "start with our friend Clifford Fitch. We had three planning sessions for the reunion, and he asked me at each of them, if I expected Cassy Rapaport to be there. She will be, by the way, and when I told him that, yes (she'd sent in an RSVP) he tried his best to keep from lighting up like that Pepsi Cola sign you saw back off 70, but couldn't it hold back. For him Cassy is yesterday's rainbow. He'll be there Friday night. God, I hope he doesn't wear his uniform and his medals. Somebody from that crowd is bound to make a crude comment about the medals and what they cost him. He wants to start life over, beginning with the night in 1963 when he balled Cassy. He actually thinks it can happen again. When it doesn't, he'll start planning for the thirtieth reunion."

I shrugged, propping my head up, trying to focus on Clifford's illusion, but he thought of Alice again overpowering everything.

"She still may not show up at all," I finally said, idiotically.

"Cassy's already in town; we're meeting for breakfast in New Buffalo tomorrow. She'll want to go sailing with us, okay by you?"

It wasn't. It meant one more contact here—another item for the hounds to sniff—but I answered:

"If I'm here that long…don't you work anymore, Ralph?"

"Want to know what yesterday's rainbow is for Cassy?"

I nodded, though it shouldn't have taken a psychiatrist to see I didn't care.

"It's you, pretty boy."

"Get outta here." I leaned back up, trying to act less interested than I was. Like anyone's, my ego still responded to stroking.

"It's true."

"Well, she never said anything to me."

"She was under orders to stay away from you, the penalty for which was losing, what else? Her car. Remember it? That turquoise '56 Bel Air with a 283?"

I nodded. "I remember she always gassed up at Ray's and wanted me to perform every check a gas purchase entitled her to."

"She was praying you would find something broken, dummy."

"Then she should have gotten an older car."

"In that week I worked for you and Ray," said Ralph, "she pulled into the station four times and looked almost crushed when I turned up to pump her gas. She never bought more than a dollar's worth and was back a day or two later to be disappointed yet again. Once, she actually dared to ask me where you were."

"I tell you, Ralph, I had no idea."

He continued: "Cassy crunched a fender one night in 1959 and her padre papa took the Chevy away from her."

"And?"

"And seeing she couldn't lose it now, she was all set to come onto you, but by then you'd met,"—Ralph paused—"her."

"I think I'll have another, Ralph," I said.

He produced a fresh bottle and extending it, noted:

"You've barely started that one."

The wind was picking up outside, and the halyards with any slack to them clanged against the aluminum masts and booms of the sailing vessels, including Ralph's. Through a porthole I could see freight cars flash by between the trees on the hill. "Is that still the Pier Marquette?" I asked, gesturing at the train.

"I don't know what they call it now, I'm just glad there's a train there. Amtrak uses it too. There's a station a quarter mile East of the Marina."

"Nice touch," I replied, "people who've never lived near a railroad don't know what they're missing."

"Maybe they don't want to know. Do you want to know the first thing Cassy asked me when she phoned in an RSVP?"

"If I'd be there?"

"Right, and when I said I doubted it, her voice went flat, like a nail had let all the air out of it."

"Look Ralph," I said finally, "let me pass on the sailing tomorrow. If Cassy still looks anything like what she once did, you're not going to want me around anyway. Hell, you won't want to go sailing at all once you get her on board." Then I remembered having not asked Ralph if he was married…or if that would have made a difference.

"Now what was this thing you mentioned in the bar about money?"

"I'm still assembling that in my head, Addison, we'll talk about it tomorrow."

"Ralph, I've got a couple of things to take care of tomorrow and I expect to be headed for parts unknown. Can we talk about it now?"

"Tomorrow will be soon enough," he replied, "You'll be here through Friday night at the very least."

"You don't know that. As a matter of fact, I don't know myself."

But Ralph only smiled. We both knew where I'd be Friday night as well as the reason.

II.
ENTER ALICE 1959

5. A REAL GEM

I'd never heard the girl I met on that March Thursday in 1959 called anything but Randy.

Once I'd learned her actual name, Alice Miranda Jones, I always addressed her as Alice in one of many attempts to make myself a stand out among those around her. I'd assumed at first that the number must be large. It wasn't, but like all things Alice, I was seldom right about anything, except that I loved her as I never would anyone else nor could anyone else love Alice as I did. It couldn't be done.

Of course, she and I began with a near disaster.

Clifford Fitch and I were waiting out a downpour at the Franklin Street Station. Clifford saw her first. She was waiting, I was soon to learn, for a passenger on the four o'clock Eastbound, one Collin Walker.

Pointing at the girl I would come to know as Alice, my best friend declared "I'd love to fuck that!" loud enough to be heard outside the station, and probably across the street. Viewing her from where we did, the back, I couldn't fault his taste. She was a stunning assembly of curves (she'd removed her coat) topped by hair that flowed downward in medium blonde waves.

She needn't have turned around and didn't. The three of us, plus a ticket agent, were the station's only occupants.

Clifford had queered more than a few such possible beginnings that I decided to rub his nose in the fact that I had something he didn't: the looks I'd always overrated.

I walked a large letter "U" through the station's interior and confronted the girl with an approach from the right. Unlike so many who look good but from just one or two angles, this girl was a knockout from any point on the compass. She was a Nordic kind of beauty who could well have been a Viking Princess, were there such things.

From the top, Alice began with the waves of medium blonde hair I already mentioned, a high forehead that made her appear taller than her actual five-foot-three. The forehead gave way to crisp, well-defined features that flowed between each other in a way that made your eyes dance across them without a misstep. Not even the braces she wore made for a ripple in this symphony. And green, deep-set eyes, so green they seemed to vibrate, rounded out the composition like glorious punctuation marks.

"I was wondering," I said, hoping my voice sounded as unlike Clifford's as I thought it did, "if the four-o'clock eastbound stops here?"

The question couldn't have been worse; every train stopped in Michigan City.

"No," the girl snapped sarcastically, "it races through at eighty miles an hour."

"Does it?" I replied, "Damn! I knew I put on the wrong shoes."

She tried not to smile but gave in halfway.

"Then you should go home right away and change them."

"Would you care to come with? My mother won't be home to tie them, and you look like you would know how to tie laces. You do know, don't you?" Already this was teetering on an abyss. Verbal fencing with this girl was the last thing I wanted; no matter how many points you think you've scored, you're guaranteed to lose.

"You're a real gem," she said. It was the first time I heard the expression I would always associate with her.

"I'd rather you call me by my name."

She turned away.

"It's Addison July—Sonny—and yours?"

"Randy Jones," she replied, still facing away, and probably cursing herself for surrendering her name to me.

The "Randy" part told me that it was probably her real one; had she said "Alice Jones," I might not have believed her.

"I'm pleased to meet you Randy Jones," I said.

"And I'm pleased to meet you Sonny July." She turned back to face me, her expression now a mix of amusement and irritation.

"There are worse things," I said, hoping to keep the conversation lit, "than a sunny July. A cold March afternoon like this one for instance, but January is the worst. It's a month of Monday mornings."

It rather amazed me that I could find words at all and spit them out in the right order. And I did spit them out because a frothy blob of spit had hitched a ride on some syllable and had come to rest on her sleeve. It was a sizable cluster of bubbles and for a moment I just stared at it.

The girl ignored it. I wondered how many such spit blobs her clothes had collected from the frantic mouths of boys trying to do what I was attempting just then.

"You don't like the cold," she said.

"I like brain tumors better," I replied.

"So you've had one?"

"I've still got it. I use it to take tests when I haven't studied; it's really good at algebra."

"I've never talked to a brain tumor before," the girl said. "What's it like to live in your head?"

"Not bad, Randy, there's a very small brain that lives here too, but it doesn't take up much room and sleeps most of the time. I've got the place pretty much to myself. It's a big head. I'm told it looks good from the outside and the surgeons say they can't evict me without killing the landlord."

The teethy smile that unfurled across her face packed kilowatts, gripping me with a compulsion to taste the saliva that glistened on her braces. It was a smile I felt I'd earned because coming up with what I had, left my brain in a state of wordless exhaustion. I couldn't have assembled another sentence for an hour.

But the smile hadn't been meant for me at all. Just then, the girl who called herself Randy stepped to her right and I was briskly bumped aside by the mass of Colin Michael Walker. I hadn't heard the train arrive or anything else.

Collin had seen me from the backside first—as I had seen him—and it wasn't very hard to guess what I was up to. He kissed Randy before turning around, hardening his rather general-issue face as he did, so as to offer me instantaneous belligerence. The fact that I was far better looking than him probably only boosted the rage he'd feel for anybody that would dare to try to take this girl away. And I could not have been the first, nor could I have blamed him for wanting to smash every bone in my face, but pleasing Collin Walker wasn't exactly at the top of my wish list. A die that would be shortly cast was already in the molten stage. I'd met Randy (Alice) and had all but sworn to myself already that I'd win her over.

"Collin," the girl said, "this is Addison July. He has a brain tumor."

"Really," Collin sneered, "pleased to meet you, Mr. Tumor."

"It's Addison July," she said as if to tease Collin by testing my name for resonance and finding it there in spades.

"Add—us—in—July," said Collin obviously holding back threats and curses until he might get me alone. "How about subtracting yourself in March, such as right now in March?

"Not just now," I said, "Mister whomever you are."

"Collin Walker," he snapped and suddenly extended his hand like a switchblade. But I didn't flinch as he had intended me to. I knew, even as I held out my own, that he was going to try to break everything in it.

But he'd missed one basic rule: when setting out to break something with your bare hands, you'd better have a good idea what it's made of. In the case of my right hand, as was true of my left, he should have seen the tiny black web work of dried grease imbedded in the surface and the mangled fingernails beneath which the first sixteenth of an inch was absolutely black with grime. They are the hallmarks of a mechanic. The only hands stronger than those on a mechanic are on robots. Colin was neither.

He seized my hand with what might have been a formidable grip in some college fraternity and studied my face. I offered no expression even when he tried to roll my knuckles and make them pop. When this too produced nothing, he relaxed his grip, tried to withdraw his hand, only to find he couldn't.

I wasn't letting go. I didn't try to crush anything as he had tried to do with my hand. I just wouldn't release him.

"Okay," he said as if it were some kind of command you'd give a dog.

"Okay, what?"

"Okay, let go." As he spoke I began to rotate my wrist while pushing downward.

Realizing he was going to either be on his knees, or see his wrist broken, Colin managed to hide his fear from Randy for a few seconds before looking scared.

"You're crazy man," he said.

"You shouldn't say things like that to a brain tumor," I replied, "it's got feelings too; you can even piss it off."

Releasing his hand, I seized his thumb. Down on his knees he went.

Collin grabbed my forearm with his left hand, trying to wrench himself free. I offered him a satisfied smirk.

"Let him go," Randy demanded.

And I did that, but only after applying a torque to his thumb that probably tore tendons and made him pale. Collin drew a long breath. Fear, pain, and rage battled for control of his face.

Randy looked scared too, and more than a little angry. And like so many absolutely beautiful girls, the anger only served to make her look better still.

"You're a real gem," she said.

"Twenty four carat," I replied, adding: "I'm sorry, the tumor hates to be called crazy. Next time I'll remember to swallow a tumor treat, I think they sell them at Kroger." But no stroke of brilliance was going to get me beyond where I already was with this girl—nowhere.

She turned to Collin.

"Let's get out of here," he said. They left the station, each carrying a duffle bag, Collin with his left hand while attempting to shake the pain out of his right.

A minute later Clifford raced up to me. "How'd it go?" he asked breathlessly. The anticipation had so tightened his face that I was afraid some of his acne might burst as I'd seen it do once before. That time my face caught some of it.

"She's in love with me," I replied. "She just doesn't know it yet." I was lying of course, at least as much to myself as to Clifford, but I believed I could make it happen and had never really let go of the idea. I set out to make it happen the next day.

"Randy" did not go to Willkie High or at least I'd never seen her there, which meant she didn't. If she lived anywhere within, say five miles of the South Shore station, she had to attend Witcomb-Riley, the only other public High School in Michigan City. Something told me she wouldn't go to a Catholic one even if she were Catholic.

Cutting the fourth-period trigonometry class, I called the Witcomb-Riley main office from a phone booth across the street from Willkie.

"This is Mrs. Jones, Randy's mother," I said, forcing an octave boost to my already high-pitched voice, which had often been confused for a female anyway. "I must get in touch with my daughter." My call was transferred to one office and then a second one, where a male voice told me to wait a minute, which of course meant fifteen.

"What is your daughter's name?" he asked when he finally returned.

"Randy Jones," I replied.

"We have eight students with the surname Jones," he snapped, "no Randy Jones, are you sure your daughter doesn't attend Willkie?"

For the first time it occurred to me that "Randy" was a nickname.

"Read off their names." It must have been obvious by now that I wasn't her mother. He should have hung up.

"What?"

"Read off the goddamn names," I barked. Instead of hanging up, as he should have, the fool began reading off the names.

"Jones," he said, "Alice Miranda, Jones, Arthur Winfield, Jones, Nathan Randolph…"

"That's it!" I cut in.

"What?"

"Alice Miranda Jones! Randy!"

"Did you say you were her mother?"

"I did, and I lied by the way, thanks asshole."

I was at the main entrance of the James Whitcomb Riley Secondary School at the end of class that day. My best guess was that Alice would exit from there.

To be on time, I had to cut the last of my own classes—I might have anyway, it was warm—and enlisted a taxi, once an almost impossible thing to get in Michigan City at that hour. But there I was, betting she would walk through those very doors at the end of the ninth period, though there were other entrances.

For the second time that day, I was right. *And Alice was alone*! Well, she was in the middle of a semi-dense crowd; she just didn't seem to be in anyone's company.

Watching her walk, I planned an interception. I'd have gone for something subtle, like being at the place I could predict by her direction that she was headed, but Collin, the jerk from the station, if still in town, was going to appear any second. Had he not imagined I would be tracking her, he was a damn fool.

I circled the crowd, poised myself directly in its path, and came on like a bowling ball.

It parted like the Red Sea as I marched straight for Alice. She was looking down and didn't see me coming. When we were ten feet apart, I came to a halt.

"Hello Alice," I said, "when are we going out?"

She was taken aback for a moment, but only for a moment, by my second invasion of her life and probably by the fact that I already knew her real name. And the surprise was gone from her face by the time she said, "Hello, Sonny July."

And she did say Sonny and not "Oh…you."

A number of Whitcomb Riley's own, who might have witnessed similar things, started to form a loose ring around us. Most of them were girls. There were boys too, whom I guessed had fantasized about doing what I was doing just then and probably hoped to see me shot down. Knowing that nothing was possible at the center of that stage, I said: "Can we go somewhere and talk?"

"I'm meeting someone."

"Collin Walker?"

She nodded.

"This will just take a minute."

She pointed to a bench, to where we then walked and sat. To my amazement, we weren't followed.

"When are we going out?" I asked. I hoped that saying "are" made our going out a forgone conclusion. It didn't work.

Alice took a long breath. She didn't seem at all angry; perhaps sadly amused at delivering the kind of thing she had to have done dozens of times: the word "no" in that many variations.

"We're not," she said.

"That's okay, next Friday then?"

"Didn't you hear me?"

"Every word, except…"

"Except?"

"That we're not going out."

"You know something, Sonny? For someone who's wasting his time, you sure don't waste much time."

"I can't," I said, "I'm a brain tumor of a few words."

"I don't think I've ever had a conversation like this before," she said.

"That's because you're talking to me, Alice Miranda Jones," I said, so as to let her know I'd bothered to find it out all of her name.

And for a very quiet half minute, no more than that, I thought Alice might reconsider. I used that half-minute to etch an image of her, line by line, surface by surface, into my head, that I could recall until the next time I'd see her.

I waited for her to say something I could get traction on, but she didn't. She only broke into that magnificent smile I'd first seen at the station. A second later, I recognized it was for the same reason as the day before.

"Waiting long?" Collin's voice came from behind me.

And like the day before, he'd seen me from my backside, but there was no mistaking who I was. I wondered what tactic he'd pick to deal with me. Handshakes were obviously out. His right hand wore a large glove of gauze and tape.

Collin ignored me as if I was irrelevant. Had I been him, I wouldn't have thought of that. It was a good choice. It placed the ball back in my court.

"No, not very," she answered, standing up. Colin kissed her.

"Done here?" he asked finally, as if to say, *"have you disposed of this garbage?"*

"Yes."

After Alice got up and they had walked about twenty feet, I called out suddenly: "Don't forget, Alice, next Friday!"

Collin's right arm was around her shoulder. His left sprang straight into the air with the middle finger extended like a flagpole.

"I'll get to that too," I almost shouted after them. I wondered when I'd next see Alice. And there would be a next time. I'd sworn to that. How it was to come about and the fact that it was the next day almost made me believe in what the preachers peddle.

6. A NOT TOO HARD THING

"You're late," Ray barked, when I showed up for work at his Gulf station that morning. I acknowledged that I was.

"Take the wrecker, here's the address. Look for a '53 Pontiac. There's a phone number here too. There could be a payoff in this, that is, if this babe looks anything like she sounds."

I took the wrecker and was off.

Rounding the corner on a street named Avalon Court, I spotted the Pontiac on a block of two flats. As I approached, Colin Walker bolted from one of them to wave me down. Alice followed closely behind.

"You!" Colin snapped angrily as I stepped from the truck.

"Yes?" I replied, as we both realized that my luck was as good as his was bad. There were a dozen other garages in Michigan City that Alice could have called.

"I had no idea you were a grease monkey," said Colin.

"I'm a mechanic," I said, "I used to be a brain surgeon, but it bored me. I got tired of ripping people's skulls open. I can still do it when the right skull needs it. Now how can I help you?"

"You can get back in that truck and get out of here," Colin answered, amazing me by slapping two dollars on the Pontiac's hood. A service call was three, but at least he wasn't going to try and stiff me.

As I reached for the money, Alice cut in, "Let's see if he's really a mechanic, Honey, we need the car."

He shrugged.

I hoisted the Pontiac's hood and was greeted by a thick stench of raw gasoline that I'd first smelled when I'd stepped from the wrecker. The air cleaner was missing and gas was everywhere. I looked for a ruptured fuel line, but not seeing one, went back to the truck, grabbed a bundle of rags, and dried off the engine. Then I told Colin to turn the starter. He did, and gas gushed from the carburetor's bowl vent.

"What is it?" Alice asked, genuinely curious.

"It's a stuck inlet valve. This car's been sitting awhile." I was now taking in that pleasant stink cars make when they burn gasoline that has partly turned to varnish.

"He just bought it," offered Alice.

"That adds."

"And what does this inlet valve mean?" asked Alice as she gave me yet another variation on the smile that I'd first seen in the station. If she'd asked me to eat the Pontiac's tires, I might have at least made the attempt. I never wanted so badly to look like a genius.

"We've got two choices," I said and pointed to the carburetor, "I can give it a sharp rap"—then throwing Colin an impossible to miss glance—"with a not too hard thing, and maybe jar the inlet valve loose. With fresh gas, the trouble could be gone for good."

"Or?"

Again I glanced at Colin.

"Or I'll hit it too hard, with the not too hard thing, and break it, and you'll have to buy a new one, a rebuilt carburetor that is, then have the gas tank taken off and flushed out, which is really the right thing to do in the first place, just more expensive."

Alice weighed this for a moment, and then asked, glancing at Collin—whose car it obviously was—"Would a snow brush do for a not too hard thing?"

"Perfect," I said. I had been wondering what I could use.

I struck the carburetor's bowl two blows where I thought it least likely to break. It didn't.

I motioned Colin to crank the engine, which roared to life after two backfires and settled down to a smooth idle. I have always liked straight-eight engines. This one was among the last of a breed that did not deserve to die.

Alice looked like she was impressed, though loathing to showing it.

Colin looked resigned and asked, "I owe you what?"

"Four dollars," I replied, watching the bowl vent for a sudden rush of gas that would ruin my moment of glory.

There wasn't one.

He handed me four dollars. I could see my tab had emptied his wallet, and probably spoiled whatever they'd planned for that day. On the way back to the truck came an inspiration.

"Oh shit!" I barked out. They turned to me.

"A service call is a dollar," I said, "it's only four when I jump a battery."

I walked back to the Pontiac and extended three dollars to Collin.

"You earned it," he said, shaking his head.

"If my boss found out I'd overcharged you, I'd get fired, he's like that. Take the money."

Colin did, and I headed back to the truck, but stopped once more. "By the way," I said only half turning about, "whoever sold you this car owes you an air cleaner—it's missing."

Passing the Pontiac's trunk I spotted a small metallic badge that read "JESSUP MOTORS CROWN POINT INDIANA." Hell of a partner, those Jessups had become, I thought.

On the way back, I hoped they might accidentally pull into Ray's for a gas fill up. They didn't of course. Colin wouldn't knowingly go near the place. But my luck had not run out by a long shot.

7. DETONATIONS

I paid Ray the four dollars I should have received from Colin, three of them from my own pocket, and wondered just how much of a hero that might make me to Alice. She had to know I was lying about the money.

At four o'clock that afternoon I had my answer.

"It's the babe from this morning," said Ray, extending the phone that I seized with greasy hands.

"Addison July?" asked Alice.

"Speaking."

"Give me your address, I'm mailing you the money."

"Not necessary."

"Not for you, maybe."

"You don't want to owe me anything, is that it?"

"That's it."

I replied, "You don't owe me anything, except you might say it was nice of me."

"It was nice of you. What's your address?"

"When are we going out?"

A moment of silence was followed by an answer that all but put me on the floor.

"Friday."

"Seven?"

"Seven's fine. You were at our house this morning, do you remember it?"

Did I remember it!

"It's the second floor. Our cousins live on the first floor, and their name is Jones too. Don't ring the wrong bell. They hate that."

"Seven then?" I asked again, unable to believe what she'd agreed to.

"Yes Seven, goodbye, Sonny July." She hung up.

Monday morning—returning to my locker for a book change—I was met by the captain and quarterback of the Willkie Wildcats, one Bobby Dardanelle. We'd shared classes, but had never exchanged so much as a nod. For a moment, I thought he might be waiting for someone else. When I'd opened my locker about ten inches, he suddenly slammed the door shut with a fist. He'd meant to catch my hand with it, but missed.

"If there's one thing that I hate more than uppity niggers," said Bobby, "it's uppity kikes, uppity kikes that grease cars and brother girls they shouldn't even be looking at."

I guessed he'd rehearsed that little speech and fumbled the word "bother" as so often happens when a line is rehearsed too many times.

"You mean 'bother'?" I asked as I wondered what his connection to Alice might be.

Bobby was a good four inches taller than me, and, right then, it looked like four feet. He must have weighed in at over two hundred. I wondered what he'd do now that he was out of words.

It was a short wait.

Bobby grabbed my shirt with his left hand and twisted it so as to tighten the collar like a noose. I would have been helpless against a skilled fighter his size, but skilled was something he obviously wasn't, and what he'd done I knew how to deal with.

Trying to look frightened, I stepped back, hoping Bobby would extend the arm he'd gripped me with instead of walking with me. His arm went straight. I grabbed his wrist with my left hand, and slammed the outside of his elbow with my right palm.

There was a wonderful, solid feel of breaking and tearing from inside his arm. The blow even took away his wind and there was a guttural yowl only when he caught it some seconds later. The hand still stayed locked on my shirt that tore when I yanked it free.

Bobby let fly a storm of curses before the pain overtook him and he staggered away trying to nurse his elbow, not an easy thing to do. I was hoping he might give in and cry, but he didn't.

I expected to be drawn, quartered, and expelled in that order once it was reported what I'd done to one of Willkie's precious athletes. Why it never happened can only be that the idea of a top jock being trashed by a peon like Addison July was so unthinkable that it couldn't have happened. It's a flimsy explanation, but there's no other.

Of course, I still have the torn shirt.

I did stay away from Witcomb-Riley though, for the whole of the next week fearing overexposure, or that Alice would change her mind. I told myself that was impossible but made innumerable reassuring trips to mirrors. My looks were the one thing about myself I'd always overrated. It amazed me how often they didn't get me what I knew they should have.

Friday Night, the last one that March, was a cold one. Borrowing the Great Frog's Chevy and wearing a corduroy coat, I rang the doorbell of the second floor flat on Avalon Court and was greeted by Alice's father: a five-foot-six gentleman whom I later learned operated Linotype machines. Her mother had a job at Sears and was working that evening.

Alice kept me waiting for just under half an hour. When she stepped into the front room, she wore a black sweater and a skirt so green that, like her eyes, seemed connected to an unseen dynamo. Of the images of Alice I would carry with me, the one of her in the upstairs front room of the second floor flat on Avalon Court stands out.

"Sorry I'm late," she said. She wasn't a bit sorry of course and neither was I. The delay was as calculated as a satellite launch.

I helped Alice into a coat that nearly matched my own, and then into dear old Dad's Chevy, the base model with the single option I wouldn't have wanted: an automatic transmission; something akin to a condom, both cheat you out of the experience.

We saw a movie called God's Little Acre at a theater in Crown Point. I remembered some of the story from a school reading assignment for which, like others, I'd used a borrowed copy of Cliff's notes…if I bothered with it at all.

And the first twenty minutes were all I'd remember of the movie. After that, they might as well have shut off the projector, locked the doors, and left us alone for a couple of years. It was that way with Alice.

I never understood why they called what we did for the next two glorious hours 'necking.' I always thought it an odd name for those face devouring gyrations that rock your molecules with detonations you'd swear were going to send pieces of you into the next county. But it was that way with Alice.

And when every brilliant line I'd stored in my brain turned to gibberish if I tried using them, because mind and mouth had ceased to connect, that too was Alice and what being near her did to me.

My life had been irrevocably split into those events before, and those after, the two hours I spent with her in that theater on that March Friday. Between dropping Alice off and arriving home, I had our children named, children that I was convinced I'd never have had before those two hours with Alice. After them, my every thought and action would have in it an Alice component. The campaign to win Alice over—that had begun in the South Shore Station—had never ended.

Over the years, I'd reconstructed that evening down to the minutes, and in some places seconds, of what was said, the very words, sometimes down to the syllables, and the time frame of each event as best I could. When exactly did I pick her up? What was the first thing she'd said to me? I to her? And where were we when she'd said this? Or I that? Was it really Alice who initiated the necking? It was Alice, of that I was certain. Often I'd sat staring at the theater stubs from that night, hoping they'd unleash a fragment of fleeting ecstasy. More often than not they actually did.

I didn't call Alice the next day, Saturday, nor the day after that, believing it bad luck, though I'd never before held a single superstition. No, it wasn't that. I worried that it all might not have happened. Or that Alice might not be as mad about me as I was about her. Or that she had changed her mind. Or that I might be overexposing myself. Or…

I waited until Monday to intercept her where I'd first done it: at the main entrance of Whitcomb-Riley, at the end of the ninth period class.

Alice wasn't there.

Was she avoiding me? I waited until the final class period—the tenth one—emptied the building. No Alice.

That night I called her.

"Hi," I began.

"Who is this?"

"Sonny."

"Oh, hi."

"Oh, hi?" I smoked the words for a minute, and combed my brain for a comeback. What did "Oh" mean? Oh? as in "Oh—you?"

"I missed you this afternoon, Alice."

"I'm under the weather."

"I'm sorry."

"It came on me Saturday, I hope I didn't give it to you."

"I don't mind."

"You don't want this thing," she said faintly wheezing.

"If it came from you, I'll take it."

"That's nice of you, Sonny, but you don't want this."

"Maybe not, but I want to see you again."

"When?"

"How about in five minutes?"

"I told you Sonny, I'm sick."

"Ten minutes then."

"No," she said laughing. A sudden rush of warmth. I so wanted to make Alice laugh.

"How about Friday?"

"No, not this one."

"Collin coming in?"

"That's not your business."

"Saturday then?"

"Are you asking me?"

"What do you think?"

"I hope you're not telling me, and if you are the answer is no."

"Then can I ask?"

"Ask me at the end of the week, can you do that?"

"Sure." This might have been a critical point: when Alice was deciding whether or not to abort what we'd started. *Please Alice, please don't do that!*

I did wait until Friday to ask, and intercepted Alice at the end of the ninth period at the main entrance of Whitcomb-Riley, having made no contact for the whole of the week.

"No," Alice said to the Saturday date she'd made me wait a week just to ask for. With a false laugh, I asked: "You made me wait a week for a 'no'?"

"Not exactly."

"Meaning?"

"Tonight's okay, if it's okay with you."

"Any night's okay, Alice, tonight, tomorrow night, either or both." Colin obviously wasn't coming in this weekend, so I might have mentioned that I was free both evenings, and any other thousand evenings.

"Seven then?" I nodded.

When I picked her up I met her older sister whom Alice had said was better looking. I wondered if she could have possibly believed that.

Alice didn't make looks out to be what I did. It was the one thing I got about her relationship with Colin and the fact that I was obviously in second place. Looks had little to do with whatever she saw in him. I racked my brain trying to figure just what that was and could never come up with a satisfactory answer.

On that Friday, the spring warmth had extended into the evening making it drive-in movie weather though most were open year round. Both of the two outdoor theaters, in striking distance, offered second-run horror jobs. Heading the bill were The *Brain Eaters* followed by *Attack of the Fifty Foot Woman*. Taking her there would have been an obvious statement of how irrelevant the movie was and what could be expected to go on in the car. I suggested it as a joke hoping she'd say 'Okay.'

"No," Alice said. A drive-in was out.

We saw a sub-titled French film instead at a theater in South Bend. Its title, *Black Daffodils*, couldn't have had any possible connection to its contents or much else.

I didn't care of course. I was there to make out with Alice again, my mission for the evening, and by now for life itself. It was exactly what we didn't do. Simply put, she'd become a different girl. We kissed once, after which Alice showed me all the passion of a fireplug.

For the better part of an hour I tried to make it a replay of the week before. It didn't happen.

"Watch the movie," was Alice's response to dozens of attempts to make it a repeat of the last time I'd taken her out. Her fending off my every advance only notched up my determination. Why had Alice cooled? Was it some strategy? What was going on?

"Something wrong?" I asked finally.

"Watch the movie," was her only response.

I did that, without saying once, that one did not need to speak French, which I did, to know how it sucked, and suck that movie did. God, that movie did suck.

Afterward, we ate at a place overrun with Notre Dame drunks or those soon to be. I guessed she'd known of the place, but hadn't been there with Collin, since no one seemed to know her, not even those who tried to buy us drinks, hoping for an opening with Alice.

"Did you like the movie, Addison?" she asked once we'd ordered. She was no longer calling me Sonny. I told her I hated it.

"It won a lot of prizes."

"Really, where?"

"Cannes."

"Oh."

"Do you know about Cannes?"

"I'm half French, we have relatives there. It's no big deal."

"I thought you might be, you don't look…"

"Jewish?" I offered. "The two aren't mutually exclusive."

"Well, yes."

"I'm actually an atheist so I must have an atheist's face. Who told you I was Jewish?"

"My cousin, Bobby Dardanelle, I think he's in your graduating class."

I smiled.

"Yes, we had a short discussion about you." Bobby had been wearing a cast and sling for about three weeks now.

A flicker of fear crossed her face as she—probably for the first time—connected the cast Bobby wore to me, and what I'd done to Collin at the station.

"You don't take it from anyone do you?" she said.

"If you mean crap like your cousin tried to lay on me, no. Some of us have learned not to."

"Some of you French?" She flashed a wonderful almost ironic smile.

"No, they never learn anything."

"And that's the part of you that's French?"

"Anyone with an asshole is part French."

I got one more kiss from her at the door of the apartment on Avalon Court when our date ended. I told her I wanted to see her the next evening.

"No," Alice replied, adding that she couldn't.

"When then?"

"Can you ask me…"

"Friday?" I finished her question, adding: "sure why not, I'll just make it a standing thing to ask you only on Fridays."

I did exactly that, wait and ask her on Friday, and once again, Alice was free for that evening, and again not for the following one.

Except for seeing a movie that was at least watchable, our date was the mirror image of the second. What had happened to passionate Alice of date number one? After trying to phrase the question in uncountable ways, I decided not to ask at all. Alice would come around I told myself; it was a matter of pushing the right buttons. I'd done it once and could again.

But I never could find those buttons, though it wasn't for lack of trying. Only occasionally did we really talk. I told Alice I didn't intend to go to College, which was one of the few things she'd asked me about. I would go to California, I told her, to get a job with a car customizing shop, and then explained what that was. I might do College for a year or so, I amended, to mollify the parents, then abscond with the second year's tuition, using it instead to stake my foray to California.

Alice told me that Collin was 22, had done a stint in the army that was now paying his tuition. He was studying law she said, hating every minute of it, but was determined to see it through like some kind of penance for a crime he may have committed in a previous life, also, he would need a way to support Alice. He'd gone into the army as a way of avoiding college, an odd thing, because most men do the exact opposite. To get into the army he'd actually contested a '4F' classification. He might have stayed in the Army had he not hated that as well, and it would have certainly guaranteed him the loss of Alice. He would shortly be taking part time work as a security guard and looked forward to it. A lot of people were in professions where they never belonged, she went on, hating it, their lives, and themselves.

"You're probably right," I said, adding that I was in no great hurry to work for the rest of my life either, even on cars.

I wondered if Collin and I might have more in common besides our taste in women, which in the case of Alice, one really didn't need anything more in common than eyes.

I believe that was the longest conversation I had in a month of dating Alice Miranda Jones. It was the most serious and probably lasted all of eight minutes. Almost all the others were five sentence exchanges that I'd try to end with some quip that would prove I was the cleverest person alive. Practically all of them flopped. So did my anecdotes: those obviously trite fantasies Alice had to have seen as such the second they were out of my mouth.

In short, Addison July, who'd so desperately sought to be suave and provocative, was boorish, if not often offensive, and losing on all fronts, his looks notwithstanding. It wouldn't have mattered, of course, had the girl been anyone but Alice. But it was Alice, and my campaign to win her was headed for a colossal crash.

I was up nights now, trying to come up with a way to turn it all around. And then I remembered the one ace still in my sleeve, the thing that set me apart from every other male at Willkie High or Whitcomb-Riley: the great thing that sat in my garage, my Lincoln Zephyr. The car, the fact that it was mine, and that I was resurrecting it myself, made me a savior no matter who did or didn't know it.

I was certain that with one look Alice would know.

Yes she would. That it didn't run yet didn't matter, it soon would. Its body was quilted with patches of yet-to-be-filed solder and primer—no matter any of that. Alice would see past all the rough spots, to its great blend of lines, planes, curves, and angles that flowed together in a glorious symphony not unlike Alice herself. How could she not see its greatness? Or mine?

That Saturday in April would be our last date. It began like all the rest with a movie. Alice parried my first moves to draw her close to me, and then appeared to submit slightly. During the movie we kissed a few times. I held myself in check. The movie ended, and we ate.

"I want to show you something," I said between bites of a hamburger.

"What?" Alice asked, with an expression, instead of words.

"A car," I replied.

"Can we do it another time? You know I teach a children's Sunday school class." Her job of misinforming children was new knowledge.

"If you'll guarantee there will be another time," I said. Her expression told me there wouldn't be.

"Okay then, this won't take long."

I'd spent much of that afternoon setting up the garage for the event.

When we entered and I hit the light switches—there were three—the Lincoln's lines formed up out of the dark offering a stunning rear three-quarter view. While Alice took in the sight, I studied her face. Nothing mattered, but that she understood what she saw. For a moment, I believed she had.

She could never, I told myself, be like so many women that regard cars as appliances that you traded in as the need arose. My Alice would understand the greatness she beheld.

"Interesting," she said, "what is it?"

"A car," I replied, stifling sarcasm I would have used on anyone else who'd have asked that question. "It's a 1937 Lincoln Zephyr."

"Oh," Alice said finally. She walked toward it, stopping when she was five feet away and turned toward me. She might have looked like an advertisement for the Lincoln Zephyrs in a magazine from when Lincoln Zephyrs were new. How many times had I envisioned the two elegant forms that stood before me together in my garage? If only

Alice would play the role I'd assigned her in my life. The metal "girl" didn't have a choice. But Alice did.

Much of the Lincoln's paint was intact, though it badly needed a re-spray. Still, what was left of the car's black paint was oddly analogous to a cocktail dress worn by drop-dead gorgeous females in the drawing rooms of countless noir films. I tried to imagine what Alice would look like in such a dress.

"Would you like to sit inside her?" I asked finally.

"It's a 'she' then?"

I nodded.

"Do you mind if I tell you that she has a big butt?" It was true, the Zephyr's trunk was enormous.

"I think it's fine."

"You like cars, and girls, with big butts, don't you, Sonny? Like me?" She was calling me 'Sonny,' again, a start.

I nodded. Alice would never believe a denial, though until then, I'd yet to consciously connect her exquisite posterior with the Lincoln's.

"It's alright, Sonny," she said finally, "men are about evenly divided on what they prefer: chests, asses, legs—once a girl's face passes muster. I guess you're an ass man."

There was no point in denying that. And I was thrilled that she'd gone back to calling me "Sonny."

"Now that that's settled, would you care to sit inside?"

"Do I have to?"

"That's not a fair question," I replied. But there was nothing unfair about it.

Alice opened the passenger door and with one foot inside, turned to look back at me, and gave a sudden start at what she saw. I spun about to face the figure of my father in the doorway of the garage.

"I heard the car, Sonny," he said, "and saw the lights."

I offered him my best 'get lost' expression. "Everything's fine," I said, "go back to the house."

"You have company?"

"You have a keen sense of the obvious father," I replied, whispering, "get out of here."

"Aren't you going to introduce us?" asked Alice. I heard the car's door click closed as she walked toward us. There was no getting her in the car now—until dear old Dad was disposed of.

"Randy Jones," she said, extending her hand. My father shook it with both of his hands in one of his ever so European gestures—the phony.

"I'm Doctor July, Sonny's father."

"I'm pleased to meet you," returned Alice, who seemed, I thought, far too pleased.

My father and I would have been twins at any comparable age and at forty-six, he still looked pretty good. I remembered how intriguing people had found the French accent, which like most things French, made me sick more often than it didn't. My father could apply it to his speech in varying intensities, though just then he had chosen to pour it on—the phony.

Though Alice would never know it, my father was probably about three-quarters of the way through his nightly bottle of cognac—the lush.

"What do you think of her?" he asked gesturing to the Lincoln. "My son has unusual tastes, yes?"

"Unusual," repeated Alice.

"But he likes beautiful women, like you, and that is not so unusual."

It occurred to me then that I had never told Alice how beautiful she was either because it was too much like a surrender, or a statement of the all too obvious.

It had been drilled into us, mercilessly, by grade school teachers, and other idiots, the notion that looks were meaningless. We were all supposed to choose our mates as if we were blind, dead, or had our heads so far up our asses that no light could get in. Just then though, I realized that my father had never insulted me by floating that kind of crap.

Alice blushed.

She had to have been told she was beautiful since before she'd known what the word meant. But being called a beautiful woman instead of a beautiful girl might still be novel. I made a note to do that at the first chance, but now I would at best be copying my father, one of the things I least wanted to do.

"Thank you, Dr.," said Alice with a look I'd only seen her give Collin Walker up until now. My father bowed slightly in his ever so

European way—the phony.

"Well, a pleasure to have met you, Randy," he said, and turned to go—at last.

"And what do you think of the car, Doctor July?" Alice fired off using the subject of my car to stop him. He halted, turned a quarter circle, rotating only his head the rest of the way: "As I said, Randy, my son has unusual tastes. My favorite car is the Citröen, but they're not seen much here."

"That's because Americans like cars that run," I snapped, "something the French"—I almost spat out the word—"haven't learned to make yet." The Great Frog smiled, shrugged, and disappeared through the doorway and into the darkness—the phony. I turned to Alice.

"Take me home," she said.

"Don't you want," I said, "to sit in, I mean see the…" I gestured to the Lincoln.

"No!" Alice replied sternly, "I've seen enough."

"But…"

"Take me home!"

"You're a very beautiful woman, Alice Miranda Jones." But no words from me were going to make the slightest difference now.

"I guess I'm going to have to walk," she replied, making for the doorway.

I blocked her. "I'll drive you," I said. That would at least give me some talking room; it was a ten-minute drive to the flat on Avalon Court. I was still using the old man's Chevy.

When we were half way there, I finally said:

"So when are we going out again?" She should have known I was kidding, but instead of picking up on the joke, Alice turned to me with a glare that could be fairly called dry ice.

"You know, I really pity them," she said in a slow, deliberate cadence as if that's what it took to make me understand anything.

"You mean my father?" I asked, "And could you speak slower, I'm having trouble with the big words." I was suddenly feeling that I'd deserved a lot better and should hit back—since I couldn't make her angrier, what did it matter?

"I mean your father, your mother, or any family you have."

"How about the girl I marry?"

"Oh God, her especially."

"Do you?" I snapped. "Well that's fine, we'll just stop, buy a bottle of cognac and a bag of dried flies, and you can deliver it personally to the Great Frog with a big red ribbon." I wondered if she understood that by the "Great Frog," I'd meant dear old Dad—the phony.

"You could learn something from that frog," she replied.

"I already know how to say don't shoot, I surrender." That's the most spoken phrase in the French language in case you didn't know."

Alice slapped my face. It was the one thing I didn't expect. And I'd have hit anyone else back, gender notwithstanding.

A silent half-minute later we drew up to the curb in front of her family's apartment. Alice fumbled with the latch lever after trying to open the door with the window crank. She was in a great hurry to get away from me, fearing what I could only guess was retribution for the slap, but it may have been a general revulsion at the course of the evening's events. The door swung open and she bolted from the car without closing it. She raced for the stairs of the two-flat and disappeared.

When I'd turned and driven a block from Avalon Court, I pulled over, having found that it was impossible to control the car and cry that hard. And I was suddenly crying like I never had before. I hadn't felt it come on. It just erupted like a volcanic storm of diarrhea that you let loose when you thought it was a harmless puff of gas.

I don't know how long I sat there sobbing amid stifled screams, but it was a good while, and when I arrived back at our house on Eleventh Street, it was well past one A.M.

My father met me at the side door. Wordless, I walked past him offering only a scowl. It should have been obvious from one look at me what had happened.

"Lovely girl," he said, and probably meant nothing more by it.

"Yes," I replied, "and by the way, thank you for nothing."

The matter of Alice should have ended that night. It had only begun.

I can't remember whether I slept or not. In the morning I couldn't really tell if I had, so it's been impossible to say since. I can only remember several early trains passing our house just as they had on any other day.

One fact however divided reality from what wasn't: Alice was gone and I'd just suffered the worst failure in this life or any others I might have lived. Alice was gone, if only for now.

It would be my worst night until two decades later when I was raped at Huntsville prison—I'll get back to that.

At nine in the morning, Lola knocked on my bedroom door. I had a phone call she said. I took it.

"Where the hell are you?" my boss Ray wanted to know.

"I forgot it was Saturday."

"It's usually the day after Friday, or have you quit and gone Orthodox on me?"

"Coming, coming." I hung up. Alice was gone.

"Don't get too close," Ray said as I walked into the office of his garage."

"What?"

"If you smell anything like you look, I don't want any."

"Which is?"

"Something that leaked out of a dead moon cricket's asshole."

"And you would of course be familiar with that." Ray started to laugh and I headed for the service bays.

"Addison!" he called out. I didn't stop.

"Come back here, Addison," he called out again, and sit down." I did.

"I know this won't do you a lick of good, but…"

"So why are you bothering me with it?" I snapped.

"That bad? The girl on Avalon Court with the Pontiac?"

I got up to go, but after one step, collapsed into the chair and buried my face in my hands.

A bell on the wall rang indicating that a customer was at the gas pumps, and as Ray got up to attend to it, he patted my knee, which like the rest of me, shook from the sobs.

"Want the day off?" he said, as he returned.

I didn't answer.

"Then what I'm going to tell you is this, and no matter that it won't do a lick of good, you're going to hear it anyway."

"What?" I croaked, trying to resurrect my voice.

"First, put it out of your head that you're going to win her over anytime soon; that's the bad part."

"And?"

"The very bad part: put it out of your head that you're ever going to win her over, period."

I wondered what made Ray think he had the right to say that.

"You wonder how I know this isn't something that will blow over in a day or so? The answer is one look at you. You've got the hurt burned so deep in your face that you'll need a plastic surgeon to get rid of it. What was her name anyway?"

I shook my head.

"I am not going to talk about it with you."

"Hurt too much to say it?"

"Alice."

"The whole name?"

"Alice Miranda Jones."

"Well Addison, you'll get over this part soon enough—the crying and all that. You'll meet other girls; you'll screw other girls. You might even have kids with still others. But you'll never be over Alice Miranda Jones, not you. And twenty years from now when someone says her name, you might even try to laugh about it. And if you do laugh, it'll be a lie to yourself and anyone who hears it. You'll know it is, even if they don't."

"And how do you know all this?"

"Because I've been there, Sonny—and because I know you. And seventy or so years from now, when you're thinking your last thoughts, Alice Miranda Jones will be first among them, along with wondering what it would have taken to win her over—maybe a silly prayer asking for one more chance at it maybe in another life, neither of which you'll get. So get used to it. End of sermon."

"Fuck you, Ray."

"Now do you want the day off?"

"No."

"Hmm," he said, "I guess it worked at that."

Alice might be gone, but only for now. I had just begun to fight.

8. AFTERSHOCKS

One month later when I called her number, Alice answered:
"It's Sonny," I said. A silence followed.
"Addison July."
She sighed. "I know that."
"How are you Alice?"
"Fine."
"I was just thinking about you and I wondered how you were and all…"
"I told you."
"That you're 'fine'?"
"Yesss," she said, ending the word with an irritated hiss.
"Was there something else?"
"No, not really."
"Well thank you for calling, and goodbye."
"Alice, wait. There's something else."
"Well?"
"One day Alice, one day, you're going to have to tell me what I did to screw things up so bad, because for the life of me I don't know, and that's the God's truth."
"I thought you said you were an atheist."
"I love you Alice Miranda Jones."
"That's not my fault."
"I never said it was, and you not loving me back isn't either, but for God's sake, can't you even like me? Right now, I'd settle for your liking me, but you can't even do that can you?"
Another silence made me wonder if she'd hung up.
"Can you?"
"No."
"Why?"
"I don't want to get serious with you. You scare me, Sonny. Goodbye."

"Alice!"

"Goodbye, Sonny."

I amazed myself by not crying all that hard after the call, a few whimpers, and that was all. I was sure she hadn't heard them.

That was at the end of May. I waited until the first week of July to try again. Alice, I was told, wasn't home. She may not have been. I tried again and was told the same. Ditto the third time. It was obvious they were screening her calls. On the fourth attempt I got through. This time, I told Alice that I had to see her. Of course, she said "no." I didn't ask why, and went on to other things.

Fortunately, there was something to talk about: Whitcomb-Riley— her school—was being condemned and raised. All its classes would be merged into those of Wendell Willkie Secondary School in the fall. Willkie was a newer building, just seven years old to be exact, though totally lacking in any character, which Riley had in spades; such was the wisdom of the Michigan City fathers.

After recounting this to Alice, I offered her a facetious welcome to Willkie High, adding that I'd look forward to seeing her. Alice said nothing.

"Did you know that they're closing Riley?" I asked finally.

"Of course," Alice snapped, "they were talking about it all year; didn't you know?"

I'd only known for about a week.

"I'll look forward to seeing you there, Alice." She breathed hard, as if to convey how much she dreaded that.

"Goodbye, Sonny."

"Alice!"

"What?"

"Nothing."

"Then goodbye, Sonny," she said, emphasizing a tone of finality.

As it turned out, Alice needn't have worried about seeing me at Willkie.

The next morning, the Great Frog announced that we were moving to Houston, Texas. I countered immediately that I wasn't going. My father almost said I would have to, but thought better of it. We'd already been through a lot of things "I had to do" that remained undone.

"Do you know where you'll live?" he wanted to know.

"Back of Ray's station, there's room for a cot."

"How will you eat?"

"With my hands."

"What will you eat?"

"Donuts and burgers, they're known to be sold here."

The Great Frog and Lola sat fuming, but the idea of being rid of me couldn't have been entirely unwelcome.

It was Lola who spoke up.

"I could talk to your aunt Dora, maybe she'd…"

"Board me?"

Lola nodded.

It was another in their bottomless cache of inane suggestions. My "aunt," Dr. Dora Fischer, was the "relative" I most loved to hate. Her son, Harry, was a classmate at Willkie and the person I least wanted to be connected to.

"I wouldn't mind living at her place if, well…"

"Go on," said Lola, slightly surprised.

"If she were dead or at least gone forever, along with her village idiot son, all her cats euthanized, and the place, fumigated. Think she'd go for that?"

My father and stepmother exchanged a familiar look of mild disgust.

"When are you going?" I asked finally.

"In six weeks."

"That's the middle of August. I'll need the garage through Labor Day."

"To finish your car?"

"Just to get it running; there's no way I'm going to finish it this year."

Finishing the Lincoln Zephyr meant acquiring skills, like upholstering, that would take far more time than that. The Lincoln's interior was ratty, but useable. I'd made some half-successful attempts at bodywork that would doubtless stick out like tumors under a coat of fresh black paint.

"I can arrange with the new owners that you get to use it," replied the Great Frog. "They're patients of mine."

One week later, about eleven in the evening, I was passing the kitchen when my father called me over and motioned me to sit down. He was about half way through his nightly bottle of Cognac, which meant he was still practically sober.

"I want to know why you won't come to Texas with us. You hate winter. Texas has none."

"I have my reasons."

"You have one reason, Sonny."

I got up to go.

"It's the Jones girl, isn't it?"

"How did you know her name?" I snapped, as if I'd caught him reading my mail.

"Her aunt was a patient in the hospital. Alice was visiting her when I came into her room. Also you remember we met in the garage."

"Yes, I remember," I snapped. I considered him at least partially responsible for the disaster that ensued.

It was a perfectly logical explanation for his knowing her last name— she had used it in the garage—still I didn't believe him, moreover, I took it as an offense that he used her first name, Alice, as if it was my exclusive right.

"Sit down, Addison," said the Great Frog. It seemed that lately, everyone wanted me to sit down. "You're making a big mistake."

I remained standing and almost told him that I regarded him as a big mistake, but that only made me the son of a big mistake, an error repeated, a copy of something that should never have happened in the first place.

"Don't bother the girl now," he said, "at least give her a little time."

"What? What the hell gives you the right to say that to me?"

"Call it the wisdom that comes with age."

"Keep your wisdom, in fact, I wish you would shove it."

"If you invade her life anymore now it will just repel her." For some reason, his accent was heavy just then.

"And what makes you an authority on repelling invasions?" I all but roared at him. "I mean, being French and all? In fact, if you French were any good at that, I might still have a mother."

The Great Frog flinched as if the words were a volley of gunfire. He started to get up, collapsed back into the kitchen chair, buried this face in his hands, and began rocking in slow regular oscillations.

"Anything else?" I said. He did not reply.

The next morning there were two bottles of cognac parked in the trash from the previous night instead of the usual one.

I continued calling Alice, through all of July, as the Great Frog and Lola prepped for the move to Houston. The two were a model of disorganization and, for the whole month, the house was an obstacle course you didn't dare try to negotiate without turning on every light in the place.

I was calling Alice with greater regularity now. After about two weeks, they gave up trying to screen her calls. Probably Alice had made that decision since I'd adopted the tactic of calling her every half-hour when I was told she wasn't home. She must have decided it was easier to talk to me, perhaps even throw an occasional bone and be rid of me for a while.

And so it went on through July and most of August. Around the middle of that month I asked her out again.

"No," she said at first.

Again I tried.

"No," again. This time Alice added that I was wasting my time.

"Do you remember telling me that before, Alice?"

"No."

"It was in March, Alice, and I'm glad I didn't listen, because if I had, I'd never know what people mean when they say they're in love. Now I'll never mistake anything else for it."

"You'll find someone else, Sonny."

"I'd rather you say that to Colin."

"Well, I'm not going to," she said, "Goodbye, Sonny."

"Wait!"

"What?"

"One date, Alice, that's all I want."

"I told you no."

"One, Alice."

"If I agree, will you stop calling?"

"Okay," I pledged, having no intention of honoring it. There would be no need to stop the calls after that date; she would want them, I was sure, all those and more.

"When Alice?"

"Friday, no a week from Friday."

"How about both Fridays?"

"One week from Friday, Sonny, at seven."

"I'll be there, Alice."

This time it would be different; I'd never been more certain of anything. First, I'd composed a list of things I'd said and done wrong on my dates with Alice—words, phrases, gestures—all studied, memorized with alternates rehearsed so mistakes or suspected mistakes wouldn't be repeated. I thought that it would be an impossible feat to remember and reconstruct that much. With Alice, it wasn't hard at all.

Second, I was no longer driving the Great Frog's Chevy. The Lincoln Zephyr was running. During the week previous to my calling Alice for the date, I'd been test-driving the Zephyr between one and five in the morning. Like so many recently rebuilt engines, the Zephyr had teething problems. That V-12, which was no engineering marvel to begin with, first propelled her in irregular bursts and jerks between backfires that had taken me a week to diagnose and cure. I would have asked Ray to look at her, but by that time I was either too proud or regarded myself the better mechanic. With her smoothed out, and several round trips to South Bend, I determined she was ready for paint. This was done in the grease stall of Ray's garage three nights before my date with Alice. Ray actually painted the Zephyr for me.

Though claiming to be "no professional," Ray had painted dozens of cars down through the years, something I'd never done even once. Watching him spray the jet-black enamel, coat after coat, with the strokes and grace of a prima ballerina, I decided he had no right to call himself anything but a maestro.

"Done," Ray said, turning to me after a final pass around the car. Afterward he didn't even walk its perimeter once to inspect for missed spots, runs in the paint, or even to admire his work. The conceited bastard left that to me. The paint job was flawless.

Black paint is unforgiving and revealed several of my first attempts at body and fender work that were far less than masterpieces.

Still, the zephyr was magnificent. Her flow of lines, so brilliantly highlighted by the black paint, more than overpowered the imperfections. After allowing her to dry for a day, I fired her up and drove her to the house on Eleventh Street, parking her in our driveway behind my father's Chevy.

The Great Frog stepped from the house and walked up to us. We'd barely spoken since our exchange in the kitchen three weeks earlier. He surveyed the car in two slow arcs from about ten feet away.

"Beautiful," he said at last, "I never realized it until now. It took the paint to make me see it."

I nodded, "Thank you, father," I said.

"But you knew, didn't you? Long before the paint showed that to me."

"Yes, Father, when I first saw her."

"Maybe because your mother was an artist," he offered.

"Maybe, you're leaving for Houston tomorrow?"

He nodded. "Have you made arrangements, where you'll live?"

"Yes," I said. Though I'd meant to talk to Ray about a cot in the station, I'd yet to do that.

"You're going to see the young lady," he said probably avoiding her name so as not to provoke me.

"Tomorrow."

"Ah," he said, turning to go back to the house, but quickly reversed his course and handed me a scrap of paper. "If things change this is our address in Houston, there's a bedroom there for you."

"Thank you, father."

He turned to go. "Father," I asked, "is that mirror in my room still attached to the wall?"

"I believe so."

"I want it."

"As you wish."

Ten minutes later I had the mirror propped against the East wall of our garage where I could gaze at myself framed by the driver's window of the Zephyr I'd parked abreast of it. There was no way Alice could reject me now, I told myself, looking in the mirror. No way she could do that, no way—none.

Lola and the Great Frog were gone before first light on Thursday morning, saying goodbye, and that they hoped to make Tulsa that first day.

The house, now empty save for the cot where I slept, and assorted heaps of my junk, seemed enormous. In two weeks, it would be someone else's. And the South Shore Line would cease to be my own personal railroad. It was the only thing about that house I knew I'd miss: my own personal railroad. "She rolls she rumbles, but she'll never roar, that's 'cause she's electric, the mighty South Shore," I said out loud, contemplating the emptiness as a Westbound rumbled by.

That afternoon technicians came to pick up the telephones and disconnect the lines. If Alice wanted to call and cancel our date for the next evening, which I was terrified she might do, she would have to call Ray's garage. I considered taking off Friday to defeat that possibility, but decided not to. Anyway, Alice didn't call.

We were on for seven o'clock. There'd been a slight chill in the evening's air that Friday. It annoyed me. We were a whole week, and then some, before Labor Day. Early chills tended to signify that a cold winter was in the offing. Mild ones were bad enough; the slightest cold front was a harbinger of the arctic horror soon to follow.

I eased the Zephyr abreast of the two-flat on Avalon Court, which I still could never have found, but for the numbers on it. The buildings were absolutely without anything else to distinguish one from another. From the second floor parlor, three pink fleshy ovals were watching the street. An arm connected to one of them pointed at the Lincoln Zephyr. It was ten minutes to seven; I sat in the car intending to allow those minutes to pass.

Two figures emerged from the two-flat the second I stepped from the car. Alice and Collin walked in line toward me. Of course, Collin was first. When we were five feet apart, I moved to sidestep him. He blocked me.

"Don't do that again," I said.

"Don't come here again and I won't have to," replied Colin.

"Tell him we have a date," I said to Alice, "and I might not have to smash every bone in his face—no guarantees though."

A faint gasp said she knew I was serious. She had to be remembering what I'd already done once to Colin and to her cousin.

"No you don't!" said Colin, as I tried once again to step around him.

This time we made contact. Colin gave me a mild shove backwards.

"Alice," I said, "we have a date, tell him that, please." She was silent. Once again I tried to flank Colin. Encouraged, I could only guess, by my failure to retaliate, he tried shoving me with his right hand. I seized his thumb, firmly applied torque to it, just as I had in the station some months before, and sent him spinning off to my right. Good God, he was a slow learner, though probably he wasn't hurt. I turned back to Alice.

"I missed you," I said. It might have been the understatement of the age. Alice's brief glance past me told me Colin had circled and was coming up from behind.

He was three feet away, both hands clenched into fists, in a sort of boxer's stance, when I spun to deliver a kick to his ribs that had to have broken at least one of them. As he doubled over and fell back, Alice screamed.

She dove at Colin as he collapsed to the ground trying to catch his wind. He lay there and began a string of long hard coughs, one of them brought up blood. Shaking, Alice knelt over him. "Baby, baby," she said, repeating it three or four times.

I walked over to them, "He's no baby," I said, "and I'm sorry I had to do that. We did have a date." The first part was untrue. I wasn't a bit sorry.

She turned to look up at me with a rage in her face I never imagined it capable of. The face, still so lovely even when this angry, perhaps maybe more so, shrieked at me:

"Get out of here. Goddamn you! Get out of my life!"

"Alice," I said, vainly hoping to calm her.

"Get out!" she screamed, loud enough to be heard, I was sure, to the end of the block.

I looked up to see five or six people spilling from the two-flat and running toward us. "Get an ambulance!" Alice screamed, "and call the police."

Her father was the first to reach me, "You'd better get out of here son," he said.

"We had a date, sir."

"Get out of here," Alice screamed again, "Get out!"

Never taking my eyes off her, I walked backward all the way to the car.

On the drive home, I was too angry to cry—at least for a while. I managed to save that until I had the Zephyr parked in the garage, and the door shut. Then I sat in the front seat and let her rip: force-five hysteria. It hadn't once occurred to me how badly I might have hurt Colin. The bastard had it coming. Alice and I had a date. A bargain was a bargain. What was wrong with her anyway? I was a hundred times better looking than Colin Walker. Hadn't she considered what her children might look like? What kind of life they might have to go through looking like Colin?

The whole horrible night that I'd been jilted was back for an encore. I deserved better, I told myself, a lot better.

I wasn't done yet. I sobbed aloud, and then screamed at the walls of the garage—empty now, but for myself, and the great car: "I've just begun to fight, Alice, do you hear? Just begun." I fell asleep sobbing "just begun" over and over again.

On the short drive to work Saturday morning, I'd made plans for the next comeback. Alice would be going to Willkie in a couple of weeks. We'd be thrown together, possibly in the same classes. She'd get over the business about Colin, who, for sure, would never interfere with any future dates I'd make. And I would get dates with Alice; she'd agreed to one, and still owed me at least that much.

Ray bolted from the station when I pulled up. "Park that thing in the back, Sonny," he hollered, "and get inside."

"What?"

"You heard me, Sonny!"

"What?"

"Park that fucking car in the back and get inside. Use the back door. You're in big trouble, Sonny." Noting his tone, I obeyed.

Once inside, Ray ushered me into the grease pit where we couldn't be seen.

"There're two dicks looking for you, Sonny," he said, in what could only be called a controlled shout, "they were here and they're headed for your place. They've got a warrant."

"For what?"

"How about assault with intent to kill?"

"He hit me first, Ray."

"You look just fine to me Sonny, but that boy you hit—he has one collapsed lung and the other is punctured."

"I didn't hit him."

"What?"

"Alright, I kicked him."

"You could have killed him, Sonny, you've got to get out of here."

"Where the hell am I going to go, Ray? I got no kin here, just an aunt I hate."

"I mean you're going to Texas, punk."

"Like hell, Ray, and don't ever call me a punk again."

At that Ray shoved me hard enough against the concrete wall of the pit to make me bounce off it and fall into a heap to the floor. For a moment, I lay stunned by the swiftness and strength I never would have guessed Ray had.

"I was defending myself, Ray," I protested, as Ray walked up to, and stood high over me. "I was…"

He planted his foot on my left arm.

"Okay, Sonny, play it your own way and tell it to the Judge. Go home and surrender to those dicks and tell them you didn't do anything wrong. And in one hour they'll have you in a lock up, then on to Crown Point, and by tonight some three hundred-pound moon cricket will have six inches of his black crank, covered with sores, shoved up your little lily-white ass. Ever been in jail, Sonny?"

"No."

"Well, pretty boy," Ray said, "let me tell you from personal experience, Indiana has some of the worst of them."

"Ray…you?"

"You never lived through a depression, Sonny. You have no idea what it will drive you to do. That's all I'm going to say about it. You're going to Texas."

Ray was right, there was no choice.

"Here's for the week," he said, handing me a thick wad of bills that had to contain several times what he owed me.

"Give me the keys, Sonny, and I'll top off your gas. Stay down here until I'm done. And don't stop for anything until you're out of the State."

"My tools are in the garage back home, can I get them?"

"Christ sake, Sonny, didn't you hear anything I told you?" After a pause, he added, "Give me your house keys, I'll try to pick them up and get them to you." There's a special thing about a man and his tools, especially if he's a mechanic.

"Thanks, Ray," I called to him, as he climbed the stairs out of the pit, "for that, and everything else."

The bell on the office wall rang indicating a customer was at the pumps.

"I just hope that's not the cops," said Ray, standing at the doorway. And do what I say: get out of Indiana as soon as you can." It was the last exchange I'd ever have with him.

Michigan's state line was far closer to us than that of Illinois, but the latter was the one I went for. A dash for Michigan meant I'd have had to drive the whole eastern perimeter of Indiana from the outside before heading for Texas, and there was no guarantee that it was, in fact, safer. Still, considering what was at stake, I took a chance and got a brief burst of euphoria as I crossed into Illinois. It was time I'd gotten away with something.

By eleven that morning, I was in Chicago, where the gleaming Zephyr scored the admiring looks it should have gotten from Alice the night before.

A little past noon, I was on the great American institution known as Route 66. I'd planned a trip down 66 as a reward for getting through high school the following summer, but the destination was to be California, not Texas. Of course, once I'd met Alice, the plan included her as a passenger, in fact, it revolved around her, as did so much else.

Now I was on that highway, a year ahead of time, with a very different plan and wanted by the law. The last item, and the reason for it, was the only thing that oddly, gave me any pleasure, though the fact that the Lincoln's engine—the one I'd resurrected from junk—never missed a stroke, should have made me ecstatic.

I made Tulsa shortly after 7:30 that evening in a downpour, the only thing that kept me from pressing on. Lola and the Great Frog had said they hoped to do Tulsa the first day, so I decided, somewhere in Missouri, to make Texas before bedding down.

But it was to be Tulsa.

I awoke with an idea. Since my plan had once been to head for California, why not just do it now? I could finish school there, or just plain forget about that. If asked to produce a diploma, I could easily have one printed. Nobody had ever checked to see who had one anyway unless they were the government. Besides, who would ever want to claim they'd graduated from a school named for Wendell Willkie? The idea of being alone was a tonic that first elated, then quickly degenerated, to something that scared the hell out of me.

I had a trucker's breakfast, determined to get on 66, point the Zephyr west, and make it all happen starting that day. As I finished, I'd come to understand that I was a long way from the fearless thing I always imagined myself. Being on my own at seventeen in a strange state nearly froze me motionless. My breathing had shortened to brief irregular bursts and I was giddy. Reaching the car, I had to catch myself on the door handle to avoid falling. I could do it, I assured myself, as I started the engine. I drove onto the feeder ramp to the highway-heading west and accelerated.

Five miles later, an overhead sign announced that the center and left lanes were for westbound traffic to Amarillo and Albuquerque. Six hundred miles beyond Albuquerque was Los Angeles. The right lane was for the turn to route 75, south through Oklahoma and then Texas.

To avoid the decision, I held the Zephyr in the center lane. All the times I'd dreamed about living in the west came back to taunt me as I drove. Californians were the most blessed people on earth and I longed to be one of them. I had been one too—in a thousand fantasies. Both Alice and I were. And now Alice never would be going to California in the passenger seat beside me. But I still had my own piece of that dream. Did I have what it took at seventeen to make it happen?

Another sign announced I was one mile from the turnoff. I held the Zephyr steady wondering that if I did turn right, would I ever again have the nerve or even the chance to turn back to the center lane one day and live where I knew I belonged, and to look out over the city of Los Angeles from that precipice jutting from Mulholland Drive like the people in the magazine ad? A quarter mile from the turnoff, I eased the Zephyr into the right lane, turned south to Route 75—to Texas, home, safety, to Lola and the Great Frog. I was more like my spineless French father than I ever cared to admit and made Houston by early evening.

III.

ENTER MAX

9. VANGUARD

On a Monday Morning in March, 1958, Alfred Cobb, a sophomore at the Judah P. Benjamin secondary school in Houston stood at his locker on the second floor, a tiny radio speaker pressed to his ear pounding in the incredible news: The Vanguard rocket, the first ever designed exclusively for space exploration, and brand new from bolt one had launched a satellite into orbit.

Alfred had tracked the Vanguard project for two years, had displayed models of it at science fairs, and had built and launched rockets of his own. But Vanguard, the world's first true space rocket had, through it all, remained his primary passion.

The Vanguard satellite launch was to be the crown jewel of America's participation in the International Geophysical Year. A great fanfare had been made of what was to be the first earth satellite and nobody outside the scientific community imagined that a brand new, impossibly complex, three-stage rocket might not work the first time out.

But on October 4, 1957, without warning, the world changed forever. The Russians, not the Americans, launched the first earth satellite, Sputnik 1. And before anyone could catch their breath, a second Sputnik carried a dog into orbit on a one-way mission. America and the world lay stunned.

A wave of hysterical paranoia followed. Could not a Soviet Union that launched satellites into space just as easily rain swarms of nuclear armed missiles down on American cities turning them into radioactive ash heaps? How could this have happened? A United States that had emerged as the world's undisputed superpower in 1945 just one dozen years later, found itself cowering under the threat of annihilation by Soviet ICBMs.

And where, oh where was the much vaunted American Satellite?

It would be launched; it was finally announced, on December 6, 1957, from Cape Canaveral where the eyes and cameras of the world would be focused.

Alfred had never imagined he would be there to see it, but he was. One week before a special delivery envelope arrived at his house containing round trip first class airfare to Florida, two hundred dollars in cash, and a note:

"Dear Alfred, best of luck to you and the great Vanguard. When you get back from Florida, you might drop by 3033 Teal Way sometime. We are very interested in building some rockets. Money is no object. Cordially, Wright Kilbourn."

Only then did Alfred remember the gorgeous youth with the wooden leg he'd seen struggling to change a flat tire on his brand new Chevy convertible in the school parking lot months before. The young man was bruised and almost in tears from failed attempts. Sensing how desperately the beautiful cripple wanted to do the job himself, Alfred offered to help, but the help he gave was deliberately minimal though he could have easily done the job himself in a third the time it took the two of them. When they were done, Wright Kilbourn identified himself, shook Alfred's hand, and then barely acknowledged him again when they passed in the hall.

On December 6th, in front of a thousand cameras, Vanguard lifted off, rose three feet, and promptly collapsed into a great orange fireball. Alfred knew enough about rockets to know that this could happen and was likely to happen the first time out. Anybody that knew anything about rockets could have foretold it. Yet, for most of the trip home he wept. To the press, this was an outrage, a study in incompetence, and worse, a swindle. How could America put its future in the hands of the kind of imbeciles that ran the Vanguard project? America was now wide open to annihilation by Russian ICBMs.

On January 31, 1958, deliverance came. An American satellite, Explorer 1, was launched atop a rocket assembly cobbled together from military hardware. Tagged the Jupiter C, it was a three stage variant of the Army's Redstone, a first generation descendant of the German V-2.

There had been a clandestine backup plan headed by the very rocket genius that had designed the V-2 for Hitler in the first place, one Werner von Braun. A dozen years before, swarms of von Braun's creations had been hurled at the population of London by a dying Nazi State desperately trying to reverse its fortunes. They failed at that, but managed to kill thousands.

No matter how many embryonic V-2s, or its descendants: the Redstones and Jupiter C rockets, had blown up on their launch pads, or made it barely into flight, the reality was that they were ready—not Vanguard—to put America on the scoreboard.

No matter that von Braun, himself, had defended and praised the rival Vanguard project for its sophistication and efficiency. Nothing mattered to the media but that Vanguard had blown up before the eyes of the world. The first true space rocket became synonymous with failure and an international joke.

Five days after the Explorer's success, a second Vanguard roared off its launch pad into a Florida dawn and for a moment it appeared that America might indeed have itself another satellite. It didn't. From the ground the explosion five miles overhead looked like the rocket's second stage had kicked in. It hadn't. Vanguard's on board detonator had been activated by a range safety officer after the 72-foot rocket developed a wobble.

There followed a fresh wave of media ridicule and faux righteous outrage. A Congressional investigation loomed. A funding termination was threatened along with the scrapping of the whole project lest America be humiliated again by yet another Vanguard flop. Politicians who wouldn't have known a rocket from a dildo vied to outdo each other lambasting Vanguard with allegations of fraud and incompetence. Media cartoonists and columnists competed as to whom could draw the most blood vilifying the great American debacle. A story was widely circulated that Vanguard was never intended to fly at all and was a hoax by defense contractors to bilk the American taxpayer out of millions. The story went that the project would be canceled after the intentional launch failures and all remaining Vanguards would be destroyed and forgotten, because, if they existed at all, they were cardboard.

But Vanguard would have its moment. The third launch was set for Monday March 17, St. Patrick's day. Alfred had not slept the night before. He kept the radio on his desk just loud enough to be heard from a foot away and not awaken his parents. At midnight it was announced that the US had another satellite rocket on the launch pad. The anchor added snidely that he hoped it wasn't a Vanguard.

Alfred having not slept, and was just about to topple from his chair, the 8-o'clock broadcast flashed the news:

> *Cape Canaveral Florida: A Vanguard rocket streaked skyward this morning. Spokesman for the Naval Research Laboratory announced that all systems appear to have functioned normally and the downrange tracking station at Blossom Point has confirmed that signals from the tiny satellite have been received.*

Apparently the third time was the charm.

Alfred Cobb let loose a great shout of joy, tossed exhaustion aside, and hurled himself down the stairs to where his parents were having breakfast. He decided only at the last moment not to jump atop the table and shriek out the news. He was unable to eat. Through the bus ride to school he kept the transistor radio he'd built pressed to his ear.

Vanguard had been launched, and was apparently in orbit. But apparently was not officially. Not yet anyway. The third rocket stage, the solid fuel one, could still have fallen short of the 18,000 mile an hour push required to turn its payload into a satellite. Or its angle of attack might have deviated enough to thrust it into re-entry and a fiery demise. Vanguard would have to make three quarters of one orbit past the tracking stations on the West Coast who could then confirm that it was indeed the world's fourth satellite. By that time Alfred Cobb would be in class. He would have to wait for the break between classes for history's verdict. Radios were officially banned inside the school, and Alfred hid his on the lower shelf of his locker on the second floor, and went to his third-year English class without it. The fifty-minute session was an eternity. Alfred sat trance like taking in nothing of the class; his mind was aboard the third stage of Vanguard as it thundered through the heavens. When the class ended, he sprinted back to his locker and tuned the news broadcast from Houston's KILT Radio.

Cape Canaveral Florida: Naval Research Laboratory scientists have stated that the Vanguard Satellite is officially in orbit and now half way through its second trip around the earth. West coast tracking stations have reported receiving signals broadcast from the satellite now called Vanguard One.

Alfred clutched the radio to his chest and shook with joyous sobs. The world's first true space rocket, brand new from bolt one and chocked full of innovations, had worked perfectly on the third time out. This was an incredible record of success. No matter that all the news fools would do now was shrug and say that it was about time somebody got it right. No matter any of that. Alfred suppressed yet another ecstatic shriek. He desperately wanted to share the news.

And then he saw her.

He had passed Courtney Provine hundreds of times between his classes, and had a pretty good idea where he was likely to see her in the hall, or better yet, get to walk behind her glorious form imagining himself one of the jocks flanking her, both trying to outdo the other with their next mouthful. If they weren't actually jocks, they looked as if they were.

Until Alfred Cobb had seen Courtney as a freshman one year earlier, he might never have believed that such girls existed. Alfred had been told, and had once believed that the ones he'd seen in magazines were created from photos with airbrushes. He needed but one look at Courtney Provine to nail that lie to the floor.

When Alfred wasn't thinking about rockets and satellites he thought about what it would be like to know a girl like Courtney Provine, to go on a date with a girl like Courtney Provine, and to touch a girl like Courtney Provine. He thought about those things a lot.

And he would think about Courtney lying in bed with his legs pressed together in a cycle of squeeze and release imagining that his thighs were Courtney's. And Courtney would giggle between gasps of breathless pleasure. And Alfred would kiss the empty air in front of him while the tempestuous throbbing between his legs accelerated to a gallop. And Courtney would writhe in glorious undulations as the pumping thunder inside him began, and Alfred would count backward 10-9-8-7-6-5-4-3-2-1-*Ignition*! And the launch pad would be showered with white liquid fire while Courtney and he soared through the heavens just like the Vanguard rocket.

He had never seen her pass his locker at this particular time and to his amazement she was without her usual escorts. He breathed deeply. He had wondered a thousand times what would happen were he to actually approach Courtney, and had concluded that there was absolutely nothing he could say that could start a conversation. But now there was something: there was Vanguard!

Courtney was alone *and there was Vanguard*! If this wasn't providence, then there was no such thing as providence.

There was a reason that Courtney was there just then and like Alfred's, hers too centered on a rocket, a bargain basement Vodka-like blend called "Moon Rocket" that left no scent, came in a bottle that sold for a dollar twenty nine a fifth at liquor stores that carried it, and not many would. Its color and contents varied from batch to batch. The ten dollars Courtney had paid an older cousin to buy this one for her should have bought something far better and would have, were his price for buying it been only money. But she wasn't ready to pay that yet, not to him anyway.

Courtney's path included a washroom stop between her first and second period classes where she could slip into one of the stalls for a few solid hits off the pint bottle she carried in a hollowed out book. But for the past week she'd been using a new route she'd discovered, where, equidistant from her first and second period classes, was an always-empty restroom. The new route, that also allowed her to avoid her unwelcome entourage, led her past Alfred's locker.

Alfred pushed the locker door closed behind him. He fumbled trying to engage the hasp of the lock with the hole in the handle and discovered he couldn't, nor could he afford the time it would take to turn around. She would have passed him and his chance would be lost. So Alfred proceeded, lock in hand.

Courtney had seen him advance from the locker, but until he was half way toward her, she didn't think he meant to confront her.

"Court-ney Pro-vine," Alfred said in a broken voice. She stopped and turned a quarter arc to face him directly. The face that spoke her name was shaking. "Court-ney Pro-vine" the shaking face said again, adding: "The Vanguard."

"The Vanguard," Alfred repeated. "The rocket. We have another…" He went blank. Alfred Cobb combed his brain and could not find the word "satellite" anywhere in it.

"We have another…another moon. The Vanguard rocket has launched another moon."

Alfred trembled at the thought of the brain behind Courtney's incredible face processing the words he could barely make. He might have expected anything but the look of utter disbelief she gave him. He had no idea that the hand with which he held the open lock was waving about erratically.

It grazed the books Courtney was holding and they spilled to the floor. The bottle leaped from the hollow one, then bounced and clinked on the hall tiles. Horrified, she dove for it. She'd heard him say only the words *rocket and moon*. How could this boy she'd never once spoken to know about the bottle she carried? If he knew, then who else did? *Who else didn't?*

Alfred sprang to the floor and began collecting the scattered books. "I'm, I'm…" He was panting. "I'm so sorry," he said handing her now empty book that had held the bottle, its purpose having completely escaped him. "The rocket," he said. "The Vanguard rocket has put another satellite into orbit!"

Courtney had retrieved the bottle and was trying to stuff it anywhere it still might not be seen. Without looking down, she found a pocket and tried forcing it in neck first. The seams gave slightly when she pushed it until the cap would go no further leaving the bottom rim of the inverted bottle pressed against her belly. It was very cold.

"Listen," Alfred said and switched on his radio hoping they might still be talking about the satellite launch. The speaker crackled to life:

"It's now official, the satellite, which was launched from Cape Canaveral Florida some two and a half hours ago and

carried into orbit by a three stage Vanguard rocket is now the Earth's fourth artificial moon. A jubilant spokesmen for the Naval Research Laboratory has said that the satellite called Vanguard One is expected to remain in orbit for hundreds of years."

Courtney's paled face assumed something resembling its normal color as she realized that Alfred Cobb was but another of an endless train of boys who would grasp at any subject attempting a foray into her life. This was the first one that had used something other than sports because all the rest knew little of anything else. But more important still, he'd missed the fact that she carried liquor in a hollowed out book.

"I'm so glad about your, your, rocket ship," Courtney said, the relief flooding her like a warm tonic. "I'm sure it's very nice. Will it be going to the moon?"

There was no trace of sarcasm in her voice. The question was as sincere as it was ignorant. She calculated that she might still have time for a stop in the girl's room some fifty feet away for a nip. She turned so as to proceed away in quickstep.

Alfred stood frozen, unable to seize upon a single thought that had a chance of becoming coherent speech when he saw that one of Courtney's books was still on the floor. He quickly retrieved it and sprinted after her. She had the door to the girl's room pushed about a foot open when he drew abreast of her. "Courtney," he said, extending the wayward book.

An enormous hand seized his arm. The book was airborne again as Alfred was spun about to face the captain of the varsity football squad, Wally Montruska. Behind Monturska stood two other squad members. Both of them sported hall monitor buttons. They were part of a student posse set up to prevent unauthorized passage through the halls during class periods. They were known also as the "Goon Squad." One of them grabbed Alfred's radio and hurled it against the steel lockers where it disintegrated on impact, spraying the floor with fragments.

Next, Alfred felt Montruska's fist slam squarely into his gut. He doubled over and the last thing he heard before crashing to the floor was Courtney's cry of horror.

An hour later Lionel Rixon entered the outer office of Myron Larch, the Principal of Benjamin High School, and rushed past secretaries with whom he normally stopped to exchange flirts. He was a tall widower of 47 with an athletic build he did little to acquire or maintain. There was an innate handsomeness to his Slavic face that was marred only by a receding hairline. The secretaries always had opening lines loaded in their chambers when he appeared. But today his gait clearly told them that he had no time for it as he sped for the door to the inner office.

Rixon entered Larch's office without knocking, something he alone was allowed do. Larch had accorded him that deference because Rixon, the assistant principal, made every decision on matters with which Larch was incompetent to do, and that included about everything. Rixon had been slated for the Principal's job when Larch had edged him out on the strength of having had a professional football career, against which Rixon could only claim thirty-three missions against the Germans as pilot of a B-24, in addition to a master's degree in English from Purdue. Not even Larch's total lack of anything resembling academia in his portfolio made a difference. Still, Rixon's resentment of this was minimal, he had seen too much irony in the war to try and make sense of it, and there were times he actually found himself half liking the man.

Larch sat behind an enormous desk that still hid most of an ever-growing paunch. Little remained of the pro-football body. The face looked as if it had once done a stint as chewing gum. He was smoking a large greenish-brown cigar the end of which hung loose and dripped saliva. A similar drip could be seen from the left side of his lower lip.

A man was seated opposite Larch. He was Frank Hollenbeck, a Physical-Education teacher and head coach of the school's football team, the Benjamin Bengals. He also oversaw the Goon Squad. This man Rixon despised. All too often he'd leaned on teachers to pass failing athletes claiming to know enough people on the Harris County Board of Education to get them fired.

But Rixon had only laughed the one time the heat was put to him, called Hollenbeck's bluff, and Larch had backed him. Hollenbeck was pulling deep drags off a cigar identical to the one Larch smoked.

"Hello Lionel," said the principal. "Care to try one?" he said, selecting a fresh cigar from a wooden box. "Jamaican, half the price of Cubans and you can't tell the difference. I would know."

Rixon held up a hand. "No, but thanks," he said. Larch motioned him to a chair, but Rixon remained standing.

"Problem?" Hollenbeck asked finally.

"Yeah," Rixon replied, "I would say there is a big problem."

Larch motioned him to proceed.

"About one hour ago," said Rixon, three of your goons—he glared at Hollenbeck—brought a student into my office because you weren't in yours, as usual, and mine adjoins it. I said 'brought,' but the right word was 'dragged.' It was pretty obvious they'd worked him over. They said he was trying to follow a girl into a washroom."

"What did the kid say?" asked Larch.

"Nothing," said Rixon. "Remember I said they dragged him in. He was barely conscious."

"Well," surmised Hollenbeck, "if he tried to force his way into the woman's washroom he got what he deserved. Hell, he should face criminal charges."

"Yeah," Rixon replied, "except for one thing: none of it's true."

"How do you know that?" Hollenbeck fired back.

"Because fifteen minutes ago the alleged victim turned up in my office and told me what actually happened. He was trying to return a book she'd dropped."

"So no problem," said the coach, "you let him go with a warning."

"It's you that needs the warning."

"Does the cunt have a name?" asked Hollenbeck realizing that there might be more trouble in this than first appeared.

"She does," Rixon replied, "it's Courtney Provine." The two seated men let loose wolf whistles.

"Yes that one," continued Rixon. No one who'd ever seen Courtney and learned here name was likely to forget it.

"Damn," said Hollenbeck after a pause, "there's a honey I'd love to poke."

"Amen to that, "said Larch.

The pair grinned at each other. Hollenbeck offered up a sexual gesture with his fingers.

Rixon fumed. "Don't either of you want to know who the kid they beat up was? His name is Alfred Cobb."

"Should that mean something?" Larch asked.

"Two things," Rixon replied, "first, he had some of the highest math scores in the state according to the most recent battery of tests." He knew this would make no impression whatever on either man, but wanted to say it before delivering the haymaker.

"So the kid's smart," said Larch, "what's the second?"

"I tried to get his parents on the phone, "said Rixon, "but there was no answer. I called in the nurse and she thought we should get an ambulance. The kid had perked up somewhat and said he wanted to leave, and not five minutes later two of his friends showed up and took him away."

"And you just let them take him away?" asked Larch.

"I didn't try to stop them, no. You wouldn't have either. The kid put on a brave face in front of them. He tried very hard not to cry. He was in serious pain."

"Is there a point to this?" Hollenbeck asked, somewhat irritated as if too much time had already been spent on the incident.

"There is," Rixon replied.

Larch's expression now hinted that he was beginning to catch on that these weren't ordinary friends. "His friends," said Larch suddenly, "do we know them?"

Rixon almost smiled while nodding his head. He suddenly found himself wanting to physically deliver the kind of gut punches to them that he imagined Alfred had received. "You do," he said. "One of them was Wright Kilbourn."

"The gimp!" Hollenbeck blurted out angrily," then taking a deep breath "that fucking gimp, ought to be put out of his misery—gassed!"

Larch and Hollenbeck looked at each other; both realizing at the same instant, that the second name was guaranteed to be coupled to the first.

"The other one was Max Morgenstern," said Rixon.

One year before, another of Kilbourn and Morgenstern's friends had been roughed up in a similar way by a pair of football players who were run down by a car on a dark street two weeks later. Miraculously, both lived, and with luck, might walk again—one day. A witness had identified the driver as Morgenstern and then recanted her statement. Morgenstern's lawyer was a twenty-nine-year-old legal hot shot, one H.S. Rawlson in the permanent employ of Wright Kilbourn, and regarded by many as among the best in Texas. The district attorney assigned the case had told Larch and Hollenbeck that trying to prosecute Morgenstern was a waste of time.

Rixon surveyed the two men and noted both were sweating beads that glistened like new ball bearings. They now knew, as had Rixon, for the better part of an hour, that there would be Hell to pay for this.

10. YOU AIN'T SEEN NUTHIN

The 1959 fall term was a day past one week old the Thursday when I walked into the Houston High School named for J.P. Benjamin, the Confederacy's Secretary of State. I was about a hundred feet inside when a couple of gorillas overtook me and demanded something called a hall pass. Each sported buttons pinned just above, and slightly to the right, of their groins that announced in bold capitals that they were "hall monitors."

I told them that I didn't have one, nearly adding what they could do with their request.

"You're coming with us," the pair announced in unison as if auditioning for some cop roles in a bad TV series.

I was still holding a ring of keys in my hand—keys are a formidable weapon if held and aimed properly. They can destroy eyes, slice arteries, or be plunged deep into an ear canal. Remembering that I was wanted in Indiana, I decided, instead, to go with them to the office of what I assumed was their den mother whose name was stenciled on the frosted glass lite of his door: Frank Hollenbeck. But Frank wasn't home so they deposited me in the office that backed up to his. There was no name on that door, but the one engraved on an upright Formica desk plaque announced I was facing Lionel Rixon, the Assistant Principal.

I told him that I was there to register, and had no idea what that entailed in a tone that told him that I couldn't have cared less, not mentioning that I was only there at the Great Frog's insistence as a prerequisite for room and board. When I was done, he responded in kind.

"Mister?"

"July," I replied, "Addison July."

"Alright Mr. Addison July, "you're from?"

"Indiana."

"All right Mr. Addison July from Indiana, you want to register here. First, we require that you show that you are who you say you are and that you have the credits to enroll at the level you claim you're at, and furthermore that you're not wanted somewhere."

I must have given a slight start at this last item and he didn't miss it. This was not a man who missed much. He pulled out a manila form from a drawer in his desk and set it on top. I read the large letters upside down: "Transcript Request."

"I suppose I'll have to get your transcript," he said. "If I leave the getting of it to you, I'll never see it, will I?" I didn't answer, and he correctly took that as an affirmation.

"Now, when and where did you last attend school?"

"Wendell Willkie High, Michigan City, the spring term."

"Indiana?"

"Check." I had just said I was from Indiana.

He pulled a loose leafed binder from the shelf behind him and homed in on a point about midway through it.

"Wendell Willkie Secondary School, 4343 Kelvyn Parkway," he said, "amazing," he mused, "I voted for Wendell Willkie."

"I'm sorry to hear that," I replied. In the 1940 election, Franklin Roosevelt had even trounced Willkie in his own hometown, though Willkie did carry Indiana. I'd guessed that most people born since the war didn't know who Willkie was. And the most memorable thing about the High School named for him was that it was so forgettable except for one thing: Alice was now enrolled there.

We spent the next twenty minutes selecting the courses I'd need to graduate based on what credits I claimed I had, all of which Rixon said would have to be verified by a transcript. I was given a small stack of blue cards that would get me temporarily into the classes that had begun a week before.

When I got up to go, he said: "One more thing, there will be a pep rally in the assembly hall late this afternoon. The whole school's going to it in shifts. Saturday is the homecoming game. Let me see those cards again." Thumbing through them he came upon one card he drew out. "So you'll miss world history at 2:30. Be in the assembly hall instead." Pushing it back into the stack, he returned the cards, saying with an ironic smile, "Participation is mandatory. They give out slips as proof you were there. You'll give that to the teacher of the class you missed."

I thought he was kidding. "I can hardly wait." My voice might have taken sarcasm to a new level. "They play football in Indiana too, as I recall."

The smile remained on his face. I gathered that he might share my opinion about the relevance of football along with other sports. I remembered, with a pang of pleasure, Bobby Dardinelle walking Willkie's halls for weeks with his arm in a sling and unable to practice, thanks to me.

"The cheerleaders alone should make it worth your going," Rixon offered.

"Not unless I can take one home and play with her," I replied. "We have girls in Indiana too." His expression told me that he liked that response.

I got up to leave.

"Mr. July, to borrow from the vernacular of the realm, I suggest that you ain't seen nuthin."

I almost told him that the same could be said for him or anyone else that hadn't known Alice. Doing that would be telling him far more than I cared to. This guy had probably surmised that I was wanted in Indiana. He wouldn't need much more to figure out why, and I wasn't about to surrender that. As I said, he was someone that didn't miss much.

And Rixon had been right about the rally. I had to admit that. Subtract Alice from the equation and I'd "ain't seen nuthin." But of course Alice was not subtractable.

The auditorium that looked like it could seat three times the school's population was filled. And Rixon said it was done in shifts.

It was also true that nothing I'd seen in Indiana could approach the waves of hysterical adulation given the varsity squad that sat on the upper level of a two-tiered stage, each of them resembling some specimen of shaved ape squeezed into a uniform a few sizes too small. Some spat as if on cue while a man whose name was Hollenbeck (the coach I later learned) pummeled us with a ten-minute harangue about the delicious carnage his boys were to wreak on the hapless opposition come Saturday. Much of it was drowned out by storms of shouting, whistles, and synchronized stomping that made me hope that whomever had built the place knew what they were doing since my seat was under a balcony. The speech ended with two minutes of bedlam, and blizzards of shredded paper mixed with a shower of powdered plaster jarred from cracks somewhere above me. A literalist would surmise from the Hollenbeck's harangue that every rival team member and every fan that had come to cheer for them would be dead, and picked over by crows at the end of Saturday afternoon.

I mention, that on the stage stood a two tier set of benches that held the twenty-two players of the varsity squad and the second string. The stage level, with the dais and microphone at the center, was flanked on each side by eight members of the cheerleading squad, the one Rixon had said would make going to this worthwhile. Their uniforms were of the one-piece bathing suit variety, dipped in a sequin bath, typical of the time. At the end of Hollenbeck's speech, they launched into gyrations that left little doubt what the lads in the auditorium would conjure up in fantasies when they were later alone and playing with their Erector sets.

Presently the principal of the school—I would learn later that his name was Myron Larch—stepped to the lectern and presented, as one would a messiah, the gorilla that would lead the charge on Saturday: the team's captain, Wally Montruska. At that point, a chant from the balcony began, "Wall-ee, Wall-ee, Wall-ee," and spread through the auditorium like a sonic plague. As he stepped down to the stage, the cheerleaders, who'd paused for the introduction, again began gyrating away without music, not stopping while he spoke.

I don't imagine anyone understood him since Wally slurred and drooled through his delivery of a roughly fifty-word speech. The one word I could make out for sure was "kill" because he used it about a dozen times. Like everyone else, I focused on the gyrating girls.

When he'd finished I thought it was over. It wasn't.

There remained the singing of the Benjamin Bengals fight song to be led by the homecoming queen whom Larch then introduced. I missed the name and Rixon hadn't mentioned her. Just then I noticed the lad in the seat next to me was pouring sweat and breathing in uneven gasps.

"You all right kid?" I asked. He ignored me, sat mute in a kind of trance while his face traversed a range of colors that reminded me of Ralph when I'd told him that Mulholland Rocket's engine was a melted lump of scrap.

A dark haired girl stepped to the center of the stage. From where I sat, she looked as if she was likely beautiful or at least close to it, though you couldn't really tell from that distance. She did not wear a cheerleader costume, but the one she did wear left no doubt that her curves, lines, and angles were a perfectly balanced composition including the nearly right angle by which the top of her buttocks parted company with the rest of her torso; that part of her resembled Alice.

"Hey!" I said, gently poking the entranced lad. "Hey, who's the babe?"

No answer. I tried zooming in on her, still not yet able to conclude whether or not she qualified as the genuine beauty I guessed she was. The rest of the assembly had long since decided that.

"Who's the babe?" I repeated, no longer necessarily addressing the lad next to me.

From one row in front of me, and one seat to the right, a voice barked out the answer as if my question was a class one felony.

"That's Courtney Provine," the angry voice said. "Thanks," I said belching half way through my reply to the unseen face. The Benjamin Bengal fight song commenced:

Onward Bengals, fight, fight, fight, fight!
Maroon, maroon and white, white, white, white!
For honor, truth and right, right, right, right!
Onward Bengals, Bengals onward. Onward to victory.

Three identical stanzas were sung. In the middle of the second, someone in a large cat costume, a Bengal tiger I suppose, ambled onto the stage and stood alongside the dark-haired girl, seized the microphone with one paw and began stroking the back of her shoulders with the other. Clearly annoyed, she attempted to brush him off several times before delivering a well-placed crack across the animal's mouth.

Larch and Hollenbeck each grabbed a tuft of the cat and threw him from the stage to the floor about five feet below where he limped off. The song was then interrupted by five or ten second bursts of laughs and catcalls before resuming. No one was sure if it was staged or not. Through it all, the cheerleaders didn't miss a beat.

The song amazed me, not because of its banality, of which all such songs are composed, but it was word for word, and note for note, the same song the Willkie Wildcats used excepting only that the Willkie colors were gold and white and their team was a different species of cat. I might mention here that I hate all species of cat.

And with a final storm of screams and yet more shredded paper, the madness ended in a rush for the doors. Since I sat about equidistant from two flanking aisles, I could wait without being pushed in the direction of either for a break in the stream of exiting bodies, one I might squeeze into, and be carried along like flotsam to a doorway. I had no idea where the slips Rixon mentioned were supposed to be handed out. Maybe he was kidding.

And had I not looked down just then, I wouldn't have seen it. And had I not seen it and just stepped over it instead, my life would not have taken a turn that had not run its course two decades later. But I did see it. And I picked it up. It was a hardbound maroon book with about two hundred pages titled *The Mathematical Theory of Rocket Flight*. On the flyleaf, was the name of its owner, doubtless the entranced lad who sat next to me and had forgotten it: Alfred Cobb.

Below the name was an address but no phone number. My first impulse was to place it down on the seat where the lad sat and hope he might retrieve it. I tried this, but the seat wasn't having any of it. The book wasn't heavy enough to keep the horizontal part horizontal. It sprang up into the retracted position and spilled the book onto the floor. Balancing the book on the end of the retracted seat wouldn't work, nor did propping it between the retracted seat and the upright; the spring tension failed to keep it wedged there. It refused to do anything but tumble to the floor. It seemed I was stuck with the damn book. I could have left it on the floor but having failed to get it to do what I wanted, I felt compelled to see that it had some chance of finding its way back to Alfred, the kid who had not even bothered to acknowledge me.

Had the address been followed by a phone number, the whole business would have ended with a phone call, but no, as I mentioned before, there wasn't one. Short of abandoning the book either on the floor or in the trash, I could,

One: Deliver or mail it to the address on the flyleaf, a bother I felt the lad hadn't earned, which would get me a "thank you" at best.

Two: I could have (and should have) left the damn book on the floor. But books with the titles this one had, carried an implicit demand for respect since their subject was one I could never have mastered were I to live ten lives. The book demanded that I do something besides abandoning it on the floor of an auditorium that had hosted the kind of moronic coronations I'd just witnessed.

Or three: I could see if the school had a Lost & Found. This was about the most bother I was about to expend on the guy who had not even said "boo" to me. I could have kept it overnight and dropped it off in the morning. But, I somehow didn't want to be burdened with this object for that many hours. The damn book had almost begun to taunt me. I had a sudden urge to rid myself of it quickly, yet do right with the matter. It's been called compulsive obsessive disorder.

So once outside the building, I asked the nearest person who looked old enough to be faculty if there was a Lost & Found. He pointed at an entrance about midway along the building's length, several hundred yards from where we stood.

"Straight down the corridor from those doors," was his reply. "It's in the middle of five offices, there's sign's over it; it's hard to miss."

I was off to jettison the book. The Lost & Found was in fact easier to miss than find on the first pass, but minutes later, I did find it, dropped off the book, and headed for the parking lot and my car, considering the business to be over with. It had just begun.

Stepping through the doorway and aiming myself roughly at where memory had it that I'd parked the Lincoln I was struck with a sudden flicker of dread. There was a medium-size crowd standing where I'd left the one thing in life I possessed that still held value for me. And the flicker burst into an inferno of horror. Standing above the crowd with their feet supported by a solid object at roughly shoulder height were four members of the football squad I'd seen on the stage twenty minutes before. The thing they stood on was the hood of my Lincoln Zephyr.

It was one of those nightmare scenarios you never see coming. I couldn't know exactly where their feet were planted, but wherever it was, they were delivering devastating hammer blows to the car's bodywork.

I broke into a white hot panic and ran for the Lincoln hoping that maybe, just maybe, I could save it from any further destruction, but knowing in my gut that I was already too late. They were jumping up and down. By the time I was twenty feet from them, I could make out the clanking sound collapsing sheet metal makes when it's pounded mercilessly. The crowd that surrounded them roared as the figure standing on the hood screamed out the same inane bombast heard in the assembly hall. They roared approval as he jumped higher each time crashing harder down on the crumpled bodywork. And then I recognized whom the jumper was; the one presented to us as Saturday's messiah: Wally Monturska. I charged towards the car at full gallop and, when five feet from it, hurled myself airborne so as to strike him as would a projectile directly into his groin. It was very hot that day, and after a short parabolic flight we crashed into asphalt hot enough to shimmer semi-liquid like.

The back of his head made for a nose wheel and the rest of him was landing gear. I hoped it would knock him cold while I took on his confederates that quickly jumped off the car. Wally lay moaning, not sure of just what happened. I climbed off him, stood up, and delivered a solid kick to his balls before three of his cohorts seized me. I broke loose from them twice before they finally had me in a grip where I couldn't free myself. Then a fourth teammate was called over to deliver the blow to my gut. My legs were still free and I headed him off with a kick to his groin. He doubled over with a muffled scream. I would have screamed too, but I seemed to have used up the last molecule of air I had in me. From behind me, I heard somebody call out for a bat.

After a long moment, I recovered enough to scream, "Get off my fucking car!"

Until now this mob might not have realized what this was about. With that one stupid revelation I'd sealed the Lincoln's fate. Watching helplessly, I saw the car begin to rock violently. An unseen crowd on the far side of it was trying, and would shortly succeed, to roll it over and smash the driver's side into a collage of broken glass and crushed sheet metal. Seconds later, it did roll over, landing with a clank that was followed by a shriek I can hear to this day. Pinned beneath the car by her legs was a girl wearing one of the cheerleader outfits whom had been gyrating in the assembly hall twenty minutes earlier. She must have knelt to tend to Wally and now both of her legs were between the asphalt and the knife edge of the Lincoln's rain gutter. It had missed the team captain altogether. The mob that had rolled the car now tried lifting it off the girl and succeeded only after a titanic struggle because there are far fewer places to grip an overturned car than an upright one. When they had the Lincoln a foot off the asphalt, they dragged her free. She'd stopped screaming and had passed out. I would have too. The part of her right leg just below the knee was missing. There was blood too, lots of it.

That was how I escaped a beating that might have killed me because any interest in me vanished with the prostrate girl who'd just lost a section of leg.

I was thrown to the pavement. There began a succession of screams, all female, that reminded me of overlapping air-raid sirens where one has not completely stopped and another starts up. I surveyed the Lincoln from about twenty feet away. The once flawless sweep of its roof was a tangle of dents that formed a depression about a yard wide and four inches deep. The hood and deck had taken a similar pummeling. Fixing them and the unseen damage to the driver's side was going to take more skill than I had. And were it done by somebody with the skill to do it right, the car would never again be exclusively my work, something people like me understand, that can never be explained to fools. My Lincoln Zephyr was a murdered goddess. I studied her wounds still from afar until I couldn't stand it and looked away.

Then came the real sirens. I wondered whom I could get to winch the Lincoln upright. After several squad cars had parked in a rough semi-circle about the Zephyr along with two ambulances, they lifted it again. This was to retrieve the severed portion of leg still under the car. Having done that, they dropped it with another clank and the sound of yet more breaking glass. Then I noticed a dozen fingers pointing at me.

A khaki clad officer approached me and told me I was under arrest.

I was patted down, handcuffed, force marched to a squad car and was half way inside when I heard the voice of Max Morgenstern for the first time.

"Sir," it said, "what are you arresting this man for?"

I might have thought the shrill, somewhat metallic voice belonged to a two-hundred-pound drill sergeant. But its owner was a slump shouldered almost melted mass of boy/troll I guessed to be my age. His face, a collection of asymmetrical features centering about a dot like pair of nostrils reminded me of a fish I'd once thrown back because it was too ugly to keep, much less try to eat.

The cop ignored him.

The troll repeated the question.

The cop's face was the mask of arrogance I'd come to associate with armed men, uniforms, and badges.

"Who wants to know?" he snapped.

"I do," said the troll.

"You want to be in there with him?" the cop roared.

"Don't mind if I do," the troll replied advancing on us. There wasn't a trace of fear about him.

A second cop whispered something to the one who'd cuffed me. He looked at the kid again.

"I'm sorry," he said to the troll, this time his tone almost apologetic," you can't come with."

"What are you arresting him for?" the troll demanded.

"Aggravated assault," relied the cop. "He tried to run down the girl with his car, and rolled it over on her."

"I what?" I screamed. "You're out of your mind."

The cop who'd cuffed me pulled a big black flashlight from a holster on his belt, poked my side with it, and told me to shut up. The troll walked up to him.

"I saw the whole thing," said the troll. That car never moved except when that mob of morons turned it over on her. Just open the hood. The engine will be cold. Now do you want to release this man or do you want to assault me too? I'm a witness to your hitting him by the way."

The cop ignored this, slammed the rear door of the squad car that dealt my right side a nasty jolt, and muttering something, got into the driver's seat. We drove off. Looking back at the wrecked Lincoln, I was suddenly gripped by the first rush of convulsive rage that I arrested so as to concentrate on recalling the faces of the three who stood on the car with Wally Montruska—swearing to myself that none of them would live long.

It was a twenty-minute ride to the Harris County Municipal Building and a holding cell. Before they locked me in, I was told that I was being charged with attempted murder, that I'd chased down the girl with the car that had turned over on her. I thought about demanding that I had a phone call coming, remembering this from some TV show I'd seen. The only person I could think of calling was Lola. I decided not to use up the call then, even if they gave me one.

I wondered how long it would take them to find out that I was wanted in Indiana, something Lola or the Great Frog had yet to discover. Ray's description of a large Negro cellmate with a sore-covered penis flashed through me.

I cursed myself over and over for coming to Houston in the first place, and second for bothering to return a book to someone I didn't even know. Had I not done that, the Lincoln and I might have been safely gone before that mob of idiots ever got near it.

I had lost Alice—and blown the chance to go to California on my own, but the Lincoln Zephyr was taken from me. No one had a right to do that and arrest me for trying to protect her. Somebody was going to pay. But first I'd have to get out of jail. At least I had no cellmate; I'd never been in a cage before. This one was a room with a steel door and a protected light bulb hanging from a plank concrete ceiling. There were no windows, hence no bars. I guessed they didn't mean to keep me there long because there was no toilet or sink. I was lying down on a platform with a thin mattress that hung from one wall by steel rods. It was the first time I felt completely helpless. And they could keep me there as long as they cared to. Usually I cried when I was this scared, but I didn't because the rage I mentioned before trumped everything. Finally, I decided to call Lola, but never got the chance.

They unlocked my cell and took me to an interrogation room. I was directed to sit at a large oblong table alongside a man in a suit that looked like it cost the price of a good used car. He was probably about thirty but had the kind of face that allowed your mind's eye to add twenty years to it, and see what he'd look like at fifty. He wore a bow tie. He looked like one of those people that would be buried wearing one. A plain clothes cop—I assumed he was that—sat opposite us, alongside the cop that had arrested me.

The man next to me extended his hand. "My name is Rawlson," he said.

"Who are you, a public defender?" I could see that he regarded this an insult in one flash of anger.

"I've been retained to represent you," he replied in a tone that said he regarded it a bother he could have done without. He defaulted to a cold stare directed at the cops that told me that I was a lot better off with him and whoever hired him on my side. He focused on the plain-clothes cop.

"Alright, what are you holding him for?"

The plain-clothes cop nodded to the one in the khaki uniform that repeated the charge I'd first heard in the parking lot, "Aggravated assault."

"You witnessed this?" Rawlson hurled the question like an ax at a target in a carnival sideshow.

"No," the cop replied, "but…"

"But what, you have witnesses?" Rawlson cut him off.

"That's right."

"And affidavits?"

"Names and addresses," said the cop in the uniform.

"Names and addresses," Rawlson repeated derisively. He opened a thin briefcase, pulled a manila folder from it and then a stack of sheets from the folder. These he slapped on the table.

"Ten sworn affidavits," he said, "with names and addresses, and phone numbers—notarized I might add. Call any of them right now," he said, in the clear tone of a dare.

"Affidavits," Rawlson went on, "that my client was being bound while a hoard of idiots rolled the car over on the hapless girl who will unfortunately lose a foot and section of leg as a result of what can only be described as mob action against someone trying to protect his property. Gentlemen, they were using his car as a trampoline."

He slid the stack in front of them. The two cops studied the spread out papers.

"We'll need to keep these," one of them said finally, "as evidence."

"The hell you will," Rawlson barked. "They're leaving right now with me and Mr. July. It was the first time he used my name. The plainclothes man realigned the sheets in a stack.

"Then we'll need to make copies," he said.

Rawlson pulled a second folder from his briefcase. "Here are your copies, he said. "The originals do not leave this room except with me." There was a strong scent of ammonia from the freshly mimeographed sheets.

He did not wait for the cops to pass the originals back to him, retrieving them instead with one quick swipe. He could have hurt a man using something similar. The cops didn't move or say a word. Rawlson stood up.

"Mr. July?" he said motioning to the door.

"I didn't say he could leave," barked the cop in the uniform.

"You didn't say he couldn't, and if he can't you'd better say it now and have a damn good reason why he can't."

"Mr. July," said the plainclothesman, "don't leave Harris County."

"Mr. July," declared Rawlson as he opened the door, "you may go anywhere you like, any time you like. We're done here."

It was still daylight when we emerged from the Courthouse. I hadn't seen a clock, but gathered it was around six-thirty.

"Who hired you?" I asked Rawlson. The question had gnawed on me since he'd introduced himself.

"This way," he replied, adding "you'll need a ride."

"I can get home alright," I said, "now who the hell hired you?"

"You're not going home," said Rawlson, adding "at least not right away. You want to know who the hell hired me? Well now, you're going to find the hell out, this way please."

11. VELOCITY JANE

Twenty minutes later we were on a two-lane road called Teal Way that wound among the mansions of Houston's River Oaks district.

To its everlasting credit, Houston is not zoned and there are no appearance commissions. Hence, in places like River Oaks, style runs the gambit from antebellum to Buck Rogers with all stops in between. The house fronted by the driveway Rawlson pulled into looked like something stolen from an ocean liner and set atop rock outcrops and concrete pylons. Two stories of balcony jutted outward from walls set so far back as to assure that nothing inside could be viewed from the ground. I imagined them fortified ramparts should the need arise. There wasn't a main entrance, at least not an obvious one. The hostile or uninvited would be at the mercy of their hosts to find a way in while sharpshooters drew beads on them.

North of the house, in one of several parking spaces beneath a canopy, the Lincoln Zephyr stood upright. After steeling myself, I walked over to survey the damage to the driver's side that I'd yet to see. Rawlson never got out of his car and had driven off having said nothing more.

It was what I expected. Both fenders and the driver's door had been crushed semi-flat by their impact with the asphalt under the car's weight. The still-shiny paint only served to magnify the damage. I checked out the dried blood still on the rain gutter that had severed the girl's leg. It covered about a third of the door. In my mind, the car had bled, not the girl. My Lincoln was a murdered goddess. Just then a familiar voice was heard from behind.

"They wanted to impound her," the voice said, "we stopped them. If they want to take evidence, they've got to come here with a warrant."

I turned around to face the boy/troll who'd tried to stop my arrest.

"Max Morganstern," he said, extending a hand which at first looked as if fire-scarred, but was in fact just a bony counterpoint to the rest of him which was more or less puffy. It was now evident who'd sent Rawlson. I started to tell him that it hardly mattered, that I never wanted to see the Lincoln again, when I noticed that I was talking to two people. In the shadow of the canopy, stood another person; it took several seconds to realize this.

Next to Max stood one of the few people I'd ever seen that I might have swapped looks with. His blonde hair embraced a masterful composition in facial geometry that would have worn well on either sex, and but for certain subtle touches, he might best be described as pretty. The first thing one noticed about Wright Kilbourn (I was soon to learn his name) were the green eyes, that, like those of Alice, suggested a connection to some high voltage source inside him. None of his other features were extraordinary, only the proportions and distances between them bespoke arrangement by some cosmic maestro of line and form. It was hard not to stare at that face.

It wasn't all that was unique about him. Most of his left leg was a tapered cylindrical peg ending far above where a knee would have been. With the other leg and a crutch, there was formed a tripod that held him erect.

"Wright Kilbourn," he said, extending his hand after wedging the small birch-tipped cigar he'd held in it between his teeth. "My friends call me Woody," and added, "my enemies have names for me too." He poked the pavement twice with the peg, confirming by the noise that it was indeed wooden.

"You're who I'm to thank for this Rawlson character?" I asked.

"Either or both of us," Woody replied. "Max saw what happened, told me, and I dispatched Rawlson. How'd he do?"

"Well I'm free, so good I guess. Yeah, he's impressive."

"May I suggest that you ain't seen nuthin?"

It was the second time I'd heard the phrase that day.

"How does he expect me to pay him?"

"Not necessary," said Woody, "he's on a yearly retainer. I'm his only client. He's paid whether he's busy or idle. This year it's been pretty quiet, but that's going to change soon enough. I think he enjoyed that little exercise this afternoon."

"Then how do I pay you?"

"Again, that won't be necessary. I heard you kicked the great Wally Montruska in the balls, and put him in the hospital, at least for observation. I'll take that as payment any day."

"It's true," said Max, "I saw it." Then turning to me he added, "You should get a medal." I told them that I thought so too.

"Tomorrow," Woody went on, "they're going to drag you down to Larch's office, that's the Principal, and try to expel you. There'll be cops and probably the girl's parents, the girl that lost a leg. I'll see to it that Rawlson is there. If anything, you should find it amusing. Max was a witness so he gets a box seat too. Damn! I wish I could be there. Larch is a total moron and a former jock. Need I say more?"

I'd heard athletes called "jocks" only once before. "You don't like jocks," I said as if it were necessary.

"No, I don't," Woody replied, "I can't imagine you would either after today, because if you do you're an idiot. The jock is animal puke. Now," he said gesturing at the car, "I'd like to know what you're going to do about this." I didn't for a moment imagine he meant fixing the car. This guy was about getting even.

"I'm working on that," I said. I wasn't about to announce to strangers the scenario I'd dreamt up in the cell that afternoon, a scenario that consisted of ripping out the bridge of Montruska's nose after passing the hook end of a crowbar through his eye sockets.

"May I offer a suggestion?" Woody asked, adding, "this way." He motioned toward an entrance of the house that would have been all but impossible to find otherwise.

No one could have begun to imagine the enormity of the house on Teal Way by what it presented to the street. The entrance led to a short corridor past some dark ancillary rooms. The end of it exploded into an immense parlor. They told me it was one of three. We passed through it and exited to one of several balconies. Only then did I really take in the scale of the place. There was one floor of balconies above us and three below where the ground dropped off abruptly. The one we stood on extended beyond all the others by fifteen or twenty feet. Had I not known this was a house I would have guessed it a medium sized resort. The ground we overlooked from about forty feet above was dead flat. There wasn't another structure or tree for about a thousand feet in any direction.

Instead, three concrete ribbons, each about six feet wide, radiated from a flat disc, also concrete, and about four yards across. Attached to the house and on poles were a windsock, and an anemometer. I was looking at a miniature airport.

Some distance from the runways stood three larger-than-life-size plywood figures: football players in the midst of some action. Around them, concentric circles were painted in the dirt.

And then I heard it.

The sound was the scream two-stroke engines make when they're being run flat out and are on the threshold of locking up or exploding. It took a few more seconds to realize that the sound was coming at me from somewhere in midair.

When the plane rushed past us no more than twenty feet away, the shriek of its engines seared my eardrums like a kind of sonic acid. I turned to Woody and Max and only then did I understand that the pilot was standing next to me. I had no idea how, or from where, Max had suddenly produced the control box he held with its two-foot chrome aerial. Once it had past us, Max held the plane's course in wide circle. Roaring by a second time, its engines churned out a shriek that if anything, pierced yet more savagely. I covered my ears. It was still accelerating when Max eased it into a straight up climb as if on a temporary waiver from gravity. At about a thousand feet above us, the climb slowed to a stop, and the airplane hung suspended, as if from some unseen hook for several seconds before rolling over on its back into a vertical plunge. When about half the distance from the ground was used up, Max eased the plunge into a shallow dive while aligning the plane's course with the plywood players on the dirt. It passed us again going faster still though farther from where we stood as he took aim. A hundred feet from the figures, a yellow flash erupted from the airplane's nose behind a projectile that slammed into the plywood, exploding into a burst of orange flame and a thousand splinters.

The whole performance had not taken a minute. With burning fragments of plywood jocks still raining down, Max landed the plane, pointed it at the house and taxied it to where I could best look down at it.

There erupted a wave of cheers and shouts from the balconies both above and below us. Only then did I realize we weren't alone.

"Mr. July," said Woody, failing miserably to suppress his delight. "Mr. July," he said pointing at the airplane, "meet *Velocity Jane*. Incidentally, what do you use for a first name? I'm guessing not your full one."

Struck dumb, I stared at the airplane while burning splinters still fluttered down.

"Sonny," I said finally, "Sonny will do just fine." A slight breeze now blew black wisps of engine exhaust past us.

I studied the shape of the aircraft on the tarmac. I guessed it to be eight feet long and about that same distance wingtip to wingtip. *Velocity Jane* was a canard, one of those designs where the small wings are set ahead of the big ones. There were two engines on pods, each one on the larger wings that directed their thrust backward so as to push the plane instead of pull it. It was a configuration well suited for carrying the rocket that had destroyed the plywood jocks. The launching racks (two of them) were arraigned above and one below the front of the fuselage so as not to queer the symmetric equilibrium when a single missile was fired. Two wheels that were the nose gear straddled the lower launch rack.

The doorway to the parlor opened and a dozen youths spewed from it, surrounded Max, and lifted him in the air. One of them began singing, and a score of voices took it up, some from those still unseen on other balconies of the great house.

Bless 'em all, Bless 'em all
The long and the short and the tall
Bless all the sergeants and W O Ones
Bless all the corporals and their blink'n sons
Cause we're saying goodbye to them all
As back to their billets they crawl
No roses or violets for dead fighter pilots
So cheer up my lads bless 'em all!

"Sonny", said Woody, "meet 'The Legion.'"

We filed back into the parlor where a beer keg awaited. Woody and Max drew drafts, handed me one, and herded me into a chair grouping which would make a crowd of anyone beyond us three. The rest of the "Legionnaires" had far more interest in the keg anyway.

Woody produced a five pack of birch tipped cigars labeled Hav-A-Tampa Jewels, selected one for himself, passed the pack to Max who accepted, and offered me one that I declined. They lit up.

"I suppose you're wondering who we are and what we're about," said Woody exhaling a deep draught of smoke, "I'm sure you have other questions too."

"Who you are and what you're about will do for openers," I replied.

"Alright," said Woody, "we're the good guys who are going to take the world back from the bad guys that stole it, and return it to its rightful owners. That's us by the way. And after today, I don't think I should have to tell you who the bad guys are. Don't imagine that what happened to you was any kind of a fluke. You happened to have walked into a war, one that's been going on since long before you and I were born. I shouldn't have to tell you where you'd be right now if Max hadn't seen what had happened and notified me."

"No," I replied, "no you don't." I didn't like where this was going. Woody had just told me that I owed him. I had the impulse to thank him and tell him goodbye, but I was going to need his lawyer in the morning, so I let him go on.

And go on he did, beginning with a description of how the world's value system had been twisted and skewed by the worship of athletes and all they stood for. One kid in a hundred didn't know who the top jocks of the day were. But Robert Goddard? In an age of satellites and ICBMs, not kid one in a thousand knew who Goddard was.

I didn't tell Woody that I didn't know who Goddard was either, but made a mental note to look him up when I got the chance.

Every evil in the world was traceable to the value system that placed idiotic games like football above intellectual achievement. That distortion, along with a heavy dose of jock arrogance had led to the outrage I'd suffered in the parking lot.

"Well," Woody said, the legion was going to change all that: beginning Saturday with the homecoming game at the stadium behind Benjamin High. What I'd seen behind the house was a kind of dry run. There would be an air raid just before half time. All those jocks and the morons that worshiped them had better understand who could do what to a world that had so wronged them. I didn't stop him to ask Woody if he meant they were actually going to incinerate people on Saturday since you could infer little else from what I'd seen and was hearing. But that moment I hoped that they meant to do exactly that.

Woody's assessment of the world's ills and what had caused them had obviously been rehearsed and refined over several deliveries. It was followed by a fine-tuned mix of grievances and a sales pitch. At particular points in it, Max took up the harangue so seamlessly that I wouldn't have realized that Woody had stopped talking had Max's voice not contained such undiluted venom that it was in a way funny. Max had taken hatred to a whole new level.

After postulating again and again that the jock was "animal puke," Max gave me some particulars of the air raid they'd planned along with an invitation that I guessed was supposed to sound like an offer of honor and privilege.

The offer was for a place in the attack party. That meant I would be in the stadium along with the pilots who would carry the aircraft controllers disguised as portable radios. Those in charge of gassing up, arming, and sending the planes on their way and back were the ground parties. The planes would be launched from the airstrip behind the mansion and would be guided to and from the stadium using a system of "reciprocal homing devices"—RHDs.

While following signals from the RHDs, the planes used a kind of autopilot that they called PAT: "Pendulum Actuated Trim." This "legion" of Woody's, like every other military since militaries were invented, had its love affair with acronyms.

If everything went as planned, the planes—there would be three— would strike just before half time. Two of them would scatter low level explosives on the gridiron, and also destroy a huge football shaped balloon that would bear the name of the captain who'd stomped on my car, the same one I'd sent to the emergency room. *Velocity Jane* would go for designated targets. One was the stadium's brand new scoreboard, or "targets of discretion"—TODs. Did I want in? It seemed like they'd revealed one hell of a lot to someone they barely knew, confident that I would say yes or at least not betray them if I refused. I didn't want to think what would happen if I did squeal.

I almost told them no.

What Woody called "the Legion" had probably once been a collection of would-be engineer types that composed those clubs that launched rockets, flew remote control planes, or just stroked their slide rules, both the wooden and the fleshy ones. They won science-fair ribbons that weren't even good for wiping the semen they would spray on the pages of the *Playboys* they kept hidden in their rooms. They were the little boys that stood in the shade and got none while the jocks—the athletes—got what was correctly perceived as everything worth having, the money, the cars, and the girls.

Woody and Max never stopped stressing over and over that the jocks were "animal puke, *animal puke!*"

So "the Legion" was a mutation driven by Max's inspired rage and Woody's obvious wealth. It may not have been the first of its kind, but I'd yet to hear of another.

I'd never belonged to a club like that or any club whatsoever, and no desire to.

I'd read all of five books in my life. No jock had beaten me out of all I wanted either. Collin Walker wasn't a jock; we loved the same girl. She had chosen him, for now. But that would change. That would have to change. *That was going to change.*

But I told Woody, "yes."

The jocks *were* animal puke; that animal puke had destroyed the thing I held most dear in life besides Alice. Woody had had its carcass towed to the motor court of his estate where I could view the sight of its mangled bodywork before hearing his sales pitch and his invitation. It was obvious what he wanted me for: another layer of cannon fodder to protect his precious pilots who might otherwise be ripped apart by an angry mob if something went wrong. And it was not hard to imagine things going very wrong.

But I'd said "yes" because there was a genuine appeal to having wonderful dangerous friends like Max and Woody who hated the same things I did and were going to do something about it besides cry out futilely for justice. And justice might just be the lady that fired rockets and burned gasoline, whose name was *Velocity Jane.*

But the "yes" I gave them had conditions:

My commitment was for the raid they planned for Saturday only. Anything beyond it was strictly my choice to make. No loyalty oaths or nonsense like that.

Rawlson was to defend me at no cost against any charges pending from that afternoon. Rawlson was to defend me against anything that might spring up from Indiana because I was wanted there too for assault with intent to kill. When I mentioned this, Woody and Max looked at each other for an instant before breaking out in broad grins.

"You were right about this guy," Woody said, "I'm liking him better all the time."

Fresh, if slurred, choruses of *Bless 'Em All* rang through the parlor for the next two hours until the keg was dry.

As Woody had predicted, my second period class the next morning was broken into by a squad of no less than four goons from the principal's office. Two of them looked like the ones that had escorted me to meet Rixon the day before. This time we went directly to that of the ex-jock principal of the school.

Max and Rawlson were waiting in the reception area and the three of us filed into Larch's office and were met by the two Police officers from the interrogation, a middle-aged couple, Rixon, and the coach from the rally whose name I'd forgotten. Max lagged behind us intentionally so as to make his entrance a solitary event. The effect was not lost on me. Larch and the coach drew short gasps and a smirk flickered across Rixon's face. When I looked to Max, he flashed me a grin as if to say, "see?"

Rixon was the first to speak. "Didn't take long for you three to become acquainted," he said.

"Yeah," Max said directing his reply not at Rixon, but the coach, whose name I then remembered was Hollenbeck. "He ran into a few of your idiots first." Nobody challenged Max's being there.

At this point, the woman exploded: "Murderer," she shrieked. "You killed my Phyllis, you murdered my baby, you and your filthy car." Even the brief glimpse I'd gotten of the girl was enough to tell me this was her mother. She rose from her chair and strode towards me. Her right arm, which ended in gleaming lacquered nails, was cocked for a swipe at my face. I braced myself. But as she passed Max, he seized her wrist and, with one leveraged stroke, sent her crashing to the floor. Everyone in the office looked at her in stunned silence until Max barked out: "Either arrest this crazy bitch or get her the hell out of here." His drill sergeant voice cracked like a whip that could slice about anything in its path. To my amazement the two cops obeyed him escorting the woman out of the office after helping her up.

Clearly, they were glad for the chance to get away lest Max turn his wrath on them and get their names. The woman writhed and twisted like a hooked fish trying to break free, all the time sobbing hysterically. The man I assumed was her husband followed. "Murderers," she screamed out, "murderers," just before the door closed behind them. There was muffled bawling and cursing heard after that. It was the first time that it actually sunk in that my car wasn't the only victim of the day before.

Just then, Rawlson took over: "Gentlemen," he addressed them in a tone that could only be called a genteel growl, "what the hell are we doing here anyway?"

"I don't know who you are Mr...." Larch began.

"Rawlson," the lawyer cut him off, "and you know damn well who I am and that I represent Mr. July in this matter." The cops did not re-enter the office.

"I'm expelling this punk," said Larch "for running over (he looked down at his desk and obviously at a printed name) Miss Phyllis Schindler with his car in the parking lot yesterday," adding, "the girl is dead." The short gasp I gave seemed to amuse Max. He shook his head as if to reprimand me.

"I have twelve sworn affidavits that say otherwise," retorted Rawlson. "The car was parked when a mob rolled it over on the girl. Mr. July wasn't in the car. It was empty."

"I'm not interested in sworn statements from this punk and his pals," Larch roared, pointing at Max, "They'll say anything he tells them to." At once he seemed to be rethinking having called Max a punk. So that was where Rawlson had gotten the affidavits.

"Maybe," said Ralson, "you'd like to interrogate them yourself."

"Damn right I would," said the Principal. "Damn right I would."

"You can start with this one," said Rawlson, unzipping the top of a leather satchel and pulling a single mimeographed sheet from it. He handed it to Rixon who was closest to him. After reading it Rixon passed it to Hollenbeck, who took a deep breath before placing it on the desk in front of Larch.

The Principal's head seemed to enlarge as it turned a rich crimson when he read it. It reminded me of Ralph's father. He ripped the sheet into four pieces, crumpled it into a ball, and threw it at us. It bounced off Rawlson's jacket and landed at my feet. I picked it up. Larch screamed for us to get out.

His last line: "you'll pay for this," was clearly directed at me.

When we were outside the office I asked Rawlson if the girl really was dead. He nodded.

"They tried to re-attach her leg," he replied. "It was risky. She would have lived if they hadn't tried that. There was a blood clot that made it to her brain." The lawyer glared at Max.

"What the hell are you looking at me for?" Max demanded. "I didn't do it," and pointing to me barked, "neither did he. So look at the bright side; she'll never die of cunt cancer."

Rawlson cringed at that. It was obvious he already resented how much Max's violence had upstaged him in the office minutes before. I got the impression that it wasn't the first time.

"We're done here," he said, and strode off.

"Mind if I read this?" I asked Max, and almost instantly regretted requesting his permission. This could become a bad habit. He shook his head.

I un-rumpled and matched the paper quadrants together. The name on the affidavit was Courtney Provine. I could well imagine how Rawlson and Max had gotten the others, but not this one.

Max told me where to find him in the cafeteria for the lunch period. We sat at a table with some of the crew that had carried him from the balcony of the house on Tealway the night before. Max and I sat together with several empty chairs between us and the other Legionaries. I was pretty sure that he wanted to be alone with me so as to find out more.

"Assault with intent to kill," he said after I'd sat down."

"Is that what they're going to charge me with here too?"

"No, you're in the clear here, I just wondered what it was about back in Indiana. Let me guess; was it over some shiksa bitch?"

"It sounds like you already know the answer," I said.

"Just a guess," Max replied.

"Did you also guess I was a Jew?"

"Yes, since you obviously know what shiksa meant. Judging from your looks I say you're either adopted or a half breed."

I didn't answer.

"Which is it?"

"My mother was Jewish," I said in an irritated tone. "She died in the French Resistance." Max nodded. He didn't need it explained.

"Ashkenazi?"

I nodded, fearing the tone of one word would betray my irritation had I said so much as "yes." I was starting to realize that giving Max any information was probably the worst possible idea. Let him get it from other sources of which he was obviously capable of doing.

"Good," Max replied. "My mother is Sephardic from Majorca. God love her, and I dearly do, but I was eight before she learned to cook like a civilized white person. I prayed before ever meal that the food wouldn't kill me. She must have learned to cook from Moors."

"So you're one of the chosen too, Max?"

"If you mean the crown jewel of the white race, yes. What did you think I was?"

"Morgenstern is German."

"Well, my parents were white, so I'll thank you not to confuse me with the niggers of Europe."

I squinted, took a deep breath and he grinned.

"Krauts," he mused, like jocks, are animal puke. They eat each other—fucking cannibals really. A kraut believes that if you kill a person and eat his brain before it gets cold, you will add his intelligence to yours. I suppose they're right if the brain they eat is from another Kraut because zero plus zero is still fucking zero. It's all been proven, very scientific."

"You're an anthropologist, are you Max?

"I like to offer my friends the benefit of my experience," he replied, his eyes twinkling. Apparently our conversation had allowed him to deliver some of his favorite lines.

"Did you have any questions?" he asked finally.

"The raid tomorrow," I asked, "three planes?"

He nodded. I only realized just then how stupid discussing it in the open was. But Max apparently didn't think so and gladly elaborated.

"Only one of them," he said, "will be like *Velocity Jane*, and that's *Velocity* herself. There's several more being built. They're all named Jane. There's Intensity, Tenacity, Virility, Tranquility, Mendacity.

"No Calamity?"

"Of course. There will be a 'Calamity Jane' silly of me to forget that."

Max paused, and seemed to be rewinding an internal mainspring before he continued: "The other two are biplanes. The projectiles they shoot are spring loaded, sort of like BB guns. They can drop small charges too. Big wing areas so they can carry a lot of ordinance, but when loaded, they're slower than chilled shit, and can barely be handled, a bad trade off really, but besides Jane they're all we have just now. They'll have to take off earlier for all of the force to arrive at the same time. Also they have to stay high: a well-aimed rock could bring one down."

"Too bad they can't all be Janes," he mused, "but only *Velocity* is combat ready, and only one person, that's me, knows how to get out of her what she can deliver, like that ATG you saw me use on those jocks last night. You think it was a lucky shot don't you? I can do it eight times out of ten. I use a system of three-dimensional triangulation that actually involves four points. I invented it myself, but I can teach it to anybody. Be nice to me and I learn you too."

"ATG?"

"Air To Ground," replied Max. Another acronym, I thought, in the legion's arsenal of acronyms.

"They're really an adaption of a model rocket motor that a company in Denver makes."

"Off the shelf," added Max. "They're fine if all they have to do is shoot straight up. The sky is a big target. But getting them to track absolutely straight and putting their payload where it's supposed to go is another matter entirely."

He went on.

"But we got them to track straight. It was a matter of refining the nozzle design and some other factors like perfect homogeneity of the fuel. Speaking of the Devil, let me introduce you to the genius who managed it for us. Addison July, meet Alfred Cobb."

The kid who'd sat entranced beside me at the rally stood before us, thighs pressed against the end of the table. I hadn't noticed him approach. He wouldn't have known me from a crayfish.

He extended his hand in my direction while still looking at Max. I shook it.

"I see," said Max to the kid, "that you got your book back, lucky you."

"Yeah" Alfred replied, "somebody turned it in to the Lost & Found."

His left hand was wrapped around *The Mathematical Theory of Rocket Flight.*

"Yeah" I said, "lucky you."

A girl was dead, my car was wrecked, I was committed to a bizarre enterprise that could among other things, get me killed. And before me stood the stupid son of a bitch blissfully unaware of what he'd set in motion with his fucking book. Thank you for nothing—genius.

12. DILLINGER

On Friday afternoon, in the largest parlor of the great house on Teal Way, I was formally introduced to "the Legionaries" by Max as "a fugitive from Indiana, wanted for the attempted murder of a jock." This got me a wave of roaring applause complete with two-fingered whistles. He did this without once asking if it was okay to reveal my being wanted. I took this as a gross breach of discretion and intended to say so—possibly while pounding the crap out him when the opportunity arose. But remembering that I would need Rawlson's consul, something Max could cut off with one word to Woody, I resolved to settle this later. And only later would I find out how physically dangerous Max was in his own right. Max also assigned me a code name which, in his mind anyway, made my membership into his, and Woody's, cabal permanent. He felt obvious pride at coming up with it too: "Dillinger," bank robber extraordinaire, also from Indiana, and one of his heroes. By now I had long since realized what a bad idea it was to give Max information of any kind. I expected that in a very short time the authorities in Indiana would learn my whereabouts if not from Max's bombast, then from the transcript inquiry Rixon would make. One way or another, I was going to need Rawlson. No doubt Max had calculated that.

A problem had surfaced. The forces of justice were not exactly about to let the business of the dead girl melt into the wind. They had rounded up eight of the Legionaires who'd signed Rawlson's affidavits and were grilling them. Max and Woody learned about this from two who'd been questioned and released. Both said that they had stood by their statements. After all, what they had sworn to was the truth whether they'd seen it happen or not. But I was sure that they would have signed anything Max told them to.

Six Legionnaires were still unaccounted for and it could be assumed they were facing interrogation. Still, I wondered about the affidavit signed by the Provine girl. What could Max have hung over her head to make her sign it or anything else? He was of course more than capable of forging her signature, but I, somehow, had little doubt that it was real.

I'd still resolved to quit this club of theirs as soon as the business from Indiana no longer threatened me and if I survived the raid planned for the next day. Any dealing with Woody or Max beyond that was a leap into quicksand.

The purpose of the meeting in the great house that Friday afternoon was a final council of war. This was the first time I saw the model of the stadium, although it was obvious it had been seen several times by everyone else. What amazed me was both how elaborate the model was and how huge the real thing had to be. Most high school athletic stadiums consisted of two tray-like seating groups tilted upward at about thirty degrees opposite each other and separated by the width of the field and a twenty-foot-wide track which ringed them. The largest ones could seat two thousand or so.

The one serving Benjamin High, Bengal Field, would have been more appropriate for a large college or a small city. Comprising it was a large oval bowl with walkways and ramps below. It had once been a municipal stadium built some decades earlier and only when it was replaced by a larger one was the high school built next to it. Woody told me it was about thirty years old and the school about twenty. His information was that the stadium cost twice what the school had. Other schools used it for events when Benjamin's schedule left it empty.

There was a toy football-shaped balloon floating about eight inches above the model with a name on it. It was "Wally," the idiot I knocked off the hood of the Lincoln. It was to be one of the targets of the biplane attack. Scaled roughly, the real balloon would be at least fifty feet end to end. Each of the biplanes Max had mentioned (the junior partners in the raiding force) featured spring powered missiles on pylons, which braced the two wings together. He explained that any one of the four they would fire at the balloon should bring it down. But four were needed to blow it apart with the desired effect. The biplanes would also drop explosives on the gridiron from bomb racks hung from their wings.

One of two sat on a ping-pong table to the side of the lectern where two Legionaries were tweaking its trim surfaces. No one else seemed to be paying it much attention besides me. It was the first time I'd seen it.

Velocity Jane, the plane I'd seen perform the night before, was the star of the event. Her primary target would be the brand new scoreboard that reportedly cost seven thousand dollars. Max intended to destroy it with one Air To Ground.

He'd also insisted that the remaining target be one of discretion. There would be so many opportunities, he said, that the final pick would be determined perhaps seconds before the ATG was launched.

Woody introduced me to the third pilot whose name was Heyward. Nobody seemed to know if it was his first or last name, and it was the only one anyone used. The three pilots, Woody, Max, and Heyward spent at least half an hour miming the attack with tiny models of *Velocity Jane* and the biplanes whose names were *Hopscotch* and *Rage*. It was *Rage* that sat on the ping-pong table.

Through it all, there was an undercurrent impossible to miss. Woody stepped away to make phone calls every several minutes and kept counting the bodies in the room. I gathered the calls were attempts to reach either the missing Legionaries or Rawlson. Max appeared unperturbed.

"I know them," he said, referring to the still missing comrades when Woody's apprehension became all too obvious. "They're good boys, smart too, true as steel, nobody's going to crack."

Woody could not be reconciled. "Only one of the six would have to admit the affidavit he'd signed was phony," he fretted, and after that, with more questioning, he'd give up the details of the raid.

I couldn't get it out of my head that if that genius/idiot Alfred Cobb hadn't left his stupid book on the floor of the auditorium, I wouldn't be there and all of this would have all happened without me.

The doorbell rang, and a moment later, the six missing Legionnaires filed into the parlor. Some grinned, some wore smirks, and one flashed

Woody a thumbs up. Apparently all had withstood whatever heat had been put to them.

Rawlson followed them in. This was not supposed to happen, and Max charged through the parlor to intercept him, but it was too late. Rawlson had spotted the stadium model, the biplane on the table, and had instantly connected the dots.

"Are you out of your mind?" he screamed at Woody. "I take that back," he recanted, then shouted: "You are out of your mind. You're out of your Goddamn mind!"

Woody's face was a blank. He turned to Max. If Rawlson said nothing, and the raid commenced, and somebody died, the lawyer could be held as an accessory. The only way the thing they'd been planning—since Max, Woody, and God alone knew when that was going to go forward—was if Rawlson said nothing. And the look on the lawyer's face said that his silence was not for sale.

Just then, every eye in the parlor focused on Max who seemed to have produced the small automatic he pointed at Rawlson out of thin air.

"Relax counselor," said Max, his voice calm, deliberate, and almost soothing, "You're off the hook. Make yourself comfortable. You can sit in that chair, enjoy a drink and our fine fellowship, or I can tie you to it. Either way, you're not going anywhere and you're not going to say a goddamn thing to anybody, understand?

13. THE WRATH OF JANE

Because I'd seen the model of the stadium, Bengal Field, its size was less of a shock to me when we filed into it from separate points and met at a prearranged place so as to avoid suspicion. It wasn't necessary; nobody paid us any attention, not even with Woody hobbling among us faster than I would have thought possible on crutches like some kind of spring wound toy. He was a common enough sight in the halls of Benjamin High.

As Woody had predicted, there was a football-shaped balloon tethered to ropes floating about eighty feet above one of the two tight curves of the oval. In enormous letters was the first name of Benjamin's crown jock, Wally Montruska.

The place where we assembled was the top tier of seats directly above the forty-yard line. There were several rows of empty seats below us. Not even the turnout for the homecoming game could fill a stadium that size. The pilots, except Woody, Heyward (it *was* his first name), and Max carried control boxes in canvas bags large enough to allow both forearms to operate freely inside. The boxes themselves had been fitted into the gutted carcasses of portable radios. Only a pair of bat-like shafts projecting upward about three inches from their faces betrayed the disguise. The plan called for them to be out in the open until someone realized that they could be worked just as well from inside the bags. So the disguise took on a layer of redundancy.

Besides the control boxes, the bags held aerials: copper wire coiled about plywood rings a foot in diameter. Woody told me that they worked almost as well as the two-foot long chrome stalks which, if used, would have been a dead giveaway.

The twelve of us Woody had called the "attack party" included the three pilots who sat with their backs to the parapet and nine others who formed a defensive half circle around them. I doubted we could have stood up to a mob of any size until I found out later that I was the only one that didn't carry a pistol. Max had feared issuing me one might cause me to back out so I was told this after the fact.

At the great house on Tealway, the planes would take off under manual control of the ground party, who would finally set Rawlson free. Once reaching their cruising altitude of five-hundred feet, they would be pulsed to follow the homing signal from the first of two RHD stations.

That one had been set up on the roof of the school where the parapets hid the station and its three-man crew from sight. Also on the roof were capped one-hundred-ten-volt outlets needed to power the RHD. The path the planes followed to the signal from the school roof RHD beacon took them directly over the stadium where the attack pilots could reclaim control once the planes were sighted and proceed with the raid.

A second RHD crew stood ready at the destination strip miles from the great house. Each plane carried two channel devices called "sniffers," that told them which signal to follow. The ground crew activated the first sniffer, the attack party switched the planes back to manual as soon as they were sighted for the raid, and when done would pulse the sniffers to follow the RHD signal from the destination strip.

Following the attack—there would be little doubt as to who was behind it—a police raid was expected at Tealway. Woody and Max foresaw a storm of cops, squad cars, and warrants within hours converging at the great house. They would find it stripped of evidence beyond the concrete runways in the back.

With the cops gone, Max had promised the Legionaries a victory party. Max might have the only one sure thing that would go as planned—his plan—but as I was soon to learn, his was the only opinion that counted that day, as well as on most others.

At exactly one that afternoon, the voice of Benjamin's principal, Myron Larch, crackled through a score of speakers positioned throughout the stadium. We were about fifty feet from one of them.

"Good afternoon," the speakers blasted. *"This is Myron Larch, welcoming you to the first official public league game of 1959, which happens to also be our homecoming game. So to all you Benjamin High School alumni out there I would like to offer you a big welcome back from all of us."*

"I offer you this welcome in the wake of some terrible news that many or most of you know about; and that is the deep sense of loss we all must bear with the death of one of our beloved cheerleaders, Miss Phyllis Schlinder, whose life was taken by the senseless cruelty of a hit and run driver who is being sought by the police. If that person is in the range of my voice, I would urge you to turn yourself in and face God's judgment lest you burn in hell for all time to come."

"I now ask we offer a moment of silent prayer for the soul of our departed sister and for a terrible and righteous retribution to the perpetrator of this heinous act."

It didn't seem to trouble Larch a bit that at least a hundred people had witnessed this "heinous act" and knew he was a liar. I wondered if he would name me, but he didn't, probably fearing Rawlson, or more likely Max.

Max tapped me on the shoulder and grinned. "Animal Puke," he said. "Is that man animal puke or is that man animal puke?" He paused a few seconds. "Gentlemen you have just heard the voice of animal puke!"

At the end of the silent minute the voice of animal puke returned.

"Please join us now," it said, *"in the pledge of allegiance, followed by the singing of our national anthem by our homecoming queen, the lovely Miss Courtney Provine."*

When she'd finished the game began.

The Benjamin team got off to a bad start that day and in ten minutes of play was down 13-0 due to fumbles, two of them by the great Wally. I hoped my "assault with intent to kill" on his groin had something to do with it. When the first quarter ended Benjamin was even further behind, 20-0.

Little happened after that. The Benjamin defense hardened and the ball never moved more than fifteen yards into either team's territory. The cheerleaders bobbed, jumped, and twirled in rote maneuvers reflecting an atmosphere born of Phyllis Shindler's demise and a game that they were losing as well.

Woody, Max, and Heyward sat with their hands buried in their satchels fingering the upright sticks of the control boxes.

I might mention here that our one communication with both the airstrips was a public telephone. At exactly two thirty, Woody dispatched two couriers each with the same message to Tealway: launch the planes.

From then on every eye of the attack party focused on the sky in line with a path back to the house. The wait lasted eleven minutes.

Sometimes, I'd been told, the sight of the planes came well ahead of their sound and sometimes you heard them first. This time both the noise and the planes came together. The triumvirate of specks in the sky came coupled with the shriek of their two stroke engines. I looked down at the audience shaped by the huge bowl in which they sat. Within a minute, scores of hands rose and pointed at the incoming visitors. Woody, Max, and Heyward pulsed their craft for manual control and executed wing wags that told the first RHD crew on the school's roof to switch off, pack up, and head for parts unknown. Their job was done.

Woody and Heyward set the biplanes, *Rage* and *Hopscotch*, into slow opposing paths directly over the field, and about two hundred feet above it while dropping small parcels, perhaps forty of them, as if planting seeds.

Before they'd cleared the stadiums perimeter, the parcels began going off. I was told they were little more than loud firecrackers. They had to have packed far more punch than that. The whole of the field seemed to erupt at once with explosions, smoke, and screams. The bulk of the players ran for the safety of the stadium's portals while a few dove to the ground. Some looked as they'd been shot. With a layer of smoke still covering the field, four figures remained on the gridiron clutching legs, arms, or part of their torsos. One held his hands over his eyes. Some of the parcels had bounced and blown up in the air. The

Legionnaire sitting next to me pointed at a figure with number "41" on his Jersey and blurted out: "Montruska." Number "41" twisted and writhed, trying to get upright but collapsed, apparently in pain and bleeding more than a little. Flame flickered from his pants. Thirty feet above them *Velocity Jane* flashed past. Max had added fan ducts that made her propellers invisible and enhanced their thrust. She was a dart like portent of sinister beauty hurling through space. The audience that Woody feared might start a stampede seemed frozen in their seats, mesmerized as might a deer be by oncoming headlights. Few, if any, seemed to be making for the exits.

Max had been handed an incredible chance. The wounded jocks lay twisting and writhing in an area no more than fifteen feet across. One well-placed shot with an ATG could easily send them all airborne into pieces just as I'd seen done to the plywood jocks at the airstrip. They were a far bigger target than Max needed. He had two rockets and couldn't have missed had he but one. *Velocity Jane* nosed up to clear the tight radius end of the stadium's length. She was no more than thirty feet above the fans, her engines running flat out. Once beyond the perimeter, Max, executing a large half circle, reversed her course, and took aim.

Back inside the perimeter, *Velocity* hurled in at her quarry. I had no doubt Max was but a second from firing an ATG at the doomed players on the field.

"Bitch!" he suddenly blurted out, "Bitch!"

I'd been so focused on *Velocity* that I hadn't looked at the target at the forty-yard line for several seconds. Another figure, a girl's, now stood among the stricken jocks.

"Bitch!" Max shrieked.

I didn't need a close look at the face to know its owner. The arraignment of the girl's hair alone left no doubt to whom it belonged. To get the jocks, Max would have to kill Courtney Provine!

Without firing, *Velocity* stormed past them, her two strokes still flat out. Along with the rest of the attack party, I turned to Max. His face, a contorted mask of frustration and rage, gave "repulsive" a whole new standard to be measured by.

"Bitch," he said for the fourth time. His voice betrayed a resignation that his chance had been snatched from him by the incredible courage of the girl that stood up amidst his would-be victims. Medics with stretchers now raced for the stricken jocks from the stadium portals. They'd never have done it had not Courtney so shamed them that they hadn't a choice. One of them was trying to beat out the flames on the uniform of number "41" amid the screams of its owner.

We had no time at all to wonder what Max would do next. Among the things I would learn about him was that he could spin on a dime. He held *Velocity* steady and then executed a one-hundred-eighty turn, bore on his initial objective, the brand new scoreboard, and fired.

A tongue of orange rocket exhaust spewed from the airplane's nose. When the ATG struck, the scoreboard became a fireball. Debris of every kind rained down on what were, thank God, empty seats. A huge pink cloud ascended from where it had stood.

Just then the voice of Larch broke from every speaker in the place.

"*You bastards,*" it raged, "*I'll get you for this, so fucking help me. I know who you are.*" He paused. Either he didn't know or he was afraid to name Woody or Max probably fearing the consequences if he did. Combing his obviously barren brain for a fresh threat, Larch had to settle for: "*I'll find you,*" he balled out, "*so fucking help me, I'll find you and I'll cut your nuts off,*" adding finally, "*You're expelled, you little fucks. You hear me? You're expelled!*" At the last line, an explosion of laughter broke from at least half of those thousands there. There followed a roar of applause but at whom it was directed was something I've yet to figure out.

I couldn't make out what he said after that, because Max did another fly-by, this one still at full throttle; once again, *Velocity's* engines drowned out every other sound.

She was no more than a dozen feet above the gridiron, and just when I thought she would slam into the seats beyond the field, she nosed up and raced for open sky, cutting it close enough to the fans that pennants and pom-poms flapped in her wake. There was no question where Max would use the last rocket. He held *Velocity* on a straight, vertical charge until she was no more than a speck in the sky, and then allowed her to stall and fall gently over, before hurling downward in a parabolic arc that would squarely align her with the press box and Larch screaming his threats. It was almost a repeat performance of what I'd seen two nights before.

I turned to Woody. His face was as a sheet of white paper. He'd obviously not figured on this though I couldn't imagine why. He well knew, as did everyone else, what Max and *Velocity* were capable of. The airplane bore in at her target opposite us on the far side of the field.

When Larch finally realized what was coming, he bellowed a great, long "NOOOOO!" through the scores of speakers the instant Max fired.

The rocket struck a bulkhead just above the windows of the press box, and a hot cloud of smoke, smashed stucco, and splintered plywood engulfed everything below it. When that cleared, the structure was a charred hulk without a single intact window. I wondered if anyone inside was alive. A wave of warm air slapped me.

With his ordinance spent, Max pulsed *Velocity* for open sky and set her sniffer to follow the RHD beacon from the destination strip. Seconds later she was gone.

Just then we heard the first sirens.

Woody and Heyward forgot about the attack on the balloon and pulsed the biplanes to follow *Velocity*. It was definitely time for us to clear out. Recovered from their trance about half the stadium must have thought it a good idea too.

There was miraculously, no panic, and though I wouldn't call the exodus orderly, it was well short of a stampede. Fortunately the ramps and walkways must have been over-designed and I don't remember any bottlenecks or backups.

Through it all, he PA system was still on and was working as well as ever.

Though he was barely scratched (I later learned) the principal's voice balled and screamed through it for six solid minutes. Certain he was dying, he confessed his sins, which included two affairs, and begged for redemption first from his wife and then God. Finally, realizing that he might live, he switched back to swearing revenge on us. A man walking several feet in front of me couldn't stop laughing. It was Lionel Rixon. If he saw me he never showed it.

The attack party did get separated, but we collected in the parking lot where incoming sirens of two- or three-dozen police cars converged from every direction. Eight of us left in two cars, and four others fled on Vespa scooters Woody had provided.

Not once did anyone connect the canvas satchels Heyward, Max, and Woody carried, with the marauding airplanes.

The expected raid at the great house by the police that afternoon never materialized. After an hour's wait, Woody and Max gave the order for the party to begin though the cops could have come crashing in anytime. But the party commenced unmolested.

There was a very short invocation by Max consisting of a single line: "Last one to get drunk," he declared, "was a nigger."

I was not the last.

Shortly after the party was underway there began a steady stream of traffic between the bathrooms and the beer kegs. The great house boasted several of each, a fortuitous thing, since beer is a diuretic. When the ones nearest the parlor were filled and I was searching out a distant one, I heard Max shouting into a phone behind a closed door.

"*Bitch,*" he bellowed. There was a pause. "*Fucking bitch!*" Another pause. "*Slut,*" he boomed. "*I should have put that rocket right up your ass and I swear to God the next time I'll do it. And I'll coat it with magnesium. You know what magnesium does? It will burn you out from the inside like a soldering iron before the charge blows your crotch first to kingdom come, you vile bitch. What? Yes he's here, getting shit faced with the rest of us, not that it's any of your business. What? No! You can't talk to him. It's not my fault if the jocks are tired of banging you. Don't come peddling your pussy here. G'bye bitch!*"

He slammed the receiver up and there followed a thud on the floor and an explosion of laughter. Only when I was half finished peeing did I realize whom he must have been talking to.

A few minutes later I was back in the Parlor drawing another beer.

Though the thing to celebrate was that we were all miraculously alive, and that we hadn't killed someone—this we learned from the radio—you couldn't have told that to anyone else there that night. Having routed the jocks, the Legionaries seemed convinced that they were at the threshold of some great golden dawn, the kind that Max or Woody must have promised them. In the morning, they would be hung over, again alone, playing with their Erector sets, and dreaming of the cheerleaders they were no closer to screwing than they ever were.

One question gnawed on me. What would Alice have thought? I concluded finally that she would not have been surprised a bit at the kind of people I'd fallen in with. But in a way I'd come home.

I'd told Woody and Max that I was in it for the raid and nothing more. But with that done, I no longer wanted out. Woody, Max, and the Legionnaires were the kind of wonderful dangerous friends I knew then that I must have always wanted. They may not have loved and cherished what I did, but they were driven by a hatred for the same things I hated. And that afternoon they had struck back at the world that I'd convinced myself had cheated me of Alice. And almost as important, they would have made the Great Frog cringe.

I was neither the first to get drunk nor the last. Though I left before it happened, I learned that the last sober Legionnaire got smeared with shoe polish. How Max made "the last to get drunk" determination was something I never found out.

After several trips to the porcelain, I bade Woody and Max goodbye. I was offered a ride in a car that would leave in half an hour. Ralson, who had remained at Tealway, was the driver. I concluded that Ralson must have been among the best paid lawyers in Texas to endure this particular degrading to a chauffeur, but I realized later that he wanted to save himself from having to defend drunken Legionaries, and all the possible mayhem were Woody to just let them loose.

I took up Woody's offer of a Vespa scooter instead.

Only when I was about to leave the great house did I hear the first cords of a grand piano ring through the parlor and Max's shrill voice begin:

No my friend, it's not the end,
No reason to despair.
There's a side of justice you never knew was there.
A side that hears your voice cry out,
A side that feels your pain.
Yes, Justice is a lady,
And the lady's name is Jane.

She'll rise to fight in the dark of night,
Or the blinding blaze of day.
She might pause for a moment,
Just to hear you shout Hooray!
No one can ever hurt you now,
Or ever cause you pain.
They know that if they ever try,
They'll face the wrath of Jane.

Taking the Vespa in lieu of a ride from Rawlson was another of my worst decisions since leaving Indiana. Driving drunk with four wheels under you is one thing. With two, it's quite another. I rode the Vespa through several loops, passing Woody's house at least three times before exiting Tealway, and realizing I didn't have the slightest idea of which way was home. I roared through several intersections on reds, and just managed to keep right of the divider about half the time.

It all ended when a chuckhole stubbed the Vespa's tiny front wheel, pitching me over its handlebar. I landed in a heap and the scooter reaped its revenge by crashing down on me a second later.

I got a mouth full of spinning tire and the kickstand in my gut. The drive chain devoured a section of trouser and a sizable stretch of skin. When I tried lifting it off, I found out just how tangled in it I was.

14. THE MATTER OF WOODY

The Ford's blinding high beams stopped inches from me. The driver's door opened and clunked shut. Presently a girl stood over me. She knelt and began untangling me from the scooter. When we'd lifted it off I stood up and faced Courtney Provine.

"Thanks," I said and went about inspecting the wreck. The fork was bent so that the front wheel was locked in way that would never allow it to turn. It wasn't going anywhere, nor was I, at least not on it.

"Come on," Courtney said gesturing to the car.

"What about that?" I asked, pointing to the scooter.

"Leave it and forget it," she answered. "Woody can afford it," adding: "and a few thousand more." Her coming upon me was obviously not an accident.

Dark as it was inside the Ford, there was no more doubt that Courtney qualified as the beauty I'd suspected she was since the Thursday rally. But unlike Alice, her face was a composition that stressed the horizontal with wide set eyes, olive skin, and black hair, a harmony in far darker shades. Though someone else might have put her in a class with Alice, I wasn't someone else, and she wasn't Alice.

Because she didn't ask my address, I assumed we weren't going there and wondered if her idea was to turn me over to the jocks. I shouldn't have worried.

Ten minutes later we pulled into the driveway of a Georgian set well back from the street. Courtney opened the garage door with a remote and we parked inside. On the door connecting the garage to the house was a plaque which read *Paris Provine M.D.*

I mentioned that my father was a doctor.

"Really what kind?" she asked.

"Internal medicine, ears, nose, and throat mainly, kind of a snotologist, yours?

"A psychiatrist," she replied, "and a world class lush," adding, "mom too. She turned him on to medicine and he turned her on to the sauce."

The Great Frog had tried having me scoped by a number of shrinks posing as friends of his before I was twelve. They were easy enough to peg by their obvious belief that no one besides themselves had made it past the second grade. Most could not stop regurgitating bromides and two-bit analogies from what seemed a bottomless cache along with a generous helping of "why's?" about every fourth sentence. It wasn't long before I'd learned which of their buttons to push so as to best stroke their monumental egos. Done right, they could be played like grand pianos.

Once inside, Courtney lit up the parlor from a bank of switches. From what I could see, the shrink business must have been good. I wanted to ask her about the affidavit she'd signed, but hesitated. She seemed intent on holding the initiative.

"The bathroom is the third door down the hall," she said. "Take a shower. There are bandages and antiseptics in the medicine chest. I'll get you a robe."

"You're not expecting your folks?"

"No," Courtney replied. "They're in New Orleans for a convention. They're gone for the weekend.

"A medical one?"

"Hardly," she replied almost laughing, "it's a convention of Spanish Civil War veterans."

The Great Frog had mentioned the Spanish Civil War a few times and how a band of American volunteers, had formed something called the Abraham Lincoln Brigade that had gone to Spain to fight for a regime backed by the Russians and opposed by Francisco Franco's rebels. Franco's patrons were Hitler, Mussolini, and the Pope. To nobody's surprise he won. One-third of the Lincoln brigade was killed before it was evacuated.

"I never met anyone from the Lincoln Brigade," I told her.

"Are you kidding?" she laughed. "When dear old Dad got over there he saw who was going to win. He joined Franco's army."

"He must have some real stories to tell."

"He has stories alright, but real ones, no. Mom told me that his job was censoring mail—perfect military logic—since he couldn't speak a whole sentence in Spanish when she met him. Also, he was dyslexic, still is for that matter."

"Your mother was in the war too?" I asked.

"She was a nurse in Franco's army."

"She was Spanish then, not American?" Courtney's looks more than suggested this; as a matter of fact, they screamed it.

She nodded. "She was a Sephardic Jewess from Majorca. A nurse in Franco's army was paid more money in a year than her family's business could make in five."

"Your Dad was her patient?"

"No, he was visiting a patient, Dwight Kilbourn. They'd gone over there together. Dwight saw some real fighting.

"That name's familiar."

"It ought to be. Dwight Kilbourn was Woody's father. Now clean yourself up before an infection gets going."

I had to admit the shower was an idea whose time had come although I had to interrupt it three separate times because Woody's beer was still percolating through me. One of the assorted things I remembered from that night was that you never regret money spent on a bathroom. The one Courtney directed me to far outclassed the rest of the house which wasn't exactly a shanty. I don't know what the robe was made of either, but the feel of it was of one that might cost a couple of times what my family's whole wardrobe did. I was close to sober when I walked back to the parlor.

Courtney had changed from a dress into white shorts and a stripped blouse. She sat puffing on a cigarette. On the table before her was a medium-sized pitcher of what looked like orange juice and a half full glass with a straw that had been poured from it. Next to it was an empty glass and a fifth-size bottle of something labeled "Moon Rocket."

"Sit down Addison July," she said, "or is it okay to call you Sonny?"

I told her to use either. I must have been staring at the glass she'd lifted from the table.

"Screwdriver," she said, tapping the pitcher and gesturing to the empty glass. "Help yourself."

"Later, maybe." There was a pause. I had my opening.

"Two days ago, you signed an affidavit about what happened in the parking lot, why?"

"I saw it happen," the girl said shrugging, "I was there, and Max asked me to sign it."

"You know Max?"

"Yes, my mother and his mother are twins. When Franco won his war, dear old Dad arranged passage for both of them to America."

"Max is your cousin?" The revelation was seismic. Swallowing the idea of Max and Courtney sharing so much as grandparents was like trying to hold down an eruption of stomach bile. My next thought was that besides Woody, none of the Legionnaires could possibly have known this, lest it douse the flames Max had taken such great care to fan.

Courtney only nodded, took a heavy pull off the straw, and swallowed. "Had Spain lined up with Hitler," she said, "they might have wound up in a death camp. But Franco was too smart. He saved Spain from the communists, used Hitler, and gave him crumbs in return. But all anyone hears about it is boo-hoo clap trap from the Lincoln Brigade about their lost cause. They should put those crybabies—the ones that are still alive—on a ship to Russia, and then sink it."

She continued, "Anyway the four of them arrived here in Houston late in 1940. They almost went to Palestine. Mom says they flipped a coin."

"Did you say four?" I asked.

"Four, including Dwight Kilbourn. He wanted to marry my aunt. She turned him down, and it's a good thing too."

"Oh?"

"Yeah, Woody would've been just another half-brew instead of the WASP God he is. On the other hand, we wouldn't have Max to deal with. He's going to be a major problem for the world if he lives much longer.

"Half-brew?"

"Max's term for a half Hebrew, us for example."

Courtney's reference to "us" meant she already knew about my parents and it wasn't hard to guess from where the information had come. I wondered if there was anything Max hadn't found out. Max and Courtney must have had a back-door communication that few, if any, knew about.

"My mother," she continued, "says that every neurotic Jew secretly dreams of WASP God or Goddess. Well, Woody was mine. Dear old Dad was Mom's. In the end, we're all chumps for goys with looks." She had yet to mention Alice. Maybe Max was saving that information for future use. He probably knew about Alice even prior to hearing about her from my liquor-loosened tongue at the party I'd just left. It was a three-minute exchange, but now Max knew everything and would forget nothing. He was the worst person to tell anything to.

"You're a neurotic Jew?" I asked.

She drained her glass and refilled it from the pitcher. Then, looking at me, she tapped the empty tumbler again. I shook my head. She tasted her drink, added some Moon Rocket to the pitcher, and stirred it.

"According to my father, there's no other kind." She went on, discarding the straw and taking gulps, "Being a shrink, I suppose some think he would know."

"Do you think so?"

"Maybe, besides a world class lush, he's an idiot, but now and then he's right about something."

"You didn't mention idiot."

"I didn't? Well he is."

"His patients obviously don't think so." I gestured to the furnishings. He might well have been an idiot, but he wasn't a poor one.

"That's because his patients are bigger idiots than he is—idiots with money—but idiots; I've met some of them. The number one job of a shrink is to prevent patients from committing suicide, which of course, shuts off the cash, so I guess dear old Dad is a success. He hasn't lost one that way yet. He gets them to feeling good enough to keep them coming back, but never well enough to quit. Skin doctors are like that; their patients never die or get well."

I wondered how Courtney would like to have been the daughter of a poor "genius" like my father—everybody said he was a genius—instead of a rich "idiot," but abandoned the thought.

"Did you, Max, and Woody grow up together?"

"Max and Woody knew each other early on, but I actually met Woody in the Class of '53."

"Hadn't heard of that one," I said.

"It was one of those rehabilitation classes for the victims of the big Polio epidemic three years before. It was especially bad in Texas."

"Yes, I sort of remember that. It hit Indiana too. I wouldn't have known it to look at you."

Holding them together, Courtney raised her legs while rotating herself. She formed a "V" with her exquisite buttocks as the fulcrum. "My left foot is a whole shoe size larger than my right. I'm the worst dancer alive, but I might have been anyway. I never cared for dancing. Of course, Woody was stricken far worse." She gave up the 'V' stance, rotated ninety degrees to resume a seated position. They tried some new thing they called 'physio-psychotherapy' on us. The woman that invented it headed the class. At the beginning of every class—there were two per week—she would read us a passage from *The Little Choo Choo That Could*. I can regurgitate *The Little Choo Choo That Could* right down to the punctuation.

"They must have stopped sometime. It can't be that big a book."

"The lady kept reading it to us over and over. It only stopped when she was hit by a car and killed."

I sighed. "And that class was where you met Woody?"

"Yes, I told you that. That's where I met Woody."

Courtney's look told me that her mind was back in the class of '53 just then, and that it still spent more than a little time there.

"Woody was the most beautiful child I'd ever seen," she went on, as if gazing at something on the ceiling. "When I met him, I stopped believing in God."

"I don't myself, but how did you get there?" I asked.

"Well, if you start by assuming God created all things, it would have to include Woody Kilbourne, check?"

"Check," I replied.

"But if you saw how this wonderful creation had been desecrated, you would have to conclude that God must be a sick, sadistic monster to have done what he had to Woody. I refused to believe that, so the only conclusion was God must not exist at all. What about you? What drove you to the same conclusion—the six million dead Jews?"

I shrugged, "My mother was one of them. She died in the French Resistance. My father is married to her twin now." Doubtless Max knew that too.

Courtney exhaled a long blue cloud of smoke, lit a fresh cigarette from the one she was smoking, and stubbed the old one out.

"I'm sorry," she said, seemingly embarrassed, then pulled in more smoke, and downed a swallow of screwdriver before exhaling it.

"You didn't know," I said, "go on."

"As I said, Woody was the most beautiful child I'd ever seen. We were both eleven. You can be smitten at eleven and God—there I go again with God—I was smitten. Of all the kids in that class, Woody was stricken the worst. His left leg was withered to a fleshy twig. When he did walk—on crutches of course—the twig swung like a pendulum and wouldn't stop right away when he did. It kept right on swinging like an unwound yo-yo. No amount of therapy was going to make a difference and that *little choo choo that could* bitch who ran the class knew it. But that didn't matter. She had a Federal grant that paid by the number she treated, and she wasn't going to miss out on even one, the greedy bitch." Courtney stubbed the cigarette out at mid length and continued. "They set up a buddy system in the class and I gave the guy they paired up with Woody five dollars to switch with him. I had to steal the money from dear old Dad. It was the first time I ever did that. I actually worried about being found out. Of course, he was always too soused to have ever missed an amount like that. So, I became Woody's partner and Dad's too. My allowance was really chintzy in those days."

"What was that like?"

"Woody? It was fireworks," she said. "First love is like that. If you've been there I don't have to describe it and if you haven't, I could never begin to anyway. I couldn't believe I was his partner. Those two classes, every week, were the only things in my life that mattered. Most of the routines they put us through needed physical contact. I could put my hands on Woody as much as I wanted. It was two hours of ecstasy twice a week. One day Woody told me that he and Max had this idea that was going to fix everything. He couldn't tell me anymore, but I was going to see something I would never believe until I did see it."

I tried to imagine what Woody and Max could have concocted at age eleven or twelve and came up blank. "What was it," I asked finally.

"Well," replied Courtney, "you know how a balloon is a limp lump of rubber until air is injected into it?

"Yes… oh shit they didn't!"

"They did."

"How the hell did they…"

"You know those things they fill up tires with? I mean the tires without tubes in them?"

"Yes," I replied, "valve stems."

"Valve stems, right. They planted valve stems into the stricken leg."

"How did…"

"Incisions," Courtney replied, "gashes really—deep gashes. They made ten of them in various points on the leg, forced the stems into the gashes and sealed them with duct tape. Then Max towed Woody to a gas station in a coaster wagon and they put the air hose to the valves. Max told me that for a time it looked like it was working. Some parts of the leg actually inflated. But when Woody tried standing, it was a bloodbath. We didn't see him for quite a while after that. Some of that compressed air made it to his lungs and his brain."

"Is that when they took off the leg?"

"No," Courtney answered as she drained her glass and refilled it, "that came a while later." She set the pitcher down but did not begin drinking right away. "When he was recovering the doctors told him that when he'd grown to his full height they would amputate the leg and fit him with a prosthesis that would allow him to walk normally. When he heard that, he begged them to do it immediately. So what if he outgrew it? The Kilbourns are an oil family, practically a dynasty; they can afford a hundred sizes of artificial legs. But Woody was told he would have to wait. He couldn't do that."

She leaned forward raised the tumbler and took a heavy pull from it. "One day, we were asked to write a theme on what we expected to do with our lives, kind of a prophesy assuming we'd all become fully fit specimens one day, which when you think about it, was kind of a sick joke."

"What was yours?"

Courtney sighed. "I honestly don't remember, but the day we read them was a day I would never forget."

She emptied her glass and set it down. I expected her to refill it again but she didn't.

"I'll always remember Woody standing propped up on the dais reading how he intended to be a General. It was the most impassioned thing I'd ever heard from someone that age. I could see him bidding good luck and Godspeed to his troops as they left for a war somewhere. He was only a few paragraphs into it when a blast of laughter crashed through the room. It came from one of the kids who'd only been slightly affected and should never have been in that class in the first place. Woody tried to ignore the laughter, but the kid wouldn't quit even after the teacher motioned him to stop. He was a big kid and I think she was afraid to do anything more."

"Listen to me, General," the kid said, "there's this thing the army has called a physical exam. Just how do you expect to get past that?"

Courtney began to shake in the grip of a remembered rage, but then collected herself.

"Woody stood there at the lectern for a minute, read a few more sentences, and then started for the kid who'd never stopped laughing. He walked like some kind of wind-up toy on his crutches and was screaming something about how he would get into the army anyway. Half way across the room he burst into tears, still walking, until he was two feet or so from his tormentor. And the kid knocked him to the floor with one quick swipe."

There were flashes of fury in Courtney's face as she spoke. "Woody lay there in a ball trembling. We all just sat staring at him like he was an unexploded bomb. I ran and knelt over to him, but he was beyond responding. He just lay there sobbing, shaking, and still gripping the pages of his prophesy; they were a tear-soaked ball. I was crying too; I loved him so much there wasn't anything I could do. Two days later Max cut the leg off with a buzz saw."

"A buzz saw?"

"Yeah, like the ones carpenters use," Courtney replied, "a Black and Decker."

"I was surprised when Max called me. We were cousins, but we almost never spoke. He was scared, let me tell you. He wanted to know if I knew how to make a tourniquet. It so happened I did. Mom had shown me. He said if I didn't want Woody to die, I was to get over to the Kilbourn place and don't bring anybody else. I didn't for a minute think it was a joke. My mother drove me there. One of the great things about her is that she knows when not to ask questions. Even then I was afraid to cross Max. But I was an idiot to keep my mouth shut. Mom was a nurse for God's sake!

Max met me at the door and took me to Woody. It's a good thing I can stand the sight of blood because I never saw so much in my life. Max had already tried making several tourniquets. There were bloody towels all over the floor. You could see the severed end of the femoral artery. Woody had passed out. When I made a tourniquet, it wouldn't work either. As soon as we put on the pressure the damn thing just slid off the end. They really cut that leg off high. I was close to hysterical. I wanted to kill Max when we saw the belts lying on the floor. The idea hit us both at the same time. We looped a belt over Woody's shoulder and through the tourniquet to keep it from slipping off. That stopped the hemorrhaging. One thing though: one person had to hold it all taught. That's when I slipped away and called the police. Max definitely didn't want the police, but by then I didn't give a shit what Max didn't want."

"I can imagine."

"Yeah, even with an ambulance it was close. A few more minutes more and we would have lost him."

"His folks weren't home?"

"They almost never are. They traveled a lot, and I mean a lot, so they hired a guardian, but Woody just paid her off to stay away. He's been alone in that house since he was ten. He ate all his meals out. When he was fourteen, his folks were killed in a car wreck in South America and things just went on as they always had."

"You saved his life. Did he ever thank you?"

"No, I don't think he wanted me to. Anyway, I didn't see him for several weeks. The class ended that spring when the teacher was killed. Woody would never have gone back anyway. He never got the prosthesis either—obviously. Max had cut the leg off way too high. They had to remove the whole leg including the hip. There was a horrible infection besides, and major nerve damage, so instead he got that baseball bat he walks around with now. And that's how he came to be called Woody, not because his middle name is Woodrow."

"You still love him?"

"Of course, I always will. He was my first love; you never stop loving your first."

"So I'm told," I said remembering Ray's telling me that I would die dreaming of Alice and was still wondering what it would have taken to win her over. "When was the next time you saw him?"

"As I said, it was several weeks later. I'd been calling him every day and he refused to come to the phone. When his parents found out that I was the tourniquet girl, they forced the issue and sent a limousine for me. When I got to the Kilbourn place and they realized I was Paris Provine's daughter, they wanted to adopt me. They actually offered my parents a million dollars to give me up. For the Kilbouns, everything had a price." Courtney shook her head, almost laughing.

"They sent me up upstairs to see Woody because he wouldn't come to the foyer. I found him in his bedroom holding a big toy airplane. There were little lead soldiers all over the floor and he was stomping them flat with that peg they fitted him with. Some of the soldier's limbs had broken off and were imbedded in the bottom of the wood. Finally, he looked up at me, tears streaming down from those green eyes of his that always seemed to me like they must be connected to batteries. And he said, "I'm going to be a general, Courtney, I'm going to be a general, you'll see." I told him I believed him, I didn't of course, at least not until now. But I guess he showed us all. And I don't think he ever cried again."

"Quite a story," I mused. "What did they do to Max?"

"Oh Max? A court sentenced him to five years of psychiatric treatment. He never did much of that though. After treating Max for three months, the shrink killed himself. Max loves to tell that story. As far as I know it's true. If you haven't figured it out yet, Max might already be the most dangerous person alive."

"I don't think you're kidding."

"I'm not. There's one more thing you should know."

I shrugged, "lay it on me."

"The kid who humiliated Woody that day, his name is Wally Montruska."

"I'd like to kill that son of a bitch myself!"

"Don't," Courtney almost snapped, "Max and Woody wouldn't be happy if you cheated them out of that. I mean it. You don't want them angry with you. They've already tried to kill Wally at least once before today."

"You just saved Wally's life this afternoon."

"What I did was to save Woody's life. Do you think that any of you would have ever gotten away with murdering a football star on the gridiron in front of everybody, and in Texas?"

"Max thought so."

"Max doesn't give a shit about his own life, much less anybody else's. And he'll take all of you down with him."

"You said they've already tried to kill Wally?"

"Mmm." Courtney finally poured herself another screwdriver offering me one which I took this time. It emptied the pitcher. She did not seem the least bit affected by what she'd consumed so far. She'd called her father a lush. I wondered what her definition of a lush was.

"A year ago last spring one of the kids in their little club—they call themselves the Legion—tried to start a conversation with me about one of those Sputnik things, what do they call them?"

"Satellites?"

"Yes, satellites. He was so nervous that he accidently knocked all my books to the floor. He was helping me pick them up when Wally Montruska and his friends showed up and worked him over just for talking to me. There's this idea people have, that I'm Wally's personal property. I barely know him, and I've never gone out, or anywhere else with him.

"Why did you agree to be Homecoming Queen anyway?" I asked.

"For the money of course, five hundred dollars, why do you think?"

"For five hundred dollars I'd put on a dress myself. That kid they beat up, do you remember his name?"

"Yes, Alfred Cobb. Do you know him?"

"We've met."

So Alfred Cobb had been another of the jock's victims. It wasn't hard to figure how Woody and Max had recruited the rest of their private little army.

"This thing the jocks did to Alfred Cobb, what did Woody and Max do about that?" I asked with a flicker of grisly curiosity.

"Well first, Wally and his friends dragged him off to Hollenbeck's office. Hollenbeck is never there so they turned him over to Rixon with a story that Alfred had tried to sneak into the girl's washroom. I went to Rixon and told him what had happened. But Alfred was already gone. Max and Woody had taken him away. Even then, Rixon knew better than to argue with them. He was a hero in the war, brave as they come, and still I could see how rattled he was at the thought of Max being involved. Little Max, Max the terrible little troll. By the way don't ever call him 'troll' to his face."

"That wasn't the end of it," I added, stating the obvious.

"Of course not, that was the beginning." She lit a fresh cigarette, this time exhaling only after I'd thought she'd digested the smoke. "Two weeks later a package addressed to Wally Montruska arrived at his house. His sister opened it. It was a bomb, and it blew half her face off. It would have been better if it had killed her. I knew her fairly well; her name was Carley, a sweet kid, and really pretty too. She was in the hospital about four weeks, facing years of reconstructive surgery. One eye had been destroyed. I visited her a couple of times."

"You assumed the bomb came from Max?"

"Where else? Proving it was another matter. There was no evidence, with Max there never is. The last time I saw Carley I brought her a pair of scissors she'd asked me for. I shouldn't have done that, it was really stupid of me."

"What happened?" I asked.

"After I'd left and she was alone, Carley used the scissors to take off the bandages. They'd forbidden her to do that but well…

"Oh Jesus," I said. Courtney stopped talking, but I motioned her to continue.

"As best they could tell, after she'd cut off the bandages, she must have looked in a mirror. They found her on the sidewalk below the fourth floor window. She'd jumped, and the fall broke her neck. I think she'd hoped for that."

"And they never did anything to Max?"

"No, I told you, no evidence. But a cousin of mine on my Father's side, not related to Max at all, is on the Houston Police force. There's an unwritten order among some of them to shoot Max for any legitimate excuse. It's one thing that fancy lawyer of Woody's can't do anything about. Remember that if you spend much time around him or Woody for that matter. It's easy to end up at the wrong place at the wrong time."

There was a long silence.

Finally, I asked: "You brought me here to tell me this?"

"That, and to sleep with you before your new friends get you killed. That would be a waste, dying a virgin, I mean."

"You're afraid to die a virgin?"

She slipped from her clothes in one quick motion as if shedding a layer of skin. "Me?" she said laughing, "It's a bit late for that. I'm going to see to it that you don't."

Denying what I was would have been an exercise in futility. Like Rixon, this girl missed little. I stood up and allowed the robe fall from me.

15. A NEW YEAR'S DAY PROPOSAL

A wave of news coverage about the raid headlined every paper in Texas the next day and lasted a week.

The great house on Teal Way was invaded that Sunday morning by a fleet of squad cars; various layers of law enforcement that advanced like waves of infantry with ordinance of every description. Woody and anyone known to have been associated with him was taken into custody, questioned, brow beaten, threatened, and finally released without being charged. Rawlson saw to the last part. It paid to buy the best.

I was arrested along with Courtney in front of our house after our night together. She was quickly released when they realized who she was.

They held me for just over six hours. After a two-hour stint by a couple of keystone cop imitators, I was "interviewed" by a psychiatrist who said he could commit me for the rest of my life if I didn't co-operate. As I'd been exposed to a number of shrinks by the Great Frog by the time I was twelve, I found it especially amusing. This one had an outstanding feature: bad breath. When I told him that, he excused himself and didn't come back. Mentioning that was the one thing I regretted. He struck me as by far dumber than the ones the Great Frog had dispatched to appraise me, and I probably missed a chance to have some real fun with him. I only hoped that they would turn him loose on Max, who, if Courtney was right, had already convinced one shrink to commit suicide. Max would have loved the chance for another scalp.

At first, Courtney was canonized by several newspapers for saving the four jocks from annihilation by *Velocity's* rockets which was certainly true.

She was invited to receive the key to several cities and villages in Texas. It shortly became a colossal annoyance since there were never any cash rewards involved, just plaques, cheap trophies, and some luncheons, along with requests for interviews. On one televised occasion, Courtney showed up with her parents. Wally Montruska, the surprise guest, still recovering from second degree burns on his legs, was rolled out in a wheelchair. Pushing him along was Myron Larch, the principal, who wore four times the bandages his injuries warranted. At the site of them, Mrs. Provine, then in an advanced state of inebriation, vomited as if on cue thus ending the plague of interview invites. I happened to have seen that one, and wished I could have taped it, but in 1959 that wasn't so easy.

A second raid was in the works when Woody's genius lawyer told him that he'd better give the idea up. The games were now under tight security by armed men who had a license to kill and were eager to use it. No amount of legal maneuvers could bring back a dead Legionnaire. Woody relented, and there followed a period of dormancy although the work on *Velocity's* sisters, *Calamity, Intensity, Tenacity, Virility,* and others went on as if the next raid was but one week away.

It all ended one day before New Year's eve and the dawn of the nineteen sixties. We were already out of classes on the first Christmas vacation I had ever seen that wasn't under assault by a mid-western winter. Still, I was toying with the idea of a trip back to Indiana for another try at winning over Alice, despite being broke.

Max called me that morning. The Legion was meeting at the great house at eleven. I was to be there—I was told this, rather than asked. By eleven, all of us were assembled in a small theater in the Eastern wing of the great house that I'd never seen before; the place was that huge. Woody smiled at us from the lectern as we assembled in fixed chairs while he pivoted nervously on his wooden leg.

At just five minutes after eleven he began.

"Legionnaires," he said, "as you are well aware, we've been forced by circumstances—the jocks and their lackeys—to lie low and bide our time for the last two and a half months. We didn't have a choice since trying to repeat the success of our raid in September would have been walking into a trap, and I'm afraid, a trap that most of us might be carried out of in bloody pieces."

Woody paused to look back at Max before going on. "A proposal has been put on the table, a proposal that I want to tell you right now that I am absolutely against, but according to our by-laws, I must allow to be placed before you for consideration and a vote. Some of you are familiar with it, but for those who aren't, Max will now lay it out for you."

I had never imagined up to that moment that the Legion had any provision for such things as proposals and votes since I'd never seen anything printed out for fear, I guessed, that it would get into the wrong hands.

Max stepped up to the lectern allowing Woody to hobble to a chair and sit down before he began. Neither Woody nor he used notes.

"Alright," said Max finally, "who here doesn't understand that what we're doing and have been doing for the better part of two years is fighting a God damn war?"

No one's hand rose.

"And the only reason you fight a war is to win it, *RIGHT?*" An affirmative mummer rumbled through the room.

"And does anyone have a single doubt in their mind who the enemy is?"

"No," barked a voice from behind me.

"It's the jocks!" screamed another. Again came the affirmative rumble, a little louder this time followed by light applause. Max extended his hands and the theater fell silent. "The jock," he continued, "has no respect for human life and therefore no right to live. He is Animal Puke."

That tripped a thunderous ovation that might have been called orgasmic as if the thirty assembled young men had all climaxed at once from what Max had stirred in them. I didn't have long to wonder where he was going with this.

"And now," he said, when the roars subsided, "we have a plan for winning the war." I had no doubt, and I was also sure Max didn't, that they would vote for anything he put in front of them.

The Benjamin football team, Max explained—the public league champions for the city of Houston—would play the champions of the

Dallas public league. The match would be held ninety miles north of Houston at Kyle Field on the campus of Texas A&M College. The varsity squad would be ferried there in a bus. The plan was to use *Velocity Jane* to fire a two-rocket salvo into the bus through its windshield.

Velocity's pilot would be at the overpass where Hotchkiss Drive crossed Memorial Freeway. Max assured us that the warheads on the ATGs *Velocity* would carry were more than capable of incinerating anything living within the confines of the bus. He didn't have to say who the intended pilot should be. Nobody was going to deprive him of that. But Max couldn't finish without a warning to Courtney, directed through me though, no one else realized it.

"That slut," he declared, "isn't going to stand in front of that bus this time, unless they strap her to the windshield, and if they do, I'll put the first ATGs right through her pussy."

He then fixed his focus on Woody, the one person he feared capable of derailing the plan. Max shifted his weight from his right leg to his left, which he must have found uncomfortable because he quickly undid the action and then began to slowly march in place. "I repeat gentlemen," he said, "we're in a war; the path to win it is open. I propose we hold a question and answer session, and vote before we leave. Who will second the motion?"

"I second the motion," came the same voice that had declared jocks the enemy a minute before.

"Questions?" asked Max. It was obviously, the one step he would have given anything to avoid.

"I have one," said Woody. Max nodded, glaring fearfully at the one person who could douse the fires he'd just so carefully stoked. "Who else will be on that bus?"

"Probably coach Hollenbeck, an assistant, the driver of course," Max replied, in a tone that inferred it wasn't worth considering.

"Who else do you think?" he asked, hoping an answer he feared wasn't in the offing.

"The cheerleading squad," declared Woody, "Do you want to take them out too? Now, not so muffled reverberations reverberated.

"They'll be on another bus," Max protested. "I have that from a good source." I didn't believe Max had any idea although it seemed unlikely they would both be on the same bus.

"Do you even know for sure there's going to be more than one bus?" Woody fired back. He obviously didn't believe that claim either. "And if there are two it's going to be all too easy to take out the wrong one. And just who is your good source by the way?"

More reverberations followed, these louder still.

"Well, what about it?" snapped Woody, "Or is killing a dozen young girls okay too as long as we take out the jocks?"

"Of course, it's not," Max replied. But there was no other answer he could give if he wanted to. "We can verify who's on the bus and call it off if any wrong people are aboard," he countered. There was no way he would call it off and everyone knew it.

Woody bristled. "And suppose your spotters screw up, what then? I don't have to tell you how many times we've screwed things like that up before…or do I?"

Max never took his glare away from Woody. Minutes before he had no doubt the vote would be for carrying out the attack, but now…

Up until then no one had yet raised the question of murdering "the right people" either: the first and second strings of the Varsity Football team, a couple of coaches and some incidental victims, perhaps thirty people in all. In a war you killed your enemy. These "friends of mine" had the means, and more than the will, to do it. I wondered what Alice would have thought. I doubt she would have been surprised at who I'd fallen in with considering what I'd done to Collin and Bobbie.

"Motion for a vote," Woody said suddenly. His timing was perfect; he'd shot a huge hole in the plan and called for a vote before it could be patched.

"Seconded," I blurted out, nearly yelling.

The vote was taken before Max had time to marshal a defense much less a counterattack. His careful planning had been no match for Woody's timing. And even at that, the vote was a near enough thing: eighteen votes against the plan including mine, and twelve for it. Meeting closed, happy holidays, peace on earth, and goodwill toward men.

I tried to avoid looking at Max on my way out but couldn't quite manage it. His glare burned with the kind of loathing that condemned men might give juries who'd just voted to hang them. Max had personally recruited me, honored me with the code name of his personal hero, and I'd betrayed him. But if I'd betrayed him, so had Woody, so had Alfred Cobb, and so had fifteen others. Max's half serious threat to murder Courtney had certainly cost him Alfred's vote and maybe the four others that it would have taken to win. But, it was too late to ponder that, he'd lost.

The enormity of what had just happened struck me in repeated waves all the way home, now riding another Vespa, one that I had acquired myself to replace my wrecked car. I didn't ask where Woody had the Zephyr's carcass taken. It was gone a week after the air raid and I didn't want to know where. Its body had been pounded into an endless tangle of creases and dents by the jocks and their imbecilic fans. I couldn't stand the sight of it, or even the thought.

I'd joined the Legion because they'd promised revenge. I had to have been blind not to realize just how serious they were about delivering on it. By a narrow margin, we'd just voted down slaughtering about thirty people most of us didn't even know. At the height of my rage, I had only wanted Wally killed.

When I got home I meant to call Woody and tell him I was out of his stupid club and considered our debt on the legal fees settled, as well as what he could do with his private army and his stupid war. I was out now, for real and for good. I owed them nothing.

16. EXIT COLIN

Once home, I made directly for the phone while completing the third rehearsal of my resignation speech to Woody, but the note that waited for me at the phone desk stopped that thought, and every other dead in its tracks. *"Call Clifford Fitch,"* it read, *"Colin Walker dead."* Beneath the words was a phone number with a Michigan City area code.

My first thought was that he'd died from what I'd done to him. And if he had, I'd need Woody's lawyer more than ever. Or should I hit the road immediately, head for parts unknown, and establish a new identity? But if I'd caused Colin's death, why didn't Ray try to warn me first? And if it was looking like Colin would die, especially from what I'd done, why was this the first I'd heard of it?

Colin—Clifford told me when I reached him—had been killed in a holdup two days before. He'd been working security on an armored car and had been killed along with a second guard. The killers had made off with over six million dollars. The police were working leads. Dozens of people had been questioned and released. Colin's burial was set for the next morning, Clifford told me, on Thursday, December 31, the last day of the decade.

Clifford then went on with rambling irrelevancies for several minutes. I heard little of it: a single thought was making my head pound. *So Alice was to be mine after all!*

"I'll see you tonight, Cliff," I said.

"What?"

"I'll see you tonight, tell your parents to expect a guest."

"Uh, Addison."

"What?"

"I don't think they'll want you staying here."

"Because of what I did to Colin?" I couldn't imagine their having heard of it.

"They don't like you Addison. I'm sorry," said my friend.

"Fine," I snapped, "I'll stay with Ray."

"Uh, Addison,"

"What?"

"You can't do that. Ray died two weeks after you left town. He had a stroke."

"Oh my God!" I'd never even called Ray to thank him for gathering up my tools and shipping them to me. It was probably among the last things he'd ever done.

"I'll meet your train, Addison, and give you a lift to a motel. Call me when you get to Chicago."

I left Lola and the Great Frog a note that said simply I was going out of town for a few days and I didn't mention where. I turned to Woody for the money. He didn't ask what it was for, or when I'd pay it back, and I didn't tell him because I had no idea. I was still in the Legion of course—for now.

Just after five that afternoon, when I stepped off a brand new Delta Airlines Convair 880 at O'Hare, winter smashed its way back into my life with a full measure of malevolence, but no matter that. Through the whole of the flight, I'd constructed a scenario for the next six months that had Alice and me together at last. I could live in any one of several rooming houses in Michigan City for the final semester at… ugh…Willkie.

Alice and I would go to the Senior Prom. Perhaps we'd marry that very night. Then, on to California and the idyllic life that included a weekly trip to that precipice on Mulholland Drive, the lights of a great city below, and twenty thousand bright tomorrows. Addison and Alice July, the way it was meant to be; there was no reason now that it shouldn't—not one, not any more. Collin was gone from the equation and all was right with the world.

When Clifford met my train, he never stopped apologizing for his parent's rolling out the unwelcome mat, recalling how many times Lola and the Great Frog had put him up when his own parents were sufficiently crocked to partially destroy their own house. Clifford offered me ten dollars that I really didn't need, but I took anyway, and some advice I might have also taken: *stay away from Alice, at least for now*. I told him I couldn't do that; the fates had ordained otherwise. I grabbed a glimpse of the Franklin Street station before getting into Clifford's car. It had all begun there. I wondered if we might get married there. I wondered if anyone else ever had that idea.

Clifford drove me to a motel.

Just after eight, I tried calling Alice. Her mother answered.

"Alice home?" I asked.

"She's not here," was the reply; a lie, I was sure.

"When do you expect her back?" I tried to select words I thought least likely to give away my voice.

"Who is this, please?"

"A friend," I said, "Where is she?"

"At the wake," her mother replied again demanding to know who I was and upon recognizing me, she let go a scream, "It's him!" I picked up a "who?" question in the background.

"That Jew bastard with that horrible old car."

I screamed for her to go fuck herself but only after slamming down the receiver.

"Horrible old car!"

I called Clifford Fitch. "There's a wake for Collin Walker tonight," I said, "I don't know where. Do you?"

"It was at our parish, Addison. It's over."

"What! Why the hell didn't you tell me?"

"You didn't ask."

"Wrong answer Clifford, I thought you were a friend."

"I was there Addison, and so was about half of Willkie High."

"Thanks for nothing, buddy."

"Did you want to crash back into her life at the wake?"

I sighed. "All right, I'll just wait until after they plant him."

"Ah, Addison…"

"What?"

"She'll be going away to Florida as soon as it's over. I'm guessing her whole family is going there to recover."

"Shit!"

"I told you to give her some time."

"What time is the funeral, Clifford? And don't fucking lie to me."

"It's at ten," he replied, without bothering to argue.

"Thank you, Clifford. See you there, goodnight."

This was off to a fine start.

I tried the motel room's TV, which quit soon after warming up. At $12.50 a night they could have done better.

I stepped out of the room into twenty-degree air. Without wind, I could stand it for several minutes and did so while reflecting on the day that had begun with the phone call to the great house, the mass murder proposal, the vote that had barely killed it, the call from Clifford, and finally, the trip back to reclaim Alice. Also, Ray was dead. It was a day of earthquakes.

I wondered how much more had changed in Michigan City. I was once told that the more things change, the more they stay the same. In the morning, I would find if the one thing that mattered had changed.

Thursday began with a brutally cold morning; the Midwest rarely gets any other kind in December. The sun was out to taunt, but not warm you a micro-degree. Though officially below freezing, snow melted by the sun soaked the wind that blew up my trousers. It reminded me of all the weekends that were trashed by the Sunday school classes that I had to walk to for half a mile in wool dress pants that chaffed savagely. I would never own another thing with wool in its weave. I was henceforth, and would forever be, a cotton man. It was during one of my Sunday school classes where I sat fretting for three and a half hours that I came up with the plan for paying back the Great Frog—who was not even Jewish—for my force-fed Hebrew education.

It was a short walk to the Church, a small half-century old Gothic knock off that badly needed tuck pointing, while the Pastor's new Oldsmobile sat in a parking slot with his name on it. I'd been no more than a mile from Alice for much of the previous evening. In less than an hour I would see her. I wondered if Clifford might be right, later being better. But Alice was going to Florida after the funeral, and I was too close to her now to turn back. A sign announcing events in front of the church read:

THURSDAY DEC. 31
MEMORIAL SERVICE 10:00 AM
COLLIN MICHAEL WALKER
1937-1959

I arrived early. There were a dozen people already there, none of whom I knew—or I hoped knew of me. I scanned the front pew where the grieving family sat expecting to see Alice among them. She wasn't there.

Alice wouldn't arrive until more than half the pews were filled— odd that was—and it would seem odder yet had I'd known that Colin was her husband.

So I sat in a back row close to the entry where I could spot Alice when she arrived, knowing she would be instantly recognizable from any angle. She might be watching for me having been warned the previous evening. It was critical that I control the sequence of events, plot her trajectory, intercept her before the service began, and before anyone could interfere.

Was Clifford right? Should I have backed off, allowed Alice mend for a month or so before moving in like a whirlwind?

I couldn't wait a month. I couldn't wait a day. I'd come too far and I was so close to her now.

But I didn't think for a minute that I wouldn't see her that last morning of the decade. This church was the one place I could be certain she would be. Still, disbelief struck when Alice finally walked by—alone—and just inches from me. We nearly touched.

It was really her, Alice Miranda Jones, the genuine article—my darling Alice. The Alice I must win over, or die trying.

When she was a few feet past me, I called out to her. Alice froze for an instant before turning around.

"Hello, Alice," I said trying to sound as if I'd last seen her just hours before and not months. She surveyed me with bloodshot eyes before closing them and, I guessed, praying I would vanish like part of a bad dream. No expression I'd yet seen on her, not anger, not contempt, nor a wish that I would drop dead, had ever detracted from the loveliness of the girl I must win over…or die trying. Alice turned around and walked all the way forward to a raised portion of the floor where Collin was on display.

She half knelt at the coffin and appeared to pray until a minister signaled that the service was to begin. She seated herself among some of the people I remembered from the night I'd kicked in Collin's ribs. There was just enough room in the pew to her left for one more person. To her right was Bobby Dardanelle. I'd forgotten he was her relative.

With the service about to begin, I grabbed a seat a few rows behind the front one where Alice sat.

"Friends," the pastor began, "I can think of no better way to begin this service than by reciting the twenty-third psalm. I would mention that it's my favorite, as well as the favorite of our beloved friend Collin, for whom we are here on this saddest of days to say farewell."

I didn't know the twenty-third psalm, of course, or any other, and might well have been the one person there that didn't.

After regurgitating the twenty-third Psalm, the Pastor continued, "A man's life has been compared to a blade of grass that shoots up strong and straight to challenge the sky in the morning, only to wilt and wither in the chill of the evening. That is as certain as God's will is divine…"

This pastor—or whatever his title—obviously had the same collection of speeches in his library as the other two clerics I'd heard preside over funerals.

"But when that blade is so suddenly, so cruelly, so senselessly, and so savagely cut down when it has only begun to reach for its place on God's earth, the sadness is so multiplied, the pain so sharp, so searing, that there are no words that can begin to soothe those left to ponder the why, and no logic that will explain it away." A woman in the row behind me, coughed wetly on my neck. "Let me tell you when I first met Collin Walker."

The good reverend—or whatever his title was—proceeded to tell us when that was, what a great Sunday school pupil Collin was, a great fund raiser for the Parish, an eagle scout, and a cache of other things so great and so good that, if true, made Collin Walker my diametric opposite—a diametric opposite that happened to love the same girl I did, that was, before he died.

That one difference between us dwarfed all the others: Collin was dead, and I wasn't. And in the end Alice would have to face the fact that fate had ordained that I, not Collin Walker, should have her. Would she understand that? I couldn't be sure. But I could to tell her. *I had to tell her!*

The space next to Alice in the pew to her left must have been open for that reason alone. A minute later, I was in it, and sat there for what had to be most of another minute, transfixed by the sheer wonder of this girl…and that I was next to her at last.

"I love you Alice," I said, placing my hand gently on her forearm. She ignored me. "And no one else ever will as much, at least no one alive ever will."

Alice continued to look straight ahead, but then said softly, "Go away." Her look was still fixed forward, not turning a single degree in my direction.

"Listen to me Alice," I said. She finally turned slowly to me with a cold stare, beneath which, I was sure a rage festered: "Get out of here, Sonny. Why can't you get out of my life?"

"I told you why Alice. I love you and Collin can't anymore, he's dead, don't you get it?"

But Alice didn't get it, or wouldn't. Between the corpse in the coffin and me, she chose the dead. Perhaps the fact had yet to sink in: *Colin was dead.*

"He's in there forever, Alice, and nobody's going to wake him up—nobody."

"Damn you," Alice screamed, and slapped my face. "God damn you!"

The Pastor stopped his sermon and signaled to the ushers to remove me, but Bobby Dardenelle two spaces away, beat them all to it. He must have thought that my still being seated while he stood over me, placed him at an advantage, and at that, he did appear gigantic. Still a quick kick to his privates was something he should have seen coming. He didn't, possibly because the last thing I'd trashed of his was a limb.

It was a really great kick—a real nut crusher—that sent Bobby tumbling on his back just as I rose from the pew. He started to prop himself up, unintentionally aligning his jaw for a second kick that— and as Ralph was to inform me twenty years later—broke it.

Six of the ushers that the Pastor had signaled, were coming at me, three from each end of the aisle. There was no way I was going to fend them all off from where I was. When the first of them was five feet from me, I sprang to a perch atop Collin's coffin.

It was still half open revealing an embalmed face. Leaping atop it might have been the only thing that made the ushers, and probably everyone else, freeze for an instant. I looked out at the one face, among the three hundred or so in the congregation, that mattered at all: the face of Alice.

Her cold stare was gone.

I was sure a mask of black rage would replace it.

But it never did. I could have *sworn,* sworn that I saw Alice fighting off a smile. A dozen hands grabbed for my feet. I stomped and kicked at them, denting the sheet-metal skin of the coffin's lid. It made me think of the Lincoln Zephyr.

I don't remember unzipping my fly at all. Even the memory of holding myself, or with which hand, is so vague, that I can only guess it was my left since it's the one I always use for urinating. I do remember the yellow waves cascading down Collin's dead face as I screamed at him to let go of Alice. She was mine! How was it that nobody understood that but me?

17. SLUTS AND BEAUTIFUL STUPIDS

No matter in which month they occurred, Max loved Fridays as he did no other day. Fridays: the launch pad of weekends and freedom.
This Friday would be the launch pad of more than a weekend, a new year, or even the new decade with all its promise and possibilities. It was a day for which Max had worked and waited for at least two years. January 1, 1960 broke with the kind of glorious dawn that bespoke the climatic perfection one couldn't put a price on. The God that Max prayed to—but had never actually believed in—couldn't have given him a better day to murder the Benjamin High School football team. It almost hadn't happened.

Just two days before, the Legion, *his Legion* had voted down *his plan* for winning the war in one brilliant stroke by using *Velocity Jane* to take out the bus carrying the Benjamin Bengals. They had voted down destroying the lynchpin of what they'd all sworn was wrong with the world. In the end, more than half of them were the gutless gang of adolescents he'd always feared they were.

Not even Addison July had gone for it, not even after what the verminous jocks had done to him. Alfred Cob was against him, and Woody himself had given him the coup de grace. The vote taken, Max went home and cried himself sick, so searing was their treachery. If they didn't know what was good for them, Max would have to show them, it was that simple. But at that point his plan was stillborn. Woody kept the ordinance, and above all *Velocity Jane* dismantled, and scattered and secured behind safeguards Max could not breach, at least with Woody in town. And then with all hope gone, providence smiled on him. He had not counted on Addison July's obsession with that slut back in Indiana. God bless them both.

Addison July, as Max had known from the beginning, was as stupid as he was beautiful. It wasn't enough that he'd been bedding Courtney Provine regularly for three and a half months. It was Courtney's face and curvaceous image that was doubtless frozen into head of God knew how many of Benjamin's lads while they played with their Erector sets half a dozen times a day in their bedrooms, and the school toilet stalls. Courtney was Addison's not just for the asking—because he didn't ask. He didn't have to.

With looks like Addison's, everything worth having was in reach if it didn't throw itself at you, as Courtney had thrown herself at beautiful stupid Addison July, because looks went for looks like money went to money.

Since childhood, he'd been bombarded by the fantastic lie that looks were unimportant. Unimportant, Max knew, to the blind, the dead, and those with their heads so far up their asses than no light could get in. No matter the gender, looks were what everyone wanted above anything else you could name. It was the one thing Max would never have in this life and in this body.

And with all that, Addison July, stupid beautiful Addison July—God bless him, wasn't happy. He had to have that one girl in a thousand that didn't want him. That slut of his in Indiana must be one fine looking bag of organs, but in the end, like all of them, a slut. Addison had spilled his guts about her when stinking drunk the night of the stadium raid. What was her name? Alice, that was it, Alice! But until yesterday, Max had never counted on Alice as the savior of all his plans, his hopes, and his dreams. Bless 'em all: the sluts and the beautiful stupids.

Woody and Max were in the largest of the drawing rooms in the great house the day before when the call came, just after eleven AM, from one Clifford Fitch of Michigan City, Indiana where Addison was being held. When Clifford relayed the details of the arrest, Max found it almost impossible to keep a straight face. Addison needed to be bailed out and had given Clifford Woody's number. Max listened, took notes, and told him to sit tight before hanging up. He then related the story to Woody, but added one critical fabrication of his own: poor distraught Addison, poor beautiful stupid Addison, Max told Woody, had tried to commit suicide.

When Woody dispatched Rawlson to Michigan City, Max knew, that the cripple would have to go too. Woody could never allow one of his legionaries to die by his own hand, or anyone else's. Woody had sworn it would never happen. That afternoon, with Rawlson and the cripple headed for Indiana, it all fell into place.

Well, it hadn't fallen *exactly* into place; Woody had taken precautions. *Velocity Jane* had been dismantled and stored in a half dozen places. At Tealway, Woody had secreted *Velocity's* wings minus her engines. A steel locker at the dispersal site where the planes had landed after the stadium raid yielded the fuselage replete with the guidance module. In four other places, Max had found the remainder of *Velocity Jane* plus the control boxes, the reciprocal homing gear, assorted hardware Woody had separated from *Velocity*, plus a litany of spare parts. All had been stored behind padlocked doors. Max had to recruit confederates and smiths from three separate lock shops so as to open them in the time frame. Breaking down the doors, an idea Max had rejected, would have been easier. Were Woody to return the same day he'd left—though this Max doubted—there could be no evidence the locks or storage points were breeched. If there was, Woody could still easily thwart him by spilling his plan to the enemy.

By eight PM, New Year's Eve, Max had *Velocity* assembled along with the controls, homing devices, and the transmitters his team would need for the attack. He never did find out where Woody had stored the air to ground rockets. He didn't need those. Max, who with Alfred Cobb, had developed them, kept spares in the closet of his bedroom along with warheads. And the warheads Max would use were unknown to Woody or anyone else. He'd designed them himself specifically for the bus attack. Crashing through the windshield, air intakes on the warheads would break open so as to force a zinc dust and sulfur cloud to fill the interior of the bus as the ATGs hurled through it lengthwise. Slamming into the rear bulkhead, igniters would set off the airborne concoction. It was a copy of one being developed for the military. There was no possibility of surviving such a detonation, although Max hoped that some of verminous jocks might live for a little while, screaming and writhing in barbequed agony.

By midnight, *Velocity Jane*—assembled and mission ready—sat in the garage behind his house. At nine on New Year's morning she was poised for take-off from the alley behind the garage. A mile away, on the overpass at Memorial Freeway and Hotchiss Drive, Max waited. Of the eleven Legionnaires, who beside himself, had voted to make the attack, he'd recruited six: four for the two ground crews and two spotters at the school parking lot where the bus would be loaded. Max himself, and only Max, was the attack crew. This time they communicated with voice transceivers, something Woody had been afraid to use. Max thought otherwise. Nobody could pick up a transmission in time to make any sense of what was about to happen. And the distance between the launching point and the target was short enough that they did not need the homing devices. Those he omitted at the last minute. The ground crew had only to set *Velocity* in the general direction of the overpass and Max would do the rest.

From the spotters who stood among the send off crowd behind the school, he wanted to know four things: "Are all the jocks on the bus? What kind of bus was it, the plate number, and when did it leave?" Who besides Jocks aboard the bus was information he didn't want. Were Hollenbeck aboard, it was a dividend, icing on the cake. Courtney Provine was on her own.

He was fairly sure she wouldn't be aboard. She wasn't a cheerleader and she'd already been paid the money for being homecoming queen. Beyond that, Courtney cared as much about football as did Max. But, were he to find out somehow that she was aboard, it wasn't going to stop him this time, nothing would.

At 9:46 the information began coming in.

The bus had arrived empty. It was a Greyhound Silversider, an older bus, the spotters told Max. He had hoped it wouldn't be one of those; its windshield was smaller than the ones on newer busses. But he told himself that it wouldn't matter. His aim was more than up to the task.

Through the transceiver, Max could hear the background rising in thunderous adulation as the Varsity team's first and second strings exited the School, helmets held to their chests and paraded past well-wishers. Max could hear the familiar chant forming up as the team, headed by its captain, filed into the big Greyhound: "Wallee, Wallee, Walleeeee." Max conjured up Wally as the charred corpse he meant to make of him, indistinguishable from the other charred corpses in the shattered hulk of the bus. "Walleee," he mused, was about to become a Wallyburger.

The wailing cheers reached a crescendo when Max heard the rush of air signal that the brakes were being released. Then the roar of diesel drowned out everything as the big Greyhound eased away from the curb. The roar faded. Max looked at his watch realizing that everybody including himself had forgotten about the license number. He switched the transceiver channel to the one that allowed him to talk to the ground crew behind his garage. In the background, he could hear *Velocity's* engines idling. They had been running since before the spotter's report that the Bus had arrived.

One word came through the earpiece.

"Now?"

"Now," Max replied.

They had all agreed that unless something went wrong there were but a few words they'd need to use.

The ground crew topped off the airplane's fuel tanks.

Max listened to the rising shriek of *Velocity's* two-strokers as she taxied to the end of the alley two houses down and turned about for the takeoff roll. She was already airborne as she roared past the garage, had cleared ground obstacles, and was circling in open sky twenty seconds later. Again the transceiver crackled to life.

"Release?"

"Yes," Max replied.

The ground pilot allowed *Velocity* to climb through one last two-hundred-foot circle before switching off the manual control. She rolled and pitched momentarily, then righted herself as her internal pendulum took over the trim and her course was set by the ground crew to a dead level path for the overpass where Max waited.

Two minutes later, he spotted her sleek silhouette against the sky. When she passed directly above him, he pulsed *Velocity* for a level, circular course and scanned the Western stretch of Memorial Freeway. Seconds later, a reflective flash caught his eye as the glitter of the Greyhound's glass and fluted sides formed up the unmistakable shape of his target just a mile away and closing. He set *Velocity* for a course directly in line with, and opposite the path of the oncoming bus. It was almost like aiming a rifle. At one hundred yards, he would fire the two air-to-ground missiles through the Greyhound's windshield. Max tried to imagine what would follow, but couldn't quite picture it. He didn't have to. He would soon see it for himself.

Velocity was a thousand yards from her target when she again roared over his head. With a sliding switch, Max armed the rockets, took aim at the Greyhound's windshield, and held his right thumb and forefinger on the two firing buttons. The shot would be far easier than he imagined. The bus was coming on at a mile a minute with *Velocity* closing opposite her at twice that speed.

The split glass windshield of the Greyhound looked to Max like two enormous black eyes, perfect for the ATGs to smash through them and everything living, or otherwise, in their path before the great bus erupted into an inferno.

Onward came *Velocity* just seven feet above the pavement directly in line with the windshield. Max pushed the firing buttons, and pulsed her for a steep climb to avoid a collision. She easily passed above the Greyhound with yards to spare.

Max counted the two seconds he'd calculated it would take for the ATGs to slam through the windshield, hurl through the bus, and detonate...

But there was no orange tongue of rocket exhaust and no explosion. Something had gone terribly wrong.

Max looked up at *Velocity* and the full horror struck him. The rockets still hung from their launch racks. The igniters, the arming circuits, or something in the control box had failed.

And then the terrible truth sank in. There was nothing wrong with the control box. Woody had beaten him by sabotaging the one thing he hadn't checked: the ignition squibs, the tiny charges that set off the rocket's solid fuel. A hot wave of rage coursed through Max with that realization. And he'd thought he was so damn smart. Woody's simple act of treachery, the substituting of dummy squibs, or severing their circuits, had destroyed all he had worked for and dreamed of incessantly.

The big bus writhed in violent oscillations as the panicked driver who'd veered to avoid the airplane fought to wrest control of her. The bus screeched beneath the overpass where Max stood, riding on its two left wheels, its windshield untouched.

When Max saw the Greyhound again, it was well beyond the overpass, its driver still fighting to keep it upright. He looked back toward *Velocity*. She was a speck perhaps, now a half-mile from him headed the other way. There was no time for another try that wouldn't matter anyway because he couldn't fire her rockets.

And then something wonderful happened. The great bus rocked one final time, toppled to the pavement, and slid a hundred feet on its right side, leaving behind it a titanic shower of sparks, torn metal and smashed glass before it finally came to rest. There were now but two ways to get out of it: by breaking open the windshield or through the upturned side windows. The only real door to the outside was held shut by the weight of the Greyhound against pavement. There was still a chance. Max pulsed *Velocity* to come about for a last dash at her target. The way was obvious. He must sacrifice her. A full half-minute had elapsed before she again rushed past him. Max pulsed her into wide circle that set her up for a plunge through the windshield. But would the impact stop her cold, or if she made it through, could the warheads still work at maybe a fourth of the speed they'd been designed for? In seconds he would have his answer.

Max had more than once tried his four point triangulation system with the plane coming toward him. It was the one situation where it hadn't worked. It still shouldn't be hard, he told himself. He couldn't see the target windshield on the far end of the overturned bus, but he knew it was huge. He would have time for just one try. The upturned bus windows were being slid open or smashed out. In a moment, the verminous jocks would be climbing through them to safety. No time for a second pass. Max eased *Velocity* from a wide half circle to a straight line toward the target who's exact position he had to guess but must not get wrong. There was nothing to do now but hold her to her course and pray. In a few seconds she would disappear from sight and crash through her target.

But *Velocity Jane* did not disappear. Somehow, Max had missed, and missed by a huge margin. He was to get one final image of her passing the hulk of the Greyhound before she slammed against a concrete pylon of the overpass where he stood. There was barely an explosion that could be called one. The warheads, meant to cloud the confined interior of the bus before detonating, dispersed their loads on impact. When set off, the flash was one of a brownie camera. Max had failed. His great moment had come and gone, his dream was destroyed. He'd sacrificed *Velocity Jane*, murdered his own child, and it was all for nothing. It was then that Max first noticed flashing lights closing on the overpass from both directions. There had been not one betrayal, but at least two. Someone had talked. H. S. Rawlson was going to have a hell of a project waiting for him when he got back from Indiana if Max wasn't killed outright. But Rawlson would handle it as he always had. It did pay to buy the best.

IV.
REUNION 1980

18. THURSDAY MORNING

The weather forecast had been right. When I woke at just after five, it was already warmer in the cabin of *Yesterday's Rainbow* than when we bedded down. A thermometer on the bulkhead alongside the hatch read 67 degrees. The daytime high might top 80. In the Styrofoam chest, there were still eight bottles of PBR floating in cold water among shards of ice. Grabbing three of them, I donned my jacket, and climbed a short ladder to the cockpit, trying not to disturb Ralph, but promising myself that the first thing he would hear about when he *did* awaken was the money he'd mentioned.

The harbor seemed beyond dark. Not a single light from another boat, or anywhere else, broke into the black. A fog blocked out any possible starlight, and there wasn't a moon. Once I was seated, and the boat steadied, a lapping noise was all that hinted of the water beneath. Sunrise might not happen for another hour, and would be on the landward side.

I opened the first bottle. Once again, the thought that I could see Alice in less than forty hours overpowered everything. To see her meant risking arrest, but I would risk that, and anything else I could still call mine, to see her. It was going to be all right after all, I told myself, though I hadn't the slightest idea why it should.

19. CASSY

The rattle and clack of approaching freight cars broke the quiet. Presently a train's headlight could be seen gliding along the bluff. It took some time for the low rumble of the diesel to overcome the clatter of the cars it pulled. And their sound quickly reclaimed the airwaves once the train rushed past the parking lot of the marina. The headlight bounced beams in a thousand directions off leafy foliage on the incline that led down to the water, where the whole of the harbor formed up out of the dark in dim flashes to quickly disappear again with the passing of the locomotive. But the light wasn't exactly gone in the train's wake. A pair of car headlights now probed the parking lot's asphalt, their beams occasionally making it to the water before coming to rest and being switched off. The interior light blinked on and then disappeared with the dull clunk of a closing door.

I rapped on the cabin hatch.

"Ralph," I said.

"Huh, what?"

"Expecting anyone?"

"Uh, no."

"Maybe you should be, have you got a gun aboard?"

"Yeah, right here."

"Give it to me."

"What's going on?"

"Someone's coming, pass me the gun please, Ralph."

He did.

I was glad it was a revolver; there was no mystery as to how to undo its safety: there aren't any on revolvers. Whoever it was carried a flashlight that defined jaunty arcs in the blackness. The arcs began dancing over the dock and the water. This person knew the way well enough that neither the darkness, nor the narrowness of the dock, slowed them. They might be headed to another slip. There were three others on our dock with boats in them, but it was us they headed for.

When the light reached the bow of Ralph's boat, the beam skimmed across it, then over the gunwales to the cockpit, and finally, to the barrel of the revolver I was pointing at it.

"Who the hell are you?" I snapped.

"Sonny?" the woman's voice came, "It's Cassy Rapaport."

"Light up your face."

She turned the flashlight on herself. It *was* Cassy, or at least someone that looked enough like the girl I connected with the name to be her.

Her jet-black hair and fair skin made for a sharp definition of features that were striking enough to begin with, but against the black and under the beam powered by four Ray-o-vacs, Cassy was downright explosive. The eyes, deep set and black as her hair, sat beneath gentle arcs from where her forehead began. Like Alice, Cassy's forehead was high, but unlike Alice, she wore bangs that compressed the dimension. You really didn't notice that the turned up nose was a touch large because the lips dominated the rest of her face. Like Alice and Woody, Cassy was defined by the kind of facial geometry that made individual features less important than the distances between them. Her blouse and tight denims left little doubt that the rest of her was exactly where it was supposed to be.

"We've got company, Ralph," I called out.

Ralph's head poked through the hatch.

Cassy stepped aboard with a practiced deftness.

"Stow this," I said to Ralph, handing him the revolver.

Cassy seated herself, drew me close, and began kissing me. I don't believe we'd ever exchanged a hundred words…and that had been over twenty years before.

"Mmmmm," she said, "that will do for an appetizer."

"Bit early for breakfast isn't it?" asked Ralph, as he stepped through the hatchway into the cockpit. "I thought we were supposed to meet at the IHOP at seven."

"It's closed this week for remodeling," said Cassy, "I came here to tell you that."

"They can remodel it in a week?" I asked.

"I forgot. You're an architect," she said, and kissed me again. "It might be just a refresh: carpets, tile, paint. What do I know about those things?"

I wondered who'd told her that I was an architect.

"How did you know I'd be out here?" asked Ralph. "You didn't get that information from a bartender named Felix, did you?"

"I called your place last night to tell you about the IHOP and you never came home. This was the only place I could think of looking."

Cassy, turned and kissed me again. "God, Sonny, it's great to see you. We didn't think you were coming to the reunion."

The sky had turned perceptibly lighter.

"I'm not sure about that yet, Cassy."

"Then, what are you doing in Michigan City?"

"We're not in Michigan City."

"Sorry," she said. "It's not my business, of course."

"I'm on the lam, Cassy," I said finally. "I'm just passing through."

"You won't be going to the reunion?"

"I didn't say that."

"Oh," she said, as if to tell me she understood, then added, "her."

"Cassy," I said, "I'm sorry to have spoiled you appetizer."

"You didn't, Sonny," she replied, kissing me yet again, this time harder. "'Her' isn't here."

Daylight was now coming on quickly. Cassy and I surveyed each other in glances, each looking for earmarks of age while trying not to let on what we were doing. It's a game of the thirty plus. As I've said, it was easy to like what you saw when you looked at Cassy—who didn't seem disappointed with me either.

We ate breakfast at a roadside shack in Union Pier. Ralph said he'd discovered it while still at Willkie and liked better than any of the chains. It wasn't hard to see why. I was about to ask him about the money he'd mentioned at the bar when he told me that he was sorry about my cousin Harry.

"Why?" I wanted to know.

"Mostly because he's dead," Ralph replied, matter-of-factly.

It was the first real surprise of the day, though nothing that would bring on tears. Lola hadn't mentioned Harry's demise in any of her letters, as she well knew how I felt about him. I didn't consider Harry a relative either. He had claimed I was his cousin because his mother and Lola were stepsisters.

"What, when did that happen?"

"Last November."

"And how did that…?"

"He got loaded one night at *The Glass Dragonfly*, or rather very early one morning, and greased the bottom of a South Shore Eastbound at Eleventh and Franklin. It was pretty grisly."

"That's bizarre, Ralph, totally fucking bizarre."

"Maybe. It's happened before, more than once in the last five years."

"Wasn't he a member of your esteemed profession?" I asked.

"You know damn well he was, and by the way, what do you think of us anyway?"

"What?"

"What do you think of us?"

"Us?"

"My esteemed profession, psychiatry and its practitioners, what do you think of us?"

"I never really thought about it," I said, slicing into pancakes that I hoped Ralph would pay for.

"That's bullshit, Addison. Give me an answer and I'm going to know if you're lying. And, you should know too that Cassy here is a clinical psychologist."

"Ralph!" Cassy protested.

"The truth, Addison!"

"A good third of you are well meaning bunglers," I said suddenly, "okay?"

"Okay," replied Ralph, "and the other two thirds?"

"Are a pack of arrogant, high-handed quacks with a God complex who like to dabble in various kinds of social engineering, the kind that get people killed."

"Such as?"

"Bussing."

"You're a racist," declared Ralph laughing.

"And you're a knee jerk, name calling, left wing ass, Ralph Falonhurst."

I was sure I'd have to pay for my own breakfast now.

"Would that bunch of arrogant quacks include your cousin Harry?" he asked, completely ignoring what I'd called him, at least in the collective sense. There might be hope for a free breakfast yet.

"Hell no, it does not, Harry was an out and out criminal!"

"Whew," said Cassy breaking in, "Want to know what I think of architects?"

"You can't have a lower opinion of them than I do," I said, "especially present company, so no, I don't."

"You do know how to head things off," Ralph offered.

The three of us hunted for a fresh topic and ate in silence. A waitress refilled my coffee and Cassy's while Ralph waived her off and motioned for the check as if writing in the air. A fresh thought finally came to me.

"Where are you living these days, Cassy?"

"Monterey, California," she replied with no small pang of pride in her voice.

"Tomorrow night," interjected Ralph, "the great class of 1960 is going to be divided into two parts, those who left Indiana and those that stayed. And those that left will be further split between those that went someplace warm and those that didn't. I salute you both."

"I think you just named three parts, Ralph," I said.

"Do you two miss winter?" asked Ralph.

"About as much as I'd miss a brain tumor," I said, remembering that the last person I discussed brain tumors with was Alice.

"For me it's more like a foot ulcer," added Cassy, "winter has its points."

"Like what?" I quipped, "White Chanukahs?"

I didn't think that worth a giggle, but Cassy and Ralph laughed hard enough to draw more attention to us than I cared for, far more.

"Cassy," I said, "can you give me a lift to Lola's?"

"Sure," Cassy said, who's Lola, by the way?"

"My stepmother."

"I didn't know that," said Ralph.

"Surprise, surprise."

"I mean," he said, "I remember pictures of you and her, Lola, pardon me, and you were a rug rat, a tiny rug rat."

"That was my mother, Ralph. Lola is her twin. My mother died in France during the occupation. She was in the resistance. When my father came here, he married Lola. I'm hoping to score some money from her so I can get on with the business of finding some place where I can't be found. And Ralph, what was it you were saying about money last night—at *The Glass Dragonfly?*"

"Oh that."

"Yes, that."

"I want you to find something for me."

"What?"

"The *Mulholland Rocket.*"

"Nothing to that. Pick up a copy of Hemmings Motor News or Cars and Parts. There'll be a dozen 1950 Nashes for sale."

"You didn't hear me, Addison," Ralph snapped sternly, "I want *The Rocket* back!"

"It may not exist, Ralph."

"I happen to know that it does."

"You know it exists but you just don't know where."

"I do have a rough idea. Did you expect me to pay you for nothing?"

"Actually I was hoping you would."

"Look," Ralph said finally, "I'll be tied up until this afternoon and then we can take The *Rainbow* out for a sail. So go see Lola, and if you're done early enough, take The *Rainbow* out yourselves and shake her down."

"You trusting me with your boat, Ralph? You don't even know if I know how to sail."

Ralph laughed, grabbed the bill, and stood up, signaling to us that it was time to go. I guessed that paying it gave him the authority to do that. I would have liked another cup of coffee.

"Hell no," he fired back, still laughing, "Cassy's the real sailor here."

"It used to be my boat," she acknowledged, "mine and my ex-husbands."

So Cassy had been the first to cheat.

20. LOLA

For me, moving back to a place that trashed you with winters like Indiana's, once you'd escaped them, was something so irrational, that it might take sane men lifetimes to explain. Yet Lola had done exactly that when my father had expired from prostate cancer five years before at the ripe old age of sixty-one.

Prostate cancer: With all the warnings, it amazed me how many doctors it had killed. The Great Frog had no right to die of it, but he did.

We'd kept in touch, Lola and I, at least during my trial and imprisonment, which meant going to see her involved risk though it was unlikely that anyone outside Max, thus far, had known that I had left Texas and was now a fugitive. Doubtless, return addresses had been copied and now hers would shortly head the list of places to look for me. It had taken Max Morgenstern to warn me of this. Many of his clients routed their mail through various drops he'd arranged. But Max had been my lawyer only of late, and I had to see Lola if for no other reason, but that I was broke.

It was no surprise that Lola no longer lived on Eleventh Street. But it was a surprise that she'd opted for a house when an apartment or condo seemed the logical choice. But Lola often did the unexpected if not the illogical. Her house was a yellow and grey prefab of porcelain-coated metal panels each about two feet square that were supposed to have solved the great post-war housing deficit by copying gas station technology. They never came close to that aim, but the houses themselves, called Lustrons, weren't half bad. Everything about them that could be made out of metal was made out of metal. You hung pictures on the wall with magnets. I wouldn't have minded owning one myself...someplace where it didn't snow.

A ten-year-old Chevy, that had been my father's last car, was parked in the driveway, as was a newer Volvo. The Volvo likely meant that my "Aunt" Dora Fisher—my late "cousin" Harry's mother—was there. Nobody else I'd ever known drove Volvos. I was going to call Lola to tell her to get rid of Dora, but at the last moment I changed my mind.

Cassy asked if I wanted her to stay in the car. "No," I replied emphatically. Dora's late son had been a dateless geek most of his life, and whose only sex would have been from rape or the purchased variety. Marching in with Cassy would be a swell taunt to the "aunt" that I loved to hate, who was in fact, no relative at all.

Cassy, who'd looked terrific in the dark of the sailboat's cockpit, looked no less so with the coming of daylight.

I rang the bell and Lola appeared in the doorway. I embraced my stepmother who I'd last seen in Houston. She ushered us in. Having learned she was actually my mother's twin, Cassy combed Lola's appearance with a curiosity she did her best to hide. It was obvious that Lola, like my mother, had once been a beauty, and many might still consider her one.

The chair on which Dora sat was a relic from our house on Eleventh Street. She had obviously been crying long and hard, and had a lap full of balled up tissues. Though I could never recall her looking remotely young, she appeared to me then, as beyond, old. Her face had a way of contorting so as to generate great tangles of lines on skin that could be described as "scrotumesque," or parchment cut from the Dead Sea Scrolls. This morning, it was as red as I had ever seen skin get. Every line in it looked about to hemorrhage.

"Addison," she croaked out, "when did you get out of jail?" She must have hoped this would be news to Cassy.

"Jail?" Cassy exclaimed, "cool." She kissed me. Lola gave us a peevish glance though it was hardly one of serious disapproval, and seated us in chairs aligned at right angles.

"You're making a big mistake," Dora said to Cassy while glaring at me. Cassy kissed me again and began to stroke my thigh.

"He's no good, young lady," declared my "aunt."

"That's not what the other women say," said Cassy. "I'm just going to have to find out for myself." She patted my crotch. "Be sure to save me some of your famous concoction, baby," she said, stressing the middle syllable.

Cassy opened her purse, withdrew a cigarette from deep within it, and lit up. She had yet to smoke in front of me, and hadn't asked if anyone minded. I didn't. In 1980 you weren't required to ask. Dora began to cough long before the smoke Cassy blew out could possibly have reached her. Lola got up and found an ashtray which she handed to Cassy.

"Sorry," said Cassy, "mind if I smoke?"

"Not if you'll give me one Honey," Lola replied. Cassy gave her one, and the two women puffed away.

Dora abandoned her faux coughs and defaulted to what must have been the subject before I'd walked in: the demise of my late "cousin" Harry.

"I know that God always takes the best ones first," Dora sobbed, burying her face in her hands. Presently tears, or snot, leaked from between her fingers.

"But why my son, and why now?" She looked up at me as if to ask why it wasn't me that was dead instead of Harry.

I didn't get what she meant by "now." Harry had been killed the previous November according to Ralph.

"He had so many friends," she went on, "so many good friends."

"That's true," said Lola, "I've never seen such a big funeral."

"Give the people what they want, and they'll all turn out," I offered.

I'd heard Harry was cremated. Somebody could have made a small fortune raffling off the job of pouring gas on Harry and setting him ablaze.

"And he never drank," Dora screamed suddenly. Somebody's lying, they're covering something up. Somebody murdered him." She might have been half right at that. Though Harry had been a lush as far back as our days at Willkie, his being polluted enough to walk in front of a train in the middle of Eleventh Street was getting pretty creative. Were Harry Fisher to have an untimely demise at all, it seemed that he would have been simply shot dead by any number of people for good reason.

Dora glared at me—as if my being alive was the reason for Harry's not being so—before she declared again that her son had been murdered. I pondered this for a moment, but only a moment, before deciding that I didn't give a shit how he died, or why; the fact that he was dead was more than good enough.

"You," she turned suddenly to me, "sure could have been a better friend. But not you. My son wasn't good enough for the great Addison July. Your own flesh and blood wasn't good enough, was it? My son was a doctor. Do you know what that means?"

Harry wasn't my own flesh and blood any more than one of Dora's cats were. She had despised Lola and my mother for the same reason Harry had hated Lola and me. We had the looks and all the privilege that they assumed went with them.

Dora launched into a series of spasms and jerks. Cassy, Lola, and I sat in silence, hoping she'd get done and leave. But, she didn't.

"You're alive," Dora said finally, as if that were the greatest injustice in the history of the earth, "and my son is dead!"

"Sorry 'bout that," I said.

"A man that rapes his own daughter is alive and my son is dead! My son never hurt anybody."

That did it. I'd had enough.

My first impulse was to calmly walk over to Dora, grab her by the scruff, slap her face, and pitch her bony wrinkled wreck of a body through the front door. Indeed, I'd half risen when I hit on a better idea and sat back down.

"If you don't count cats," I said.

"What?"

"You heard me: if you don't count cats." Dora had never fewer than eight felines prowling her rather large house, every interior surface of which, except possibly the ceilings, reeked of cat urine. They had long since become the substitute for the three husbands that had left her and possibly the reason for their departure. But then again, and as I said, Dora was a study in ugly and the fact that she'd ever had husbands at all was a source of wonderment, even with her being rich.

"What do you mean by that?" she shrieked accusingly at me.

"Well my dear aunt," I said, "not all of the ones that you thought ran away, ran away." Some of them, and maybe all of them in fact, met a different fate, one in which your beloved son figured prominently. There was, for example, Clarence." Doubtless Dora had wondered about the disappearance of her great favorite, a half Siamese that had once torn into my wrist and left a scar I still have. "Clarence," I went on, "Clarence, the combustible cat. Did you know what a great patriot your son was? How he celebrated our day of independence with, how shall we say, organic fireworks?"

Dora's continual shifting in her seat suggested a hemorrhoid, but she hadn't stopped staring at me. I'd hooked her.

"Harry, your precious Harry," I continued, "attached a string of ladyfingers to old Clearance's tail, tied him to a tether, and took wagers on how many laps he'd do before the M-80 lashed to his belly finally finished him. You see, my dear Dora, your son was a great entrepreneur. He really cleaned up on old Clarence. And Clarence wasn't fixed yet—was he? No, he wasn't, so just before Harry lit him up, he cut off the poor cat's nuts with a rusty X-Acto!"

Dora sat trembling at the realization that what I said, was possibly, no probably, true. For a moment I thought she had lapsed into hyperventilation. Lola wrapped on my hand to signal me to shut up, but there was no stopping me now.

"Of course your son didn't blow them all up auntie, just the lucky ones, he was nothing if not an inventor. Shall I say that the makers of chemistry sets never imagined to what uses their stuff could be put. Then there were the awls and the electric probes, all of them brought great results, I was told, and I was told, first hand, by dear cousin Harry."

Dora began to choke or gag.

"But his piece de resistance was that silver tabby you called Pewter. That was the one Harry duct-taped to one of the South Shore rails and spray-painted concentric rings around it on the roadbed. He took bets on how far a piece that measured at least an inch-and-a-half would fly, and which space between the rings it would land once the trai,n ran over him, like a game of darts."

Dora was trembling with what I was sure were visions of her cats' last moments.

"How do I know? Well auntie, as you recall, Harry's other hobby was photography, and he'd always slip me a free picture of his latest doings in hopes that I'd think he was so cool that I'd introduce him to girls like Cassy here. Of course I never did. One day though, I'll compose a commemorative album and send it to you. You see—I kept all the pictures." (Actually I hadn't.)

The word "liar" must have come from the bowels of my dear aunt's very soul as she rose from her chair and marched toward me, her right hand extended to deliver as hard a blow as she could pack. Her red-lacquered nails glistened, and I was sure she meant to tear into my face with all five of them, and if possible, scar it. She really hated that face, as had her son, and all the sexual privilege they imagined it got me.

When Dora was three feet from me, and taking aim, she suddenly lunged foreword, soared past me, and her belly flopped on the carpet with a resounding thud. I looked at her and then to Cassy whose foot was still extended to the place from where it had tripped my dear aunt. Cassy grinned and blew me a kiss. Lola got up and rushed to her prone stepsister who groaned as she rolled over.

Dora propped her torso upright and glared at Cassy, contemplating a strike.

"Come any closer to her and I'll deck you, you bitch," I said. But my dear aunt had already decided against it. Cassy was fit, perched for a vigorous defense, and needed no help.

Once again, Dora again burst into tears as she collected her gear (leaving the balled up tissues on the floor) and made for the door, where she paused to call me names, for most of a minute, before storming out.

Shortly, a roar was heard from the Volvo's engine, and a brief screech of tires signaled she was gone.

"Don't tell me that wasn't necessary," I snapped at Lola, who gave me another look of mild disgust.

"You didn't have to…"

"What, Mom?" I asked, "Just tell me what I didn't have to do, I'd like to know, so pleeeese tell me."

"Let it go, Sonny," said Cassy.

"They only let it go when I'm right, Cassy," I said, forgetting that "they" included my now deceased father. When I'm wrong, it's always time for a month-long analysis, and I'm always wrong aren't I, mom?"

"Okay," I said, holding up my hands with fingers spread wide. Lola excused herself and returned minutes later carrying a Samsonite attaché case that looked new.

"What's that?" I asked.

"What you came here for, Sonny."

She set the case on a divan I remembered as having also been from the house on Eleventh Street, and opened it to reveal stacks of bound bills.

"It's all older money. It should be easier to spend without people recalling who spent it."

"I'm going to pay this back, Mom," I said, with no idea of how I ever could.

"No, Sonny," she said, "your father left it to you with instructions to give it to you on an occasion like this."

"How did he know there would be an 'occasion' like this?"

"Because he knew you, Sonny."

"How much is there?"

"Just over fifteen-thousand dollars."

"I'm sorry I can't thank him," I said. "Sometimes I think he deserved better than I gave him."

"He certainly did, Sonny. You could have been the greatest joy in his life. Instead you were the greatest hurt. One day I hope you'll realize just how much he loved you." She closed and latched the case. "Now, I think you should go. And don't come back. Dora may be making a report to the Police right now. Even if she doesn't, they're going to be here sooner or later, likely sooner."

Tears streamed down Lola's still lovely face when I kissed her goodbye.

As I reached for the door handle, Lola suddenly said something she must have been trying to hold back: "You could have come to his funeral, Sonny. It was the least you could have done. And you would have been amazed who showed up there, really amazed."

I almost asked her who it was that would have so amazed me, but wanted this to end as soon as I could make that happen.

"I'm sorry, Mom, you're right of course," I said. I might have gone to his funeral too had Lola not brought the Great Frog back to Michigan City where her family plot was. My mother was buried there too. Her body had been exhumed and sent back from France a few years after the war. I was eight then, and there for that burial.

I checked the case into a locker at the Franklin Street station after detaching a hundred in twenties, fives, and singles.

When I withdrew the key after inserting four quarters, Cassy and I looked at each other. The only, and absolutely only, sensible thing to do now was to take the money, be on the first train out of Michigan City, and evaporate. Fifteen thousand dollars was more than enough to do that, and about five times what I ever expected to get from Lola.

I looked at a schedule that told me I'd missed the last train going in either direction by twenty minutes. The next pair of trains wouldn't arrive for over an hour.

"I should leave now," I said, knowing that I wasn't going anywhere.

"You should," Cassy agreed. "There's no reason to wait until tomorrow night. If you must see Randy, she's got to be in a phone directory. After that, I'll drive you to Chicago, South Bend, or anywhere else you want to go. It's a bad idea anyway, to take public transit. Screw the reunion, I won't go either."

"No!" I snapped. "It's got to be at the reunion." It had to have some semblance of being a chance meeting no matter how obvious it wasn't. I had no right to invade Alice's life with another direct assault. Or was it that I expected another disaster and wanted to put it off so as to fantasize for the day and a half remaining, that this time it would be different. I turned to Cassy, "Let's go sailing," I said.

21. WHAT'LL YA HAVE?

The fog had yet to burn off the harbor, as it seemed to have from everywhere else we'd been that morning. Cassy set me to removing the main sail's cover and after that to the supply shack for fresh ice. Two slips away from *Yesterday's Rainbow*, a couple of late middle age were adjusting the mast guys on a sloop slightly smaller than Ralph's. They waved to me as I stepped back aboard Ralph's boat with ice to restock the Styrofoam chest. I returned the wave, and they let it go at no more than that. Hopefully they didn't know Ralph well enough to wonder what strangers were doing on his boat. The encounter at Lola's had left me short on patience and explanations. Cassy was in the forward cabin.

"Got the ice." I called out to the boat's former owner.

"Down here," was the reply, "and close the hatch behind you." The request seemed odd only until I stepped into the cabin facing the bow. There, Cassy sat stark naked to my right on a side cushion, drawing deeply on a cigarette through a black holder.

"If there's any beer left," she said pointing to the chest, "I'll take one now." I opened it, withdrew two still slightly chilled bottles, uncapped them, and handed her one.

"Aren't you overdressed?" she asked.

Cassy stubbed out the cigarette in an ashtray on a shelf above the cushions, and set the bottle alongside it, having taken but a single sip. Then she went about undoing my belt with deft, precision moves I could barely feel.

"You should have been a pickpocket," I told her, as she finished with the belt, unzipped me, and began probing my crotch.

"You do the shirt, Sonny," she said, adding: "how long has it been?"

"Been since what?"

"Since you've been laid, Sonny!"

"If you don't count being raped at Huntsville, two years."

"Then it would have been your wife?"

With my trousers already on the floor, and my unbuttoned shirt hanging loosely on my shoulders, Cassy began tugging downward on my briefs, but it wasn't as easy now as it would have been half a minute earlier when I'd yet to snap to attention.

"Yes, her," I replied.

"That's a long time," she noted, fondling my erection. "I'm going to have to make sure you're in shape for tomorrow night."

She giggled and we continued probing each other.

"Isn't that using you, Cassy? I'm supposed to say that I don't like doing that."

She sighed. "Dear Sonny, didn't you know that everybody uses everybody? As for me, I mean to discover what I've wanted to know for the last twenty years in the next few minutes. If that's being 'used,' then by all means use me."

Cassy paused, took a pull of her beer and set it back on the shelf. She looked marvelous, knew it, and handled being naked without the slightest fear that there was anything about her to disappoint whomever looked. I knelt to her belly and kissed the sweet flesh below it. My tongue inched lower to wade into her wet crotch. I pressed my bottle of PBR to the outside of her thigh and rolled it back and forth.

Cassy jerked, squealed sweetly, and broke in a marvelous little laugh. "Poor Randy," she quipped, "she could have had all this for the last twenty years but passed it up."

I poured some of Milwaukee's finest on Cassy's belly where it cascaded down to her portal to trickle inside. My tongue followed to lick the beery blend of juices from her vagina. Cassy lapsed into a pulsating groan that rose through the octaves as I probed her ever deeper. I poured another splash on her belly and set the bottle aside.

"Whatever you call this, Sonny," she said between ecstatic moans, "I love you, and don't stop."

I backed off, rose to align my face with Cassy's, and extended my tongue.

"What I call it, my dear girl, is the only thing you can call a Pabst smear." Cassy burst into a wild, glorious laugh.

"Well, Sonny," she said finally, "like they always say about Pabst Blue Ribbon, what'll 'ya have, mister? What'll 'ya have?"

"I'll try one of everything you've got Missy, and I'll make the tip as big as I can."

An hour later, under Cassy's expert captaincy, *Yesterday's Rainbow* knifed through the harbor channel and out to the light chop of Lake Michigan. Cassy slid into a giggle that I queried her about with a glance.

"I was just thinking about what my father would do if he knew I was sleeping with you," she replied to my unasked question.

"Oh? Where's your father now?"

"Florida," she replied, "and if he saw us together, he'd probably jump into the shark pool at one of those sea museums."

"I'm sorry about that, Cassy. He seemed like a nice man. He wasn't the target anyway, but I guess he took the worst of it. When I was thirteen, I didn't worry much about who I hurt so long as I got to the Great Frog."

"Coming about," Cassy said, motioning me to duck. An instant later the boom swung past, just inches above my skull.

Cassy had me hold the wheel while she trimmed the jib. That done, the sloop healed to port and accelerated steadily.

"I never did get the whole story," she said taking back the helm that I was more than glad to surrender, "except in bits and pieces. The one time I asked my father about it, I thought he'd have a stroke. So I'd like to have it from the beginning, from the mouth of the perpetrator, if you please."

"It's no big deal, Cassy."

"Out with it, Sonny."

"Here…now?" I asked, reaching for my zipper.

"The story, Sonny, from the beginning," Cassy giggled, "save what's between your legs for later."

That set us both to laughing again.

"Now," she said, "what exactly did you do?"

"From the beginning?" I wanted that affirmed.

"The beginning."

"Well, Cassy, right after the war, my French Catholic father made it his mission to begin undoing the holocaust by making a Jew out of me. By and large, the French sold the Jews out. Dear old Dad never got over it like most of the frogs did."

"Your mother was Jewish wasn't she? So you are Jewish. Wasn't that a menorah in the bookcase at Lola's?"

Of course. My mother's first name was "Shiloh." You can't get any more Hebrew than that. Mom was a first generation American and went to France to study at the Sorbonne when she was nineteen. She met my father and they were married the day the war started. They could have gotten visas, left Europe, and come here even after France was overrun…but they stayed. I understood it was my mother's decision. She joined the resistance as soon as it was organized, was betrayed, and killed two days before Paris was liberated. My father was a Doctor at the second largest hospital in Paris. During the occupation, it was full of wounded Germans. He may well have saved the same men that went on to slaughter Jews...or had already done it. There's a high probability of that. Ironic isn't it? Germans killing Jews, Mom killing Germans, and dear old Dad saving them.

"He was a doctor," Cassy interjected.

"Lola told me that in her letters, Mom never held it against him and she knew about the massacre of Jews from fleeing refugees. There was regular mail from France for that year-and-a-half until Pearl Harbor. Dad was probably treating the very Germans her resistance cell had shot. I was told that they took down quite a number of them. Something else: There was a sizable plant outside Paris that supplied the German Army with canned rations. Some of their soldiers that 'disappeared' wound up being 'processed' there. It was a huge risk, but they did it anyway to keep up morale. 'Fritzburgers.' If there's one thing you can't fault, it's the French sense of humor."

Cassy held a hand over her mouth as if stifling vomit, but finally burst out laughing.

"Does this have anything to do with what I asked you about?" she asked finally.

"You did say you wanted to hear it from the beginning."

"You're right, I did. Go ahead."

"I was three years old when the war ended and Mom was dead at the hands of Germans. Then the full story of the holocaust came out, and dear old Dad, who'd suspected the worst all along, held himself personally culpable having saved so many Kraut lives. So I became his salvation…or scapegoat—take your pick. He was determined to make me as Jewish as he could, which meant Hebrew school, Sunday school, and of course doing the Bar Mitzvah thing. I had other ideas."

"But you complied."

"Like most lads, I went with a gun to my head. You remember: *"**thou shalt teach them diligently unto thy children?**"* The Great Frog was a Catholic by the way; he never converted, and died with his cock intact.

"Coming about," announced Cassy, easing the wheel clockwise. *Yesterday's Rainbow* rocked upright, then healed to starboard as her bow again swung across the wind. This time I managed to work the jib ropes once the boom swished past me. The wind had risen and Cassy, noting my tenseness, slackened the main. The boat slowed and settled to a less threatening angle.

"Proceed," she said.

"What?"

"You went to Hebrew School with a gun to your head."

"That? Oh yes. Well, you remember there was Sunday school as well, and the big drive to get us all to have pen pals in Israel? Of course you would, your father was the Rabbi."

"I remember," she said, "My pen pal kept demanding I send her denims. When I didn't, that ended it. I didn't mind. The pen pal thing had gotten to be a pain in the ass."

"Well," I said, "I had a little better luck. My pen pal, Ari, had a sense of humor much like mine, and we cooked up a little gag."

"Which was?"

"I sent him a copy of *Tropic of Cancer* with certain very graphic passages underlined and had him translate them into Hebrew written out phonetically in English characters so I could read them. And that's what I delivered for my Torah and Haftarah readings at my Bar Mitzvah. After four years of Hebrew School I couldn't read a word of it, by the way."

With eyes open wide, Cassy shook her head in faux disgust trying to suppress a laugh, then nodded her head signaling me to proceed, which I did.

"You could tell who in the audience understood Hebrew right away," I said, "by the shade of purple on their faces. Of course most of them didn't understand what they heard. Your father certainly did. His face bore the darkest shade in the place." I paused. "It was my way of getting back at the Great Frog for forcing the Hebrew thing on me. I never imagined it hurting anyone else, but I would have done it anyway. I was thirteen, remember? The Great Frog made me tear up the checks the relatives gave me, some of them from France. I managed to keep a few. But they'd stopped payment on them anyway. The letters with the cash were another story. There was no way they could make me give that up. I bought my first car with it, a Lincoln Zephyr. I'd long since learned to laugh at sanctions and threats."

"And the 'Great Frog' was your father?" Cassy asked.

"Um hum. I always wondered whatever became of my accomplice. We stopped writing shortly after my prank. I hope he wasn't killed in one of those wars with the Arabs. His name was Ari, Ari Abraham Kauffmann. He lived in Beersheba."

"He wasn't," Cassy said, her voice suddenly an icy monotone, "not in a war anyway."

"You know that?"

"Yes, I know that. I saw to it, he was my cousin." Her voice now took on an edge that could have sliced metal though it hardly seemed directed at me. She yanked in the main sail and the sloop healed violently to port. I tumbled from the seat and lay sprawled on the floor of the cockpit, deciding it was a bad idea to inquire about what *did* happen to her cousin.

But whatever had gripped Cassy left her as suddenly as it had come. I might have sworn it never happened, and for the next two hours, she tutored me on the fundamentals of sailing theory and on Lake Michigan itself. "Michigan," said Cassy, "offered the best sailing, was the prettiest of all the Great Lakes, and like a woman wronged, the one most likely to kill anyone that failed to give it the respect it demanded."

Cassy and her ex had owned *Yesterday's Rainbow* for nine years, had sailed her on all of the Great Lakes, and had won a score of races. I asked her what the sloop's name was when they'd owned it. She offered a wistful look, then said, "We called her the *Wayward Wind*. Do you remember the song?"

"Who doesn't?" I replied. "Great piece, the *Wayward Wind*; it sounded so much like an anthem that you forgot it was a country song. Who sang it?"

"Gogi Grant sang it, and I loved it." Cassy concurred. "I don't know anybody that didn't. Then I found out how literally my husband took the title. He was a manufacture's rep and on the road a lot. This though, was his favorite love nest, when he was in town. "*The Wayward Wind*," Cassy mused, "was his real mistress. He loved her much more than me if he loved me at all, or any of the girls he screwed aboard her, and I do mean girls. There's a piece of teak trim inside with commemorative notches. Frank—that's my ex—never allowed anyone besides himself to work on the *Wayward Wind*. I would love to have gotten her in the divorce, but it's better that Ralph did. At the time, I would have burned her and sent Frank a picture. So you see, Sonny, getting to screw the man I've wanted to for the last twenty years aboard the one thing my ex loved most was hardly 'your using me.' Maybe Ralph would consider re-naming her one more time as the *Last Laugh*."

I remembered Ralph telling me that Cassy was in fact the first to cheat without actually naming her. There was no way of really knowing. I doubted that either Cassy or her ex knew who was first for sure. I doubted that her ex spending money on a shrink had anything to do with an addiction to pussy.

At one-thirty, Cassy eased the boat back into the slip at Snug Harbor. Twenty minutes later, Ralph joined us at the dock clad in the same sailing gear he'd worn the night before at *The Glass Dragonfly*.

"I thought you might be early, Doctor," said Cassy.

"And I thought you two might be hungry," replied Ralph as he swung a knapsack over to me. I lowered it to the cockpit and spied several McDonald's bags inside. Ralph stepped aboard and proceeded into the cabin, pausing half way down, to ask what we were drinking.

"Beer for me," I replied.

"Well, I just wondered who might like a Hot Tody," said Ralph.

"Great," said Cassy.

"Addison?"

"Beer, Ralph. PBR, preferably."

"Don't like Hot Todys?"

"Never had one, I don't like the name. It sounds too much like a piece of shit. And don't ever offer me a tootsie roll either; they *look* too much like it."

"Thanks for nothing," said Cassy, as he made a face and slapped me playfully.

"Uh, Ralph, on second thought, make mine a Pabst too, a Pabst Blue Ribbon smear."

We ate.

"Are you free now?" Cassy asked Ralph.

"Until Monday," he replied.

"How's Randy?" Cassy asked looking straight at Ralph as if she expected no reaction from me. It was obvious that Randy had been part, or all, of Ralph's morning agenda. Why had he mentioned it to Cassy, but not me?

"She asked about you, Addison," he said, turning to me.

"That's what you met her to discuss?" I asked, "me?"

"No, it was a professional matter. She's part of a defense team on a murder case. They're considering an insanity plea. I met with her client and they don't come any worse. When he needs to kill he doesn't hesitate, and likely enjoys it."

He paused, probably wondering whether to say any more, then decided to: "I told her that no jury would buy insanity. All his killings were purposeful ones, very rational, no fetishes, nothing like that. Besides that, jurors have become especially suspicious of Doctors lately. The more education you have, the more likely they are to believe you're out to con them." He got up, crunched his hamburger wrap into a ball and began collecting the leftover lunch papers.

"You were only mentioned in passing," he said finally turning back to me. "She wanted to know if I'd heard from you. I knew that if I told her yes, she might avoid the reunion, so I lied."

"I'm starting, just starting, to like you, Ralph."

"You always were so generous, Addison."

I was going to bring up the money Ralph mentioned for finding the *Mulholland Rocket*, why he thought it might still exist, and where it might be. The fifteen thousand Lola had given me placed me in a far better bargaining position. If I didn't think Ralph's offer worth the risk of being in any place where I'd be vulnerable for capture, I would tell him to forget it.

"How's Sharon?" asked Cassy, derailing my whole plan. I guessed that "Sharon" might be Ralph's wife. He didn't have any sisters.

"She's in Las Vegas," Ralph replied, "actually Boulder City. Her parents have a home there."

"A little R & R?" Cassy suggested.

"She's finalizing our divorce."

"Wow!" Cassy clapped her hands, "do you realize we're three for three?"

I couldn't remember having told Cassy that my marriage was over also, but she must have gathered that from what Dora and her big fucking mouth had implied.

Ralph breathed hard, "I'm seriously proposing to one of the Junior Colleges here that they add a full credit course to every curriculum on the mechanics of going through a divorce. I wish they'd had one when I went to school. I'd offer to teach it gratis, but only to men, of course."

"Do you think you're qualified on the legalisms?" Cassy asked.

"If I'm not, I could make myself qualified in a couple of evenings. I don't think what lawyers do is all that special."

"How are your kids taking it?' asked Cassy.

"Mark died just before Christmas—drugs."

"God, Ralph," said Cassy, "I'm sorry."

"Yeah Cassy, me too," responded Ralph ruefully.

"He had a running battle with the needle for just under two years, at least that's the time I knew about it."

"I'm sure you did everything you could."

"I think that a non-medical parent might have done a better job. In a way, I was smug about it as if I could outsmart his habit. I thought I had everything in my arsenal to break the back of the beast that had seized my son. I knew all the tricks. I was the one people came to make their worlds right. I underestimated the beast, overestimated myself, and the beast won. I don't know Cassy. What if I'd been somebody that just worked in an auto plant and beaten Mark to within an inch of his life when I found the junk? He might be alive now. Maybe Addison here is right, that I'm nothing but an arrogant quack along with the rest of my profession."

"Don't blame yourself, Ralph," said Cassy.

"My soon-to-be ex-wife certainly does."

"Do you have any other kids, Ralph?" I asked, actually hoping that there might be better news on another front.

"Yes," Cassy interrupted, "How is Rhonda?"

"When she turned sixteen, my daughter went to Israel to work on a Kibbutz for the summer. She decided to stay and finish high school there."

"Mazeltov," declared Cassy.

"She's seventeen now and has moved in with an Arab. I have a picture of them holding my grandson. The lad's name is Mohammed." Ralph smiled at us as if the story was so sick as to be a dark joke.

"Of course my father doesn't know, continued Ralph, and he must die not knowing."

I almost accused Ralph of kidding us, but I could see he wasn't.

"Now," he went on, "I have two children to say Kaddish for…how's the world been treating you, Addison?"

"About the same," I replied. I didn't know how common the knowledge of my arrest or the particulars of it were. But I was in no mood to be serving them up for dessert. I hadn't asked for Ralph's biography, or Cassy's for that matter.

"I'll tell you after tomorrow night," I said, abandoning the subject of money and the *Mulholland Rocket*. They seemed dead questions for the moment.

Cassy refused to take the *Rainbow* out until an hour after we'd eaten. She was long past sea-sickness she said, but assured us we weren't. Once under way, we replaced the boat's jib with a much larger Genoa sail. Cassy set the sloop for a "close haul," sailing almost directly into the wind. Properly trimmed, *Yesterdays Rainbow* slit the surface of Michigan with a grace and speed that astounded me.

Cassy guessed we were making twelve knots and said we could reach Sheboygan if we sailed all night, and still be back in time for the reunion. I couldn't tell if she was stating a fact, or was actually for trying it. Ralph vetoed the idea, as it meant being out of sight of land for hours in the dark. Back in Snug Harbor, dusk was coming on as we tied her up.

Ralph sent me ashore to the supply shack for batteries, which I thought odd at the time. When I returned to the sloop, Cassy was glaring at Ralph red faced. I meant to ask her what it was about later when we were alone, but forgot to. The prospect of seeing Alice blotted it out along with everything else.

"You're welcome to stay here tonight," Ralph told us. "I don't think anyone followed me.

"How many people know you have a boat here?" I asked.

"A few."

"Felix knows, of course," I said, certain that I'd stated the obvious.

"He only knows I have a boat," Ralph replied, adding, "I don't think he knows it's here."

"You can bet he knows it's here, Ralph, don't kid yourself."

"Well, dear hearts, and gentle people," I said, "I propose that we stay away from the harbor until after the reunion. When it's over, everyone will have seen me; I'll be a spent issue and long gone."

Cassy groaned.

"I'm sorry," I said, "staying here beyond the reunion is too risky." I had absolutely no idea of what I would do if my meeting with Alice really was a success. How could I then leave? Yet I would have to.

"I'm paid up for two more nights at a motel in Michigan City," said Cassy. "I guess I won't be staying there either."

"Not if you're coming with me."

"I am. It's my rental car, don't forget that," she pointed out.

I had forgotten.

"And Ralph," I said…

"Yes?"

"It wouldn't be a bad idea for you to stay somewhere tonight where you never have been before. If anyone comes looking for me and talks to Felix, they won't care much about how they get information, and I don't mean bribing you with Girl Scout cookies."

"Understood," Ralph said. "Hadn't thought of that, I'm glad you did. Until Willkie then, and by the way…" He reached into a duffel bag and produced a slightly misshapen envelope with diagonal stripes. "Here's your ticket, and no, you don't owe me anything. Call it a professional courtesy. You will register at the gate so your name isn't on any list yet. And if I don't see you beforehand, good luck." He extended his hand. I shook it, and we separated.

I called Max Morganstern from a service station's pay phone in Union Pier. It was a little short of amazing: all that had happened in the day since I'd called him from Chicago. Since so many of Max's clientele were like myself, men on the run, he'd established a kind of clearing house for his incoming calls that routed them through a series of wireless links, making them untraceable, or so he believed. What it did make was for a rotten connection.

I told Max what had happened, not even omitting the fifteen thousand Lola had given me. It wouldn't begin to pay what I owed him, besides, I needed it. Since Max had become my lawyer, I thought it best to withhold nothing. Most of the time though the information was already known to him. I told Max I intended to stay in the Michigan City area until after the reunion, and told him why. Max was familiar with the matter of Alice since our days in the Legion.

There was a short pause when I'd finished, then:

"Mr. Dilllinger," said Max, "would it do any good if I were to materialize in front of you the way they do on Star Trek, and scream at the top of my lungs that you are a fucking imbecile?" There was another pause while Max caught his wind and rewound his mainspring. Decades of cigar smoking had left him with a rumbling wheeze.

"Do you have any idea what it took to get you out of Huntsville? No, none of you clowns ever cares what it takes to get them out once they're out. You've been free for just four days now and you've already forgotten what being in the joint is all about."

"I haven't forgotten, Max," I said. "Do you know if anyone's on their way yet?"

"No, I don't, half-breed. You don't have to worry about bounty hunters yet, unless you piss me off since I'm your bondsman and I am, by the way, pissed off. If you had one ounce of gray matter in that pretty little skull of yours, you'd get as far from Indiana as you could while the getting's good. But you won't, will you? No you won't, the prettier, the dumber."

"I'm not in Indiana at the moment, Max, as a matter of fact I'm in Mi..."

He cut me off. "Why don't you just tell whoever might be tapped in, where you'll be sleeping tonight, pretty boy? Make their job that much easier. And one more thing…"

"Yes, Max?"

"Why didn't you kill that son of a bitch when you had the chance?"

By that, "that son of a bitch," Max meant Courtney's present lover Pillepe, the one who along with her, had framed me.

"Calm down, Max."

"Fuck you pretzelputz. I'll decide when to calm down. It took my fucking brains, my talent, and my shekels to get your well-reamed ass out of Huntsville, and now you're going to flush it all down the toilet along with the rest of your life chasing some shiksa that can't stand the sight of you. I'm telling you this right now, pretty boy, get caught and sent back to Huntsville and I won't help you. I swear to God I won't. You'll leave that place on the installment plan."

"On what, Max?"

"The installment plan, in pieces, do you need me to paint you a fucking picture with oils?"

"Done, Max?"

"I should say, 'fuck you, Sonny,' but you're going to do that all by yourself, so good luck."

"Thanks, Max. I'll send you an invite to the wedding."

"Schmuck," he barked, and hung up hard. I hung up too, knowing full well he'd loved every second of his rant. I might have given him the best three minutes of his week.

I didn't exactly ignore his advice either. I was going to buy Cassy a proper dinner in a decent restaurant with some of the cash I'd deducted from Lola's gift. But instead, we ate at a drive-in where we declined carhops and Cassy bought the food from the walk-up service. She understood, she said. Caught, I was no good to either of us. By ten we'd taken a room at a motel she'd known from girlhood. It was on a back road, nearly picturesque, and had gas fireplaces, that once lit, you'd swear were wood burners.

Cassy knew how to undress. I would have thought that seeing her stark naked all at once in the cabin of *Yesterday's Rainbow* would have taken any excitement out of a disrobing now, but I couldn't have been more wrong. It's one thing to see your lover stage it with overpriced translucent bedroom garb, but quite another when it's done with the clothes you've watched her wear all day. There's no turn on to equal spontaneity. Cassy must have sensed I liked it done from the top down from the way I'd looked at her that morning. She began with the simple untying of her hair, allowing only half of it to fall, while she undid the buttons of her blouse, all the while taking faux puffs on an unlighted cigarette. The open blouse hung in place while I unhooked the bra strap for her. Cassy whirled about and went to work on my shirt, and with a shimmying undulation, her bra, slacks, and blouse fell to the floor. She stepped from them and walked to the night table and finally lit the cigarette. She had the full, still high, firm buns—Max had called them afterburners—that one might see on a young black woman. Inhaling smoke, Cassy turned slowly about so as to display, once again, the fact that she hadn't a single bad angle.

"You really didn't want to take Ralph and me to Sheboygan?" I asked.

She shook her head to let the last of her hair tumble down. The shake rippled through her curves as she exhaled a stream of smoke that almost formed a contrail. The only garment remaining on her was the black panties, the one thing I wanted to remove myself.

"No, but I'd like to go there with you sometime," she grinned. "They have a terrific marina, with about ten great restaurants, one of them practically out on the jetty." She smiled mischievously. "We could have weighted Ralph, pitched him over the side and just kept going, first up the St. Lawrence, then down the New England coast to the inland waterway to Florida or even the Caribbean, and then who knows? It would also be a way of getting my boat back."

"What naughty thoughts we're thinking tonight, young lady," I said, suddenly fixating on the exquisite way her navel blended with her sweet belly. Young women had lately begun piercing their navels so as to wear rings in them which reminded me of bathtub plugs. My trousers dropped, and I stepped from them fully erect.

"Do you like naughty girls?" Cassy asked. She pulled down a fresh draft of smoke and parked her cigarette in an ashtray.

"Right now, I don't believe I like any other kind."

Instead of walking to her directly, I detoured to a knapsack on the floor hoping she had yet to see its contents. I hoisted two now warm bottles of PBR I'd snatched from the boat by their necks. Reaching Cassy, I hooked my free arm about her splendid mid-section. She laughed musically at the sight and clink of the beer bottles as I kissed her bosom.

"Well, my dear girl," I asked, "What'll ya have?"

It was no small comfort that no matter what names Max called me, we both knew well that I had what it took to go places he could only dream about—the troll.

22. COUNTDOWN

The downpour we awoke to on Friday meant we couldn't have gone sailing anyway. It was a relief that my situation had spoiled nothing and we remained at the motel until check out time. Cassy declared she was going to squeeze the last drop of love juice out of me, and proved it with a leg lock that I expected to make welts. Leaving the room, we limped with our gear to the rental car hoping a recharge might emerge from some part of our bodies we never knew existed.

Since no drive-ins offered breakfast, we settled on eating at a franchised restaurant deep enough into Michigan that nobody looking for me might go, and it was too far out of the way for anyone headed to the reunion. Of course, I was wrong.

Once we'd ordered, Cassy asked me if I'd thought about what I'd say to Alice. I told her I wasn't sure, as if I hadn't considered it. Between our frolicking, and wondering how close I was to being caught, I'd thought of little else since hearing about the reunion from Ralph.

What would I say to Alice? There was a short list of topics: I could say that I was glad to see her, and sorry about pissing on her dead husband—whom I didn't know was her husband at the time—and since all was sure to be forgiven and forgotten, how would Alice like to abandon her life and career so as to run away with me and hope I wasn't caught, since I was, by the way, a fugitive wanted for child molestation and attempted murder? And oh yes, no other person alive would ever love her as I did—nobody.

"You look deep in thought," said Cassy.

"All my thinking is deep, Cassy. That's why most people get the sudden urge to pull on a pair of boots when I share my great thoughts."

She giggled. "Well, Sonny, if you come up blank when you see her, just tell her to ask me what you're like in the sack. You wouldn't believe how many girls in the great class of '60 wanted to know that. And I'd love for all of them to know that I know firsthand. Does anyone else from our illustrious class know by the way?"

"No Cassy," I said, "I left Michigan City a virgin."

"What? You are sooo full of it."

I smiled, "It's true."

"Boots please," said Cassy.

At first I thought the fat pair of thighs standing next to our table belonged to the waitress, but the thighs wore jeans that the waitress had not. Also, no food was set down in front of us. I looked up at the face of a black woman who looked down at me intently before shifting her gaze to Cassy.

"Well," she said, "if it isn't Addison July and Cassandra Lee Rapaport, and don't we look just fine together? Tell me, is everything right with the world?" She glared back at me. "I know you don't remember me," she said. "All of us look the same to you, don't we?"

All of them didn't. There were millions of black women that looked fantastic, but this was not one of them.

"Hello Cosmoline," said Cassy.

My memory was jerked into alignment. Cosmoline Brown was one of a half dozen Negro students at Willkie from the class of 1960. 'Cosmoline' may have sounded resonant or poetic to whoever named her, but they should have known that Cosmoline is a kind of packing grease that happens to be the color of shit.

During my freshman year, President Eisenhower had sent troops into Little Rock, Arkansas to enforce court ordered integration. The overseeres of Willkie High, which had no negro students due to its location, suddenly decided that they needed a half dozen or so Negroes on the Willkie rostrum…and fast. Cosmoline and five others were appropriated from a district well outside the one served by Willkie and were provided door-to-door shuttle from their homes to our fair institution.

And that wasn't all.

Willkie High, in solemn tribute to its namesake Wendell Willkie, a legendary debater, ran a kind of intramural debating tournament at the end of each October. Participation by the freshmen and sophomore classes were mandatory as was the forced assignment of teams and topics. Higher classes were strictly made up of volunteers who liked to argue, and wanted to be lawyers…or politicians. There was never a shortage of them anyway.

It was decided to nail the lid on segregation once and for all that year by assigning the worst student in each of eight sophomore English classes to a team that was to make the case for it. Students with top grades were assigned to the team that would annihilate them. I was to head up the team of fall guys defending segregation. When I met with my crew—none of whom I'd yet known—we decided that we were damned if we were to be the chumps they'd assigned us to be, and set about constructing our line of attack.

It was simple enough.

"How," I opened speaking before a full audience in the school's auditorium, "could the faculty and students of Willkie High sit in judgment of an entire region of the United States when we hadn't, until three weeks before, ever admitted a Negro student? How could we demand that the neighborhoods of cities hundreds, and in some cases, thousands of miles away, be integrated per the specifications of politicians whose children attended private schools that in some cases wouldn't hire so much as a non-white janitor?" Finally, as our piece de résistance, my teammates read off sales and rental ads for properties placed by a real estate office owned by the parents of Willkie students, one of whom headed our team of opponents. The ads stated clearly: "Whites Only." It was about time, I said in summation, after the list was read to admit that segregation existed not simply because the South wanted it, but so did we.

When the debate ended, our side got a standing ovation and the opposition was all but booed. Exiting the stage, my team and I were confronted by the principal of Willkie High, the buxom but, otherwise unattractive, forty-four year old Miss Lilah Coincap who, after delivering a short tantrum, expelled us on the spot.

When the story of the expulsion hit the newspapers, it was rescinded after a threat from the local ACLU provided I, and the members of my team, made a public apology. The team all deferred to me. I refused, of course, and got the usual storm of empty threats from the Great Frog. And for two days our phone rang off the hook with kudos and death threats in equal measure until our number was changed to an unlisted one. Lola approached me and pleaded with me to apologize if only for my father's sake.

"Mom," I said, "I'm trying to teach that cowering Frenchman you married something about not caving in the first time you're threatened. I will not apologize."

Lola burst into tears. "One day, Sonny," she sobbed, "one day I hope you'll understand just how much he loves you."

That was too much. I pulled Lola toward me. "Alright, mom, alright," I said, "for you I'll do it," adding, "not him."

And the next day in a cold Northern Indiana drizzle and a threat of snow on the steps in front of the Wendell Willkie Secondary School, before a crowd of about a hundred, including two reporters and camera crews, I did apologize, sort of:

"On behalf of the debate team," I said, "the debate team who was conscripted and given no choice but to defend segregation in the south, I hereby apologize for not being the band of beaten baboons you set out to make us. From the bottom of my digestive tract, and I assume you know where that is, I apologize. I apologize to that body of negro students hastily snatched from schools out of our district who were made pawns in this hypocritical display of brotherly something or other."

Pausing, I scanned the faces in the crowd.

"And I apologize to the parents and teachers upon whom this fraud was perpetrated by a supremely cynical gang of district supervisors and political hacks who wanted to be able to say "seeeeeeeee, no segregation in our schools."

At least one or two people in the audience began to clap, but quickly halted amid angry glares.

"And finally," I went on, "I would like to extend a deep and most profound apology to our esteemed principal, Miss, miss…" I hesitated before delivering the moniker that would stick to Lila Coincap like epoxy for two decades now and counting, "Miss Pile o' Cowcrap!"

"What do you want Cosmoline?" I asked.

"I thought you should see something," she said, and placed a wallet sized snapshot of a young black boy in graduation garb in front of me.

I looked at the picture, tried to figure out who it was and gave up.

"That was my brother, snapped Cosmoline Brown. It's a good thing we took that picture—and it wasn't easy to pay for either. You see, a year later, my brother died in Vietnam."

"I'm sorry," I said, and I was.

"Yeah," said Cosmoline Brown, "I'm sorry it wasn't you. You're here and he's dead. You weren't in the war were you? You weren't even in the army—were you?'

I didn't answer.

"Were you?"

"No," I said.

"Well, why not?" It was not a question, but a full tilt accusation, delivered in a shout.

I tried to look straight at Cassy, but, with a quick sideward glance, noticed that half the restaurant was watching as if they too believed they were owed an answer.

"They didn't invite me," I said, "and I didn't ask them why they didn't invite me." This was a lie of course. I'd moved heaven and earth to stay out of a uniform.

"Shiiiiiiiiiiiiit," said Cosmoline. She then knelt to face Cassy, "And how's the cracker bitch head of the cheerleading squad?"

"Fine," Cassy replied evenly.

"Yeah," said Cosmoline, "fine. You got what I call the just-fucked look."

"And you've got the 'just-fed look'," Cassy fired back, "very well fed, which is why you didn't make the squad, sweetie, it wasn't your skin color, there was just too much blubber under it."

"You made the squad," rebuffed Cosmoline, "you made the whole damn team—the first and the second string! I heard you gave some to the coach too."

With that, Cassy cracked the black woman's face with a blow so well-placed that it looked staged. Cosmoline's balance was precarious due to her great mass and kneeling position. Cassy's blow sent her crashing backward to the floor with the thud bowling balls make when they're dropped.

When the black woman finally raised herself, Cassy faced her with a fork gripped with an overhand fist.

"You better get out of here," I said, and Cosmoline did, hurling us hateful glares for the whole trip back to her table of friends. Thankfully, they included no men.

Our food arrived and we asked it be boxed so we could eat it in the car.

The rain, which had eased to a drizzle when we'd driven up to the restaurant, rebounded to a downpour harder than the one we'd awaken to. We sat in the car. An opaque wash of water on the windshield left us to ourselves. Cassy closed her wrap tightly around her.

"I'm sorry," I said, after downing the sweet rolls I'd ordered. "I guess what can go wrong, will."

"Well," said Cassy, "for what it's worth, I'm glad she showed up. Cracking her in the face did me a world of good."

"Do you think she'll be at the reunion?"

"I couldn't care less," Cassy replied, "My guess is no, but if she is, fine, I wouldn't mind slapping her around all over again, the bitch."

"I wonder why she didn't call me a child rapist," I said finally.

"She didn't have time to fit it all in."

"It's common knowledge around here, then, isn't it?" I asked. Cassy told me she knew it wasn't true.

"Want to hear about it?" I asked.

"Only if you want to tell me."

I didn't, but if anyone had a right to know, Cassy did. Whatever she'd heard, she'd had dismissed as lies, and slept with me at the first opportunity.

"Well, Cassy, "here goes"—I looked at the window, caught my reflection for a moment, and then turned to her—"I was married ten years, and happily I thought, when I discovered that Courtney was cheating. That was in '78."

"Courtney was your wife? Sorry," she said embarrassed, "what else would she have been?"

"Uh huh, it had been going on for at least half the years we were married, so I later found out."

"With the same man?" asked Cassy.

"She'd been doing others, but she was with him through all of it and had settled on him by the time I knew. He was from Louisiana; his name was Phillipe Bienvenue, and was what they used to call a 'Dandy.' Sometime back he'd inherited a slug of money."

"Just as an aside," said Cassy, "was your wife Jewish?"

"Both of them were, well, Courtney was a half breed like me."

"Sorry," said Cassy. "I'm just having trouble picturing it."

"I confronted her and told her that I was willing to forget what she'd done if she'd end it, or we should get a divorce. I wasn't going to go for counseling, which, as far as I was concerned, was snake oil. Also, counseling assumes mutual guilt, and I'd done nothing wrong. Courtney suggested a trial separation. I nixed that idea since it meant moving out of a house which I'd just finished paying for—and having the Dandy screwing her there, if not moving in outright. Three days later, I was served the divorce papers which charged me with everything but bombing Pearl Harbor."

"Did they accuse you of molesting your daughter in the suit?"

"No. Since that was a criminal matter, they sprung it on me sometime after the preliminary hearing, kind of a one-two punch. One day—it was a Thursday I think—a couple of deputies showed up at my office, broke into a meeting I was having with a couple whose house I'd just been commissioned to design, read the accusation, and dragged me off in handcuffs.

I wasn't frightened at first, furious of course, but scared, no. But it didn't take long to realize just how beautifully they'd constructed the frame-up, and the fact that bail was set so high that I wasn't going to see freedom until I'd been proven innocent. I still didn't think that would be too hard to do, since there couldn't possibly be any evidence for something that never happened. Besides, I thought I had a good lawyer, but he only charged me like he was good."

"But there was no evidence?" Cassy insisted.

"So I thought, dear girl, so I thought. Do you have children by the way?"

"No," Cassy replied.

"You have to imagine," I continued, "the sight of my seven-year-old sitting on a pile of cushions in a witness chair and describing to an enraged jury how I first started probing her when she was five, and then graduated to stuffing myself into every opening in her big enough to accept me. What amazed me was how they'd staged it to look so spontaneous. If I hadn't known better, I'd have believed it myself. I still don't know how the hell it was done.

"Drugs and post hypnotic suggestion," declared Cassy without hesitation. "They may have used hand signals too in a very finely tuned combination. I've read about similar cases. We can ask Ralph if you want to. He's been involved in a lot of criminal defense. He might even know who your wife and her lover used to pull it off."

"I would pay for that information," I said, sure that it wasn't hard for Cassy to realize what that implied.

"But didn't your lawyer cross-examine your daughter?"

"He tried, but they had to have anticipated that too. They had Shiloh—that's my daughter—programmed to burst into tears with every fourth or fifth question. Anyway, the cross examining did more harm than good."

I reiterated, then, that I would really like to have known how they did it and who they used."

"And why," added Cassy.

"Why? There's' nothing to figure out there, Cassy. They wanted, and got, the house, that's why there's nothing to figure out there at all."

"Didn't you say the Dandy was rich?"

"I don't know what he had, but I gather he was going through it fast enough. Anyway, being rich only makes the greedy greedier. And putting the vanquished husband in prison probably helped them both sleep a whole lot better."

"So you were convicted?"

"Convicted, yes, and sent to the maximum security prison in Huntsville, Texas. I was given ten- to twenty-five. The judge said that if anyone made the case for surgical correction, I did. This was also the opinion of four psychiatrists that interviewed me. They said I was a sociopath and a sexual predator, along with compulsive obsessive and schizophrenic. The order of them on their lists depended on the individual shrink. And, of course, anyone convicted of child molestation and sent to Huntsville never has to worry about serving his full term; no one sent there for that crime lives anywhere near that long."

"Do I want to hear the next part?"

As I continued, I stared at the cascading water on the windshield.

"I'll make it short. They do to you everything you've been accused of in spades, and with variations you could never imagine."

"Oh Sonny, I'm sorry." Cassy leaned toward me and with her fingers, brushed a stray hair from my forehead.

"I'm not going back, Cassy," I said, trying not to sound melodramatic or cry…both of which took some doing.

"But you're out, did you escape?"

"I would have, were it I could, but I made a deal with the Devil instead, or at least a reasonable facsimile. In Huntsville, you'll make a deal with the Devil just for a chance to make a deal with the Devil. My Devil's name is Max Morgenstern. I knew him from high school."

"That was the man you called from Union Pier?"

I nodded. "He had me out in seventy-two hours. Nobody but the smartest lawyer in Texas—or the Devil—can do that. Max is one half of each. So I was free, pending a new trial."

"Who put up the bond money?"

"Max did, flight risk and all, it was ten thousand dollars, total."

"How did he manage that?"

"Simple, he got the bond hearing transferred to a venue where he had something on the Judge."

"Ah, why didn't you use him in the first place?"

"I didn't want to be involved with Max, Cassy. He's the most dangerous man I ever met, and I say it without reservation. Once you use him you're his property. Even now I wonder if I should have."

"You shouldn't wonder about that, Sonny. I don't care what kind of deal you had to make, and when you see him, thank him for me."

"If I do, I will." I turned to kiss Cassy lightly on the cheek and then pulled back.

"So why are you on the lam?" she asked.

"I got out just last Saturday. I met with Max who told me what I was in for once he'd arranged for a new trial. Since he'd gotten me out with such apparent ease, I thought that undoing the conviction would be just as easy—for him anyway.”

“And?”

“And he told me what they’d have to do to Shiloh, namely have a team of shrinks rip her head apart and wrench out the truth! At that, he said he couldn’t guarantee success.”

“Eventually,” said Cassy, “she would have to know the truth anyway.”

“Eventually, yes, but in the compressed time frame of a trial, Shiloh’s head would become a battlefield, with our shrinks and my ex-wife’s going in with tanks and dynamite.”

“That’s probably right,” Cassy agreed.

“So,” I went on, “Max laid out ‘Option B,’ the one I took. Simply put, I was to disappear.” Max suggested this strategy frequently, he told me, and the bulk of his vanished clients have remained at large, some now for a dozen years. Also, he had set up a system of paid informants within the County and State prosecutor’s offices that warned him if a cold case was being re-opened. If it were, he would send out an alert. It’s sort of a witness protection plan in reverse. The down side is how much he has on you should you fall out of his favor. His name for that little fraternity of fugitives of his is the ‘Stern Gang.’”

“But that was less than a week ago,” noted Cassy, “Why, with them thinking you’re going to fight it out in court, would they be after you now?”

“Because Cassy, since I was going to go on the lam anyway, and had to abandon everything I had claim to in the world, I figured that I should settle up with the Dandy that framed me.”

“Which you did.”

“Eh, yeah.”

An almost vengeful rain hammered the car and waves of wind shook it. Cassy started the engine and turned on the radio. Presently we caught a local weather forecast. The line of thundershowers, it said, was expected to sit on the south shore of Lake Michigan for hours before a letup.

Cassy kissed me grinning. “You know,” she said, “I was kind of pissed when they told me at the rental place that all they had left were the big cars with four doors. But now,” she said, giving the back seat a glance, "I don't think that was so bad. She hoisted the back door's lock button on her side. I copied the move, and we dashed outside and were in the back seat an instant later, dismantling each other's garments between kisses.

"Well, Sonny," she said, when we had each half-undressed the other, "what'll ya have?"

There was no letup in the rain until two p.m. when we awoke from a nap that left us somewhat rested, and almost pleasantly stiff from the odd positions we'd slept in. It was stiffness reminiscent of drive-in movies.

"Two o'clock!" The reunion would start in five hours. In five and a half I would see Alice.

"It's two o'clock, said Cassy. Five hours to show time."

"That obvious?"

"You can't help how you feel, Sonny, neither can I. I'm a psychologist; give me a little credit for reading you. Don't feel guilty either. I got a day and a half of what I wanted, and that's more than some people get in a lifetime." She handed me a business card.

"I've got a terrific townhouse on Cass Avenue in Monterey. It's walking distance from Cannery Row. If you ever change your mind, Sonny…"

"How did you pick Monterey, California anyway?"

"I fell in love with the name. It was my only reason for going there. But believe me, once you've seen it you'll realize the name doesn't begin to do it justice. It means King's Mountain."

"I like it myself."

"Then look me up," said Cassy as she buttoned the top button of her blouse and brushed back her hair. "Oh, by the way, what are you wearing tonight when you meet the great Randy?"

I pointed to the duffel bag I'd been carrying along with a knapsack since leaving Texas. Cassy pulled it over, opened it, rifled through the last of my clean clothes and gave me that, now familiar, look of playful disgust.

"Men!" she said, "We're going shopping."

An uncle of Cassy's owned a haberdashery in Lakeside Michigan where we selected a pinstriped shirt, a blue blazer, grey slacks, a fresh pair of socks and more underwear than I normally kept in my home dresser drawer. We'd tried combinations other than the blazer, but none worked as well. When I told Cassy, who paid for it, that I'd reimburse her from the stash in Michigan City, she insisted it be a gift. She hoped I'd think of her when I put it on. She knew I would too.

At four-thirty we were back in Cassy's Motel room in Michigan City, meaning only to shower and freshen up for the big event. I was nervous going there, but told myself that no one besides Ralph and Cosmoline had yet to connect me with Cassy. Among other things that brought us up to seven p.m.…we actually did take separate showers.

When we stepped from the Motel room, another warm front greeted us along with the kind of sun we'd yet to see that day. The weather was too good not to walk the half mile to Wendell Willkie Secondary School.

Countdown!

23. OF GREAT THINGS YET TO BE

About half of the walk to Willkie was along Eleventh Street. We paused for several minutes when passing the house where I'd lived. It looked far better cared for by whoever owned it now. White vinyl siding that looked brand new had replaced the sagging clapboards that the house wore when the Julys were its occupants. I stopped to study the lines and proportions of the façade, something I'd never done twenty plus years before.

"Anything special take you back?" Cassy asked.

"Nothing special," I replied, but there were in fact about twenty or thirty things that came to mind. Each of them had a greater or lesser connection to Alice.

I'd wondered if, for example, the built-in-phone shelf in a nook off the hall, where I'd made most of my calls to Alice, was still there and still in use as such, or were there phones in every room now? Our cracked concrete driveway, which had featured irremovable oil stains from the Zephyr's differential, had been replaced with one so clean as to look surgical. I recalled the last time I'd raised the garage door and drove the Zephyr through it over twenty years before, to be soon told by my boss Ray that I was wanted for assault with intent to kill, just one of several things I would be charged with if caught now. That door, wooden then, was now a steel one that gleamed under semi-gloss baked enamel and was embossed with a faux-wood texture. It probably carried one of those lifetime warranties. Still it was our house. The more things changed, the more they didn't.

We were still standing there when a six-coach West bound rumbled by, its horn making soft hoots as it passed the streets that intersected Eleventh before braking to a halt at the Franklin Street Station. We walked on, saying almost nothing for the rest of the way.

A plywood signboard on 4x4s driven into the dirt at the main entrance of Willkie High, announced the reunion for the classes of January and June 1960. The class year had seen several paint overs from other reunions. At the bottom, in larger letters than any others on the sign, was the Willkie High School team's fight slogan: "Woo Woo Willkie!"

"Woo Woo Willkie," I said. If there were a meter that could measure sarcasm, my voice would have broken off its needle.

Cassy, probably embarrassed remembering the number of times that, as a cheerleader, she'd shouted that idiotic chant in front of thousands, said she was a little fearful that they'd demand she do it for old time's sake.

"You can always fake laryngitis," I suggested, "or tell them to fuck off."

We walked up the entrance stairs. Then I remembered something.

"Cassy," I said, "if there's trouble, and there damn well may be a lot of it, I could get arrested. If I am, call this number in Houston." I pressed a slip of paper into her palm. You know his name: Max Morgenstern. Tell him what happened. Expect about five minutes of nonstop laughing, but after that he'll help."

"Understood," she replied.

From accounts I'd heard by anyone that had returned to their high school for a reunion—to visit a favorite teacher, or settle a score with the other kind—everything was supposed to look half the size of the things in their memory. Lockers would look like they served midgets, writing chairs for the diapered set, and classrooms or assembly halls shrunk to a third of their remembered dimensions.

For me, Willkie High had somehow managed to resist the great shrinking it had twenty years to do. Everything in my memory of the place that included missing wall tiles, beat up bulletin boards, and pushed-in locker doors, formed up to a crisp, distortion free realness that could by itself strike alternate chords of nostalgia...or more often disgust. Had twenty years and some months actually elapsed?

A large paper sign with the word "REUNION" and an arrow pointing towards the gymnasium was taped over a glass cabinet that contained athletic trophies. When I turned the corner to face a long hall ending with the gym entrance, I saw clusters of alumni dallying about. I wondered who would be the first I'd recognize, when suddenly, music broke from an overhead loudspeaker. The speaker's delivery was one laced with the same hisses and cracks as when I'd last heard it. Probably it was the same music being played by speakers in the Gym. A song started with a familiar lead in which I couldn't quite place, until the vocalist began:

Never thought a time might come,
Never thought I'd see,
A time when one so fair as you,
Might want someone like me.

It was the recording of a local group from Michigan City, a really good '60s garage band that I thought had deserved much better than the crumbs such bands wind up getting if they're that lucky. Its name was *Lord Essex and the Terraplanes* and the band's symbol, a white triangle, was lifted directly from Hudson, the maker of Essex and Terraplane cars. I'd always thought the song *Great Things Yet To Be* worth of at least a slot on the top forty. Of course it never got close.

When we'd walked half the length of the hall, someone broke from a cluster of bodies and made for us with great deliberateness. It was Clifford Fitch. I recognized him before the face filled out with familiar features. The left sleeve was empty. Thankfully, he had not worn any of the military decorations I feared he might. They could easily precipitate the kind of tactless remark that would make me want to smash in somebody's face.

"Sonny," he hollered, but his eyes were riveted on Cassy.

"Hello Cliff," I said in a moderated tone as he drew near.

"And who have we here?" he said as if he didn't know.

"Hello, Clifford," said Cassy.

Dreaming of those days ahead,
And great things yet to be.
So sweet dreams fair lady,
And let your dream be me.

He didn't reply to that right away: The sight of Cassy had overwhelmed him. He might have rehearsed a thousand possible openings but now seemed dumbstruck by the realness of her presence. He'd lost an arm trying to prove he was worthy of this girl.

The loudspeakers broke into an ear-piercing squeal of feedback then resumed:

If I could only tell you,
If you could only see,
How the sight of you can set,
Explosions off in me.

"How are you Clifford?" I asked finally.

"Fine," he replied, "at least what's left of me. You?"

"Been worse, been better, been younger," I answered.

"No one thought he'd come," said Cassy.

"Yeah, I'm surprised myself," said Clifford, adding in a low monotone: "She's in there, Addison." He wanted me gone of course but feared I would take Cassy with me. My faux quizzical look fooled nobody, if anything, Cliff and Cassy were amused.

"Go get her killer," said Cassy, "Clifford and I have old times to catch up on." At this, Clifford glowed in disbelief until Cassy seized and kissed me hard. I wished she hadn't done that in front of him. I spun about, without pausing to check Cliff's reaction, and headed quickly for the gymnasium doors where the corridor's end intersected to form the letter "T," wondering as I had for two days, what seeing Alice would do to me.

So let me share my vision,
Of great things yet to be.
And sweet dreams my lady,
Please let your dream be me.

When I reached for the handle on the gymnasium door, someone called out, "Sir, you have to register." There were two tables pushed end to end at the right of the gym entrance. On them were rosters for the January and June classes of 1960. Two women, whose names I couldn't remember, sat at the desk. Had I registered in advance, my name would have been on the roster for June. It wasn't.

I took the envelope Ralph had given me, removed the ticket, and placed it on the desk, "Addison July," I said, my voice barely audible. The women exchanged looks before one of them offered a welcome. The other looked at her as if to say, "Him!" Opening the door, I paused for an ever-so-brief glance down one end of the corridor that formed the top of the "T." If I hadn't, I wouldn't have seen a woman talking in animated frenzy into one of two telephones that hung from the wall. She'd aged considerably since I'd last seen her, but there was no mistaking Lila Coincap.

I stepped into the gym. The music was louder now, and the song was in its final refrain.

Smile my love, I'll whisper of
Those great things yet to be.
So sweet dreams fair lady,
Please let your dream be me.

There were about a hundred and fifty people in the gym, which included some teachers I'd remembered, none of them fondly. "*Of Great Things Yet To Be*" ended and the DJ eased a fresh 45 onto the turntable. It was a Billy Vaughn instrumental called *Look for a Star*. Its opening chords were played on a xylophone, before a saxophone took over and the tune melted into dreamy notes from warm summer nights two decades past when Dwight Eisenhower was the President of the United States and the folks living in them still knew where their place was.

I scanned the room in two arcs before zeroing in on four female backsides that might have been Alice. The four became two, and the two, one, and only then was I sure I was looking at Alice Miranda Jones in a tight black dress that displayed her curves with the effect that had never let go of me. I remembered the two times I'd seen Alice in black, once in my garage beside the Lincoln Zephyr and once at Collin's funeral. And her hair was the same symphonic sculpture it had been when I'd last seen her.

I was sixty feet away, momentarily frozen, and breathing as if I had forgotten how.

Alice stood talking to two men and a woman. To my relief, one of the men was Ralph. The second was Bobby Dardanelle. The woman looked familiar but remained nameless.

I made straight for them in quickstep, with no time for last minute strategies, second thoughts, or great opening-line rehearsals. I would say to Alice the first thing that entered my head as she surely would to me.

Ralph spotted me when I'd closed to twenty feet from them, but mercifully gave no indication. At ten feet, Bobby's head snapped left twenty or so degrees to face me with a white-hot glare of malevolence. Alice turned slowly about to see what had prompted Bobby, and the full force of her loveliness struck me as it so often had over twenty years before.

Ralph had told, no, had warned me that she looked sensational. He knew full well the kind of mesmerizing power girls like Alice wielded, whether they wished to or not. But no one had known any of that better than me. Twenty years had nothing to diminish it. I doubted that forty would. My eyes danced across her incredible features as they once had, without a single misstep.

Alice bolted backwards with a slight gasp when she saw me. She'd gambled in coming to the reunion that I wouldn't, and lost. My gamble had won. And my opening line, the first words I said to her in over twenty years tumbled from my mouth as if programmed: "Mrs. Walker," I said, "may I have this dance?"

She was still looking at me, her disbelief diminishing, before turning to face Ralph as if he'd betrayed her with his prediction that I wouldn't come. And I must have shown a disbelief of my own—the disbelief that I was really standing next to her. Alice, the genuine Alice Miranda Jones, my darling Alice, right down to her molecules.

"May I have this dance, Mrs. Walker?" I repeated. She had yet to say a word to me.

"No," Bobby interjected, "You can't."

I turned to him. "I didn't ask you, you son of a bitch," I said, "and if you don't shut that hole in your face, it's going to get a big brother."

I stood combing that face for some evidence of the jaw I'd broken twenty years before. With any luck it might had been set ever so slightly askew. But no such luck had prevailed.

"I'll dance with him," said Alice, as if only to defuse the detonation that loomed. Still she'd yet to address me.

An instant later we were together on the floor. I felt as if everyone in the gymnasium was watching us and prepared to rip me from her if I made a false move. I assumed that a number of them had been at Collin's funeral and the rest must have heard about it.

We danced saying nothing.

Look for a Star is a short instrumental, but the DJ blended it so seamlessly into the next number—*The Twelfth of Never*—that the dancing continued without a break. Still Alice and I had yet to speak in a direct exchange, and now that I was as alone with her as I ever expected to get, and just like Clifford, I was reaching for words that refused to come.

Finally, I managed to seize on a few, "Are you really that surprised to see me?"

"Yes," she said, smiling slightly, "and that you can dance." The smile, so unexpected, filled me with a fresh wave of wonder.

It was really her I was touching. Alice Miranda Jones, the genuine Alice, Alice right down to her molecules!

"Most men can't," Alice continued. "You never seemed like the type that would bother to learn."

To her everlasting credit, Lola had forced me to learn.

"That's because you never knew me at all."

She gave an irritated sigh, "Why did you come here, Sonny?"

"Isn't the reason obvious?" I asked, "and…"

"And?"

"Well, I don't think you ever knew me at all. And Alice, it's not too late for that." It would never be too late. *Never!*

She said nothing but appeared to be weighing my words.

"And no one alive will ever love you as I do. No one alive, will ever love you, as I…"

The music ended suddenly with a loud pop and a protracted screech of electronic feedback. Then Bobby's voice burst from the speakers by the DJ's table, and probably the ones in the corridors too, reverberating off the ceramic tiles that lined them.

"Ladies and gentlemen of the class of 1960," he barked, "I would like to call your attention to one of our distinguished alumni, who is in fact no alumni at all, and I'm sure most of you never expected to see—and hoped to never see again. But here he is, fresh from beneath the rock he crawled out from under, just in time to ruin your evening and mine. I speak, of course, of that vile low-life child molesting jailbird: Addison July."

Alice broke from me in one quick motion. She stood surveying me with horror at the accusation, which for some reason she'd apparently not yet heard, the same one that Cassy had dismissed as a lie out of hand.

"I swear to God, Alice," I said, "IT'S NOT TRUE! I swear to God," only then remembering that I'd once told her I was an atheist.

Her look told me that she believed it. My gamble of undoing a twenty-year old disaster had ended with a bigger one. For two decades, I'd clung to the belief that I could rekindle feelings for me inside Alice that I'd known had been always there. I'd wanted only one chance to do that. Bobby Dardanelle saw to it that I didn't get it.

And there was still something I could do about him.

"Excuse me, Mrs. Walker," I said as I turned toward the DJ's table where he stood.

I expected him to cut and run for his life, which I was quite ready to snuff out with no hesitation. But Bobby didn't run. He stood in a mocking stance alongside the table, not even trying to anticipate how I would come at him so as to prepare a defense.

I was soon to learn why.

Whatever it was that hit me on the head from behind had serious mass. I still don't know exactly what it was that struck the off-center blow that bounced from my skull to land on my shoulder, and send me face down on the gym's maple floor. I rolled a half turn to face three gorillas that had to be the middle-aged remnants of the 1959 Willkie Varsity football squad—Bobby's one-time teammates. A horrific wave of pain charged through my left side, and settled in my neck. The goons stood grinning, as if daring me to try to get up. I struggled and made it to a kneeling stance, forcing myself not to cry out from the pain. The middle gorilla set his right foot on my shoulder as if taking aim for a drop kick. He grinned and looked at his fellow goons for approval. "Woo, Woo, Willkie," said one of them. The gorilla laughed and turned to the other who offered him a "thumbs up." When he stepped back to make the delivery, I sprang from the floor, crashed against his chest, and took him down with both my arms around his neck.

As we plummeted to the floor, I found his cheek, bit a hole clean through it, and spat out the flesh. He let go a wail that would shame a squad-car siren. Some of the air shot through the fresh hole in his face to spray me with spit and blood. I sprang from him, ignored the two other dumbstruck goons, and made straight for Bobby Dardanelle. This time he did try to run. He spun about, forgetting that the DJ's table was directly behind him. When its edge dug into his thighs, Bobby toppled forward, his face slamming into a turntable. An instant later, I landed on him and the table collapsed under our combined weight sending a cascade of wires, equipment, and 45s into the chasm. And for the first time that evening, fate did cut me a break. Bobby wore a ponytail that I seized, and using it for a handle, smashed his face into the wrecked turntable's innards at least four times before they could tear me off him.

There was no breaking away. I was being restrained by a half dozen goons with a second layer of many more for back up, ready to grab me if I somehow did. A few of that second layer reached through the first and tried to land blows on me. Others were spitting. And then the last sound I ever wanted to hear reverberated through the gym: whistles blared as the powder-blue uniforms of Michigan City's finest marched in. A hundred fingers pointed at me.

Less than a minute later I was being led back to the halls of Willkie High in shiny steel handcuffs past jeering throngs of my former classmates. One face alone stood out among them: that of Lila

Coincap. It was more than obvious now who was on the other end of her phone call.

"Pile O' Cowcrap!" I screamed at the top of my lungs as we passed her, "Pile O' Cowcrap!"

V.

THE IRON AND THE CLOCK

24. HEAD AND SHOULDERS

Had I not fled Indiana for Texas in the late summer of 1959, I might have found myself in the same holding cell I did two decades and some months later since it was one of the same four that had to have been there for half a century. The charges to be filed against me would be violations of the same sections of the same penal code, with different dates and victim's names inserted in blank spaces over dotted lines.

"Assault with intent to kill." I couldn't imagine how or why it differs from attempted murder, but I suppose there is some rhetorical division and indeed Max had told me that the charges I'd face in Texas if caught included the attempted murder of my ex-wife's lover. The difference may have something to do with premeditation. Anyway, Phillipe hadn't died. In the end, I couldn't finish the job I'd pledged to myself at Huntsville that I would finish.

Holding cells vary little in the two States where I've been a guest. There is an identical stench that radiates from wall-hung stainless steel crocks that are rarely serviced like the one where I was being held and which overflowed. Unable to get close enough to it without wading into the high tide of an advancing urine puddle, I simply emptied into it directly. There's got to be a law against pissing on jail floors, but that would require witnesses.

The person that could save me now was the one who swore he never would if I went through with my pursuit of Alice, and that was, of course, Max. I trusted that Cassy would have called Max by now, but a personal plea from me would likely sweeten the incentive. Max loved nothing more than desperate pleas from people scared shitless.

I had no hesitation of reaching out to Max. His threat to leave me twisting in the wind notwithstanding, there was no way he was going to pass up the chance to gloat and call me sixteen different kinds of stupid. His appetite for doing that was insatiable. But having done it, Max would help. The question was how quickly he could spring me before the long arm of Texas justice came to drag me back.

I knew I was entitled to a phone call, but nobody else that mattered seemed to. Around midnight I started to make my case for it.

"I'm entitled to a telephone call, do you people hear me?" I began this demand first in normal tones, certain that it could be heard in the adjoining office where I assumed somebody was posted.

By the fifth chorus, I'd added "*fucking*" to "*phone call,*" upped my demand to a mild shout, and added banging on the bars with my shoe to the performance. To my amazement a deputy responded. He was rail thin, ugly, and about 25.

"Mr. July," said he, "your request has been noted. You can make your call at nine, tomorrow morning. Will that be satisfactory?"

His voice, a heavily accented New England Yankee's coupled with the information, came as a mild shock. Nine A.M. was more than I had a right to expect, considering I'd invited this disaster and I didn't want to mention that nine in the morning might well be too late. Not even Max could get me out of this instantaneously, and nine AM, instantaneously might not be good enough.

Then I thought of Clifford.

"Deputy," I said, "Do you know Clifford Fitch?"
He nodded.
"Can you get in touch with him?"
Another nod. "He has a pager," the ugly man replied, "but it shouldn't be necessary, he's scheduled to take over in half an hour."
I felt a flash of giddy relief. "Can you page him and have him call back to confirm it?"
"I suppose so."
"Please do that, now," I said, adding another "please."

Clifford didn't respond to the page, nor to two more the ugly man said he made after that. And he didn't arrive on time either. I was beginning to imagine that he'd anticipated my pleading with him to let me loose which could cost him the only job he could ever expect to get. I had no right to ask him, but I would anyway. If he let me out, Lola's fifteen thousand was his. How I'd live on the lam without it was an issue I'd deal with once I was out.

I couldn't hide with Cassy without making her guilty of harboring a fugitive. Also, she had yet to make the offer.

When Clifford did show up, it was after four in the morning; I'd twice added to the advancing urine puddle, and was wondering what to do with what else that would shortly demand to exit me. When Clifford did arrive, the ugly man delivered a tirade that consisted of one line repeated about ten times: that Clifford owed him. Then he left. When he did, I called over a wall that separated the quartet of holding cells with the office and did not quite make it to the ceiling.

"Clifford," I bellowed. No Answer. "Clifford!"

"I hear you, Addison," he said.

"I want to talk to you."

"Do you?"

"This is serious, Clifford."

"I can hear you, Addison," he called over the wall, "talk." There was a trace of amusement in his voice. Payback, I imagined, for the staggering number of women he'd assumed I'd laid (the actual number was two and until recently one). And there was the business of the arm he'd lost trying to prove something to the second of them: Cassy. I suppose he had a right to enjoy hearing me beg. I just didn't imagine he was the kind that would.

"Listen to me, Clifford." I pleaded. "I'm wanted in Texas and by tomorrow morning they're going to know I'm here. And tomorrow night I'll be back in Huntsville and that's it for me, Clifford, lights out. I'm a dead man if they take me back. I might as well slit my wrists now."

"I can't help you there, Addison," replied my friend. "They won't let me give you anything sharp. I did notice," he went on, "that you had a nice belt."

"You want me to hang myself?" I shrieked incredulously. "Fuck you, Clifford." At that a woman's voice I'd yet to hear burst into laughter. It was Cassy!

The office door swung open. Cassy walked behind Clifford who had a key extended in the hand of the arm that remained.

"Well," said my friend, unlocking the cell, "if that's the way you feel about it, you can get the hell out of here right now. Who wants your company anyway?"

I stepped from the cell, jaw agape.

"How…"

"You're released on your own recognizance, Addison," said Clifford.

"I've got a very good friend who's a Judge that lost his son in Vietnam. When I want something from him, I can usually get it. I woke him up and told him it couldn't wait for a hearing. Of course, you'll never show up for a hearing, which will be slightly embarrassing for us, but no big deal. Just don't get caught in LaPorte County anytime for the next fifty years."

"That's one hell of a friend you've got," I said.

"I'm one hell of a friend, Addison, in case you haven't noticed, and yes he is. His name is Pettigrew Brown. Cassy tells me you met his daughter yesterday at a restaurant."

"Ah, yeah, we did."

None of us three could think of a single relevant word for the better part of the next minute.

"Alright you two," Clifford said finally with a last longing gaze at Cassy, "Out! And Cassy, if you…" He paused, looking for a moment like he just might cry, "nah, forget it."

Cassy seized Clifford and kissed him hard. When she withdrew, my friend looked as if twenty years had been subtracted from his age. I half expected the missing arm to regenerate itself. It was probably the worst thing Cassy could have done to him, but I could well appreciate why she'd done it. The poor bastard—I'd already amended the pledge to myself to give him the fifteen thousand. I was going to need it.

"Where's your car, Cassy?" I asked when we stepped from the municipal building. She pointed to where it stood: among a half dozen police cruisers.

"I've got things to pick up at the motel," said Cassy, "and you'll have to get your money from the station, which, by the way, doesn't open until 5:30 now."

"It used to be open 24 hours," I recalled, almost in protest.

"Someone told me last night that they were going to close it up and tear it down."

"Sons of bitches," I snapped; the South Shore station was the place where I met Alice.

I was actually less afraid of going to the motel than I'd been the previous evening, although I shouldn't have been. My legal freedom in Michigan City meant nothing next to what threatened me from Texas…and I'd been in just one place for over two days now.

At the Motel, Cassy gathered her gear with a mechanical efficiency I had to admire. We were loaded, had checked and idiot-checked the room inside of ten minutes. I was standing in the doorway, the knob in my hand having started the stroke that would close it behind me when the phone rang.

We stared at each other knowing that answering it might be the biggest mistake I'd ever make.

"Let's get out of here," she said.

I could not imagine what compulsion it was that made me tell Cassy to answer it.

She shook her head.

"Then I will."

From somewhere had come the mad notion that it might be Alice calling to tell me she believed me innocent.

I'd broken off our stare and was half way across the room with my hand extended to pick it up when Cassy overtook me.

"No," she shrieked, and parked half her body weight on the receiver.

"It's got to be the bad guys, Sonny."

"Give me the phone, Cassy."

She reached for the cord and tried to rip it from the wall. The cord held, but her shifting weight sent the receiver flying off the cradle to land on the bed where we starred at it as if it could wrap its cord around our necks and strangle us both.

"Hello, hello, is anybody there?" the handset pleaded for a response.

"It's Ralph," Cassy said finally, having recognized the excited voice an instant before I did.

I picked the receiver up from the bed. "Yeah, Ralph," I answered.

"Addison?"

"Yes, Ralph."

"I tried to get you at the jail. I had a lawyer ready to get you out first thing."

"That lawyer wouldn't be Mrs. Alice Walker would it, Ralph?" I snapped, knowing this to be impossible. "Anyway it would seem you're a bit behind events, my friend Clifford Fitch turned out to be a better friend than I ever imagined."

"You're right about that," Addison. At first he didn't even want to tell me that you were already out, much less where you'd be. I called here on a hunch."

"Now that that's settled, Mr. Hunch, what is it you want. And by the way, I'm in a bit of a hurry."

"Addison," he said, "do you remember our talking about money yesterday morning?"

"No, I don't, Ralph."

"Oh," he responded in a deflated voice, "you don't?"

"No, I don't, Ralph," I went on, "because it was Thursday morning that we talked about that, two days ago, not yesterday."

"Would you still be interested in finding the *Mulholland Rocket* for me? For money, Addison, for a lot of money?"

"Thanks no, Ralph, right now I have a pressing engagement with parts unknown, but since I've already said 'no,' just for shits and giggles, how much money?"

"A lot of money, Addison, a lot of money."

"Goodbye, Ralph, and as they say, thanks for the memory."

I pulled the receiver from its nest on my shoulder, and had it halfway to the cradle, when I heard the earphone bark out, "*a hundred thousand dollars, Addison, do you hear me? A hundred thousand dollars.*"

I was now holding the receiver midway between Cassy and me.

"*A hundred thousand dollars,*" it screamed a third time, "*do you hear me, Addison?*"

"I heard you Ralph, and you don't have to shout," I said amused at having made him squirm without half trying.

"Tell me, Ralph, how is it that a 1950 Nash is worth a hundred thousand dollars to you? Fifteen hundred will buy one in decent shape and four grand will buy the best one in the world."

"It will take too long to explain now," he said, "but come to my office tomorrow at one-thirty and I'll lay it all out for you."

"It's going to be too hot for me around here tomorrow, Ralph. Forget it unless you want to meet somewhere else, and by the way, if you mean Saturday, it's already tomorrow."

"Where then?"

"I haven't said, 'yes' yet Ralph, and if I do, I'll call you and decide then, got it?"

"Let me give you my number."

"Fine, Ralph," I replied, and took it.

"I'll meet you anywhere you want, Addison."

"I'm beginning to like your attitude," I said, glad for a chance to have Ralph beg; the 'Doctor Ralph' who thought himself oh so smart.

"But" he added, if it's at the office, "I can arrange for Randy to be there."

"God damn you, Ralph," I barked, "God damn you to hell!"

"See you then," he said in a dead flat voice, adding "at my office, one-thirty."

I hung up the phone and cursed myself for having ever gone near it. There was still more than half an hour until the station opened and I could retrieve the cash from the locker, whose key I checked for with a quick probe in my pocket once every five minutes or so. We parked in an empty lot next to the station where once stood an office and bus shed of the Indiana Motor Coach Company. When she'd shut off the engine, Cassy turned to me and said in measured cadence so as to allow each word to sink in:

"Sonny, that phone never rang, and you never answered it." Ralph had spoken too loud for Cassy to have missed any part of what had been said.

"It rang and I answered it," I replied, adding, "and it's a long way to one-thirty."

"That's right," she said, "we could be half way to St. Louis or De Moines by then. We could put most of another state between us and Indiana. Even if Ralph is on the level, it's way too dangerous for you to stay another hour. A hundred thousand dollars is no good to anyone in jail or a grave, Sonny."

"I know that."

"Sonny, get your money and run like hell."

I sat mute. Had Randy (Alice) not been mentioned, I would have done exactly that—run. Cassy knew it and so did Ralph.

"Please, Sonny."

There was a pause, then: "You're not going to, are you?" she said finally. "It's the bitter end for you, and it's going to be bitter for me too. She'll see to that. She's poison, Sonny. Why can't you just let go?"

"Don't blame Alice," I said. Whatever happened was my fault, and whatever happens now is my fault too."

"Alright," she declared, "If I can't blame her, is it alright if I hate her fucking guts? Will you at least allow that?"

"Sometimes I'm not so sure I don't myself." That was of course, impossible.

We'd stopped talking for at least three or four minutes when Cassy suddenly blurted out: "I fucked Clifford by the way."

Somewhere between surprise and shock, I turned to her, "In exchange for getting me out?"

"No, he'd already decided to do that," Cassy answered, "which is why I fucked him."

"He had the release writ from the Judge," she went on, "and we were on the way to spring you when I told him to stop the car. We did it in the back seat."

"It was a reward then?"

"You could call it that, maybe it was just nostalgia. Anyway it was better than the first time seventeen years ago; I didn't have to worry about zits bursting. This time there were only craters the zits left. And he's got fabulous TDM."

I'd heard of 'TDM' once before. It was some new kind of system for rating a man's coxmanship. I almost asked Cassy exactly what it meant, but let it pass because I had a fresh thought: "You didn't call Max then, did you?"

"No," she replied, "we didn't need him. But I did mention Max to Clifford and they've known each other since you got arrested at Colin's funeral. He's the one Clifford talked to when you had him call

Houston for help twenty years ago. They knew each other in Vietnam too, not well, but they did know each other."

"If they knew each other at all, I must have been quite the topic of at least one discussion."

At that we lapsed into silence again. Cassy was madder than hell about the grip Alice held on me, but I'd been up front about it. I didn't blame her for screwing Clifford. And he'd certainly earned his piece of what Ralph had called "yesterday's rainbow." Had he ever.

A light rain, that had begun when we were at the motel, settled over the still dark intersection of Franklin and Eleventh Streets. The light from *The Glass Dragonfly*—where I'd met Ralph Wednesday—barely burned through the rain as a yellow blob—from which music rose and fell in gentle waves—though never quite loud enough to allow for picking out a distinct tune.

Suddenly, the music rose sharply as the yellow blob brightened with the *Dragonfly's* door opening and three silhouettes were highlighted before melting into the darkness outside. It was impossible to make out anything else, except that two of the figures seemed to be propping up the one in the middle. After moving from the light, they were invisible for several seconds until lightning flashes revealed them walking diagonally across the intersection and directly for either us or the station.

They could well have been three buddies, two of which helping the third to a car, but there wasn't a single car, besides ours, parked in the lot or on Eleventh. There might be a hundred reasons three drinking buddies would be headed in our direction after having left a bar. But one of those reasons could be that they were after me and the staggering drunk was an act to be abandoned at the last second when they would dash for us, guns drawn. I'd been in Michigan City two plus days and I worried about bounty hunters no matter what Max had said. How they could know I was in that car was a point I didn't stop to consider.

Cassy had missed none of this and may well have imagined the exact scenario unfolding, because she started the car, shifted into drive, and sat with her foot on the brake while the engine idled.

Another flash showed the trio; the middle man still staggering across the intersection and our view of them soon to be blocked by the great terra cotta mass of the South Shore Station.

"Go?" Cassy asked. I shook my head.

"Not yet."

From the East, the belch of an air horn, announced that a Westbound train had entered Eleventh street and would be in front of the station in less than a minute. Our company might well have been simply three revelers waiting for that Westbound who simply stopped for a few drinks since it was raining and the station was still closed.

The air horn belched again. The train was now perhaps two blocks from where we sat. Then a headlight beam drilled its way westward through the dark.

"Cassy" I said, "watch that corner. I'll look behind us, they could have gone around the back to come at us from there." In fact, they could just as easily come from both directions. It was obvious that we should have run the instant the bar's door opened. There was still time to do that, but we'd now have to back up and rush down a side street since the westbound would block us from the front.

Presently, a six-coach train eased up to the station. Its first two cars would stop beyond the intersection at Franklin Street. The center pair, to a point abreast of us, and the final two would stretch beyond us to the east for some one hundred and fifty feet. Conductors, who hung from the doors of every second coach, stepped into the street some seconds before the train halted.

From some point blocked from our view by the station, there arose a scream so piercing it was impossible to determine its gender. The conductors raced for the source. Passengers began trickling from the coaches to do the same a minute later. Shortly after that, the trickle became a flood. Cassy and I looked at each other with expressions that said we should know better than to join them. Then we got out of the car to do exactly that.

We found ourselves in a crowd looking at the mangled remains of a human being that had been roughly halved, quartered, and squashed to gristle by the wheels of the train. I could only guess that they belonged to the "drunk," whose "buddies" where either long gone or melted into the crowd.

Under the probing of flashlight beams, there could be made out savaged body parts and sections of clothing they still wore. Guts, gore, and severed bone oozed from the cloth cylinders. It was futile, of course, but I had no doubt that each of us in that crowd was trying to mentally assemble back into a person what was spread out on the pavement in front of us, much of it like margarine. I looked for a head, or what remained of one, and couldn't spot it. I turned to Cassy, sure that she was as close to puking as I was.

It was far easier to walk North on Franklin and around the back of the station to the car than negotiate the crowd that had gathered along Eleventh. Minutes before, I was afraid that the three men meant to do exactly that, charging the car at the last second.

Thirty feet from the corner, lying alone—and as yet undiscovered— was a shoulder attached to most of an arm, a section of chest, and that elusive head. There was a pool of bloody pulp draining from it, though a smaller one than I might have imagined, reasoning that the heart was still somewhere under the train. The wheels and track had made for the immense compressive force that had sheared off the man's top quarter and sent it flying to where we had been the first to see it. Cassy propped herself against the building breathing in great gulps of air while still looking down at the carnage. I flopped over the head with my shoe so as to view the face.

Breathless, she asked if I recognized him. Had she been from Texas, she wouldn't have needed to. The lifeless face of Jarret Traff, one eye open and the other out of its socket and hanging on tendons, stared at the sky or at me—I couldn't say which exactly. "Yeah, Cassy, I do," I replied, adding that we were looking at about one fourth of the most famous ex-ranger/bounty hunter in modern Texas who'd once had his own TV series. "Howdy partner," I said and kicked the jaw closed on a protruding tongue.

Back at the car, we stood beside it for several minutes, sure that puke was coming and determined to rid ourselves of it before getting inside. A few minutes later it did in short, mighty bursts. Only after we were sure that the last of it was gone did we get inside. Sirens were converging on the train, the crowd, and possibly us. Cassy pointed to an ambulance and set me to laughing when she said, "they better have very good medics." I barely managed to thwart another volley of puke.

I'd have to retrieve the cash from the locker later. Cassy started the car and had it rolling when I told her to stop, got out, walked to the train, and kissed the side of it. My ally: the train.

We ate breakfast, or tried to, ten miles from Michigan City but found that we were unable to down a morsel of what we'd ordered once it was placed in front of us. Beyond that, we were both exhausted; neither of us had slept and knew we must whether I met with Ralph or chose the only rational option left me, which was to run like hell.

But first I called Max.

"If you're still not in jail don't tell me where you are," Max screamed.

"Okay, I won't," I said, "Did you know about Jerret Traff?"

"Know about him? I sent him, fool," Max replied.

"What, Max? To do what?"

"To spring you, stupid, I knew you'd be in jail if you went after that Shiksa bitch."

"He was here to get me out?"

"Yeah," said Max, "didn't he?"

"Not exactly Max, somebody threw him under a train. I'm looking at a splash of his guts right now that's still on my shoe. I guess he owes you a refund. Don't hold your breath waiting for it."

"You threw him under a train?"

"I said somebody, Max, as in somebody else, *somebody else*, get it?"

"Yeah, he said finally, it isn't in you, too bad. I was just starting to think there was hope for you."

"You sent a bounty hunter to get me?"

"You know something, Dillinger? You are dumb. I mean for a half breed, you're a dumb half breed, and you might be the dumbest white man alive, and that's saying something."

"Would you care to explain yourself, Max?"

"Look, Sonny," he replied, his voice shifting to a slow, condescending sarcasm, "No bounty hunters are coming after you until there's a bounty. That means either a reward for you or your body, or one posted by your bondsman for bail jumping. In your case, there isn't any reward yet and since I posted your bond, no skip tracers are on their way either since you haven't failed to appear in front of a judge yet. As of yesterday, there is a warrant for your arrest for what you did to Phillipe Bjenvenue, thanks to the fact that you didn't have the gonads to finish him off…so he identified you, but there's no reward that would make anybody interested yet.

"You're not telling me I'm a free man?"

"Hardly, Sonny. Didn't I just tell you you're being wanted for attempted murder? Just now though, there's nothing about you to interest anything but a cop. I sent Traff to spring you, knowing you'd be in jail inside of a day at the rate you were going, and they would have you on the wires as being held in Michigan City and then our great beloved State would send out the cavalry.

"Your man worked both sides of the street, Max?"

"Gosh, Sonny, did you figure all that out by yourself?" Max snapped.

"Do you have any more great revelations for me, Max?"

"I do Mr. Dillinger, I do."

"Jerret Traff was an ex Texas Ranger. Nobody knows I hired him to spring you." Now somebody will be up there and asking about him and they'll hear that he was looking for Addison July just before he greased the wheels of that train. You will then become priority one. Rangers consider an ex one of their own."

"You sent him, Max so now get me out of this mess, and by the way, why did you send such a heavy anyway?" Clearly Max or his man had screwed up, Max knew it, and was loathe to admit it.

"He wasn't busy, and he owed me, Addison, and I thought you might need some muscle. He was ready to break you out if he had to."

"He could have used some muscle himself, Max, or a few more gray cells. His brain was smeared all over the tracks and there wasn't much to it at that. Who do you think killed him anyway?"

Cassy barely stifled a laugh at hearing my bogus description of Traff that she knew Max would likely believe. It was time I had a little fun with this arrogant bastard, guardian angel or not.

My lawyer breathed hard which meant that at best his answer might be one he'd have to eat later, a thing he hated to do above all else. "He had even more enemies than I do," Max said finally, "certainly more living enemies. It might not have had anything to do with you at all."

Since Max told me not to say where I was, I didn't say anything about Ralph's offer of a hundred thousand to find the *Mulholland Rocket*, or where I'd be at one-thirty that afternoon, or that the money was actually secondary, since Ralph had promised Alice being there. At least I didn't tell him that then. I was getting a little sick of his calling me the same names over and over ever since he'd gotten me out of Huntsville, and also the fact that his screw up had wrapped a dead ex Texas Ranger around my neck like an albatross.

"Is there anything else, Max?" I asked finally.

"Yeah," he replied, "How did you get out of jail anyway?"

"I carved a gun out of a piece of soap, counselor. I'm John Dillinger, remember, or don't you read the papers?"

25. THE PROPOSITION

Cassy made no further protests about seeing Ralph at one-thirty. The one hundred thousand might not be bait enough by itself, but the idea that Alice would be there made my attendance a forgone conclusion.

Ralph knew better than to set me up…I hoped.

He opened his office at just before 1:00 to find us already sitting in the waiting room. Cassy was finishing her second cigarette since we'd arrived. Ralph did his best to hide surprise at the sight of us. It was obvious that we'd broken in.

"Hi, Ralph," I said. "We had some time to kill so I thought I should look your place over. Can't say I care much for your taste, but I sort of wanted to know the layout in case we needed to make a quick exit. And don't worry Ralph, we didn't hurt anything getting in, locks were once a hobby of mine."

Ralph sighed. "Is that my gun from the desk?" he asked, pointing to a bulge in my jacket.

"Actually, Ralph, it's the revolver from your boat, but you can give Cassy the desk gun."

Ralph obeyed after escorting us into his office. He loaded a chrome automatic he produced from a drawer, and asked Cassy if she knew how to use it. Cassy replied that she did. I was glad of this because I didn't know, though there's little to it.

"Did you think I asked you here to set you up?" Ralph asked as he passed the automatic to Cassy. That question had been hanging over us until Ralph sprung it.

"No Ralph, I don't. But this involves other people, doesn't it? How many other people?"

"Two," he replied.

"And Alice is one of them?"

Ralph nodded.

"And who is the mystery person?"

"Bobby Dardanelle," Ralph replied after a hesitation.

"You're not wondering why I'd want a gun are you?"

"He doesn't know you'll be here," Ralph countered. "I haven't told him."

"Did it occur to you that he may have figured that out himself? And having done that he may pack heat of his own? Sorry Ralph, but paranoia does have its appeal."

"You're not paranoid, Sonny, as far as I can see," Ralph countered. "You're a bunch of things including the most obsessive neurotic I've ever met, but paranoid, no. Anyway, Bobby isn't expecting you; he and Randy think they're coming to discuss their client, the one I examined. They still want to try for an insanity plea."

"Didn't you already tell Alice no way, Ralph? And by the way, how is Dardanelle involved?"

"He's a senior partner in the firm she works for and yes, Addison, I did tell her that I doubted a jury would buy insanity because the person he murdered was his wife. For many people that alone proves he's sane. But I called Alice this morning and told her that we may be able to work something out, however there were ethical questions involved and to bring Bobby. She was a little miffed at the slight, but she wants to win of course."

There was something wrong here. "Who's paying them to defend the creep?" I asked.

"Nobody, Ralph replied, "it's pro bono. Charlie Novak is notorious enough that firms line up to defend people like him for the P.R. it gets them.

This was the first time I heard Novak's name. "So, you want to tell me how this involves me, a hundred-thousand dollars, and the *Mulholland Rocket?*"

"All in good time, Addison, this way please."

Ralph led Cassy and me to one of two other rooms he probably used for interviews. "You'll be here," Ralph explained, "and I'll be next door with our guests. The walls are supposed to be sound proof, but don't say anything anyway. You can hear us with these." He produced two pair of headsets that looked like the ones pilots wear and flipped a switch somewhere on the desk. The middle of a matched set of three pictures on the wall vanished to become a window into the next room.

"From that room," Ralph motioned with his hand, "all you see is a picture. Mirrors are so overused that they're a dead giveaway that somebody's watching and cameras are impossible to hide. These things use polarized light. They're almost unknown."

I suppose it shouldn't have surprised me that Ralph used the kind of cheap theatrics I'd seen on 60 Minutes. And having said what I did about shrinks, I guessed that Ralph expected it wouldn't either. But Cassy was surprised.

"That really sucks," she snapped at Ralph, "it violates every ethical standard we're supposed to uphold."

"If it helps, Cassy," Ralph replied, "it was here when I rented this suite, it cost the previous tenant something like eight thousand dollars, and I had to agree in the lease not to remove it. Believe me, until today, I've never used it."

We said nothing else until all three of us were seated back in Ralph's office. Cassy turned to me. "I don't believe him," she said, "please Sonny, let's get out of here."

"You're right," I said. "Thanks anyway, Ralph. Give the man his gun back, Cassy."

Cassy got to her feet and laid the automatic on the desk. I did likewise with the revolver, got up and we walked to the door.

I had already stepped through it when I stopped and turned back to Ralph. He knew I was bluffing. His promise of Alice trumped everything. He sat trying to stifle a gloating smile. I walked back to the chair and sat down. "Okay, Ralph," I snapped, "this had better be good."

"It's a lot more than that," he replied, "you'll see."

Per Ralph's instructions, Cassy and I waited back in the darkened viewing room saying nothing. Ralph needn't have worried about the soundproofing. We never heard Bobby Dardanelle or Alice enter the suite of offices thirty minutes later. Without the headsets they would have been a silent movie. Through the faux picture we watched Ralph open the door, seat them, and offer drinks from a hidden wet bar. To my surprise, Alice accepted. Bobby—his eyes already glazed from previous drinks or painkillers—asked for a double. Besides a shiner, his face was a canvas of my work from the previous evening. I pointed at it and grinned at Cassy who flashed me thumbs up.

Alice was as ever, lovely. I suppose I sat for a couple of minutes taking in whole the girl I'd fallen in love with on that March day in 1959.

With her a dozen feet from me, the twenty-year separation shrank to a blink, just as it had in the gym. Every other play of light on her features and her movements replaced details I'd remembered for two decades with real ones. The seventeen-year-old girl I must win over or die trying had become a thirty-eight-year-old I must win over or die trying. That she probably believed every lie Bobby and others had floated about me, and with what I'd done at Collin's funeral notwithstanding, I'd kept telling myself, that somehow, I could undo it all in a stroke. How to make that stroke was another matter. Ralph had promised me only that she'd be there that afternoon and on that he'd delivered.

Alice nipped at her drink while Bobby downed half his double with a gulp and then belched.

"How do you feel, Bobby?" asked the psychiatrist.

Alice cut him off. "The Novak case," she said, "what's it going to take to make you testify he's crazy?"

"You get right down to it don't you?" observed Ralph.

"I'm paid to," she replied, but nothing like what you charge."

Ralph reached into a desk drawer and pulled something from it I couldn't make out until he set it on top and shoved it across to Bobby. It was a cast aluminum model of a 1950 Nash sporting maroon paint. I knew that only because I once owned one like it. Dealers gave them out to the children of prospective buyers. They were called "promos."

Alice looked at him, doubtless wondering what this had to do with Charlie Novak.

Ralph turned to her. It's a "1950 Nash," he said. "I used to own a real one like it, same color and everything…but it was stolen." Bobby and

I used to double date with it. Its front seat converted into a bed. We had some great times in it. Its name was the *Mulholland Rocket*. Once in a while, I'd even loan it to this genius here, like when he crashed that new Pontiac they bought him with school funds."

"Charlie Novak," said Alice.

"Patience counselor," replied the psychiatrist.

"Anyway, about three weeks ago this paragon of justice and I met at *The Glass Dragonfly* and got to talking about the good old days. We had a very unusual friendship way, way, back when, seeing as he was a jock and I was class valedictorian. But there was a weird kind of hierarchy that showcased big brains and big brawn. We jointly hosted the graduation rites if you'll recall. We each had what the other seemed to want. In my case, it was the women that the jocks had, and as it seemed, more than they could possibly use. I can't imagine what it was Bobby wanted."

"That's right," said Bobby, "if it wasn't for me you'd never have poked that Heeb cheerleader; what was her name?"

Cassy flinched, and mouthed the words "son of a bitch."

Ralph was noticeably uncomfortable at this. It was clear that he'd never expected it to come up.

"Your point being?" Alice interjected; she'd obviously taken the crack about Cassy as a general affront on her sex.

"Anyway," Ralph said, trying to regain control. "We got to talking about the car that somebody ripped off twenty years ago. I thought it might still exist and Bobby was sure it didn't. We were well along on our drinking and the speculation turned into wagering.

"Which you wimped out of," Bobby recalled.

"I didn't have the money to cover the amount you insisted on, and I don't bet money I don't have. It was two-hundred-thousand dollars, wasn't it? Do you remember what you called me then?"

"No," Bobby said, "I was a little wasted."

"Do the words 'cheap little kike' mean anything to you Mr. Captain and quarterback? Would you like to know what they mean to me?"

Alice shot Bobby a look of mild contempt, although like myself, she must have wondered how Ralph was going to tie together all of the ends he'd tossed out.

"Look Ralph," Bobby came back in an almost conciliatory tone. "I said I was drunk, and as you well know, my wife's Jewish, or half Jewish, or some shit, and one of my sons was Bar Mitsoid.

"It's Bar Mitsvahed," corrected Alice.

"Whatever."

"Well," said Ralph, I still don't have the two-hundred-thousand, and I have no idea of how to find the *Mulholland Rocket* and prove it exists. But now I have someone who I'm ready to bet can. So what do you say to wagering that I can have the *Rocket*, the very *Rocket*, my *Rocket*, in the Snug Harbor parking lot ten days from today?"

"You said you don't have the money," interjected Randy.

"I have something more valuable to you than that."

Randy and Bobby looked at each other and then at Ralph as if to say, "What?"

"My testimony that Charlie Novak is out of his mind, of course," Ralph answered.

"Whore," Cassy whispered, her rage instantaneous, "Whore."

I motioned her to stow it, although the fact that Ralph was ready to treat life and death testimony as something for wager came as at least a minor shock to me as well.

Ralph sat impassively and allowed the proposal to sink in. Alice and Bobby looked at each other, each waiting for some signal as to what to do. Neither said a word.

"You said a jury won't buy it," said Alice.

"I'm offering you my testimony," Ralph responded. "Making a jury believe it is your problem. Maybe you can, maybe you can't. If you do, my hat is off to you."

There was another silence, while we, all of us, may have paused to note how simple bar-room reminiscing had led to a threshold nobody wanted to be the first to cross, nor could anybody turn back. Ralph had weaved a kind of double-dog-dare from a whole nasty tangle of two-hundred-thousand dollars, a 1950 Nash, and two men's lives hanging in the balance, one a murderer's and the other as I would shortly learn, my own.

"Look" said Alice finally, "if money's what it's all about, how about we pay you for your testimony? You get what you want and so do we."

Ralph smiled. "Okay, counselor," he said. "My testimony will cost you two-hundred-thousand."

"But," Alice protested. Ralph cut her off. "What I want counselor, is to win two-hundred-thousand dollars from this son of a bitch—he pointed at Bobby—and to give the both of you absolutely nothing. I want to win and you to lose. Get it? Still don't understand? Do you want it stated in another language, Hebrew perhaps? You ought to be careful whom you call a 'cheap little kike,' Mr. Captain and quarterback. Now have we a bet or don't we?"

"How," Alice asked, "do we know that you don't have that car in a garage two blocks from here and all ready to make magically appear in ten days?"

"Or," added Bobby, "that you don't have a ringer for it?"

"First," Ralph replied, "if I had the car, I would have taken the bet when it was offered in the bar. You'll just have to believe that I haven't found it between then and now. The idea of resurrecting the bet came to me two days ago when I found the person I believe can find the *Rocket*. Right now I still haven't the slightest idea whether or not it exists at all." Ralph opened the top drawer of the desk where he sat. "Secondly," he added, "here's the registration from 1959. The serial number is on it."

Bobby protested that a new body plate could be made if Ralph already didn't have one.

"True," said Ralph, "but the engine number has to also match and that's in raised numbers cast into the block, impossible to fake. The AMC plant in Kenosha will give you the ones that match the engine serial number. I don't even know them. I'm gambling that the engine hasn't been changed. If it has, I lose. I'll ask again, have we a bet or don't we? I have a patient due in twenty minutes, and I need to prep for it."

They sat without saying anything for most of a minute.

"Well?" Ralph demanded.

"You want to make a game out of a man's life," Alice declared flatly.

"Life is a game counselor," replied the psychiatrist, "if anyone should know that, it's you."

"Take it or leave it," snapped Ralph, "Ten, nine, eight, seven, six, five, four, three…"

"Okay, Okay," Bobby cut in.

Alice exhaled hard, possibly contemplating how many laws the three of them had just broken and the loss of their licenses should any of it ever get out. But all that registered with me was how, with each expression or gesture, she seemed to take on a radiance that outdistanced the previous one. Bobby sat empty-faced. The winner of the bet notwithstanding, Ralph had totally defeated him, and would have, had he not taken the bet. I almost caught myself liking the creepy little shrink. What should have screamed at me just then was how saving Charlie Novak could be worth two-hundred-thousand dollars to anybody and where it would come from.

As if an afterthought, Alice asked whom Ralph thought could find the *Mulholland Rocket.*

"I thought you'd never ask," said the psychiatrist.

"Well, anyone I know?"

"You do," Ralph replied, "or at least you think you do, but you never knew him at all really."

"Oh, Jesus Christ," Alice burst out.

"Wrong," Ralph said, "not Jesus."

"What?" said Bobby who looked as if he had been paying only half attention.

"He means Addison July."

Bobby glared at Ralph as if it should have been a surprise.

"Who the hell did you think I would get to find it?" he asked.

"The man's a wanted criminal," said Bobby, "for raping his own little girl."

That had been aimed at Alice, who flinched.

I started to get up, but stopped when Cassy seized my arm with the strength that surprised me.

"Would you like to make that accusation to his face again, Bobby?" asked Ralph.

"And since he's going to get half the two-hundred-thousand I win from you, I wouldn't be entertaining any thoughts about stiffing us. Now get the hell out of my office, I have something to say to your partner that doesn't concern you.

One more thing," Ralph snapped at Bobby when he was almost through the door. "If this place is surrounded by police in the next ten minutes, or if for an instant I think that there's been any attempt on your part to interfere with retrieving the *Rocket*, the bet's dead, and if I know Addison July, you could be too."

Bobby left, probably wondering if he should search the suite for me or let the law do the work of bagging me for him. I'd proven fairly good at getting sprung from more than one jail.

Ralph and Alice faced each other.

"I was taught once to respect Doctors," she said, "but after today, I'll know better."

"I knew early on about how much respect to give lawyers," added Ralph. "My father was one. Now that that's settled, I just want you to know some things about Addison July."

Alice turned away as if she couldn't be less interested and seemed about to get up and leave.

"The first thing," Ralph almost roared at her, "is that he is absolutely innocent of those lies that have been floating around. He is innocent, do you hear me?" Ralph rose and walked over to the chair where Alice sat. "He is innocent," Ralph screamed at Alice, his face a foot from hers. Only after several seconds did he back away.

"And what would you want to bet on that, Doctor?" Alice snapped in a voice acid enough to eat holes in metal, "your good name maybe, your word, or what cash amount do you want to place on that?"

Ralph went back to his desk and sat down. "He's innocent," declared Ralph.

"You knew he'd be at the reunion last night," Alice snapped accusingly. "I asked you specifically. You knew that he would be, and you lied to me."

Once more, anger only served to enhance her loveliness. The fact that it was directed to anything connected to me seemed the irony of all ironies. The girl I'd never stopped loving for twenty-two years still refused to admit her feelings for me.

"That's right, I knew," said Ralph. "I met Addison in a bar Wednesday. He's on the lam. He had no idea there was a reunion. He had some business to take care of and meant to leave in a hurry. When I mentioned the reunion, and that you would be there he had no choice but to go. It was risky as hell to stay in town, but that meant nothing to him knowing that you'd be there. I felt he deserved at least that so I didn't say anything. How long was he with you? Thirty seconds—sixty? He almost paid for that with his life."

"He's listening to us right now," asked Alice, "isn't he?"

"That's right," Ralph replied.

"I call that rotten," she said.

"It's no worse than recording this conversation to blackmail me into giving you the testimony you want. This is the first time I've seen you carry that humongous purse.

Alice reddened with embarrassment and disgust.

"You don't have to tell me it was Bobby's idea," said Ralph, "and it won't do any good unless it has a white-noise filter which won't fit into anything that size."

Alice opened the purse, produced the recorder, and pulled back a plastic panel to reveal an empty battery compartment.

"I just happened to forget the batteries," she said.

"Would you like to see him?" Ralph asked.

"No," Alice replied emphatically.

She holstered the recorder back in the purse that contained nothing else and stood.

"Is that all?" Alice asked.

Ralph seemed about to shake his head "no" but ended the motion with a nod.

Alice rose and made for the door, pausing to face the picture Cassy and I were looking through. Had she figured that out too? Apparently, she had.

"Good luck," she said to the picture and left the room.

Those two words may well have sent me to the floor had I not been sitting in a chair with arms and a back. Ralph turned to look directly at Cassy and me.

"Stay there," he said, "while I check that the place is empty."

Minutes later he walked into the room where we waited and escorted us back into his office.

"You know something, Doctor?" I said. "I wish my lawyer could have heard you just now."

Ralph smiled anticipating thanks for the performance on my behalf.

"Oh?" he said smiling.

"Yeah Ralph, because five hours ago he called me the dumbest white man alive, I'd like him to know that there's at least one that's dumber."

Ralph looked bewildered if not a little hurt.

"Need an explanation, Ralph?"

He nodded.

"Well?" said the psychiatrist after I failed to respond.

I realized then that I didn't have one a second or so after Ralph called my bluff.

"OK, Ralph, who the hell gave you the right to commit me to this little enterprise of yours?"

"You don't want the hundred thousand?"

"I don't want to land back in prison."

"Yes or no, Addison?" asked Ralph making it obvious he didn't intend to do any begging.

I looked at Cassy who mouthed the word "no."

"No Ralph," I said.

"All right, Addison," he said, "Goodbye and good luck to you."

I stood there, half expecting a counter offer: say a hundred and twenty thousand. But Ralph only sat down at his desk and replaced the model of the Nash in a drawer. He looked up. We'd begun to walk out of the office but had stopped under the transom.

"Didn't you have to be somewhere?" he asked.

I turned to him. Ralph tried to look preoccupied with some folders he produced from an attaché case.

"What are you going to do now?" I asked.

"My problem," Ralph replied.

"Very true," I said, turning around. With her hand on my waist, Cassy tried to push me through the doorway.

"But to answer your question, I'm going to call somebody that would like to make an easy hundred thousand."

I halted again.

"You know where it is?"

"Come back here," he said, "both of you, and sit down."

We did.

"You know where it is?" I repeated.

"Roughly," Ralph replied.

"Roughly?" Cassy repeated. "How rough is 'roughly'?"

Ralph pulled a magazine from the folder that I'd assumed was a patient file. I'd seen the magazine, ironically, at the prison library. Like so many magazines, it was, thin, packed with advertising, and overpriced. Ralph opened it and slid it across the desk. "The picture on the lower right," he said.

It was bad as photographs come. Worse than the ones I'd taken with the only camera I ever owned, a Brownie with a flash attachment that didn't work more often than it did. For most architects, photography was a second career connected to our genetics. I'd never taken it up.

In the snapshot, somewhat to the right of center poking its egg-crate-like grill, sat between a pair of late model Chevys, was the faded, but unmistakable, maroon nose of a 1950 Nash. I handed the magazine to Cassy.

"It's the *Rocket*," Ralph said. "Ladies and Gentlemen," I give you the great, and certainly not yet late, *Mulholland Rocket*. Ralph handed me a magnifying glass.

"Want to know how I'm sure?" he asked.

I didn't answer.

"First," Ralph said, there's a z-shaped crease just below the right headlight. "Bobby put it there, the one time I loaned him the car. His new Pontiac, a jock perk, was recovering from its second collision that month. It chewed on me when he claimed it was old damage, and there wasn't a damn thing I could do about it, but that makes this car the *Rocket*, no doubt about it."

Cassy passed the magazine back to me. With the magnifying glass, I studied the scar Ralph had described on the fender.

"Are you sure Zorro didn't pay you a visit?" I mused.

"I tell you it's the *Mulholland Rocket*," declared Ralph, still believing I needed convincing.

I didn't. Ralph was right. I was as sure as he that the picture was of the Nash I'd first seen a panic-stricken Ralph drive up to the pumps of Ray's garage on that warm Thursday afternoon more than two decades before. Immediately in front of the cars was a landscaped strip separating the parking from a sidewalk from which poked the kind of plants that grow in sand. Though the Nash had no license, both cars that flanked it wore California plates. It didn't take a genius to see that we were looking at a parking lot somewhere in a Southern California desert.

"Did you see it, asked Ralph?" His tone suggested disappointment that I apparently missed something major.

I had.

"The sign," Ralph said finally.

There was indeed, a section of maroon sign extending perhaps a quarter of the way into the photograph's width from the left. The four off-white letters that could definitely be made out were "—GIO'S."

"I'll give you the short version," continued Ralph. "I went through several phone directories for Southern California cities at the library. There were eighteen possible restaurants with names ending in "GIO'S." Believe it or not *Delmagio's Steak & Lobster Shack* was the first one I looked into. They're something of a chain and have six locations in the L.A. area. I called one of them. The picture shows something more arid than L.A., although that used to also be a desert. They have a location in Barstow, which is about as desert as it gets. I called that one, told them I was planning a family reunion there, and could they please send me a menu, along with directions on how to get there coming in on Route 15, the main highway between L.A. and Las Vegas. I asked specifically for landmarks to spot."

"This came two days later," he went on as he tossed an envelope to me on which was the full replication of the sign fragment in the photo. The colors, shape, and lettering could not have been a better match. "There's more," he went on after indulging himself with obvious pride on his detective work. Read the last part of the directions."

I did: "South side of Main Street, (Route 66) next to a Chevron station, just east of the intersection with Route 91," it read. I held the magnifying glass over the photo, and the sign unmistakable in the background. There was no arguing that this was the place where the *Mulholland Rocket* had been, though God only knew how recently.

I glanced at other pictures on the page of the magazine that was titled "readers random shots." There was a caption underneath each of them identifying the contributor. Of course, the name of the *Rocket's* photographer was not given. It was simply captioned "49 Nash," wrong by a year.

"Ralph," I asked, "did you call the magazine and ask when this shot was taken or who sent it in?"

"It was the first thing I did. Getting hold of the guy who shot it would have gotten me the location with a lot less work." He shrugged. "They'd only say that it was sent in about two months ago. That kind of plant in the picture you're looking at has no seasonal phases, so there's no guessing the month from that. With a better photograph, you might figure the month from the lighting, especially if there were a time/temperature sign or something. The temperature in say, January in Barstow, could be forty degrees or so, while eighty-five puts it somewhere between April and June. Over a hundred and it would be June through September. But of course there's no such sign."

"What about the Chevys?" I asked.

"Well," said Ralph, "what about them?"

"There's plate numbers on them," I said. "Monday morning we call Sacramento, get the department of motor vehicles, act pissed, and tell them you just got a renewal notice and that your plates shouldn't come due for another ten months."

"And?"

"And with any luck they'll ask you the plate number, and you'll give the Chevy's. And then with a the same luck they'll punch it into a computer and two minutes later they'll ask you if you're John J. Snakeface at 1151 Pit Road in San Shitmore, California, which of course you'll record."

"That's amazing," said Ralph, "Does it work?"

"It does in Texas."

"You figured that out yourself?"

"No Ralph, I know someone who's a road warrior, and when he has an incident, he uses that technique to find whoever he's been in a dogfight with. Then he settles the score."

"Nice guy," noted Ralph.

"He's a son-of-a-bitch," I replied without saying anything more about Max.

"Do you think the Chevy people can tell us anything?"

"I don't know. They could say when they were there. They damn well may know who's got the *Rocket*. They may know nothing, or know everything and not want to tell us squat. Of course, you called the restaurant, you asked about the car."

"Of course," Ralph replied.

"And?"

"No information, and yes. I offered a reward for the information."

"How much?"

"One hundred dollars, anything more would probably have purchased made up information if nobody had anything real. Anyway nothing came of it."

"Then why, Ralph, didn't you go straight to Barstow and post a reward yourself? Make facsimiles of this snapshot and put them wherever there's a bulletin board?"

"It wasn't until fifteen minutes ago that the *Rocket* became something worth two hundred thousand dollars," he answered.

"Actually Ralph, it's been worth that for about three weeks."

"I hadn't yet seen the magazine, but even if I had and took the bet, what then? What if I went to Barstow, and everything turned into a dead end? I'd freak. I hadn't thought of betting the testimony in lieu of the money 'till a couple of days ago. I only came up with a plan when you mentioned needing money in the bar Wednesday night…and it all fell into place. You were the man to find the *Rocket* if anyone could. Still, you almost blew it last night getting arrested. I tell you, Addison, God wants us to have that money. I still don't have it to lose, and quite frankly, I needed you on board to make sure the *Rocket's* found, and besides that, Bobby would be too afraid of you to stiff us."

At this my look at Ralph hardened. "Look Ralph, forget about the 'us' thing. If Bobby stiffs you, don't look to me to be your enforcer.

You will owe me a hundred thousand and it's from you I intend to collect. We are not partners, get it?"

Ralph nodded, attempting an expression of injury or betrayal. "It's that way, is it?"

"Yes."

Silence followed. I'd grilled Ralph enough about why he'd done this or that, why it was a good bet that I'd find the *Rocket*, get my hundred thousand, and still have enough luck left to melt into oblivion. It was time to either take the deal or leave it, although for all intents and purposes, I was already in.

Cassy broke the quiet.

"I didn't hear anybody mention that if you two lose, a murderer goes free."

It was true. I'd forgotten what Ralph had wagered, and that any code of professional ethics had been cast into a toilet. By agreeing, I was Ralph's bedmate. He obviously didn't give a shit about whoever Charlie Novak's next victims might be should I fail to find the *Rocket* and the wagered testimony sent him into an institution instead of where murderers go. Charlie Novak would be free inside of a decade, or more likely he'd escape in far less time than that. Ralph had made it contingent on what I did. If refused, Ralph lost the bet, and a monster was free. If I accepted and failed, the same happened. Ralph had ensnared Bobby, Alice, and me with our own greed.

I could still say no, of course. But whom was I kidding? It was just too much money to pass up. A fugitive life loomed, along with false identities, and minimum wage jobs. Cash was king. The only surprise in any of it was how important winning the case was for Alice. And although she had to have been unprepared for what Ralph had proposed, none of it seemed to have bothered her much.

I was suddenly amused that, more than once, I'd lamented having taken up architecture and not medicine or law. Knowing people like Max Morganstern should have cured me, but if there were any lingering doubts, they were removed that day.

"They should lift your license and throw you in jail, Ralph," said Cassy. "You're a disgrace."

"What about that, Ralph?" I said smiling. "Are you ready to cut a killer loose if I don't find your car?"

"Charlie Novak has killed his last victim," Ralph declared, "Three more states are lined up to charge him with bank robbery and assorted other crimes. And as I said, not guilty by reason of insanity is a long shot here, even with my testimony."

"Alright, Addison," Ralph said finally, "will you get the *Rocket* for me, yes or no?"

I nodded.

"I'm coming with," Cassy blurted out.

I turned to her. Ralph extended an upturned hand in my direction so as to indicate that it was my call.

I shook my head. "Too dangerous," I said, "Bobby will try to interfere, and he's not going to worry much about who gets in the way."

"You might want to reconsider that," said Ralph.

But I shook my head.

"O.K., Sonny," he said, "let's say you find the *Rocket* tomorrow. How will you get it here? You'll likely have to trailer it."

I shrugged, "so?"

"For the rental, you'll need a valid driver's license and credit cards. Or do you want to gamble our money that you can drive it cross-country, and don't forget that you might not find it right away. Do you have a license and cards?"

"*I* do," Cassy jumped in, adding, "I've got a firearms license in California. We can take Ralph's guns on a plane if I declare them."

I looked at her in mild shock.

"I've needed a gun from time to time," she explained. "I've had those kind of patients."

"You're welcome to the guns," said Ralph, "but I wouldn't try taking them on a plane. If you declare them, there will be all kinds of questions. Don't take any baggage either. Buy whatever you need, discard it when you're through, and for God's sake pay for everything with cash."

I abandoned any protest. They were right about my needing a legal companion. "Alright," I said, "she's in. And Ralph, any expenses come out of your hundred thousand."

He nodded, "Playing it hard, are you guy?"

"I am. I have a right to," I said, implying that it was self-explanatory.

"Perhaps you do," said the psychiatrist. "Anyway down to cases. I've booked two seats on a flight from Indianapolis to L.A. that leaves at seven tonight. There's a good turboprop shuttle out of here in an hour for Indy. I've used it. No reservations, you just show up. I'll drive you to the airport."

"A few steps ahead of us, were you Ralph?"

He only smiled.

"I've got a rental car to return in South Bend," Cassy advised.

"What company?" Ralph asked.

Cassy told him.

"I'll drop it off for you, and take the South Shore back, nothing to that. It's settled then?" I nodded. Cassy did too. Ralph reached into the desk, produced a thick envelope with a fat green rubber band around it. I removed it to examine the contents. It was cash of course.

"It's ten-thousand, said Ralph, "you can count it. The guy's going to want something for the car, the rest is for expenses, and keep the change, okay?"

This reminded me that I still had to retrieve Lola's fifteen thousand from the locker in the station. It might be impossible to return for it later.

"What if he doesn't want to sell it, Ralph? What then?"

"You'll take it, of course, by whatever means," he replied as if regarding the question more than a little stupid.

"Don't forget, it was stolen from me in the first place."

"Well then," he said, "if nobody has anything else, shall we adjourn to the airport?"

"Ralph," I said, "you do know about the man that went under that westbound at four-thirty this morning?"

He nodded. "When I called your motel from the bar, I was about a dozen feet from a guy that I'm pretty sure was him."

"You were there, Ralph?" I asked surprised at first, before remembering that it was where I'd met him on Wednesday night. It was becoming plain to me that Ralph spent more than a little time at *The Glass Dragonfly*.

"Did you see anyone with him?" I asked, "such as the two others that threw him under the train?"

"No, when I saw him, he was by himself."

"He was a Texas Ranger sent here to get me," I announced, omitting the fact that Traff's mission was benign.

"Well," Ralph replied, "he won't be taking you back to Texas, now will he?"

26. APRIL IN BARSTOW

We used Cassy's rental for the ride to the airport figuring that Ralph's Citroën was too easily spotted, though anyone that wanted to would have had no trouble following us. But it didn't look like anyone was making the attempt. I imagined that when the trouble came we'd be well out of Michigan City.

A few minutes into the ride, I said, "he was murdered," offering no other context and studied Ralph for a reaction.

After a short pause he replied, "the Ranger so you said?"

"Yes, Ralph, the Ranger, two men threw him under the train. I saw it happen…almost. Not many people get drunk enough to allow themselves to be thrown under a train. Certainly no Texas Ranger would. He had to have been drugged."

Ralph nodded, "Sounds like it."

"This means that it's also a near certainty that my cousin Harry was done in by the same people…and I'm the only real connection between the two."

"Weren't you in Texas when Harry went under the train?"

"That is correct, Ralph."

"So you can't be accused of doing in Harry."

"Ralph, you've never been in the joint aside from business like Charlie Novak. I have."

"And?"

"Well, in the month I was there, I met men that did twenty year stretches for crimes committed while they were in jail and couldn't have been near the scene. The evidence screamed at anyone who cared to listen. No judge would, figuring they probably were guilty of worse things, so they did the time. I heard some ended up in old sparky."

"They didn't have lawyers like yours, Addison."

"You talked to Max?"

"That's right."

"When?"

"This morning, Addison. He called my office."

"Does he know about the *Mulholland Rocket*?"

"Not from me, he doesn't, but my guess is he already suspects you're involved in something you haven't told him about, even though you weren't yet when we talked. This Max fellow is that good, and I might add, more than a touch obnoxious, a kind of much smarter version of my father, if I had to put a label on him. It's as if everything he says is either an accusation or threat."

That was true, Max might only say that it looked like rain, and you'd get a vision of yourself being struck by lightning.

"You ain't seen nuthin,' Ralph," I said. And he hadn't.

Had anyone else been boarding the plane in Michigan City, Cassy and I might have had a problem since there were exactly two seats left open by deplaning passengers. The Air Indiana turboprop arrived and left for Indianapolis full. Only as we began the take-off roll, did I remember that my fifteen thousand was still in the locker in the South Shore station! I checked my pocket for the key. It was there.

We had a comfortable two-and a half hour layover in Indianapolis. Cassy and I transferred the bulk of Ralph's money into a new carry-on bag she bought, while I toted only a few hundred of the cash. In the spring of 1980, passenger searches were a perfunctory, random, and haphazard business. If stopped, Cassy would be in a far better position to talk her way out of why she carried so much cash. If she was detained, I would carry on, try to link up with her in California and wire Ralph for more money. I tried to shut out from my mind the ever-increasing threat of being caught on outstanding warrants. It was starting to eat holes in me.

Ralph had booked our flight to LAX under our own names, a good risk as calculated risks go. It's always better to have identification that matched who you said you were.

We ate real meals for the first time that day having been unable to down any of the breakfasts we'd ordered in the wake of Jerrat Traff's dismemberment by the train on Eleventh Street. By now, that memory was fast fading, and neither of us mentioned it.

When she'd finished eating, Cassy lit a cigarette after inserting it into the holder she'd used to smoke on the boat. She pulled on it in deep even drags, exhaling only as needed to breathe. It reminded me that not that long before, smoking ads promoted a chic and daring kind of decadence that implied women who indulged were amenable to other pleasurable pastimes.

Nobody needed to tell Cassy this. At the moment, still in her reunion clothes, her lovely face wreathed in billowy wisps of blue smoke and slices of her terrific ass peaked thorough the slats of a chair back. Cassy Rappaport looked not unlike a travel poster and more desirable than any images I might conjure up, apart from the one of Alice. Sitting across from her for the first time in quite a while, I didn't mind being exactly who I was and where.

At the boarding gate we sat apart as if strangers, and continued as such aboard.

I didn't expect Ralph to have booked us first class seats, but he did. I sat two rows away from Cassy, who was, for the first half of the flight, hit on by a half-century old Jerseyite who repped men's accessories and was consumed with convincing her to spend the next week with him, all the while making no attempt to hide his wedding ring. I wanted to get up and suggest that his health required he stop bothering her, but the last thing we needed was an incident. For the second half of the flight, the drinks he downed on the first half kicked in and he slept.

At just 9:35 Saturday evening, we taxied up to the Delta terminal in Los Angeles. We went to the car rentals once finding out we had missed the last air shuttle to Barstow. It was just as well that we rented the car in L.A. anyway; we were far less likely to be remembered there.

It's a two-hour roll, much of it across California's Mojave Desert, from the city limits of L.A. to those of Barstow.

I had never been to California before although I'd been close to going enough times. For many, it's that place where some lucky relative lives that you can crash in on when the kids will go no further in life without that first trip to the empire built around the world's foremost rodent. It is in fact, a state full of people's relatives that also contains more per capita of all things artificial than any other part of the known world.

But sometime around my fifteenth birthday, I'd promised myself I'd live in California because it's still the most beautiful place in all of North America. At seventeen, it was that I'd live there and be married to Alice. For the previous twenty years or so, I'd cursed myself at least once a week for failing to deliver on either promise.

So my first experience with the place where I'd always intended to live was one of sand, unlit asphalt, and some very interesting road kill. Cassy initiated me into a game she'd played with her husband on business trips that consisted of a point total for which side of the road's lane divider contained more of the region's late inhabitants. Even at night it was possible with the high beams on. At the end of the trip, or some decided upon number of miles, the one with the most carcasses won. If you had daylight and time enough to stop and look, a point scale could be assigned to various species. We didn't try that, but Cassy swore that her ex-husband had at times insisted they do. A dead human being, a cow, or a horse on your side is an automatic win. The game is called "Roadkill" of course.

It's been said that if you can get lost in Barstow, California, you have genius for it and also are an idiot. Still, we twice missed the turnoff from I-15 east and were well back into the desert before realizing we had to do two double backs before finding *Delmagio's Steak & Lobster Shack* exactly where the post cards we'd gotten from Ralph had placed it: on Main Street (Route 66), just south of 1st next to the Chevron Station, where incidentally, is found the real Barstow not the Interstate that plows through the city about ¾ of a mile to the south.

Delmagios itself looked to be open, but wasn't. A cleanup crew that did not speak English was just leaving. A schedule posted left of the doorway showed that the place opened at six-thirty AM and served breakfast from a menu or a six-dollar buffet.

Cassy and I had not slept since Friday afternoon and it was time to crash. We did this at a Motel called the Super Chief on Hwy 66 roughly a mile to the east. We arose at six and were seated by seven in the main dining room.

Both of us still wore reunion clothes, but unlike me, Cassy hadn't slept in hers and had showered. Too exhausted to bother so much as disrobing the night before, and too much of a hurry to get going when we awoke, I must have reeked like the road kill we'd counted that previous evening.

We opted for the buffet breakfast, each selecting eggs over-hard on top of which we piled huge helpings of bacon.

"I suppose that I'll probably go to hell for eating this," Cassy remarked and guided a double-thick strip of the crisp red meat into her mouth. But if they have bacon there, I won't care."

"As sins go, it's a misdemeanor," I replied. "You can have a glass of milk with it and not be hit with any more demerits if you do it at the same sitting."

"No need to cross that barrier," she replied. "I hate milk. Who told you all this by the way?"

"Max," I replied, "he was a Talmud scholar. I'll check with him when I get to Hell, which is where both Max and I are headed. I'll drop you a post card."

"Maybe I should call my father and ask him if it's okay to have a bacon breakfast with Addison July, seeing as I've been having sex with him for the past three days."

"You really must want to do him in. Tell me, is there an insurance policy involved?"

Cassy laughed.

I unzipped a flat leatherette pouch, withdrew Ralph's magazine and hailed what looked like the manager.

"Is something wrong sir?" he asked.

"Does this look like anything you remember?" I asked. He gave me one of those "What are you talking about?" looks.

"The car," I said, handing him the magazine.

"Oh, the owner's car," he replied.

Cassy and I exchanged drop-jawed glances.

"He wouldn't happen to be here, would he?"

"I'll check," the man said, and disappeared.

The "owner" he returned with, looked (uncomfortably for me) too young to be one. Since passing 35, I found myself guessing the age of people who I'd determined had "made it" and comparing their mileage on their faces with my own.

This "owner" was a good five years younger than myself unless he'd cheated the looks clock as I told myself I was doing.

"Frank Delmagio," he said, extending a beefy hand. I shook it.

"You are?"

"Addison July," I replied, telling myself that this was a family business that Frank's father must have started, or maybe his grandfather had.

"You came about my car," declared Frank irritably, "you brought a check…finally?" This was clearly not in the script and could only be explained by Ralph's having located the car while we were in transit and negotiated a price. But why had Frank mentioned a check when we carried so much cash, the undisputed medium of strangers?

"Can I see it?" I asked.

Frank Delmagio threw up his hands in exasperation and motioned us to follow him.

Halfway through the dining room, he stopped cold and turned around to hurl his very red face at mine halting the charge six inches short of a collision. It was obviously a practiced technique, designed to intimidate, and clearly among this man's weapons of choice. I would have flinched, but it all happened too fast.

"I've insured forty vehicles in eleven years with your company, Mr. July. This is the first claim ever over five hundred dollars, and what do you do? You dick me around for ten weeks, fuck me over on the loner, and now you want to have the car bondoed over by some Taco garage after even your own appraisers admit that it's totaled, can't be made right, and never was worth fixing anyway. You want to tell me why I should ever pay you another premium? And you got the nerve, the fucking nerve, to send out a rep just yesterday who wants to insure my business?"

He finished with "Ah shit," then led us down a corridor to a rear exit.

Cassy and I followed him through a door to a small service court, one corner of which was occupied by a mangled lump of metal recognizable only as the remains of a car by melted tires that peeked out of wheel cavities that were both smashed and distorted by heat. The roof was caved in flat to the level of the hood.

"There," he bellowed, extending a hand. Besides whatever had impacted it, this very unfortunate vehicle, a fire had consumed anything that would burn on or in it including the paint, and left it with a coat of bright orange rust where it wasn't a charred black. I assumed that nobody had been on board at the time of the occurrence. Frank certainly hadn't.

I stared at it for no more than ten seconds. It might have once been one of any number of makes, but it had never been the *Mulholland Rocket*.

"Well?" said Frank Delmagio, glaring at me.

"Mister Delmagio," I said, trying to summon up the most apologetic of faces, "I'm not from any insurance company. I'm looking for this." I held out the magazine to him with my left hand, while pointing to the picture that contained the *Mulholland Rocket*.

"That's it!" Frank insisted.

"It can't be," I fired back.

"Alright," he said, "look at the fucking license number!"

"Mr. Delmagio," I said, "there isn't any license number on the car, there isn't a plate."

"What the fuck do you call that?" he roared at me, practically pushing a finger through the page.

It was now, a whole five minutes since I should have realized that Frank Delmagio had owned one of the Chevys parked next to the *Rocket* in the picture. That Chevy was now the melted wreck in the corner of the court. Apparently his insurance company didn't want to pay for a new one for one reason or another, probably the usual reason, which was they just didn't want to pay.

"Mr. Delmagio, I'm here about that car," I said, tapping the page.

"Oh." Recognition crept over his face beginning from the top. He was an only slightly bigger imbecile than I was. "What is that piece of shit anyway?"

"It's a 1950 Nash," I answered, ignoring the insult. I hated to hear an old car, any old car, degraded. From most people, an elderly car gets the same respect an elderly person without money gets.

"My friend called here about it," I said, "The car once belonged to him. I'm from Indiana and I'm here to buy it for him. From the picture, I'm guessing it was here sometime recently. I was hoping that someone could help me." To my great relief Frank did not ask for an explanation as to how I knew it was the same car.

"This is your wife?" Frank asked, nodding at Cassy.

"She's my friend's sister," I replied. "We want to buy the car and ship it back to Indiana for his birthday next Saturday."

It was obvious to us both, that Frank Delmagio, although he wore a wedding ring, had been contemplating a tryst with Cassy since first seeing her. Helping us with the car might advance that plan, and we passed each other a glancing signal to play this for what it might get us.

"It's really important," said Cassy, adding, "it would mean a lot."

She offered a pose of dumb innocence with upturned hands that called attention to (as if it were necessary) a torso that hadn't lost a shred of appeal since she'd been a cheerleader. Frank fixated lecherously on the chest in a way ass men like myself never did, staring unabashedly for several seconds before his eyes broke away.

"Come with me you two," he said finally, and back we went through the same service door and corridor to a leather-lined office lit with chrome-trimmed incandescents. He seated us.

"Do you two have any idea how lucky you are that you came here today?" Frank asked, refocusing his gaze on Cassy's chest.

"How lucky is that, Frank?" I asked.

"Damn lucky, real damn lucky," he snapped at me. Clearly my presence was now a bothersome detail to be disposed of in the most expeditious way so he might get on with the business of seduction.

"I mean," he said backpedaling, "that it so happens, I can tell you exactly when that picture was taken, and I'm leaving town tonight for three weeks in Australia. If you had come tomorrow, you'd been shit out of luck."

I nodded sheepishly. Disputing so much as a syllable might be all it would take to shut off what help Frank might offer. He was obviously not the sort that gave anything away, including, and perhaps especially, information. Knowing exactly when the *Rocket* was photographed might be a dead end anyway, but we would never know that without pursuing it.

"When was it taken?" Cassy asked. She produced a cigarette, which Frank sprang up to light. She drew in the smoke suggestively, exhaling with equal expertise. Frank was close to drooling.

"It was Valentine's Day," he said as he walked back to his desk. "It was the day I bought the Chevy. I parked it in a reserved space miles from the main entrance where there's almost never a customer car parked, so there would be no danger of some fucking asshole throwing open his door and putting a $200 dent in the side of my brand new car. That Chevy was one hour off the showroom floor and this asshole with that, what is it, a '50 Buick, parks a foot away from me and punches a fucking dent in the side."

I arrested the impulse to correct him by saying that it was a Nash. With the Chevy now a melted wreck headed for the crusher, Frank Delmagio was still ready to beat the hell out of whoever put the first dent in it. I sat, nodding in tacit agreement with him. It so happened I hated people that went through life dinging the sides of other people's cars at least as much. I imagined that prolific door dingers might do something like ten-thousand-dollars damage a year and yet have no idea why they will burn in hell when they die.

"Anyway," said Frank, "let's check the reservation log for Valentine's Day" as he wrestled a huge, loose-leaf binder from a desk drawer, rifled through it for a minute, and zeroed in on two sheets that he detached after splitting the rings. "It's a busy day for us, as much traffic as any other major holiday, believe it or not."

There was no reason not to believe it. He passed the two sheets to me. I couldn't imagine why they hadn't been discarded at the end of each day unless kept for some sort of tax audit.

"Lucky for you we require numbers," said Frank, "it cuts down on no-shows or at least it forces them to bother canceling. Like I said, you're lucky."

I had to agree.

"Where do we go from here?" Cassy asked.

"Well, Honey," said Frank, "you call each of these numbers and say that you saw this piece of shit which you'll call a terrific old…what the fuck is it again?"

"Maroon 1950 Nash."

"Yeah, Maroon Nash, which you saw, you want to buy, and got a tip that the person you're calling might know who owns it. You could even offer a bribe, which you'll call a reward—that ought to smoke something out if anything does." He obviously considered this most astute and his face mirrored the delight with himself.

This advice of his reminded me that Frank had yet to mention Ralph's offering a reward, or even inquiring about the *Mulholland Rocket* there in the first place. Frank did not impress me as one to forget much, and if Ralph had inquired at all, as he claimed he had, the information would have gone to Frank or somebody would be in deep shit.

I scanned the two sheets Frank handed me. Each side contained about twenty names in the first of three columns. In the second were the phone numbers, in the third, the number in the party.

I was scanning the second side of the first sheet when a name about halfway from the top struck me in the face like a line drive: "Paul Pfengston, party of six." There was a phone number, which I tried to etch into a brain now doing barrel rolls. Repeating it to myself again and again, I looked up trying to hold my face in neutral.

Frank got up and slowly walked to where Cassy sat. She blew out a long blue plume of smoke before stubbing out her cigarette in a tray on Frank's enormous desk. Frank lingered behind her chair and began lightly dragging the knuckles of his left paw across her shoulders. He had all the subtlety of a Rhino in heat.

"You're gonna need a lot of quarters, fella, he said to me." In fact, I needed none at all, having spotted Paul Pfengston's name.

Cassy reached up and covered Frank's hand with one of her own.

"This is a nice little town," she said. "What do you say to letting Frank here show it to me while you make the calls?" Give him twenty-five dollars and just make the calls from here.

Cassy hadn't seen what I had, had missed my signal to break it off because we had no more need for Frank, his office, his phone, or the papers.

Frank gave Cassy's shoulder a gentle pinch, figuring that on some days scoring was just too easy. He may well have bought the whole story we gave him about the *Mulholland Rocket,* which was close enough to true anyway.

"No need for that, Sonny," he said. I wondered when he had picked up on the name. I couldn't remember Cassy using it in the previous five minutes, but she must have.

"I pay a monthly charge for unlimited local calls," he explained, "and

I've got a watts line for the long distance ones. Keep your money."

"That's sweet," said Cassy. "Is everyone here as nice as you?"

"Everybody that works for me better as fuck be," said Frank, "or they don't work for me long."

Cassy tried to keep a straight face while giving Frank one of those "I am impressed" looks.

She couldn't quite hide her amusement, but by now Frank's focus had shifted from her face to a different part of her anatomy and he missed it completely.

"Give me one minute," said Frank. "Gotta tell my dumb-fuck manager a few things, Honey, and we can go." He winked at Cassy while strutting from the room as would one who'd just purchased planet earth for a penny on the dollar.

"How the hell were you going to get out of that?" I snapped at Cassy, adding, "never mind, let's get the hell out of here."

"Got something?"

"The jackpot," I replied. "All we've got to do now is get rid of that gorilla."

"We were halfway to the doorway when Frank appeared in it."

"Going somewhere?"

"The motel," Cassy said, and turned to me with an expression that was a mixture of exasperation and amusement, all of it fake.

"Tell me something, Frank, is it all right to call you 'Frank'? What do you do with heart patients that don't or won't take their medicine? And it's not like it tastes bad." She gave me a disgusted look. "It's a pill for Chrissake!"

"It makes me nauseous," I protested, and started to sink where I stood, arresting my faux collapse by grabbing the doorknob.

"Shithead," Cassy snapped, and slid an arm around my waist. She groaned at a genuine attempt to lift me, and then turned to Frank. "Help me get him to the car," she almost demanded.

To my amazement, Frank bought it completely and did as she asked. After loading me in the car, he asked Cassy what else he could do.

"Nothing," Cassy replied, seating herself behind the wheel, "except wait here for me. This isn't as bad as it looks, he's just got to take his medication and he should be fine. Believe it or not this is the third time this month."

She blew Frank a kiss, started the car, shifted into drive, and we were off. When we were a block from *Delmagio's* I turned to her, "An Oscar for you lady, an Oscar."

She smiled.

"Wadja find?" she asked.

"A name and number: Paul Phengston," I said trying to remember the number.

"You think he's got the *Rocket?*"

"All but know it."

"Any special reason?"

"A Paul Phengston lived on the first side street to the east of our house in Michigan City. He's got to be the one who stole it twenty years ago."

"I'll be God dammed," she said.

"No, my dear girl," I replied, "we are blessed—BLESSED!"

"Should we check out of the Motel first?"

"Let's make a pit stop there and decide then." Hydraulic pressure had been bearing on me since we'd sat down in Frank's office. I didn't want to ask for so much as a piss break as long as Frank was feeding us information while we fed him crap. Any pause in that flow of favors could have ended it cold. Now a toilet was a got-to-have.

While I attended to myself, Cassy collected our gear that included snatching the Barstow phone directory. It was new and they're always impossible to get on the road when you need them, even if this one was only good for the first thirty miles. There was no way of knowing if the *Rocket* would need to be trailered, or whatever else would be required for it. But it was a good bet it would be in no condition for a cross-country run. "I checked the listing for Paul Psfengston," said Cassy, as I exited the bathroom. "743 Yucca Parkway, want to call him first?"

"Hell no, girl!" I snapped, if the man's a thief, forewarned is forearmed. We might very well have to take the car. Is there a street map in that telephone book?"

"Didn't you notice, Addison?"

"Notice what?"

"This motel."

"No, what do you mean?"

"We're on the corner of 66 and Yucca, Sonny. '743' is probably three blocks from here. Yucca stops at the freeway and then picks up to the south."

"The next time I say 'we're blessed' girl, will you believe me?"

"We could walk there," Cassy offered.

I weighed this and decided that I liked the idea. Pedestrians attract far less attention than does a car in a parking maneuver. There was also the chance that Frank would be looking for us and spot our car on the street. A sign on the room's door posted check out time at noon, which was over four hours away. Things were going a bit too well. I didn't know what waited for us at 743 Yucca, but if the winning streak was to end there, I wanted it to last perhaps a few minutes longer. Life lately had been a series of slam-dunks, and I felt another looming.

Cassy was already outside and I was pulling the door shut, just as I had in Michigan City, when the phone rang. We looked at each other for the same reason that we had in Michigan City when the phone rang in her room there.

"Who the hell?" exclaimed Cassy.

"Frank," I speculated, "either we were followed, or there's a hellava grapevine in this town."

"He wants payment," I said, "and I wouldn't bet against him showing up here to collect it, which can't happen now. You'll have to fend him off. Oh Hell, what's the matter with me anyway? Why don't we just check out?"

"It could be Ralph," she offered. "He found us in Michigan City."

Cassy walked to the phone, which we both knew, was a bad idea. The kind of compulsion that had gripped me in Indiana apparently had now taken hold of her. She lifted the receiver, listened to it for an instant, and handed it to me.

"Good morning, Mr. Dillinger," said the voice I knew all too well, "fancy finding you here."

"Hello, Max," I replied.

"Just wondering how you were managing to further fuck up your life since I last talked to you. Can I say that I'm impressed?"

"How did you find me?"

"Shrinko here told me where you'd be."

"Where are you?" I demanded as if I had a right to.

"Nice little place of yours, this Michigan City, but I thought it was supposed to be a state. Like Michigan State—no that's a school isn't it?"

"How did you get him to tell you?" That was a silly question.

"It wasn't hard," Max replied. "Does this sound familiar?"

A firearm's mechanism clicked in the phone's earpiece.

"It's a nine millimeter, Pretty Boy. Its muzzle is right against his left temple. Did I mention that as your lawyer, savior, and chief guardian angel, I don't appreciate being kept out of the loop?"

"Listen to me, Max," I said.

"Anyway," said Max, cutting me off, "Shrinko here didn't want to tell me where you went, or why, but he wanted to live even more. So he tells me the "where you are" part. But the reason you're in California, I figured I'd hear from you because, even though he told me, I don't quite believe him. And if the story you give me is different from his, he's going for an interview with his hero, Dr. Freud, on that big analyst's couch in the sky."

I had no doubt that Max was holding the muzzle of a pistol to Ralph's head and was more than ready to make good on the threat. While I disliked psychiatrists, Max's sentiments toward them took hatred to undreamed of heights. It was a matter of great pride that the one who treated him when he was eleven had committed suicide.

"You're a son of a bitch, Max," I said, hoping it was what he wanted to hear. It was.

"I always loved the way you say that," Max replied. "Now what are you doing in a stupid little railroad town in the California desert?"

"I'm here to find a car, Max, Ralph's high school car. It's called the *Mulholland Rocket*. He's got a bet that I can find it and bring it back to Michigan City by a week from Tuesday. The bet's two hundred thousand. If he wins, I get half, and you get paid."

I hoped that the last part might make some kind of difference to him. I had no idea what I owed Max, and doubted that kind of money meant much to him, next to owning people as he must now figure he did me. He'd probably tell me to keep the money. But I didn't want it all to end three blocks from what I was pretty sure would be the *Mulholland Rocket*. I waited, wondering what Ralph had told Max I was doing.

There was no reason for him not to have told Max the truth, especially when he was staring down a gun barrel.

"Liar!" Max snarled a second later. I couldn't decide which of us he meant.

"Max, don't."

"Lying little shrink!" said Max and his gun roared.

"Goddamn you, Max!" I screamed, "Goddamn you!"

I envisioned the contents of Ralph's skull spilling into a widening pink puddle, roughly trapezoidal on the surface of the desk where we'd sat less than a day before. I could see brain tissue pouring over the edge, dripping down the side and dissipating on the gray carpet before soaking in.

"Goddamn you, Max!"

"There you go again," said Max, "getting all worked up over nothing."

"What did you say, Max?"

"You heard me, Sonny."

"You just killed a man!"

"You mean 'another man,' don't you? Get it right for Christ's sake. Oh yeah, you flunked English, didn't you? Say, you don't like being joshed do you?"

"Where are you, Max?"

"In a bedroom, of course with a very pretty whore, just like I imagine you are."

It occurred to me that I hadn't once heard Ralph's voice.

"You said you were in Indiana?"

"Oh, that, uh, well I'm not. I had to find out what you were doing in California."

"You son of a bitch, Max!"

"I still love the way you say that, Sonny. I swear to God, I love it! Anyway, April Fool Pretty Boy, or should I call you 'Rocket Man'? I know it's not the first, but it's still April, and you're a fool if there ever was one."

"Fuck you, Max!" I yelled in all sincerity.

"This is going to be one interesting week Rocket Man. Come Watson, the game is afoot. Say hello to the Rocket Man, Dr. Watson. C'mon, say something, Doctor."

Whoever Max was with said nothing.

"I don't think she's really a doctor," said Max, "but she's got one helluva snatch." I could still hear Max laughing when I slammed the handset into its cradle.

"Asshole," I snarled.

"How did he know we were here?" Cassy asked.

"I couldn't even begin to guess. But he was letting me know how easily he can track anybody. Also, his ego is bothering him that his Texas Ranger who he thought was such a big gun was disposed of so easily by a couple of thugs in Michigan City. It hurt his southern fried pride. He had to demonstrate to me how he could still bluff me by pretending that he was in Indiana, holding a gun to Ralph's head, and then pulling the trigger. I swallowed the whole act. Actually he was home in bed, or that's what he wants me to believe."

"Are you Okay?" Cassy wanted to know.

"I gave him what he wanted," I said, "calling him a 'son of a bitch' to his way of thinking is an admission that he's fifty times smarter than me. It might even keep him from meddling for a while, but of course he will sooner likely than later, it's just a matter of what direction he comes from. To Max, this is one big game, and he couldn't be happier." "Sound's like a very angry man," ventured Cassy. "Who's he so mad at?"

I shrugged. "God maybe, for making him so ugly. There's one thing you never call him: it's 'Troll.' Use it on him and he'll bring down every resource he has to destroy you. I've seen him do it. C'mon, let's find the *Rocket*."

We stepped through the Motel's doorway, uninterrupted this time, left our gear there—practically none, except of course the cash— and headed up Yucca. Cassy, as she had on our breakfast sortie, and since Indianapolis for that matter, carried the bulk of our cash in the tote bag we'd bought at the Airport, from which the end of a soiled handkerchief dangled. I thought this a passable ruse, but I sure didn't want it put to a test.

The three blocks turned out to be long ones, the first two part of a '50s subdivision whose developer must have gone belly up about the middle of its execution, since the line of nearly identical stucco homes ended abruptly half way up the second block which offered only half-built walls probably two-plus decades old. The houses themselves, though, were better than anything the 1980 generation of architects I belonged to had produced. The seven hundred block of Yucca contained still older houses from an earlier development. But I'd quit paying attention when we crossed the last street and saw the bulbous maroon outline of half a car projecting from one of those attached carports roofed with undulating green fiberglass panels screwed to wooden uprights. Even from half a block away, Cassy and I both knew what we were looking at.

We tried hard but could not keep from breaking into a run and then sprinting the last quarter block which left us breathless by the time we reached that driveway on which sat the *Mulholland Rocket*.

Cassy, the smoker, recovered before me. I put my hand on her shoulder as we looked at each other, faces frozen in disbelief.

So there it was. Cassy walked up the stretch of driveway and pointed out the 'Z'-shaped scar on the fender that Ralph had said cinched this car as his in the magazine.

I might have felt better had he Xeroxed the registration with the VIN number Ralph had held in his hands and do a check against the body plate. There was no reason we couldn't have done that, except that I'd thought of it about eighteen hours too late.

But it was the *Rocket* all right, no question about that. I was starting to pick out small blemishes that I'd first noted myself twenty-two years before. The two gouges on one of the hubcaps, that were still in filled with orange paint from whatever had made them, struck a fresh bolt of memory, as did a fracture in the cloth welt that was used to seal off the joint where the right rear fender met the body. I'd forgotten about the trailer hitch too, and was reminded of it when it dug into my left shin. And there was something I didn't remember at all because Ralph must have added it later: just above a chromium belt that held the tail and directional lights on the trunk lid in expertly painted script that matched the raised Nash Airflite emblem of the factory, was the car's name: "*MULHOLLAND ROCKET*." Not bothering to remove it was like leaving on a sign that said "stolen car." Ralph may not have mentioned it, sure that it was the first thing the thieves would have removed. Yet there it was for all to see.

I was well inside the carport, and although it was open on three sides, I was trespassing and had no idea what kind of reception the thief who had stolen the *Rocket* might give me should he appear.

It wasn't a long wait. To my right, and just outside my peripheral vision, the clacking of door hardware sounded. Following that, came the kind of wheezing creak doors make when they're old aluminum.

I looked up from the painted script to what I imagined was the face of Paul Pfsengston. The look on it was hardly the one I give someone I caught poking around my carport. He offered me what could have passed for a smile.

27. THE PHENGSTON ODYSSEY

"How ya doing this morning?" he asked.

Cassy advanced up the driveway and called out: "Hi."

"Hi, yourself," said the man.

"Addison July," I said extending my hand.

"Paul Pfengstion," he replied reaching for it. The wrinkled skin of his hand matched that of his face, the obvious consequence of years of life in the Mojave sun. His hair, still quite black, looked as if the ends had been singed into tiny balls from being held over a flame. I wondered how he managed to comb it.

But his smile bore genuine warmth, not the kind people like Max wore just before producing a weapon.

"I know you," he said, and looked up as if reaching back.

Returning to me he said, "you're the Doctor's boy. You worked at Ray's garage in Michigan City."

"You knew my father?" I asked.

"Hell yes, I knew him, Addison. He took care of my whole family, finest man I ever met."

"He had his points," I replied."

"That he did," confirmed Paul. "My parents worshiped him, and my older sisters were in love with him."

"He's dead you know," I said.

"I know that," Paul replied. "When my mother called to tell me, she was choked up so bad that I could barely make out what she was saying."

I could not remember myself crying at the news, and hadn't attended the funeral. Dear old dad had died in Houston, but Lola shipped him back to Indiana for a burial next to my mother. I was too busy to attend.

"Say, Addison, do you remember…" Paul cut himself off with a quick and embarrassed laugh.

"So what the hell do you want, Addison?" he asked, still laughing. but indicating that he was already as tired of small talk as I was.

I decided to show him the same courtesy. "Paul, I said, I was sent here by the guy that you stole this car from twenty years ago. He wants it back. We're ready to pay you cash for it, and I'm also ready to take it if I have to. What'll it be?"

Cassy squeezed herself through a space between the *Rocket's* right quarter panel and a 4x4 that supported a section of the carport's roof so as to join us; the twin mounds of her buttocks made for a delightful path in the car's dust.

Paul surveyed her as one would a painting, or something two dimensional, instead of attempting to calibrate the projection of her bust or buns through the instinctive kind of trigonometry most men use.

"Normally," he said, "I don't much cotton to threats. But you're right, I stole the car and it's time it went back to whoever it really belongs too. I'd always meant to return it myself. Whose car is it anyway?"

"His name is Ralph Falonhurst," I replied, repeating: "we're ready to pay you for it."

Paul shook his head. "Falconhurst," he said, "the lawyer's kid. You may tell Mr. Falconhurst that I can hardly sell him back something that was his in the first place. It's a wonderful car, and I'll miss it. You could say that I owe it my life."

I avoided correcting the pronunciation of Ralph's surname for fear of queering the man's demeanor. It was going too smooth so far to last.

"Would you like to tell us about it, Paul?" Cassy asked. I'd wished she hadn't said that.

"That might take a little while," said Paul. "We'd best go inside."

I might have been, perhaps, a little curious myself how it was that somebody selected this very unlikely car for stealing, and kept it twenty years without any attempt at all to erase the evidence of the car's former life. But it was far more important how it ran and if it didn't, to find a way of getting it back to Indiana. Listening to what could be a long stupid sentimental story was a time luxury I felt I could ill afford no matter how much a flying start we seemed to be off on.

We went inside where I was nearly struck dumb by the framed portrait of a very young Negro face fitted out in graduation garb that was sitting on a mantle opposite the divan where we'd just sat down. I walked to the portrait to further cinch the features since I found blacks, like Asians, nearly impossible to tell apart. I was sure now that it was the same portrait the enraged Negress implored me to look at in the restaurant in Michigan. I took it from the mantle and turned to Paul as if to ask: "who?"

"Calvin Coolidge Brown," Paul rattled off in near mechanical cadence.

"My brother-in-law, Class of '66, Wendell Willkie High School, Lance corporal United States Marine Corps, killed in action, age nineteen, city of Hue, Republic of Vietnam, February 1968 during the Tet offensive, awarded the Bronze Star posthumously."

I studied the portrait, which somehow seemed to demand from me an explanation for being alive, and offer some account of how I spent the last twelve years during which the boy, whose likeness it bore, lay in a grave, while I lived, breathed, and had occasional sex. One thing was a fact: his death, coupled with Clifford's lost arm, were the very reasons I was free at the moment.

"Sorry," I said, not sure of whether I was addressing Paul or the picture. I set it back on the mantle, reminding myself that I had once decided that I owed nobody an explanation for being alive, not Ralph, not Clifford, not Paul Pfengston, and especially not some dead soldier's picture, or even Alice for that matter. I was a draft dodger, not proud of what I did, nor sorry, not a bit.

Next to Calvin's portrait was one of a much younger Paul Pfingston, so much younger that recognition was a tough call. He was tuxedoed out, and the expression he wore bespoke an ecstasy he had to fight off for the kind of dignity a shot like this demanded. It was his wedding picture. Next to him was a very pretty negress in white lace who seemed to be having the same problem controlling herself.

Clearly, neither showed a hint of buyer's remorse, or last minute trepidations. I remembered my wedding portrait with Courtney and was suddenly more than a little jealous. I guessed my expression would have looked like his had I been able to marry Alice.

Cassy and I looked at each other both remembering our encounter with Paul's sister-in-law, who, back in the restaurant, would have shot us both dead with the greatest of pleasure.

"What's your wife's name, Paul?" I asked.

"I'm a widower," he replied. "Her name was Nell. She died in February. We buried her on Valentine's Day. Her family came in from Indiana, and we used the Nash for the family car. Nell would have liked that."

"Did you hold a luncheon at *Delmagio's* afterward?" I asked, but I needn't have.

"That's how you found me?"

"That's how," I replied, "some roving old car nut with a camera snapped the Nash in the parking lot, sent the picture to an old car nut magazine that put it in their random shots section, and lo and behold…"

"The real owner bought the magazine," said Paul, "Amazing."

I had to admit that it was little short of that. There was no need that I could see for mentioning anything about two-hundred-thousand dollars.

"I suppose you'd like to hear about why I stole it," said Paul. "It's the only thing I ever stole in my life." Cassy nodded as did I, reluctantly. Paul left the room for a moment and returned with a tray of soft drinks.

"How old were you in '59?" he asked after we'd seated ourselves on a divan.

I replied that I turned seventeen in October of that year. Cassy just nodded, indicating that she didn't care to say exactly. She might have been slightly older than me.

"Then you were old enough to know what race relations in Indiana were like then."

"About the same as everywhere else." I offered an upturned hand.

"And do you recall what that was?" asked Paul.

I could see I was in for a short preachy history of the world. Two years before the time in question, I'd won a debate, when I argued in favor of segregation.

"I married Nell in June of fifty nine," said Paul taking up the narrative. "The first thing that happened when we came back from our honeymoon was get fired from my job. Two days later, Nell, was fired from hers."

"It might not have been for that," I offered. Paul gave me the irritated smile that my banal piece of B.S. deserved. I told myself it was something Ralph might have come up with and that I'd been around him too much in the last few days.

"I worked at a company that prided itself as being of the most progressive in Indiana," said Paul, "but they still held separate white and colored picnics. When we showed up together at the white one, we were a problem that they dealt with by firing me. It was really stupid of us. We weren't trying to make a statement or anything like that. It would have been so much simpler to just not go to either of them."

"Where did you live?" I asked.

"With Nell's folks for a while. But then I came into enough cash for a down payment for a place off Eleventh, a nice place, sort of midway between where each of us had grown up. But it was a little too close for some people's liking. The threats started the first night."

"What kind of threats?"

"The usual: 'move to Gary where you belong or we'll kill you,' that kind of stuff. What amazed me was that not all of them were from whites. I think the worse threat anybody felt was that their kids might imitate us. I think the colored neighbors resented us at least as much, even though the neighborhood had been mixed for some time. An integrated couple was something new and not at all welcome."

"What did you do?" Cassy asked.

"We ignored them," Paul replied, "or tried to. After a time, the threats subsided as did minor vandalism."

Suddenly, Paul got up and began pacing furiously in rough figure eights pounding his left palm with his fist. Then he blurted out in a fury: "Hell, we were both Michigan City born and raised. Our people were too. I'm a veteran of Korea for Chrissake. I'm a Baptist, so was Nell. Her kid brother, Calvin"—he pointed to the now dead Marine's portrait I'd held a minute before—"couldn't wait to get into a uniform and serve his country." You'd think Nell and I would have the right to live together in a fucking city we grew up in. This was Indiana for Chrissake, not Mississippi."

Cassy and I listened intently.

"Indiana," he mused, "I suppose that it shouldn't have surprised me. The Ku Klux Klan once ran Indiana. They never ran any ex-Confederate State. But they fucking once ran Indiana."

Paul's face was now pumped up like a crimson balloon. He sat down, paused, took several deep breaths, and picked up the story.

"One night late that December, I was dropped off at home from my third day on my fourth job for that year. They gave me the second shift that put me home at eleven. I noticed something odd about my house. All the windows were apparently open and this was, as I said, December, late December. In an instant, I realized that there just weren't any windows, or any glass left in them to be exact, and the front door was ajar. Something else too: there wasn't a lit house on the street for a block."

I looked at Cassy whose expression showed me she'd known at least something about this.

"I suppose I should have called the police, but, of course, by the time I even thought of it, I was through the front door and reaching for the light switch. I shouldn't have expected it to work, but I was surprised when it didn't. Something hit me in the face, or seemed to. It took me a second to realize nothing had actually touched me. It was the beam from a flashlight, one of those big, black, hard rubber ones that hold about fifty batteries, you know, the ones the police use."

"These were cops?" I asked incredulously.

"No," Paul replied with a half laugh, "they weren't the cops. Funny, I'd never seen Klan robes before, except in movies and newsreels. It struck me how well made they were. I've been in the garment trade all my life, and you notice things like that even with what was going on. You might even focus on it because you're so damn terrified of what's in front of you. Your mind grasps for any piece of normalcy it can. I can remember the stitching being so nice and even…"

"How many of them were there?" I asked.

"Four," Paul replied, "the middle two had shotguns pointed at me. The scariest thing about them was that the guns were shaking. They held guns on us and they were scared. I realized that they were waiting for me to say something first. So I screamed the thing I probably was most afraid to ask, which was: 'where is Nell?'"

"The one holding the flashlight directed it away from me and past some smashed furniture to a corner of the room were Nell was sitting on the floor. They had her all tied up, gagged, and a noose that wasn't attached to anything else was around her neck. I ran over to her. She shook so that it took me a couple of minutes just to get the gag out of her mouth. She couldn't speak when I did. I don't remember saying anything to her either, not even anything stupid like 'it's going to be alright.' How could I when I expected us to both be dead in the next minute? I was taking the noose off Nell when one of the Klansmen ordered me to stop. He was the first one of them to say anything, and his voice sounded like a twelve-year-old's. You could barely understand him through the hood. The other three looked at him as if he might have some idea of what to do with us, which they obviously didn't. They were kids for Christ's sake."

"I almost said to them something like, 'Hadn't you boys best be on your way before somebody gets hurt?' Something magnanimous, like the hero would say in one of those Frank Capra movies. But seeing what they'd done to Nell, I wasn't much in the magnanimous mood. I didn't want any of them leaving my house alive. They were mumbling among themselves, pointing the barrels of the two shotguns in every direction like you'd point a finger in a debate, forgetting that they were guns at all. I didn't need an invitation to gather myself into a two-legged ball and charge them like they were bowling pins. When I hit, one of the guns went off and blew a hole in one of their chests you could pass a grapefruit through. He collapsed on the floor except for a section of his guts that were pinned to the wall by the pellets. For a minute, we all froze, literally, like you do in a dream. I knew that the first one to come out of that dream was going to be the one that lived. I broke out just as the one who held the other shotgun was trying to take aim at me, but I was so close to his buddies that he should have been afraid to fire. But fire he did, just as I grabbed the barrel and pointed it away from me. That blast took the arm off another one of them just above his elbow, and he let out a scream I can still hear. Paul smiled wryly and was quiet."

"And then?" I asked.

"And then," said Paul, "they ran like hell, and get this, one of them turned around when he'd made it halfway down our sidewalk and came back. I faced him at the doorway and he was spurting blood like a fuel pump from the stump that was all that was left of his arm. He screamed at me: "white nigger, give me back my fucking arm!" I did, but it took time to find it, there were no lights, remember?"

"When I found it, I gave it to him like it was something he just forgot, like an umbrella, and off he goes. He dropped it when he reached the street, and was trying to pick it up when he collapsed and was probably dead in the next minute, or at least well past saving. Anyway that's where they must have found him." Paul stopped.

I looked at Cassy who was shaking now, not doing at all well, and trying to hide it. Paul's expression seemed to ask if I wanted to hear the rest. I offered another up-turned hand, which he took as a signal to proceed.

"Well," he continued, "I untied Nell and we found the one lamp they hadn't smashed and plugged it in. Then we pulled the hood off the kid with the grapefruit-sized hole in him. And he was a kid, my God, was he young, and his face was familiar. It took me a minute to place it. That face had been on the sports page of practically every paper published in LaPorte County for most of the previous year. That kid had been the star running back of the Willkie Wildcats who'd just graduated the previous June. And here he was, dead of a shotgun blast, lying in a huge puddle of blood and pulp right in my living room."

"Nell was sobbing. She was scared, like I was, to be sure, but knowing Nell, she was crying for the dead boy and how the kind of hate that had infected him made him lose his life before it had started. That was Nell for you. If the kid wasn't a football jock, he probably would have died a virgin. I didn't mention to her that there was another boy probably just as dead lying in the gutter alongside his blown off arm. In a few minutes we heard sirens. That tripped one impulse that ran through the both of us like electric current: to get the hell out of there. Anyone else would have said to themselves: thank God, we're going to be safe now."

"You would think that," I said.

"Yeah," said Paul, "that's what we're taught to think, you and I. Living with Nell for six months taught me a whole new way of hearing a police siren."

"I've learned to react to them differently myself."

"So you ran?" Cassy asked.

Paul nodded. "We had no idea what we could expect to come at our house next: a mob, the police, the Klan, or all of them at once. I guess we were running in the general direction of Nell's folk's place. After a couple of blocks we stopped to catch our breath. I told Nell that we had no right to place her whole family at risk seeing that none of our kin, hers or mine, had approved of us. She agreed. We tried to think of somebody that might put us up. Your father's name came up incidentally. But it wasn't fair to ask anyone. There might have been a thousand things we could or should have thought of, but we couldn't think of one. Everything we had was back at the house and yet we didn't dare go there. And then I saw it parked in a driveway with its trunk lid up. I guessed somebody was packing or unpacking for, or from a trip.

Paul gestured towards the carport calling the Nash "it," again. I shook my head in amazement. Paul began smiling now. I think that he could hardly believe it himself.

"When I saw that it was running, I didn't need an engraved invitation. It was fucking providence. I slammed the trunk lid shut. Nell and I got in and we just drove."

"I take it you didn't have a car of your own."

"We did," he replied, "but it had broken down and our mechanic had died that fall. His garage was closed."

I didn't have to ask if his mechanic was Ray. It had to have been.

Paul paused again as if to pull up a fresh image. "At first I only meant to use it to get out of town, or Indiana maybe, and then abandon it. But when and where do you decide to do that and become a pedestrian in December? We sure didn't know. And then I remembered that Nash cars had beds built into them. So keeping it a while was hardly a tough decision. There was nothing really to connect it with the dead boys. Once out of Indiana, the plates were relatively cold. This was 1959, remember? Two-way radios were state-of-the-art then and what they called computers used tubes, and maybe even gears or rubber bands."

"We made the first stop for gas about six hours later, half way across Illinois. Nel went to stretch out, walked to the back of the Nash, and a minute later gestured me to come over. And low and behold, the great revelation: painted right across the back was what you were looking at when I came through that door.

"*Mulholland Rocket*," I said.

"You got it." Paul replied. "Providence strikes again. Everybody knows where Mulholland Drive is—everybody! Go West young man, go west. 'No color line in California,' somebody once told me. And since we were flat out of ideas, it was all we needed."

"California," said Paul after another pause. "That's where we went and never looked back. For a while, until I could buy a used Airstream, the Nash was our house. It wasn't a conscious decision to keep it, but after a while, we started feeling like it belonged to us. It was something from home, and since we learned from our kin that the bank grabbed our house, we figured our hometown owed us something. I suppose that's why we never took the car's name off the trunk. Maybe we were subconsciously daring somebody to catch us with it and extradite us to Indiana so we could tell everybody what had happened. We always wanted to do that."

"But the good State of Indiana wasn't exactly anxious for the information. There was no way we could be convicted, evidence being what it was. A dozen years later we negotiated giving a statement to the LaPorte County Sheriff's office with Nell's father, a judge by then, acting as a liaison. The two reps they sent to take our statements looked like they were still in High School. We did it at the city Hall in San Bernardino. I thought it might be a trap, but it wasn't. I think they were actually afraid I'd demand a hearing, or go to the papers with the story."

"What did they do about the dead boys?" I asked.

"The whole story was buried along with them. That was the bizarre part," said Paul. "Even the town clowns had it all figured out by the next day. The two kids that escaped alive had apparently broken down and talked. A botched home invasion that was repulsed was as American as American cheese on white. Funny thing, those kids didn't belong to the Klan at all. There wasn't a real Klansman in all of LaPorte County. The robes were borrowed and the whole thing was some kind of fraternity prank. Why the hell did they have to take shotguns? I suppose they figured I'd have a gun and wanted some insurance. What they expected to do with us is something I never figured out and I don't think they knew themselves. They couldn't have lynched us in our house, the ceilings are too low. It bugs me to this day that I just don't know."

I stared at Cassy. All of what Paul had just described had gone on two days before Colin's funeral and I hadn't heard a murmur of it until that morning in April 1980, more than twenty years later.

"The newspapers just let a thing like that go?" I asked.

"Oh," said Paul, "another amazing aside. That very afternoon, somebody robbed an armored car, killed the guards, and stole six million dollars. Do I have to tell you what the editors were told to focus on? Apparently everybody fell into line, lest the memory of a Willkie super jock be dragged through the mud. Something like that could be hushed then. Hell, how about Kennedy and Marilyn Monroe? Old Jack was dead eight years when somebody blew the whistle on him. Say, didn't both of you live in Michigan City at the time?"

"I did," Cassy replied. Her voice was steady, and her shaking had subsided. I guessed that she knew something about this and was afraid where Paul might be going with it.

"You knew about it then?" Paul asked.

"I went to one of their funerals. I was a cheerleader. The jock that died in your living room was Thurmond Gratt. I went out with him a few times. The guy that died in the street was Thurmond's cousin or something like that. The story was that they were killed in an accident. There was talk about that not being what happened at all at the funeral, but nothing beyond that."

"You never mentioned any of this to me," I said to Cassy.

"No," she replied, "you were focused elsewhere. Anyway, you didn't seem interested in gossip or dead jocks, and all I knew up to now was that they were dead."

"You might have mentioned it," I said, a little irritated, but she was right, I couldn't have cared less and she hadn't known this fantastic angle until now. I did wonder if Thurmond had done her though. I turned back to Paul.

"So you kept it?" I asked, meaning the Nash.

He nodded.

"Like I said, it was our house for a little while. I bought a surplus army tent and we camped in the Mojave about ten miles from here for the next month. After that, came the Airstream, which that Nash pulled handily. The twins were born in the trailer. They were conceived in the Nash." Paul motioned to the mantle where a series of pictures traced his two daughter's progress from infancy. The most recent showed them in their late teens. They bore a strong resemblance to the very angry Cosmoline from the restaurant. We all looked at them through a couple of quiet minutes.

"How long have you lived here?" Cassy asked finally.

"Nineteen years," Paul answered. Over time, we used the Nash less and less, not that it gave us any trouble. I started to think of it as an antique that should be in a museum or something. I had that tiny Quonset put up out back to store it about ten years ago. We still drove it periodically. About five years ago I stopped licensing it. Today's the first day it's been out in several months. Last time was Nell's funeral. You'll need a new battery if you're going to drive it to Indiana."

"You think it will make it to Indiana?" I asked. It seemed almost too much to hope for.

"I wouldn't be nervous about it myself, but that's just based on how she drives. I forgot; you're a mechanic aren't you?"

"Used to be."

"Well, it's what, a three days drive? Give yourself four or five. Go easy on her and I bet she gets you there without a complaint. It's what we were going to do."

"You were going to take her back?"

"Actually we were considering it, seriously. Nell loved the car, but the way we got it ran against her grain. We thought about trying to find out who owned it and then we hit on an idea." Paul smiled as if asking me to ask him.

"Which was?"

"We were going to drive her back to Michigan City, put the old plates on her, and park her exactly where we found her. We even thought about doing it on the twentieth anniversary of taking her. But we let the date slip by. It was the winter that kept us from doing it. Neither of us wanted to do it one day of a Midwest December and Nell wasn't well. She died in February. I used the car once this year and that was for the funeral. As I said, today's the first time since that day it's been out of the garage." Nell's family came out for the funeral, including her Dad. He's a judge now as I told you before."

I didn't think it necessary to tell him that I was on the lam and his father-in-law had signed for my release. I wondered how I could avoid hearing any more details, especially any about Nell's demise.
"I'm right with you on that," I said, "winter sucks squid."
Paul either got the hint or didn't want to talk about it himself.
"It's still not licensed," he said. "We'll have to do that if you're going to drive it to Indiana. I'll need some time to find the title which I'll endorse over to…who did you say owns it?"
"Ralph Falonhurst," I replied adding almost sarcastically: "Dr. Ralph Falonhurst."
"A medical doctor then?"
"They're called that. He's a psychiatrist actually."
"That is a doctor."
"So they claim."
"You don't like them?"
I chuckled and shook my head. "How did you get a title anyway?" I asked.
"Just applied for it, said the old one was lost, forged a bill of sale and signed a few affidavits, nobody checked. It was a lot easier to tell lies before the damn computers invaded everything."

There was nothing left to say anyway. Paul told us where we could buy a tow strap, a new battery, and a set of road tools. Cassy would run chase with the rental car back to Indiana. We could use it for a tow should the *Rocket* crap out. What Alamo Rent a Car didn't know wouldn't hurt. We debated about getting temporary license plates.

When we stepped from the house, the Mojave sun struck us with a full force made even more intense by the fact that it had been overcast up to the time we'd gone inside. I took a final glance at the *Rocket*, and turned to look at Cassy, when I suddenly stopped in mid arc at the sight of a Ford Mustang parked directly across the street from 743 Yucca.
Mustangs never did anything for me from the day they bowed at

the 1964 World's fair. The five million people who bought them since their introduction, disagreed. This one must have arrived since we'd gone inside.

Long before 1980, people were beginning to collect Mustangs and there were some pristine examples showing up at drive-ins on nostalgia nights. This model, on top of being one of the uglier ones, had obviously led less than a pampered life. About a third of it was covered with dark-red primer under which could be seen abandoned attempts at body repair. The windows were tinted absolutely black and the whole car bore an acute tilt that placed the nose no more than four inches above the pavement. Huge chrome coil springs gleamed from beneath its jacked-up rear. The coarse growl of the exhaust bespoke the potential of an ear splitting shriek when the moron owner—he had to be a moron—slammed down the accelerator.

I gestured toward it and offered Cassy a disgusted shrug. The Mustangs' driver likely saw that and treated us to the shriek I'd feared since first seeing the car.

We were walking a brisk pace back to the Super Chief Motel and I turned around to take one last look at the *Rocket* that was now better than a block behind us.

"Shit," I snapped. Cassy started to turn around when I barked at her not to.

We walked on and she said, still facing straight ahead, "*Delmagios*?"

"He's parked in front of the *Rocket* blocking it. He's looking right at it. He'll be there when we get back; that's for sure."

We walked on, down the incline, turning off Yucca Street at the next intersection, and hoped Frank had not seen us.

Finally, Cassy said: "I can call his restaurant from the motel. They'll page him. And when he calls in, he'll get the message that I'm on my way back to his office for fun and games."

I considered this, but: "No good, Cassy. Paul Pfingston is going to tell him we were there; he has no reason not to. Even if he were in on it and lied for us, saying we hadn't been there, Delmagio is too smart to buy it. By now he's got to figure I was faking it. We're going to have to deal with him.

We reached the motel without resolving anything. Cassy said she wanted to use the bathroom one last time, but I went directly to the car, leaving her to gather what gear we had. She emerged from the room a few minutes later, slipped the key into a slotted drop box and we headed for the parts store.

They had one six-volt battery left on the shelf, a nice assortment of emergency tools, and no tow straps. By now I was too consumed with the prospect of facing Frank to care much about the strap. We considered phoning in a bomb threat to his restaurant as a way of getting him back there and away from the *Rocket*, but I figured he'd see through that too.

Back at the house on Yucca, Frank's car still blocked the driveway where the *Rocket* stood.

"C'mon," I said to Cassy in a tone of resignation. "He might just be amenable to a cash bribe." What the hell, I was going to tell Ralph I bought back the car for ten thousand and keep the money he said I could keep anyway. Frank has no claim on either of us but could make our getting out of there very sticky indeed since he probably had connections with the local police and might well have sensed that we wanted to avoid them at all costs."

The Mustang was still there too, but only momentarily. As I eased up behind, its tires let out an ear-searing shriek as its engine erupted in an orgasm of torque and exhaust. Then it was gone. I hoped a large telephone pole might just be the next thing to get in its way.

28. BLOOD LAKE

Ringing the doorbell of 743 got us no response. I rang it again, listening this time. The bell did sound, but again summoned no one. A third ring produced the same odd quiet. I tried the door; it was locked, but the one leading in from the carport wasn't, so in we went. Halfway through the kitchen, we saw that the living room contained a holocaust.

On the far wall, the one that we first faced directly, there was what looked like a half-finished painting by some self-described modernist who'd begun with random splashes of very red paint. The bigger ones ran down the wall in long tapered drips to end in puddles on the floor. Of course, none of it was paint.

The wall was gray, and the brain tissue splattered on it blended in to the background so well that there was no noticing it from more than ten feet away. I reached down to remove a hairy something that had stuck to my shoe and found it was a section of Paul Pfengston's skull. Just beyond the end of the sofa was the rest of his head, still attached to his body. The left eye, which stared upwards, was slightly askew in a way that reminded me of Jerret Traff. The right one was where the bullet had gone in. The back of Paul's head, at the 'exit site,' there was missing the section that I'd stepped on. One of the red splotches on the wall had a black slug in its center.

For a minute, I wondered if Frank could have done this, until I saw Frank sprawled out face down in the hallway. It had apparently taken several slugs to end his attempt to escape. I counted five holes in his back and the wall-to-wall blood for much of the hall's length meant that the slugs had gone clean through him as well.

I hadn't heard Cassy approach me from the rear, so when she touched me, I sprang several feet forward to land on Frank's back where I lost my balance and splashed into a heap alongside him. The dead face, aligning with my own, stared at me while fresh blood, squeezed from him by my landing, gurgled from his mouth and nose. Cassy extended her right hand to help me up while holding her left over her mouth. When I was half way to my feet, she let go a mighty rush of vomit on Frank and me before sinking to her knees into the bloody lake where I'd landed. After a moment, I hoisted her, and the both of us staggered, dripping blood into the front room leaving crimson hand and footprints everywhere. As we collapsed breathless on the couch, a telephone next to me rang. There wasn't a reason in the world to pick it up and a thousand excellent ones not to…

"Don't touch it," Cassy screamed in a voice made uneven by what I guessed was residual vomit and bile.

She was right of course. It was plain madness to touch another thing much less answer it, had I not instinctively known who was on the other end.

"No, Sonny," Cassy cried out, in a final protest, as I lifted the hand set. A voice in the earpiece said: "Dillinger?"

"Yeah, Max," I replied.

I didn't even bother to ask how he'd found me this time. It had become a given that he could do that whenever he chose.

"Did the Rocket Man find his rocket?"

"As a matter of fact Max, I'm looking right at it," I said, though I wasn't.

"So you don't need me."

"I didn't say that Max," I replied.

"So what is it now, Goyface?"

"If I turn my head a little Max, I can see two dead men that were alive twenty minutes ago.

"How?"

"Shot Max, one through the head, the other a bunch of times in the back."

"Are you inside, Dillinger? Can anyone see them or you?"

"We're inside Max, and the drapes are drawn."

"And I suppose your prints are all over the place?"

I remembered leaving prints in places I could never remember, besides the bloody ones on the wall. "Yeah Max."

"You'll have to burn the place, Sonny," he said with a resigned tone that almost masked his delight. "This is a house, am I correct?"

Had I not known it was Max, I might not have guessed the voice. It had assumed the cold, flat, professional tone of exactly what commanded it, the best legal mind in Texas. No matter that it shared a brain with a certifiable psychotic. I had stepped into the last place I wanted to be beside the State Prison in Huntsville. I was now in the kingdom of Max Morgenstern and he held the only map that showed a way out.

"Yes, a house, Max."

"Attached Garage?"

"Carport."

"Has it got a door into the house?"

"Yes."

"Okay," he said. Check the stiffs for car keys, and for God's sake, don't get prints on anything else." It seemed to me that wouldn't have mattered.

Cassy, who'd overheard everything, went to fish the bloody ring of keys from Frank's pocket and held them up over his corpse.

"Find the stiff's car," Max went on, "back it into the carport, cut off a length of garden hose, and run a siphon from the gas tank into the house. Just let it gush out onto the floor of the front room. You're going to need a timer. Check for a clock radio in the bedrooms, one with an accessory outlet in the back for a Mr. Coffee or something.

"Cassy," I said, "look for a clock radio."

"Uh, Max?"

"Dillinger?"

"What about the car, Max? The *Mulholland Rocket*. It's in the driveway with a dead battery. When I went for a new one, the men were killed. I'm taking it back to Indiana, Max. I didn't come this far to leave it here."

I expected him to hurl a storm of curses, names, and threats at me, demanding I forget the *Rocket*, do as he said, or he was abandoning me then and there. To my amazement he didn't. Instead: "How long to make it run, Dillinger?" he said, still in the flat tone.

"Ten minutes, Max," I replied, not having the slightest idea.

"Alright, Sonny," said Max, ten minutes, if it doesn't start, leave it in the carport and use its gas to blow the house. Every minute you're there, your chances of getting caught quadruple."

I wondered how he came up with that number. I imagined it accurate; with Max everything was a calculation.

Cassy returned from the bedrooms and while cautiously stepping over Frank, announced that there was no clock radio.

"No clock radio, Max," I said, but spied something on an end table. "Wait a minute, there's one of those things that turns on a light when you're not home."

"Perfect," he said. Set it to go off in an hour. Plug a lamp cord into it. Cut the cord and strip off two inches of insulation. Twist the raw wires together. Set it by the gas siphon. It'll do for an igniter. Check the fuse box, and if there are real fuses instead of breakers, jam a penny under the fuse that controls the front room circuit and screw it back in. If it's circuit breakers, forget it. It should work anyway. Got it?"

"Yeah," I said, "anything else?"

"No, wait, yes. See if there's a gas range. If there is, blow out the pilot lights, and turn on the gas for the ovens and burners full tilt when you leave. Now get to work and get out. Call this number when you're a hundred miles from there. I'll know by then what kind of arsonist you are."

"How will you know that, Max?" I said, copying the number he then gave me on my arm.

"Because I'll call the phone you're talking on genius, and it better be out of order."

"Can't I call it?"

"No genius, you can't. If you get stopped the number to that place can't be on you. Get it?"

"Right, Max," I said sheepishly and hung up.

After a quick hosing in the shower with each other alternating as lookouts, Cassy and I snatched clothes from a gorgeous antique bureau set and went to work. Paul had kept his dead wife's wardrobe as if he expected her to return. It fit Cassy well enough, and I had needed a change well before my dip into Blood Lake.

It was Cassy that found the fuse box, which it turned out, contained circuit breakers. Forget the pennies, nothing to do there. With any luck, there would be a good enough spark before the breaker was tripped. I set her to making the igniter. She stripped the lamp wires with a butcher knife from the kitchen, while I went out and installed the new battery in the *Mulholland Rocket*.

When I touched the starter button, the big inline six came to life with the same robust rumble I first heard in the service bay of Ray's station twenty-one years before when Ralph fired her up after the rebuild. I'd listened to a thousand engines start before and after hearing the *Rocket's*, yet told myself that I remembered its sound specifically, and believed I had. I left it idling, backed Frank Delmagio's new Cadillac Seville out of the way and eased the Nash into the street. Then I backed the Caddy into the carport where the Nash had been, noting that the fuel gauge showed the tank was three-quarters full.

Finding a garden hose, I got to the business of turning 743 Yucca into a bomb. It took several tries to get the siphon going, but once started it gushed gas into a puddle that I had no doubt would slosh through the whole of the house by the time the lamp cord lit it up. We set our bloody clothes near the end of the siphon. When they were saturated, we covered the dead men with them.

With that done, it was time to go.

As she stepped through the front door, Cassy and I looked at each other and then the telephone, half expecting it would ring again. It didn't. The gas puddle surged, exploring the floor for low areas. Throw rugs in its path, that first tried to drink in the flood, were drowned by it.

"The range," Cassy blurted out. Apparently she'd overheard Max's instructions.

I ran back into the kitchen, blew out the pilot lights, then turned the burner and oven dials on as far as they would twist.

Once again Cassy stepped through the front door ahead of me. I gave the door a hard tug and felt it click shut. It occurred to me that the Nash still had no license plates and there wasn't a prayer of getting legal ones now.

But the whole issue was suddenly dwarfed by an elderly couple standing beside the *Mulholland Rocket* and studying it with great and very unwelcome interest.

29. AN ENCOUNTER
WITH THE MULLIGANS

"Howdy Folks," I said approaching them with an extended hand.

The man shook it. Hopefully he didn't know Paul Phengston.

"Like my car?"

"What's your name son?" the man asked in a way that made me believe he'd once been a cop. His upper dentures dropped from the gums as he spoke. He pushed them back in place with his tongue. There was a cloudburst with every other word he spoke.

"Bobby Dardanelle," I replied, hoping he would remember the name, and not my face.

"Homer Mulligan," he said, "and I owned a Nash just like this until I stopped driving five years ago, a Nash Statesman just like this."

"I see," I said, faking interest.

The *Rocket* was an Ambassador, a higher model, but I didn't want to say anything that would prolong the conversation by as much as a syllable.

"I almost thought that this was my car, but mine was cream color," he went on through frothy spray.

"Easy to make that mistake," I said, trying not to look at the house. The *Rocket* was maroon and had probably never been anything else. Cassy was already seated in the rental car, but had yet to start it.

Just then I had the idea of us leaving it some miles from 743 Yucca and appropriating its plates.

"The Mrs. and me'd be right obliged if you'd give us a ride for old time's sake," said the old man in a tone that suggested that he had a right to expect it.

I sighed, trying to put on the most sincere, "Gee I'm so sorry but…

"expression but had a minor inspiration.

"Are you free this afternoon, Mr. Mulligan?" I asked.

He turned to (what I assumed was) his wife: a small singularly ugly woman, who nodded "yes" with acute vertical jerks.

"Yup," he replied.

We were standing downwind of the house and a slight breeze was bringing with it a scent of gasoline.

"What's your address?" I asked, "I can be by your place at two this afternoon and give you a proper ride. Just now I've got to be somewhere."

"And just where is it you gotta be?" said the woman who spoke for the first time, her tone one that presumed I owed her an answer. Now I wondered if it was she who'd once been the cop, or had both of them been cops?

I'd had enough. "That's my business," I replied.

"You smell something, mother?" said Homer to the old bitch.

"Kerosene," she replied, "it's coming from the house."

"Look," I said, "I think there's time enough for that ride you wanted after all." I stepped around them, opened the back door of the Nash, and smiled apologetically.

It was too late. Homer was marching up the driveway with sharper gait than I'd expect from a man his age. I rushed up, overtook him ten feet from the front door, and jerked him about more roughly than I'd meant to. He stumbled and was on the ground.

"You can't go in there," I said to him.

I hadn't any choice now but to force both of them into the car and drive them too far away from there to get back before the place went up. I yanked Homer half way upright and started to drag him back toward the Nash.

The old man's next words made me freeze in my tracks.

"Mother," Homer bawled out, "shoot him!"

Lifting him by his shirt, I landed a powerful jab on his jaw that may well have broken it and should have put him out cold. It didn't, but did send his dentures flying across the lawn. Homer swung back wildly at me.

Twisting his arm, I forced him between myself, and his wife. She'd already dug a shiny automatic pistol from her purse and was aiming it. With Homer between us she should have been afraid to fire.

But sweet old "Mother Mulligan" wasn't.

The shot passed clean through her husband's torso and deflected off me with a nasty sting. Homer let out a gasp. I released him, sure he was dead before he hit the ground. Cassy leaped from her car. The bitch had already fired again when Cassy reached her. That shot split the air inches from the right side of my head, crashed through the largest of the front windows and set off the gasoline.

The siphon had been working no more than twenty minutes of the hour Max wanted for it to work. I cannot imagine the inferno *that* would have produced. Twenty minutes, it seemed, was more than enough.

I was struck to the ground by a wall of heat, stucco chunks, and glass shards. The flat roof of 743 Yucca rose what looked to be a whole foot above the rest of the house, and hung suspended in the air before coming back down on the walls that had once supported it. When it landed, half of them collapsed. The hot wall of air reversed and tried to suck us into the blaze that made what was still standing, implode. Debris of every kind soared twenty feet into the air. I imagined the bodies of Frank and Paul or anything else not bolted down got at least part of that ride. Homer lay on the lawn. A section of spine dangled from a hole in the back of his shirt. Exit Homer.

I raced for Cassy. She was still struggling with Homer's thrashing spouse, who'd gotten off a third shot that threw dirt into my face. Cassy bit down on the wrist that still held the gun. The old lady howled and I landed a blow on her jaw like the one that I'd clocked her husband with. She collapsed as Cassy wrenched the gun from her.

Cassy and I looked at each other. That block of Yucca Parkway was filling with people all headed for 743, the Nash, and us. We made for our cars as the remains of the house erupted in successive puffs of fire and low roars. When I hit the starter button the *Rocket's* engine rumbled to life and I was off. Cassy followed, knocking aside a neighbor with a corner of her car. He rolled and settled in her wake on the curb. Before we reached the corner, a second fireball rose from the collapsed carport. I guessed the flame found its way to the gas tank of Frank's Cadillac. I made a left turn at the corner of Main and Yucca and started to head eastward into town, exactly where I didn't want to go. Cassy, following me, honked and pointed at the right direction. I executed a one eighty in the middle of the next block and headed west.

We were already accelerating down the entrance ramp onto I-40 when I heard the first sirens.

30. THE ROCKET LAUNCHED

We weren't followed. No one from the swarm of Police cruisers that arrived at the inferno at 743 Yucca could have connected it to the Maroon Nash or the Alamo Rental that followed it of town. We were too far from the scene by the time they got a chance to get anything from witnesses.

I was going to pull over and tell Cassy to follow close enough so as to hide—at least from the rear—the fact the *Mulholland Rocket* had no plates, but being there was none on the front either, the ruse wasn't going to last long. As it turned out, it wouldn't be necessary to tell her. Cassy rode the *Rocket's* tail indicating she understood. I wondered if we might just steal plates from a hapless car in some parking lot and retain the rental car for back up or a tow.

But ten miles east of Barstow I decided that hot plates were a risk I didn't need to take. We'd chuck the rental car and use its plates. Of course they wouldn't match the *Rocket*, but they wouldn't be hot either, for a while anyway.

Ralph's Nash cruised along at fifty-five—the national limit then— not once missing a beat. There were, of course, vibrations, which came and went while I accelerated through the gears. I'd ground them slightly just once, shifting into third, indicating worn synchronizers, which if good, would have prevented this. Small matter, any of that, the thing to watch out for was the oil pressure and the fuel pump. Pumps have been known to work fine for a short while on cars that have been catatonic but then die soon afterward. But you couldn't really watch a fuel pump, one minute it worked, and the next it didn't. I would buy an electric pump in the next major town and graft into the gas line should the need arise. I'd get extra tools too. But that ten miles had lulled me into the idea that it wouldn't be necessary. I found myself instead unconsciously counting road kill as the *Rocket* ambled east with the grace of the Goodyear Blimp. The ride you got from a 1950 Nash was exactly what you'd expect from a car shaped like a pillow. It had always seemed to me that Ralph's naming it "Rocket" was typical of his talent for either irony or misnomers, some deliberate, most of them not. Periodically, I glanced back at Cassy who would give me the high sign when she saw me looking in the rear view mirror. The ten miles from Barstow became twenty, the Mojave not changing perceptibly with the slight rise in elevation as we rolled east. A lack of events in twenty miles made one thought bubble to the surface like bath water flatulence: Who the Hell had killed Frank Delmago and Paul Phengston?

There were now three murdered men in my wake and to not believe them to be connected was to believe cows jumped over the moon, even if murder number one was over two thousand miles distant from numbers two and three, and the methods of dispatch couldn't have been less alike. Also, numbers two and three had a prime suspect: whoever drove or rode in the Mustang.

Could I have been the target? No. The killings were anything but botched. I wasn't supposed to be dead—not yet anyway.

I conjured up a short list of suspects with a total of three names: Max Morgenstern, Ralph Falonhurst, Bobby Dardanelle, or someone hired by them. The major, but not only reason for including Max, was because I'd already seen him kill not one, but two people, calmly, and with mechanical deliberateness as if he were squashing bugs that threatened his picnic. One of them was a young woman. This had been eight years before, in 1972 in my first months of architectural practice when I was uninsured and being sued. With the threat of being wiped out eating holes in my gut, I had turned to Max. Thinking back, there was little that could have been taken from me, but I'd never been sued before, and at the time, it seemed I faced a cataclysm.

I remember meeting Max for the first time since high school on a wet December Thursday in his office. I'd brought with me two cartons of folders containing documentation of every kind that if you spent enough hours digging through them, and understood something about buildings, contracts, construction documents, and specifications, they would prove that I bore no responsibility whatsoever for the fact that a couple of kids had managed to start up a bulldozer left unattended at a construction site. One of them died having been run over by the other, who'd managed to start it. As I said, the papers filled two small cartons. I had collated the material and was in the process of laying the folders out on Max's conference table explaining the particular significance of each as I went. When I'd spoken for a couple of minutes, having laid out the logic of my defense as I saw it, Max held up his hands, "Will you do me a favor, Dillinger, and stow that shit back in your car? You can burn it for all I care."

"What?"

"Stow that shit in your car. When you're done, come back here and tell me exactly what happened." I realized only then that I'd yet to do it.

"But Max…"

"I mean it, Dillinger, get that crap out of here."

I did, and having done that, told him what had happened adding that architects I'd talked to told me that a properly selected jury was my best chance for a favorable verdict. I talked for about ten minutes, and Max could not have appeared to listen more attentively. When I was done, I held out an upturned palm so as to invite a response.

"If you believe that shit, Dillinger, then let me tell you right now that you've come to the wrong place."

"What am I going to do, Max?" I said, trying to hide the fact that I was close to tears. "They're going to take everything I have." Actually that was little more than one-tenth equity in a house—which they couldn't have taken anyway—ten thousand cash, a five-year-old car, and some office furniture. Beyond that, a simple bankruptcy could wipe out any future claims. But Max didn't tell me that.

"They will if you turn this over to a jury."

"What? Why?"

"Let me ask you something, Dillinger, do you know what 'being what you are' means?"

"What I am?"

"An architect, Dillinger, do you know what being an architect means? Because I don't think you do."

I shrugged, deciding not to bother giving Max any of the usual reasons about changing the face of the earth.

"It means," he continued, "that you're what about half the adults dreamed about being at one time or another when they were kids. It also means that you're what the other half thinks they should have been as they look back, but for some non-existent reason that stopped them. And finally, it means that they will hate your guts for living their dreams. And for that, Sonny, a jury composed of those people will make you pay."

Max leaned back in his chair until the tilt threatened to spill him. He re-lighted a cigar he'd been chewing on and eased the arch of a shoeless foot to the edge of his desk. His shifting weight furthered the tilt. When I thought that he had passed the point of no return, Max stabilized himself by propping two fingers against the wall and proceeded to rock back and forth, all the while puffing on his cigar.

"I wanted to be an architect myself," he observed, "so did Hitler. They should have let him."

With a quick sweep, I took in his office and decided that it rented for about eight times the one my practice occupied. The furniture was new, save for his antique desk that probably cost what several new ones did.

"You haven't done so shabbily," I said.

"I'm a licensed extortionist, Sonny, like every other lawyer."

I started to protest, but Max only held up a hand.

"But I'm what you need to get yourself out of this mess. How much cash can you raise?"

"Eight thousand," I replied, "besides that, I've got some equity in my house that I can probably get a loan on."

Max shook his head. "Give me the eight thousand. We'll offer them four, and the other four I'll keep."

The suit was for 2.2 million dollars. Was he out of his mind? "You think they're going to settle for four thousand dollars?" I asked incredulously.

"If they don't, they'll wish they had," Max replied. "I'll call you after I arrange a meeting with them. And Dillinger, you'll do exactly as I say and keep your mouth shut."

"That's it?"

"Yes, except that when I say to keep your mouth shut, it means to keep your mouth shut. Now, who has this piece of shit got for a lawyer? I told Max her name and asked if he knew her.

Max's response was a nodding grunt. "Yes, I know her, a cute little bag of organs." He reached for a phone. "You'd probably like her if she wasn't trying to take off your flesh," he paused, "terrific afterburners."

Max set up a meeting with the plaintiff three nights later and the "cute little bag of organs" who represented him. Her name was Penny Thatcher. She could not have been more than twenty-eight and, indeed possessed among other things, terrific afterburners. It was also the first time I stood face to face with the father of the kid who'd been run over by the hot-wired bulldozer. He was a light skinned Negro. The expression he gave me said that he'd somehow convinced himself—or his lawyer had—that I had personally wired the dozer that flattened his kid. I noticed him stealing glances of Penny's posterior at about the same frequency as I was. I tried to imagine what the proper flaunting of those hindquarters would do to a jury of a dozen men. "Dead meat," I thought. I was dead meat.

We sat in Max's waiting room for some twenty minutes without exchanging a word before he called us in apologizing, almost curtly, for the condition of his conference room, where plastic drop cloths covered virtually every surface with the exception of the ceiling. Three days before, I had noted that the room looked almost freshly painted. After a moment I realized that there was no attributing this to decorating, since there was nothing not covered that could be painted. I almost said something before remembering that I'd agreed to keep my mouth shut.

We seated ourselves facing each other with Max, the last to sit down next to me.

Penny Thatcher began by saying that Max hadn't mentioned I'd be present, and that she didn't appreciate surprises.

"I'll try to remember that," Max replied.

"Now to cases," he went on, "which is something, by the way, that you don't have."

"That's not for you to decide, counselor," snapped Penny. Max stubbed out a very foul cigar that had about three-quarters of its length left to burn.

"What the hell do you expect to get out of this anyway?" he fired back. "Don't you know what kind of a pittance architects make? Where the hell do you expect my client to come up with money like that anyway, that is, if you won, which you won't? Why don't you go find some goddamn doctor to sue? And how the hell is it that you hold him—Max poked me, probably without meaning to—responsible for some imbecilic punks bent on killing themselves? What the hell was he supposed to do, take the engine out of that bulldozer and store it in a locked vault overnight?"

At the words "imbecilic punks," the dead boy's father rose angrily from his seat. Max roared at him to "sit the fuck down," which he did. Then he continued.

"But," he said finally, "we're reasonable men. My client doesn't have the time to defend himself from frivolous garbage like this, and quite frankly, the creative mind, and the only kind by the way, in my opinion, worthy of any respect at all can be seriously derailed and have its juices sapped by the trauma of an irrational lawsuit filed by people that regard the law as a mechanism for acquiring the price of cars like the Benz you drove here, Miss Thatcher."

I wondered how Max expected this rambling tirade was ever going to get Penny Thatcher and her client to settle for the four thousand he'd said they'd wish they had. Were he to deliver anything like it in a court, we would lose hands down. Max reached for the cigar he'd stubbed out a moment before.

"Done?" asked Penny Thatcher.

Max didn't answer.

"Done?" she repeated.

This time Max nodded.

"Well, counselor," she began, "creative geniuses may be all you respect, but the rest of us peons respect something called human life, especially ones with about ninety percent of their time left to live. We respect it, we cherish it, and when we see it recklessly squandered by "creative geniuses" that act as if they couldn't care less, we say they must pay. And the courts have agreed, and agreed in the form of some substantial awards, by the way."

Somewhere in her monologue, Penny Thatcher had stood up and

was prancing back and forth with something akin to the gait of a show horse. I don't think that either Max or the kid's father took his eyes off her fabulous ass for more than ten or fifteen seconds at a time. Certainly I didn't.

"Mr. July," she snapped suddenly.

"Yes Ma'am," I responded, jerking involuntarily to attention. Noting this, Max threw me an amused scowl. Penny was herself amused.

"Mr. July," she went on, "you wrote the specifications to the project in question, did you not?"

"I did."

"Are you aware Mr. July, that it's now a standard clause in architectural specifications to instruct contractors that if powered equipment, particularly heavy equipment, is to be stored on the jobsite, contractors are to see to it that either a watchman be posted on said premises and/or extraordinary measures are to be taken to see that said equipment is rendered inoperable for such time during which it is left unattended?"

"Yes," I replied. Actually I didn't know.

She reached into a Samsonite case, withdrew the set of specifications I'd written and tossed it across the table at me. It landed with a slap.

"Would you care to tell me, Mr. July, where that clause appears in these specifications, which we've established you yourself wrote for the project in question, the project at which the only son of Mr. Earl Fowler died—and died because a six-and-a-half ton piece of equipment was left in such condition that it took no more than an unbent paper clip to shunt its ignition and make it fully operable?"

I was mute. I didn't think that lawyers laid out their whole line of attack prior to a trial, but it may have meant she considered this one so indestructible that she didn't believe that Max could figure any way to put a hole in it. On top of that, she might have another entirely different one in reserve. Either way, Max notwithstanding, I imagined myself dead meat. I looked down and back at her face. It bore a self-righteous arrogance that was both intimidating and rather flattering. For a moment we stared at each other before she looked away as if to say she was done with me.

"Counselor?" she said to Max, her tone of voice that of someone who had already won.

"Four thousand dollars," Max declared, his tone one of not being open to negotiation.

"What?" Penny's face bore an incredulous rage once it was apparent that this was our offer to settle the case.

"We can settle this tonight," Max said as if he expected them to go for it.

"Four thousand dollars!" Penny's voice bordered on a shriek. She appeared fighting the urge to leap across the table and attack Max, or me, or anybody, who dared to insult her with such an offer. Max might as well have just requested a two-dollar blow job. I turned to him. He was devouring every second of it like a chocolate bonbon.

"You!" Penny barked at Max. "You think you're a goddamn comedian don't you?"

"I guess I know a joke when I see one," he replied. "Want to know what my idea of a joke is?"

Penny didn't answer, but Max went on as if she had: "My idea of a joke is a twenty-eight-year-old slut that got her law degree by sucking the penises of every law school Professor in New Haven, won a few cases because she knows how to strut an ass that God meant to be put on some nigger bitch, and now thinks she can come into my office and dictate terms to me. Earl Fowler rose and put one foot on the table and was transferring his weight so as to lunge across it and go to work on Max.

"Sit down Boy!" Max commanded him. The words struck as if they had physical mass.

"Not now, Earl," Penny almost pleaded, "please." With both arms, she coaxed him off the table and back into his chair. His glare at us told me that Max and I were at that moment the embodiment of three hundred years of every indignity blacks had suffered from beatings to rape and murder.

I wondered why Max had arranged for a meeting at all. The whole premise that he could settle this lawsuit for four thousand dollars was shone to be as preposterous as when he'd first mentioned the figure to me. Was it just great sport for him to deliberately antagonize the opposition? Whatever strategy could there be to that? Had he one at all? He couldn't have.

If the idea was to goad her into a physical assault, Penny didn't rise to the bait, in fact, she said nothing at all as she assembled the papers she'd set out in a stack, retrieved my spec book from in front of me, and—as if there were no one else in the room, not even her client— snapped shut her case and got up to go. I hadn't a doubt in the world that she was pledging to herself to nail me if it was the last thing she ever did. But it wouldn't be.

Penny could not resist breaking her silence for a parting shot. I could hardly have blamed her. Glaring at Max, she smiled, "well, it's been a pleasure, counselor, and by the way, now I know why they call you 'The Troll.'"

When Penny reached the conference room door she found it locked. She probed the escutcheon plate for a release. Finding none, she did not turn around right away. I imagined she was deciding what degree of rage to display when she did turn about and demand the remote lock release be tripped.

I was for once, right. And again the anger flattered her features, but only for an instant before she broke into the terrified realization that calling Max a 'troll' was the worst mistake she'd ever made in a very short life. I had never seen a person die before, and indeed the experience was so oddly surreal, that for several seconds I thought that Penny and Max must be playing a colossal prank on me.

They weren't.

The gun roared and Penny's green suit just below her bosom erupted in a crimson splash as the force of the bullet threw her body against the plywood sheet. Her skull slammed into it with a crushing thump. I saw her blink once on her way to the floor where she collapsed into the corpse-like form of the dead. Though I couldn't be sure because the table obscured my view, I believe that once on the floor, she never gave so much as a twitch.

Earl Fowler must have watched with the same disbelief as my own, because when we looked at each other, I was sure that his expression was akin to the one I wore. We faced each other, jaws agape. It took an instant for him to realize that what he had just witnessed had in fact sealed his own fate. When he did realize it, Earl rose, raced for the same door Penny had, seized the handle and yanked futilely at it. Of course, it remained bolted fast. His feet wrestled with Penny's body as he tried to keep his balance. Finally, he turned around, his face as white as I ever saw a black man's get.

Max was by now aiming his gun directly at it. "Boy," said Max, "give my regards to your son," and calmly pulled the trigger. The bullet destroyed the bridge of Earl's nose before charging through his brain, which splashed in a foot wide circle on the plastic drop cloth backed by the plywood. Earl stood there as if the gore had acted as some kind of adhesive that held him erect. Then he began to sink. Just as the man's chest slid beneath his line of sight, Max pumped a second slug into it. Earl, who was probably already dead, gave but a mild jerk backward and a groan before he was on the floor, his body draping Penny's much like a shawl.

I clasped my mouth, certain that a great rush of vomit was on its way, and discovered that none was. I turned back to face Max. He sat impassively. Had the two dead people arisen and with Max howling hysterically, I would have been less shocked, than at the nonchalance with which my lawyer selected his next words:

"Dillinger," he said, "I believe you owe me eight thousand dollars; I advise and expect prompt payment. He motioned at the bodies adding, "Case closed." As he spoke, Max depressed an unseen button beneath the lip of the table and a click could be heard from the door's lock. Two gorilla like men in janitorial kaki entered the room and a moment later carried a corpse apiece out over his right shoulder. A second pair of men followed, and with marvelous efficiency, rolled and folded the drop cloths into neat bundles. Behind the place where Max had shot both Penny and Earl, was a four by eight sheet of one-inch thick plywood that had absorbed the slugs that had killed them. There was but one plywood sheet in the room. Max had anticipated exactly where they'd be when he shot them.

"Burn that," said Max to a short, powerfully built man who smiled pleasantly. The scent of gunpowder, that had at first been so strong as to burn my eyes and nostrils, was already beginning to dissipate.

I got up. "I suppose they know what to do with their cars," I said, sickened and amazed at how easily I'd adapted to what I'd just witnessed. Max responded with a frowning nod as if my comment impugned his professionalism. "Can I go?" Just seeing what Max was capable of had triggered this request for permission, something I'd done only a few times, and silently cursed myself for what amounted to sucking up to the class bully who's just done an outrage to somebody else that could have been me.

Max noted this and with no small amusement. "Dillinger," he said, "wherever that dead boy is now, he's going to need a father. A boy should have a father to keep him out of trouble. Now he has one again. This time the old man can't go off and start six new families. And as you ought to know, Negros are not an endangered species, nor are arrogant bitches, even ones with great afterburners." Max began a laugh that he broke off abruptly. One of his gorillas stood in the doorway holding the Samsonite case that contained the legal briefs Penny was going to nail me with. "Give that to my friend here," said Max. The gorilla laid the case on the table in front of me. "See that you get rid of that," said my lawyer. Apparently he hadn't the slightest worry about me not reducing it to its molecules.

"You'd better," I said, and got up realizing he never meant for me to leave with it.

"All right, Dillinger," Max replied, unable to conceal his amusement.

Outside, I stared at the two empty spaces in the parking lot where Penny and Earl's cars had been parked. The gorillas were already gone with their load of gore. In an hour or less, nothing but ash and melted plastic would be left of either of the corpses or what they were wrapped in. I shuddered at the thought of how I'd hold up under a grilling by the police over their disappearance. By some mechanism, Max would see to it that there never was one. I paid him the next morning with a cashier's check delivered by messenger and swore I'd never so much as think of using Max Morgenstern again. I'd try if possible to forget his name. Eight years later, after being raped at the State Prison in Huntsville night and day for a week, I reconsidered.

The *Mulholland Rocket* ambled East on I-40. Great green overhead signs that announced 'Needles, California' came and went along with Needles itself. I'd have refueled there only if I needed to, but I didn't. More signs said thirty miles from Kingman, then it was twenty five. In her Alamo rental, Cassy continued to hug the *Rocket's* rear, still masking the absence of a license plate. My watch said we were some two-and-one-half-hours out of Barstow. The idea of the state line offering the kind of jurisdictional safety it once did for outlaws was about as stupid as I had been for the last several miles. A scene of sudden horror, hidden until now, greeted me as I topped the last rise in California and began a gentle quarter mile slope down to the Arizona border where Khaki figures with side arms mulled about between four lanes of stopped cars. I should have planned a strategy for this about ten miles back, but my mind had been too busy with reminisces about Max. The plateless *Rocket* was in plain sight of the State Troopers or Agriculture Cops and it was too late to snatch the ones off Cassy's car and abandon it. One of the khaki clad men was pointing at the *Rocket*.

Wanted for child molestation, assault, and suspicion of murder in three States, I was about to be busted by the dauntless diligence of the Arizona fruit and bug cops. I downshifted so as to allow the *Rocket's* engine to serve as its brake, disengaging it fifty yards from the roadblock. And I had been correct about where the khaki man was pointing. He walked toward me in a brisk, deliberate cadence, his finger aimed at the bumper of the Nash. In his other hand was a transceiver with its chrome aerial extended.

He'd begun a downward flagging motion at me as if to say 'halt' when a blast of air horns from my left cracked through the *Rocket's* interior like a bullwhip. I turned, expecting the great steel wall of a semi-trailer truck to be about three feet from my face. There was a truck. But it wasn't a semi at all, just an oversized pick up on which some asshole had hung air horns. One look at the driver's face told me that he had to be that asshole. It was a face that said there wasn't a thing you could possibly like about its owner, the kind of face from which venom drips like drool.

It was a face that hated anything that it looked at for more than five seconds and I had just passed goal. Another blast of the air horns crashed through the *Rocket* with enough force to rumple the headliner. The face screwed itself into a mask so tight that it had to ratchet back just to swear at me, which it proceeded to do while a finger of the driver's right hand circled in tight angry orbits. I hadn't the slightest idea of what he wanted until finally, he floored the pickup so as to force his way in front of me.

That was what it was all about, a place in line. The same issue as when somebody cuts in front of you with a shopping cart at a supermarket. When the truck stormed by to cut within inches of the *Rocket's* fender, I saw it was bumper-to-bumper scars from exactly what I'd just avoided. The pickup's driver likely saw life as a war and every other being that breathed an enemy soldier to be humbled or killed outright. Once ahead of me, he cut the truck's ignition and quickly switched it on again so as to make for an earsplitting backfire that hurled soot at my windshield. With that, he nosed up to the khaki man in jerks that made what was left of his tires bark and shriek against the pavement. Waiving the car ahead of him through, the cop ushering my lane of cars walked to the pickup's window and, to my great relief, turned out to be the one who'd just been so interested in the plateless *Mulholland Rocket*.

I couldn't, of course, hear what was said, but the cop's gestures seemed those of a professional that expected no particular trouble. A few seconds later voices rose to near shouts, although all I could make out was: "Sir, will you please exit the vehicle?" The driver's left arm then extended through the window, its index finger poking at the cop's face. That was enough.

The khaki man yanked open the door, seized the arm, and in a single motion hauled the ape-sized driver out and threw him on the ground. A second Khaki yelled into the transceiver and within seconds four more were racing for the pickup. I glanced into the rear view mirror where Cassy gestured to me with upturned hands so as to say, "What?" I shook my head and refocused to what was ahead of me. There were now six of the Khakis standing over this prone gorilla—he was gigantic—though not one had his gun drawn, the first thing I would have done. They must have thought their numbers were enough to quell any ideas the ape might have had about resisting.

Wrong guess.

The prone figure at once erupted into a whirling juggernaut of kicks and thrusts, not one of which missed a head, torso, or groin. Among the first things to go flying was the transceiver which landed abreast of my driver's window to shatter on the pavement as if glass. The next things to take it were the cops themselves. One of the blows alone was enough to send two khakis staggering backwards to crash against the nose of the *Rocket* with the force necessary to dent it before they passed out. They were the lucky ones. Lucky, because being unconscious, they wouldn't have to explain later why they'd left their comrades to absorb any more of the ape's work which consisted of among other things, jaw smashing punches and nut crushing kicks. Had it been timed, the whole performance wouldn't have been three quarters of a minute. Only in the aftermath did one of the prostrate cops reach for his sidearm. He looked too dazed to know what to do with it. Before he could begin pointing, the ape was at him, stomping the gun hand and most of its unfortunate appendage to a gelatinous, branch-like mass of red and pink. A final kick sent the pistol airborne to discharge upon landing and blow out the side window of a Chevy two lanes away. For a moment, I thought he'd saved the worst for last: me. With the *Rocket* blocked by the pickup in front, and Cassy's rental in the rear, he aimed the glare I'd seen a minute before back at me and began an almost casual gait toward the *Rocket*. I spun, and frantically motioned Cassy to back up and allow me room to escape. Instantly she understood this and did just that. I had the *Rocket* in reverse, and was revving its engine so as to burst forward from the trap and run over the ape if I had to. But the Ape's face was suddenly and incredibly drained of belligerence. He turned about, as if obeying some radio signal from God, got into his truck, and with a blast of burnt rubber, roared off as if at a drag strip. Whatever powered that truck was more than equal to the job.

A minute later, two state troopers in cruisers lit out after him with what I am sure was no real desire to overtake. It took the honking of the car behind Cassy to make me realize that the border was now unmanned and I could enter Arizona unmolested, which of course I did, stealthy inching the Nash past the smashed up khakis the ape had left in his wake. Only one of the six had begun to stir as I rolled passed. A last look in my rear view mirror as I accelerated into Arizona told me that no one in any of the cars that followed me had stopped to assist the stricken officers. Far ahead on a distant rise, I caught a last glimpse of the chase. If anything, it looked like the pickup was stretching its lead. I wondered how long it would be before there were roadblocks and helicopters, deciding, that so long as I wasn't stopped, I couldn't have cared less. Cassy hugged the *Rocket*'s tail until we were at least five miles from the state line and I signaled her to pull off to the shoulder. We got out. The look she gave me must have mirrored the one she got. I glanced at my watch. Was it really possible that the morning that had begun in the dining room of *Delmagio's* still had a whole eighteen minutes to go before noon bells somewhere declared it over? We embraced each other in a quiet disbelief beside the mound like shape of the *Mulholland Rocket*, a hot spring Arizona sun beating down on it all.

"Sonny," Cassy asked, "did it all really happen?"

"Yes, Cassy, it sure as hell did," I said, and then, as if it were necessary, rattled off the morning's tally: Three men killed, one of them shot dead while in my arms by his own wife, eight more beaten to within an inch of their lives, an exploding house, a fantastic story of a stolen car, and now the car itself, stolen all over again—this time by me.

Finally, I added: "And don't think it's even started," not sure myself what "it" was. I knew that somewhere Bobby Dardanelle, either personally or by proxy, was going to play his hand. Whether or not Max had yet to meddle was an open question.

As if on cue, a swarm of six state police cruisers, sirens wailing full tilt, hurled past us at what looked like Mach One. Whoever the ape in the pickup was, I hoped for their sake that they'd never catch him. Probably they hoped so too.

There was no time for more rehashing. We were running a fresh risk for each second we remained at the side of the road. All I needed now was some well-meaning state trooper stopping to render assistance and note the *Rocket's* lack of plates to land me in prison for good that very day.

Still, all things considered, my luck had been just short of incredible. With no more than five percent of the trip behind me, I was starting to count the hundred thousand and suddenly slapped myself. At that, Cassy gave me a quizzical look.

"Cassy," I said, "we're going to have to lift the plates from your car and leave it behind the next abandoned building, best if it's way back from the road. You'll call and report the car stolen when we get to Michigan City. Let's get going and honk if you spot something you think I missed."

"Sonny," she said as we separated.

"Yes?"

"These last four days…have been the best ones I've ever lived. Whatever happens now, I want you to know that."

"For me too," I replied, sure it was what she wanted to hear. I'd read somewhere how some women had a death wish and hoped to share their end with some hapless idiot they thought they were in love with. Cassy didn't seem to be the type, but who knew?

"For me too!" Jesus, I might have become a bigger liar than Ralph.

We rolled east. It was time to think navigation. I'd actually started to do this on the plane to LA, but having never expected to have gotten this far this fast, I had put the thought aside in favor of complementary drinks. Cassy carried a Rand McNally in her gear bag that we'd bought in Indianapolis.

It was a matter of making Michigan City on the route "they" would least expect. And the one we were on hardly qualified as that. I was headed down that group of interstates that had all but replaced Route 66, although here and there you drove sections of the original road. Were I to stay on it, I needed no map at all to get to Chicago; signs even this far west told you where to turn or go straight. One of them had just announced "Chicago 1922;" the mileage was implied. From Chicago, Michigan City, and my hundred thousand was but sixty miles further east on I-90. The most glaring glitch at this point was that the route I was on ran straight across the Texas Panhandle, One-hundred-eighty miles through a state I never wanted to so much as go near for the rest of my life.

There were alternates. The first of which was to swing north at Albuquerque and up through Raton Pass to La Junta, Colorado. From there the road due east virtually followed the Amtrak route past Hutchinson, Newton, and Kansas City. From there…

Braaaaap!

I bolted slightly at the sound of Cassy's horn, recovered, and glanced at the rear view mirror. She was pointing to the right where an abandoned motel stood about a quarter mile south of the highway. Apparently the road's rerouting north by just that much was enough to sever the umbilical cord that kept it in business. I imagined we'd probably pass dozens of others like it. Again we pit stopped on the shoulder. Except for a gully you couldn't get past without all-wheel drive and monster tires, this was exactly what I'd had in mind as a place to stash Cassy's rental car. She looked embarrassed at having missed the detail that really couldn't be seen from the highway. "Nice try, girl," I said smiling. We drove on and found what we were looking for about three more miles to the East, an abandoned Texaco station behind which the *Mulholland Rocket* got its first, albeit less than legal, license plates in a number of years. I wondered how long it would be before they found the rental we would later report as stolen.

With us both seated in the *Rocket*, I asked Cassy if she wanted to try a nap. We were invisible from the Highway and I was exhausted.

"No," she snapped with sharpness that both energized and shamed me. She was right. We had to put as many miles behind us as we could. The events of the morning, while unbelievable, had given us an advantage we didn't dare throw away. Our pursuit of the *Mulholland Rocket* was still an hour less than one day old. Bobby, or his proxies, would have had less than a day to mobilize and couldn't possibly know we'd come this far.

But if that was so, who had killed Frank and Paul? I desperately wanted to rule out Max. He didn't have a motive I could fathom. And he'd said he was in Houston. Maybe he actually was.

The nasty puzzle flew in the face of all the rosy logic that said I was winning the game, unless the murders had nothing to do with me, the *Rocket*, or anything else I knew about. From what I could see of Frank Delmagio, he might well have his share of people that wanted him dead with husbands of his bedmates heading the list. As for Paul Phengston: wrong place, wrong time? Maybe.

But connected or not, the ancient Nash and its driver were the first things people back in Barstow would remember.

"You're right," I said, touching the starter. The Nash rumbled to life. "Do you think we should call Ralph?"

Cassy looked at me as if I'd lost my mind. "No, what the hell for?" she snapped. The distinct anger in her voice surprised me.

I nodded without answering, having forgotten that the building was abandoned and there wasn't a phone there anyway. I'd already made up my mind to tell Ralph that I'd spent his whole ten thousand buying the *Rocket* just for the pleasure of lying to him. Only after all was settled, would I mention that the car's most recent "owner" was a murdered man and Ralph had best forget any sentimental crap about keeping it.

When we were just half way back to the road, we determined that no car could be seen behind the station's ruins. Heading East, I kept us in the right lane and held the *Rocket* at just over fifty. Though widely ignored, fifty-five was still the national speed limit. An hour and three quarters later we exited at the first of three turnoffs leading into Kingman and gassed up miles short of the city.

There was, thankfully, an attached convenience mart that also carried road accessories. Cassy shopped for provisions while I bought two five gallon gas cans that I'd forgotten to buy at the NAPA store, and filled them. Any and all stops carried a risk, so the option of reserve fuel was one I definitely wanted. I'd have bought and filled five cans, but that would be something likely remembered. The store didn't have radios for sale, and offering to buy the clerk's seemed to carry the risk of an inquiry as well. The Nash's radio hadn't worked even when Ralph owned it. It would have been nice to know what was being said in our wake about what happened on Yucca Parkway, though the thought of police alerts was something I kept trying to shut from my mind.

A medium-sized man in a car one lane away had not taken his gaze off the Nash since pulling up. He had the look of a cop or an ex-cop. I shuddered at the idea of nostalgia about to strike again. Cassy was stowing provisions into the back seat when he got out and began walking toward us. Suddenly, a vulturesque female barked out a storm of words from the passenger window of his car. He spun about after flashing me thumbs up. Bless that bitch. As he reversed course, his trouser rode up high enough to reveal that the left leg was prosthetic. I lurched slightly when Cassy closed the door. I didn't notice she'd finished loading and had gotten in. "Roll," she said, and roll we did.

Maps show one hundred thirty five miles from Kingman to Flagstaff Arizona that, with strict obedience to the double nickel, translates to two hours and twenty-seven minutes. What maps don't consider are thirty year old Nash Airflites, underpowered even when new, going most of that uphill highway in second before reaching that plateau in the San Francisco Mountains where Flagstaff is perched at just over seven thousand feet. I deemed it a major victory doing it in four hours. I'm told, and can confirm from glancing snippets, it's some of the most beautiful country in all of the American West, which makes it among the best scenery anywhere. But when I wasn't watching the asphalt, the road signs, or overheating threats from the Nash's instrument cluster, I kept seeing images of Frank and Paul with occasional bursts of Jerret Traf, the Ranger sent to help me, who wound up greasing the bottom of the Eleventh Street Train.

I took the second of four exits into Flagstaff, again stopping well outside of the city itself. This time it was at a gas stop, road store, and McDonalds grafted together in collage so grotesque that it could well induce nausea on whoever looked at it too long. I'd read in a book once that Road Architecture was a planned visual assault that if really good, was memorable for having left gastric trauma. This then, was the work of a maestro. An agitator I didn't know I had begun to rotate deep within me.

"Something wrong?" Cassy asked.

I pointed at the building.

"Interesting," she said, adding, "cool." Then: "I've got some cancellations to call in, you know, patients I can't see this week."

I nodded, setting the gas pump to dispense regular, and wondering if it contained the lead that the Nash needed to keep its valves from eventually burning. Most fuel sold in 1980 still contained lead or it said otherwise somewhere. I noticed it was a lot colder in Flagstaff. A time/temp sign read thirty-six degrees. Western temperatures are much moderated by dryness, which means that cold can sneak up on you, whereas the Great Lakes kind can carry a nasty bite even at well above fifty. The darkness that would descend in an hour would easily subtract twenty degrees. That meant buying blankets or sleeping bags for a night in the Nash after finding secluded parking where a helpful cop wouldn't be tapping on your window at three AM…and after doing his good-Samaritan thing, would check the license plates.

Across the road, and half a mile towards town, there glowed green neon letters that spelled out 'MOTEL.' I wondered how much greater the risk was staying there if we parked the *Rocket* in the back. And there would be television to tell about any alerts out for us, or worse, a description of the car whereupon we'd flee. It was easy to make the case for the room versus a night in the Nash…and we had a ton of money.

I went inside and saw Cassy at the phone in a far corner behind several aisles of grocery racks. I paid, and headed back to the *Rocket*, hoping she would remember we'd agreed to keep our stops short ones. I hadn't checked the oil since Barstow, and that was stupidity all by itself. I hoisted the hood and was amazed that the dipstick still read full. A double check confirmed this. I wondered if Blake's machine works that had built that engine twenty-two years before was still in business and I hoped they were. This world needed people like them or my late boss Ray, much more than it ever did people like Ralph, Max, or myself for that matter. I lowered the hood and its latch gave the sharp metallic clack of something made before the great plastic onslaught had gripped civilization.

"A fifty, right?" came a voice from directly behind me. It would take most of a hundred eighty degree turn to view its owner, not that I especially wanted to, but I had a terrible vision of the prosthetic man from the gas stop at Kingman, which all the arithmetic said was impossible. His car was a modern one that should have put him at least two hours further east of us unless he'd stopped for a leisurely lunch or dalliance with the hag I'd seem in the passenger window at Kingman. And that was if he'd been going east at all.

I spun about to lock eyes with the face I least wanted to, all the reasons for this being impossible notwithstanding. Shit, and double and triple shit. He was Mr. Kingman alright or Homer Mulligan minus twenty-five years, plus the same number of pounds, all muscle but for the plastic leg or whatever it was made of and the same most unwelcome interest in the *Mulholland Rocket*. The face, including the dentures, could have been borrowed from Mulligan, except Mulligan's teeth might have been soaked a few times in the last decade. His hadn't, so what he sprayed through them carried a distinct tint, not to mention a deadly stench.

"Man," said he, slapping a vertical face of the hood, "I screwed so much great crack in these pieces of shit you wouldn't believe it." I wouldn't have believed it either, though it was possible that he'd screwed a large number of pieces of shit in old Nashes that deserved better. The pieces of shit certainly did.

"Wanna trade?" he asked, launching a shower of spit meteors. This surprised me; the man was driving a two-year-old Pontiac worth at least four times what the *Rocket* was.

"Can't," I replied, "Not my car."

"I mean't bitches," he said. "I seen the doll you got with you."

"She's my wife," I replied.

"I don't mind," he fired back, "course mine's on the rag now, in fact she's in the shitter screwing in a fresh cunt cork. But if you can get past that, she'll crawl under you like a reptile, you know what I'm say'n?"

"I think so, but no thanks," I replied, quite sure he wasn't kidding about the reptile part. I turned about and headed inside.

"Could sweeten that with some cash," he called after me and farted. I paid for the gas and made for the phone where I'd spotted Cassy.

I found her still facing the wall and was gesturing with emphatic arcs of her free arm, indicating this was no casual call.

"C'mon, girl," I said, "We're either out of here now or we've got problems." She froze, clapped a hand over the mouthpiece, and slammed the handset on the hook so hard it amazed me that it didn't break. When she turned around her quite lovely face was white as wonder bread. "Jesus Christ," she snapped, "What the hell are you doing here?"

"I'll explain later." But it was Cassy that owed the explanation. "There's a very ugly guy out there that wants to trade for your butt. And he likes the car too by the way. We're out of here."

I grabbed her forearm and we made for the door and gas pumps in a forced march. I expected the man from Kingman to be waiting for us, with a new offer or possibly a threat, although I couldn't imagine what that would be. But the man and his Pontiac were gone and I assumed the hag I'd seen in Kingman was too. I pulled in and exhaled some great lungfulls. We got back into the *Rocket*.

"There's a motel down the road," I said, pointing at the glowing neon, "I'd like to go farther, but it'll be dark before we make Winslow. I think we're as safe here as anywhere. We'll park in the back. Okay?" Cassy nodded as if the words had been snatched from her mouth. We were just realizing how exhausted we both were. This motel was—I noted the irony—called the 'Super Chief,' although decades older than, and doubtless unconnected with, its namesake in Barstow. I stayed in the car while Cassy registered. Paying cash meant that only minimum identification was required. She listed me as David Rappaport, a brother, whom she told me I'd once actually met.

Just across road from the Super Chief was a line of puke-green stucco buildings with fake log projections, one of which advertised western wear. Cassy headed for it telling me to take the first shower. She'd shop for both of us having remembered my sizes from her uncle's store. We were each more than a little sick at having to wear garments borrowed from the dead Phengstons, not to mention that they were evidence.

Once in the room, I plunge dove into the bed and had my first fresh thought in hours. It was as welcome as a migraine. I should call Max. It wasn't that I wanted to, but I'd said I'd call him a couple of hours out of Barstow, and Max took such delinquencies as betrayals. I dialed the number he'd given me in Paul Phengstston's house. Max answered on the first ring.

"Yeah, Dillinger," said Max as if we'd spoken a moment before. If he was mad, his tone didn't hint at it. If anything, he sounded bored.

"I'm in Flagstaff, Max," I said. "We're staying the night here."

"I know that," he replied and I hadn't a doubt in the world that he did. He might damn well be able to rattle off the number of our room that I'd already forgotten. After Barstow, nothing about Max could surprise me. I imagined that there wasn't a government on earth that could track people like Max could.

I started to tell him about the inferno in Barstow. He cut me off.

"That's old shit, Dillinger," he said.

"It'll make the national news once tonight, but speculation is that it's a mob hit. One of those stiffs was Frank Delmagio, a very bad boy. Nobody's said anything about an old car yet, much less a Nash. Give me something new."

I told Max about the Mulligans still grinning at the thought of him calling anybody a very bad boy. Of course mentioning the Mulligans wasn't necessary either.

"The old man died," Max said, but I could have told him that. "The wife was too hysterical to remember anything besides shooting him. There's no alert out, you're clear at least for now on that score. Give me something new."

I mentioned the brawl at the State line, which Max called irrelevant. "You're past that, and halfway through fucking Arizona, Dillinger. You should have made Winslow tonight." I wanted to argue, but didn't.

"What's going on now?" he asked through what sounded like a yawn.

I told him about encountering the same scumbag at gas stops in Kingman and now Flagstaff. This, I thought, might interest him at least slightly. It didn't. Finally, I mentioned Cassy's sudden start when I broke into her phone call.

"Um hmm," said Max.

"You think I should press her about it?"

"Um hmm," said Max.

"You mean yes, Max?"

"Um hmm, as in 'yes you should genius,'" he replied as if my asking that placed me at the remedial third grade level. "Anything else, Rocket Man?"

"No, Max, nothing that I can think of," I said, silently cursing myself for sounding like, if not thinking like, somebody that worked for him. The man's capacity for control was astounding. It seemed to me as if I'd somehow reduced myself, and all by myself, to awaiting instructions.

"Get a good night's sleep, Dillinger," said Max almost benignly, adding: "You're going to need it."

Coming from Max Morganstern, the last statement was, for all intents and purposes, a threat I could take to the bank. He hung up without waiting for a goodbye. I slammed up the receiver, showered, and lay naked on the bed waiting for Cassy to return with our new clothes, and wondered about the best way to dispose of the old ones we'd borrowed from the dead Phengstons.

Cassy didn't have to be told to keep her public exposure brief. We both knew that we should remain as unseen as possible. She was back in half an hour with a pair of shopping bags one of which contained two changes of outer clothing and six sets of underwear because they'd been packaged that way. I thought Cassy a rare woman indeed being able to discipline her clothes shopping to one bag full for each of us.

"They had some great looking outfits," she said as I tried out one of two identical pair of denim trousers. "I bought the blandest stuff they had. We're too attractive as it is. No point in letting that be our undoing." I had to agree, but for someone vain, I cared little for clothes. My wife had taken on the role of outfitting me and I'd taken to wearing black almost exclusively even during summers in Houston.

It was time to bring up the nasty business of her phone call and who it was that should not have heard my voice.

"Cassy," I said, "who were you on the phone with back there when I broke in?"

Her expression told me that her answer would be true enough, but not one I'd like. "A man," she replied.

"Sorry girl," I said, "you'll have to narrow it farther than half the earth's population."

Cassy swallowed, and angled her head downward and away as she spoke, "A man that feels about me the same way you do about Randy Jones. And like you Addison, he can be a little dangerous. It might not have occurred to you that you don't have a monopoly on obsessive love."

"Clifford Fitch?" I asked realizing before I even gotten it all out, that it was a stupid guess.

Cassy shook her head, "but since you mentioned it, the poor bastard deserves better friends than either of us."

A wave of shame briefly cracked through me like a whip and was gone. "What was it you once said Cassy, about everybody using everybody? I guess it's true enough."

"Especially true," she said, "when your face looks like the surface of the moon. Those people seem to get used a lot more than the rest of us, don't they?"

"I need to take a shower," she said after a long pause, and smiled as if the taste from some bad medicine had passed. "Do me a favor, Sonny," she said stepping into the bathroom, "take off the pants, and don't put on anything else, I'm sure it'll all fit. There's something for you in the other bag. I walked over to it, reached in, and felt the cardboard handle of a six-pack. Hoisting it from the bag I stared with mild surprise at the dark bottles of PBR.

This time, Cassy and I were spent after twenty minutes in bed. Two bottles of PBR sat opened but ten percent drunk on their respective nightstands when we lapsed into sleep. It was our third night in bed together and we'd come a long way towards a routine. Though she'd yet to mention it, Cassy must have known by now that I snorted like a road grader.

And for the first time in about a year I had what I'd come to call an "Alice Dream." I'd labeled it that for cataloging in my imponderable junkyard that passed as a mind. It was one of the few instances where I sometimes called Alice "Randy," the name that everybody else used.

But for its principal and only players, Alice and me, it was never exactly the same. Nor did it contain that stretching and shrinking of time and distance that allowed events like the Battle of Gettysburg to be fought on the drain board of a kitchen sink. Nothing in it was unlike the size and shape of things I knew when awake.

"Alice Dreams" might begin on a street, in a church, a mall, the parlor of the second floor flat on Avalon Court, the South Shore station on Eleventh Street, places where we'd actually been together, or ones I'd never been to before. Suddenly, or just as often gradually, I'd realize that I'd entered the physical space where she existed. And with that, the world became one of sacred objects any of which might be ones Alice touched, would touch, or might have touched. Trees, fireplugs, car bumpers, chairs, even toilet seats were henceforth "Alice things." I wanted to rip each of them from their moorings and cart them off for enshrinement.

It might have been because Alice and I had never exchanged gifts of any kind and for that reason I saved the clothes I'd worn on our dates, some of which still fit. Items like receipts from twenty years before, the ink, now bleached to invisibility, still languished among things I'd have otherwise thrown out, but never did.

Sometimes, I wouldn't see Alice at all. If she appeared, it was in the very last part, possibly because she'd always be late when I'd gone to pick her up. I can't remember her making an entrance. Only suddenly,

I was staring at the face of the girl I'd fallen in love with that March afternoon with the same disbelief as I had at the reunion or Colin's funeral, my mind numbed by the realization that it was the genuine Alice. Looking slightly upward, the face I'd so longed to caress wore the irritated expression that demanded to know why I'd once again invaded her life. And I'd answer the unasked the same way I had all the other times: "Because I'll love you forever Alice Miranda Jones. I'll love you forever, and no one else could, or will ever, as I do."

31. A CONTINENTAL BREAKFAST

I slept in bursts through most of the night and as usual Alice occurred in the last of them. When I broke into irrevocable consciousness, Cassy was already up and told me she had been up for just over an hour. It was twenty minutes after seven. I wondered if we hurried, we might make it to the car without a harassment call from Max. I'd made no commitment to call him the previous evening, and barring trouble, could do with a day void of his particular brand of brilliance.

The phone rang.

Cassy and I gave each other a look of resignation as I picked up the receiver.

"This is the office," said a voice I could only imagine belonged to a squirrel in a cartoon. "We are serving a continental breakfast in the office until nine AM."

"Really?" I replied, "I've never eaten a continent. What do they taste like?" The squirrel hung up hard.

"You're in a swell mood," said Cassy. "Sounds like today is going to be a ton of laughs." She started to gather our gear. I looked around and, besides Ralph's money, couldn't remember taking anything else from the car. We poured the undrunk PBRs down the sink.

I got up and started to dress myself from Cassy's self-described selection of bland western wear. She pulled two plastic trash bags from a tear off roll and filled them with the Phengston's clothes. Cassy was staring at me the whole time I dressed. I was pretty sure of the look.

"What is it you're deciding whether or not to ask me?"

"It's that obvious?"

"Um hum."

"Do you think you'll ever get married again, Sonny?"

I sighed, and offered a rueful half smile. The last thing I needed now was a marriage proposal, no matter how indirect.

"Look, Cassy Rapaport," I said, deciding that to do anything but slam dunk this notion while still embryonic was cruel. "I think you're one hell of an attractive girl, but I've…"

She cut me off with a burst of wild laughter.

"Addison July, you poor, vain, son of a bitch."

"What?"

"Addison July, you really are a poor, vain, son of a bitch, aren't you? You think every girl in the world except Randy wants to marry you?"

"That's not what this is about?"

"No Addison July, you poor, vain, son of a bitch, it certainly isn't."

"Then what?" She had now called me a poor vain son of a bitch three times and I was not about to let her make it four.

"I just wanted to tell you that if you ever do get married again, your wife better get used to the idea of your telling Alice in your sleep that you'll love her forever."

"I did that?"

Cassy nodded with a sardonic smile.

"More than once?"

"I stopped counting at seven. What your wife did was rotten enough, but I thought you should at least know the reason. If it were me, I'd have taken a blunt object to you."

We didn't say anything else while each of us surveyed the room another time for forgotten items. There weren't any. I wondered what the best way was for us to dispose of the two bags stuffed with the dead people's clothes that I suddenly had a great compulsion to be rid of. I could do without any more revelations from Cassy for the rest of that day as well. Were there anything other than what was in the bags, I'd have just stuffed them into a large green Dumpster two spaces away from where the *Rocket* was parked. Now doing so came with the worry that the motel's manager might well go through anything I discarded, looking for ways to get even for my wise guy brilliance. The clothes would be in the hands of the police by ten AM and an alert for us out by eleven; never mind that they were nothing but the same dirty laundry everyone on a road trip accumulates.

"Why," I would be asked when apprehended shortly thereafter, "did I throw away perfectly good clothes?" Of course, once they discovered the *Rocket's* "borrowed" plates, they would connect the car with Barstow, and that would be that. Clearly, we would have to jettison the sacks later either wholly or in dribs or drabs. I longed to be rid of them and the *Rocket* too as soon as possible.

Still slightly irritated with Cassy and her revelation, I turned on the television and discovered that the great Max Morgenstern, who was always right, had been wrong as hell in his prediction that the Barstow mess would be blown over in one telecast.

The screen lit up with an overhead shot of what I recognized as Yucca Parkway, although a huge rising column of black smoke in the center obscured much of it. The audio did not come on for several seconds and the first whole word I made out was "Mulligan." Next, a reporter's face that could pass for a model's, filled most of the screen with the smoldering rubble of 743 as a backdrop.

> *"The police have announced," said she, "that they are pursuing several leads including one that this was not a professional hit at all, that a vintage car was seen racing from the carnage, driven by persons now being sought. The death count stands at three, including one Homer Mulligan of 5777 Blazedale in Barstow, believed shot by the same alleged killers when he tried to intervene. One of those sought for questioning is reportedly a young woman."*

"What the hell?" I said, turning to Cassy, "now the bitch is saying we did it?"

"Wouldn't you?" she replied. "Do you think they can match teeth marks? I really bit her hard you know, and that's the only reason she missed hitting you all those times."

Cassy was right, she'd saved my life and I'd yet to thank her. That tripped a fresh thought that must have struck us both at the same instant: Mother Mulligan's gun.

"Where is it?" I held my right hand up with the index finger extended.

"In the car," Cassy replied, "under the front seat, I forgot to bring it in."

"All right," I said, "no reason to panic," we'll wipe it off and throw it into some trash heap, bury it in the sand, or just pitch it, whatever's easiest."

Cassy nodded in agreement.

Nothing yet seemed problematic, until I opened the door, and stepped into the daylight to face a sight that froze me in my tracks: it was the broadside of a State Police cruiser forty feet away and parked abreast of the only driveway out of the parking lot. It was obvious that its driver meant to check out anybody who entered or left.

I was motionless for some seconds before stepping sideways and then backwards so as to close the door. "Cop," I said in a loud whisper, and started to swing the door shut, when Cassy snapped, "stop."

"Is he looking at you?"

"No."

"Then turn like you're calling out to me, and then go. You can be a little curious, but don't look at him too long. Just tell yourself, nothing's wrong. Close the door now and you might get his attention."

She was sounding a little too professional, and a lot more than a little like Max.

"Go now," she said, "drop off the key. I'll take the gear and meet you in the car."

I obeyed. Cassy followed several seconds behind me. When we were fifty feet from the room, I detoured to drop off the key in the office that fronted on the main drag while she made for the Nash. When I'd opened the office door half way, I realized there was a drop box at the end of the bank of rooms. But now, I didn't want to do anything that looked like breaking stride. As far as I could tell, the cop had yet to look in my direction.

Once inside the office, I faced a nasty mountain of humanity in old clothes manning the desk that looked as if he'd been waiting for me. The face was jowly, fortyish, and inherently dislikable. A cap emblazoned with a small Confederate ensign topped off this fleshy behemoth.

Setting the key with its acrylic tag on the counter, I turned to leave when my eyes swept past a television suspended from the ceiling from which the face of Frank Delmagio stared down at me. Just below it, his name and the words "murder victim" were flashed. I walked toward the door.

"Number twenty-eight," squealed the voice I remembered from the phone call. It belonged to the great fleshy dreadnought; there was no one else there. "The comedian," squealed Squirrel Voice, "the comedian from California." He pushed open the pass through and was between the door and me before I could get to it. "You're from LA aren't you, smart ass? Don't you want some breakfast?"

"Indiana," I replied, "maybe you'd like to take it up with the cop out there?" God! Why did I say that?

"Those plates don't belong to your car. Want to know how I know? I had the cop out there call the numbers in. He's my brother. You're not going anywhere. You're going to wait right here," he said as if I were an employee or a dog from which utter obedience was expected. As he stepped through the front door, the TV flashed Mother Mulligan's face captioned by the words: "witness dies." I would have breathed a grateful sigh, and wished her peaceful passage with no last words like Nash for instance. She might well now be reunited with the asshole husband she'd shot for all I knew, but events had made her irrelevant. I prayed that Squirrel Voice had not heard the words: "vintage car" from the newscast.

No sooner was he outside, when a Ford Mustang, half of it covered with primer paint, and nothing resembling a muffler, roared past doing no less than eighty in a speed zone I recalled seeing posted at forty the night before. I said *a* Ford Mustang. It wasn't "*a Ford Mustang*" at all, it was "*the Ford Mustang*" that had been parked across 743 Yucca twenty four hours before.

The State cruiser at once erupted into an explosion of flashing lights and sirens. Whatever the cop's plans were for me, they played second fiddle to a juicy speed bust.

Squirrel Voice began jumping up, down, and sideways, seized his cap by the visor, waved it, and made a kind of wild yelping sound I hadn't heard since a high school field trip to a slaughterhouse in Chicago. The cruiser lunged forward with a screech of tires and incredible torque.

I guessed that the unfortunate quarry would be bagged inside of a minute, and its driver shortly, poorer by at least two hundred dollars if he were very, very lucky. But he wasn't. No indeed, he was far more than lucky.

The cop who Squirrel Voice had called his brother wasn't but a second in pursuit and may never have realized that he'd bolted from the motel's driveway squarely into the path of a semi that might as well have been a locomotive!

Had I seen it coming, I might have instinctively blinked, but it was an option I never had since it happened too fast to allow even the poor trucker a split second of braking before he clocked the cruiser amidships. The first sound to register was one metal objects make when two of them try to occupy the same space at the same time. The semi hurled past losing but a shred of momentum from an impact that tore the car's body off its frame and squashed it into a metal rag one third the size it had been an instant before. There followed a hailstorm of glass. The car's frame, now minus the body, lodged beneath the trailer's wheels and was dragged several seconds before its gas tank ruptured and the contents burst into a lush orange ball of ascending flames. Heat from it charged through the doorway that Squirrel Voice had yet to close. The great truck continued on another hundred yards before coming to a stop.

Squirrel Voice ran screaming after that most beautiful carnage while I sprang from the office, unable to resist calling after him loudly as I could, that I would be right back with the marshmallows. I made for the *Mulholland Rocket* in a sprint and noted that, but for some glass, the motel's driveway was clear of any real debris. It seemed that this was one Monday that had started out right after all.

32. GAS STOP

Cassy was standing abreast of the *Rocket's* rear bumper. She'd have seen the crash had she been looking the right way when it happened. I turned around and caught the sight of a great black funnel rise several hundred feet from the street.

"Did you see it?" I asked her. I took her mute straight-ahead stare for lingering disbelief at our luck. She seemed almost unaware of me.

"C'mon girl, I said, this place is going to turn into a cop convention in no time. I had my hand on the driver's door handle when I called out to her again. "Cassy!" Only then did she turn around.

"Sonny," she said, "we've got company."

I peered inside the Nash and was greeted by a prosthetic leg hanging over the upright part of the *Rocket's* front seat. I turned back to her without bothering to look at whom the leg was attached to; I had more than a good idea. Cassy gave a clueless shrug. She hadn't until now seen who'd offered me his hag plus money for her at the gas stop. I motioned Cassy to get in while I opened the driver's door and confirm my guess as to the leg's owner. It was him!

"Morn'n," said the man from the gas stop. Thought you might be going my way. If you weren't, you are now, so let's get the hell out of here, unless that is, anybody wants to talk to a bunch of cops."

My first thought was whether or not Mother Mulligan's gun was still where Cassy said she'd left it. The answer would have to wait. Above all, we had to get the hell out of there. This guy would be a lot easier to dispose of in the desert and I was sure he figured we'd be too were that his aim, and he'd had a lot longer to work it out.

"Do you mind getting that thing out of here?" I asked, gesturing to the limb while touching the starter. The Nash rumbled to life. I had never imagined until then, that prosthetic limbs could stink. This one must have been used to stir sewage. "Gas Stop" withdrew it, though managed to brush it against Cassy's hair. She recoiled. He belched out a laugh.

"We're going east by the way," he said. I turned the Nash around and all but coasted down a slight grade to the driveway and onto the street avoiding the largest concentrations of the cruiser's glass. A bottleneck had formed around the wreck and colored lights were blinking a mile or less behind us in our rear view mirror.

The crashed truck had held a straight course and not toppled to become a roadblock, although the trailer was now a great inferno. Oncoming traffic had compressed itself to a single lane that allowed our side to use the other to get past the blaze. But cars still waited until there were several clear lengths at each end of the wreck before running the gauntlet. When our turn came a minute later, the sirens and lights had all but overtaken us. I revved the *Rocket* and accelerated hard through a scorching wave of heat. I'm sure that we were among the last cars to get through before cavalry arrived to block off everything. I spotted Squirrel Voice, and what I took for the semi's driver standing as close to the crushed body of the cruiser as the heat would allow, looking for some sign of life.

We were on the entry ramp of I-40 heading east when I took a last look toward Flagstaff. The smoke funnel seemed identical to the one we'd left behind in Barstow. Gas Stop watched it too; his expression told me he was loving it. Considering everything that was pretty easy to do.

On I–40, we passed several westbound state cruisers and emergency vehicles, all of them with lights ablaze and headed for what I was sure we were putting behind us as fast as we could. It was several minutes before anyone spoke.

"Okay," I said to him finally: "What do you want?"

He didn't answer.

"What do you want?" I was in no a position to demand answers, but tried to sound like I was.

"A ride," Gas Stop finally replied.

"Where?"

"I haven't decided, exactly, when I do, you'll be the last to know…

Dickhead!"

"Where's your wife?" I asked, remembering the apparition in his car. He kicked me hard through the seat back.

"At breakfast," replied Gas Stop, "or rather she's breakfast. I hope prairie dogs like theirs well done."

"You burned her!" Cassy said in the midst of an involuntary gasp.

"Beyond recognition I hope," replied Gas Stop, almost smiling, "the car too." His belligerence had diminished for some reason allowing me to peg the accent as a Gulf Coast Texan's.

"Relax," he added and brushed Cassy's hair this time with his real foot. "I always kill food before I cook it, even dog food." His tone suggested that not burning her alive qualified him for a humanitarian award.

"I'd do the same to you," he said facing Cassy, "if it came to it, but it doesn't have to. Dickhead here is another matter." He kicked me through the seat cushion again.

I wondered if Cassy was thinking of Mother Mulligan's gun but hoped she'd wait to act on it though Gas Stop had yet to display a gun…he certainly acted like he was carrying. Either way, he was for the moment on full alert where he couldn't stay indefinitely unless more questions kept him there. I decided to let him do more talking, if he cared to, but it turned out he didn't. I was already toying with ways to get rid of him, none of which had him departing alive. His story seemed riddled with holes. I would have imagined his wife's murder, by itself, an all-consuming business without singling us out for his mode of escape. His having just come across the *Rocket* parked in the back lot of the motel while fleeing the murder scene was too far a stretch even with his knowing we were wanted…and how could he have known about that? Burning his car along with the wife made no sense unless it had also been stolen. I had the damnedest feeling that no matter where we'd spent the night he'd still have been in our car as if there was a script everybody had read but me.

The *Rocket* rolled east.

Except for the rise in temperature, I might not have noticed that Winslow, Arizona is two and a half thousand feet below Flagstaff because the drop stretches over fifty-seven miles.

We didn't stop at Winslow except for a roadside piss break some miles east of the city. Gas Stop took the keys, had us stand some five feet from him facing away, and played his urine stream in the sand just short of my heals. I could feel a faint spray of droplets. And still, I'd yet to see a gun. I only assumed that his baggy jacket concealed one and so I obeyed him as if it did. That done, he returned to the car and left us to relieve ourselves, apparently unconcerned that we might make a break for it. He had the keys and where would we go anyway?

Returning to the *Rocket*, we found Gas Stop had spilled the contents of Cassy's tote bag onto the rear seat and was counting what was left of Ralph's ten thousand dollars. "Who the hell are you two anyway?" he asked. "Bonnie and fucking Clyde? You picked a hell of a getaway car. A cop on a bicycle could run you down."

"You picked the same car," I reminded him, "and the money's ours, I don't trust credit cards or banks."

Gas Stop kicked the seat again. "It's who's?" He laughed. "It's got a new owner, funny man, drive."

"Look" I said, take it all, just leave us a few hundred and we'll drop you off anywhere you want. Buy yourself a car."

"Oh, I intend to—In Cairo,"

"What, where?"

"Cairo."

"This car doesn't float."

"Cairo, Illinois, I got a brother there."

I guessed we were twelve hundred miles from there and told him so.

"We're going straight through if we have to drive all night in shifts," declared Gas Stop as he waived a fist full of bills laughing, "I'll spring for the No Doz."

I didn't tell him that "Cairo, Illinois" was pronounced "Kerro" or that the "s" in Illinois is silent, either of which would have netted another kick through the seat back, and I was tired of those.

But we did stop in Holbrook, and over a tense breakfast, exchanged names.

The name Gas Stop gave as his was Wilson Killian. I had no idea if it was real and didn't ask for anything that said it was, because I was in no position to, and didn't care anyway. Cassy and I gave him our own names, which I had the impression he somehow already knew.

"So you're not married," he said.

"What?"

"You told me that she was your wife."

Only then I remembered having done that. "We're divorced," I said, hoping I hadn't lied my way into yet more quicksand.

"So what the hell are you doing together?" Killian demanded. "You're supposed to hate each other."

"It's a trial reconciliation," said Cassy.

"Yeah right," Kilian's dentures were flopping all over his mouth and mixing with gobs of food and brownish saliva. Once or twice he seemed on the verge of either swallowing or spitting them out. Halfway through his food, he yanked several cigarettes from a pack Cassy had set on the table, wedged one over each ear, then lit a third, and continued to eat between coughs and drags. I was hoping he'd step away for a moment so that I could ask Cassy about the gun. But Killian didn't, nor did he seen particularly nervous about our trying to escape now, even with the car, since he'd only have to make an anonymous call to the Police—several calls just for insurance—to effect his revenge. He may or may not have connected us with Barstow, but my guess was that he had.

But he relaxed his leash sooner than I'd expected, and when Cassy announced she was going to the rest room, he only nodded. He didn't stop me either after she'd returned. It might have meant nothing or maybe he wanted us lulled for when he put a bullet through my head, and perhaps Cassy's too, after raping her.

But just then, things stood in a kind of equilibrium since we held identical threats over each other's heads. Each of us was connected with murder, so no one could afford the attention of the police. Neither could one ditch the other alive and free to inform, although there was nothing in Killian's being caught for us besides revenge which I'd have gladly given up to be rid of him.

Still, the surest and safest way to accomplish that was kill him and stash the body in the kind of place where we did Cassy's car before there was anything to connect him with us. The local wild life would take care of the remains. I was starting to feel ashamed at taking his orders, *and there were two of us*.

We topped off the tank and continued east at just after eleven. Signs now announced distances to places in New Mexico, Gallup, Grants, and Albuquerque.

I worried about what kind of obstacles the good State of New Mexico would have set up at its border. It was true that we had license plates now, and that only Killian had yet pegged us as wanted, but it hardly meant that we weren't being sought and that every pair of eyes that fell upon us wasn't a threat.

There were painted lanes at the border that led directly beneath canopies identical to the ones we'd seen at the other end of Arizona. But they were unmanned for some reason, even by the fruit and bug cops. We drove through them, barely slowing down.

33. SCHOOL BUS AND THE TROOPER

At twelve-eighteen P.M. Mountain Time, the *Mulholland Rocket* and its fugitive crew invaded New Mexico, a.k.a. the *Land of Enchantment*.

I'd first learned that the forty-seventh State to join the union was called that in a book from the school library that, like others, I'd taken out and never returned.

And in fact, if you are not running from killers and cops there is a lot about the *Land of Enchantment* to enchant. Traveling west to east you enter on the Colorado Plateau and exit to the Texas panhandle. Between them lie three hundred miles of high red desert and the zig-zag of mountainous horizons that you think you'll never reach until you realize you're either in them or you've past them.

West of the Rio Grande, which splits the state roughly in two, the road will snake between rock outcroppings that appear to have been aimed by some subterranean force at the road or whatever was on it only to have the road take an evasive turn at the last instant. And another line of zig-zag horizons looms ahead of you indistinguishable from the one you were looking at two hours before, and you wonder if you've entered some gigantic loop, so you check the road atlas before realizing that, no, you haven't entered a loop at all, you're still headed straight.

The outcrop of red mesas, so dense in the west, becomes sparse East of the Rio Grande valley and thins out the further east you roll. The glorious rich-red of the West somewhere becomes a not so rich-red, eventually taking on the color of the Great Plains which is ochre in April. The zig-zag horizon melts to a flat and featureless line occasionally punctuated by road kill, rocks, and tumbleweed; I've seen paintings I thought captured it. There's not much in them to look at.

The memorable things for me about the *Land of Enchantment* are the names of the places in it. There was a pop song played with a Jew's harp about a place named 'Tucumcari' at the East end of the State on old Route 66. There are a couple of dozen stories about the origin of the name, but I'm convinced all of them are wistful horseshit. 'Tucumcai' for me is just a cool assemblage of syllables akin to a preposition at the end of a sentence. It breaks the rules of good writing and sounds great.

And there's 'Albuquerque,' a name that mimics the rattle and squeak of a tired transcontinental train rolling on a stretch of neglected track. It's also the place where I meant to swing north with the *Rocket* up Raton Pass thru Trinidad, La Junta, and the plains of western Kansas where, as far as I knew, there were no warrants with my name on them. I'd sworn to myself that I would not go through any part of Texas.

We had crossed nearly half of the State of New Mexico in a most welcome silence when I learned it was not what our guest Wilson Killian had in mind. Killian, who'd been studying the *Rand McNally* in the back seat, announced we would be heading due east across the Texas panhandle, through Oklahoma to Joplin, then east through the Ozarks on a course south of old 66. This led to Cape Gerardo and finally Cairo where he'd abandon us or more likely abandon our bodies having first killed us with the gun I still only assumed he had because he acted like he did.

"Killian," I said, "the car has bogus plates and I'm wanted in Texas." This met with the kind of silence that was as if I hadn't said anything.

One minute later, I repeated this and the reply was instantaneous. It was a shot to my back through the seat that threw me gut first into the steering wheel and set off the horn. Breathless, I plopped back into the cushion certain that a bullet was lodged in me. Cassy shrieked in horror.

"Bastard," she screamed at Killian. The Nash veered left into oncoming traffic where the first in line was the enormous bread-loaf shape of a Greyhound bus closing fast. In reflex, I'd retracted both hands from the wheel. Then when I reached for it, my back exploded like an overloaded transformer at a power station. My arms recoiled as I bent over backwards and all I can remember was looking at the headliner of the Nash and bracing for the impact I was certain would shortly flatten the three of us.

But no impact came. Instead, the Nash executed a hard right lunge that threw me against the driver's door and set off a second explosion in my back far worse than the first. The blast of the Greyhound's air horn and the roar of its diesel shrieked in my left ear with a force I was sure would send my eyes flying from their sockets as the great wall of fluted aluminum rushed by. Only then did I know we'd missed being crushed by it. Cassy had seized the wheel and was fighting to correct the car's oscillations that followed the hard right she'd saved our lives with. Still bent in a backward "U," and looking almost straight up, I caught a flash of white lettering on a green backdrop through the sliver of windshield at the bottom of my vision. "Albuquerque," it read, "next 10 exits." The *Mulholland Rocket* still whipped violently left and right before Cassy could correct it and set it on a straight course. She'd done it all with one hand.

We were headed downhill now, on tires that had probably been on the car since Ralph owned it. How long it took me to realize my right leg had jammed the accelerator to the floor was only a few seconds. But moving it the two inches to get it off the pedal sent a third shock wave through me that awakened everything back from the fight at the Willkie reunion. Killian—that son of a bitch—had shot me with the gun's muzzle jammed into the seat back which was why I hadn't heard the discharge.

I eased my foot off the gas, made several jabs at the brake pedal, finally connecting, only to have it sink to the floor without the car slowing a bit. Bracing myself, I reached for the ignition switch and a jolt from my back sent me reeling convulsively. A wave of mauve puke rushed straight up from me to spray the windshield. But Cassy had the *Rocket* on the road's shoulder, found the ignition key, and turned it to the off position. Still on a downward incline, but with the engine functioning as a brake, the Nash coasted to a halt on the gravel. I toppled sideways to the center of the front seat, wondering when Killian would fire again. He peered over the seat back and down at me.

Cassy knelt to face me. "Well done, girl," I whispered wondering what organs Killian's bullet had torn through. I was likely finished and knew it. Cassy took my hand and kissed me. I mouthed the word "gun" to her and realized she was already probing below the seat for it. She shook her head. I knew it could be anywhere in the car by now. I had written myself off and only wanted to stop Killian before he could execute his designs on Cassy. Then I thought of his wife and prayed I would expire before he burned the *Rocket* with me in it.

"Lose something?" Killian asked, "this maybe?" He dropped Mother Mulligan's automatic on my cheek and it bounced to the cushion. Was that what he shot me with? Cassy seized the automatic, and with a single motion, pointed it at Killian, pulled the trigger four times, and got a click with each pull.

"Thought you'd like a souvenir," said Killian. "The bullets are on the road back in Arizona." He sprang up and slapped Cassy's face hard. When she recovered, Cassy spat a huge, frothy blob on his face. He plopped back to the seat with an angry laugh. "That's all I ever got from bitches like you," he said. "You think you're so Goddamn special, don't you? Let me tell you something bitch: without people like me you'd be eating rice behind a goddamn wire fence and breeding baby gooks nonstop for some Commie warlord right this minute. That's where I left my leg, Honey, in a gook cage while people like you were burning flags and sleeping with people like Dickhead here. I don't guess you were ever in the army were you, Dickhead?"

Here it was again. Killian had unmasked the rage that drove him. He'd likely gotten little or no action before his sacrifice and less since. I wondered if the same sort of thing dwelled to a lesser degree deep in Clifford Fitch. If so, I could hardly blame either of them, though I still wanted Killian dead. I rolled forward slightly on the seat anticipating the next shot, the coup de grace with a second gun, the one I'd yet to see.

Suddenly, I longed for real air. The mustiness of ancient upholstery, once an elixir, stifled me and I began to gasp. With Cassy as a crutch, I managed to stagger outside. Pain shot through my back in waves. I coughed hard and collapsed as I heard the back door of the Nash open and shut. Killian wasn't letting us out of his sight for a minute, not even now. The bastard wanted to watch me die, squirming, without having to waste another slug. For a moment, I just lay prone with my head on the right front tire where I felt a pool of wetness spread about my buttocks. I wondered about the exact location of the wound. "Death on a New Mexico interstate," I mused—a fitting end to a life gone so wrong. The one person who might have saved me now was long past being able to. "Father," I sobbed, "I'm sorry, I'm so damn sorry." I felt the ground behind me and the pool of blood must have doubled in size in less than a minute. My thighs were wet. How long, I wondered, before I passed out for good? Cassy knelt beside me. I could see a purple bruise forming on her cheek.

"He shot me, Cassy," I said as if it were necessary to explain. I'm going to die, baby." I took her hand and pulled it into the wet. She gave a mild gasp at the sensation of the liquid. For a moment our hands remained in the puddle and it occurred to me that I had hemorrhaged some very cold blood. Cassy raised her hand and held it up. My "blood" was an almost jet black kind of very foul, light oil mixed with rusty orange chunks that would have given sewage a bad name. Cassy's expression of horror began to melt into a quizzical one but stopped somewhere between the two. "What is this crap?" she asked.

"It's brake fluid, Cassy," I replied, now remembering the unresponsive pedal. "And it's probably as old as the car." The wet had nothing to do with my back. Killian peered down at me. He braced himself on a door handle, raised his faux leg over her shoulder and by some unseen motion made it snap like a switchblade to a point an inch from my face. "Like it, Dickhead?" he smirked. A machinist hopped it up for me. It's spring-loaded and can break two by fours. And you thought I used this on you." That's when Killian displayed the gun I'd only assumed he actually had. There's no mistaking anything for a Luger. Even the most avid of gun haters cannot help but admire the menacing beauty of Lugers. They'd been around for the better part of a century and still looked like something out of the next one.

Killian's had a well-used look, which I doubted was from shooting paper targets at a range. The pain in my back was still rising with no sign of leveling off. But it would eventually, I thought. There was no bullet lodged in me and I had not been shot.

Killian put the Luger back into his jacket pocket. "What is that shit?" he demanded pointing at the puddle of liquid.

"It's brake fluid," I replied. "We probably don't have brakes. It wasn't 'probably.' There was no way the brakes could still work. Killian walked around the car, opened the driver's door, and must have punched the brake pedal, because a gush of filthy fluid from somewhere on the bottom of the car showered my left side. I motioned Cassy to lower me so as to have a look underneath. Without being asked, Killian hit the pedal again. More fluid gushed from a rusted out length of one of the steel lines that connected the brakes to the master cylinder.

"Goddammit," came a growl from the interior of the Nash. "No fucking brakes!"

I heard the driver's door swing open and slam shut. Killian stood over us an instant later looking at me as if I were responsible.

"It's a rotten line," I said. "Press on the pedal and all you do is pump fluid on the ground."

"So fix it!" Killian demanded after a brief pause. "You're a Goddamn mechanic!"

How the hell did he know I was a mechanic? I wondered if telling him doing it right there was impossible might get me shot for real. Actually, with some basic tools it could be done in about an hour. "I can't do it here, Killian," I said.

"Well, where can you?" he fired back accusingly. Lying to Killian and his Luger was a bad idea, but so was giving him bad news.

"There." I pointed to a green sign about 20 feet ahead of us on which was printed "Albuquerque" along with the number of the upcoming exit. The back pain had downgraded a couple of notches, but I shuddered at what would happen when I tried to move. When I did try, I found that I could, and thus emboldened, announced that I intended to drive the Nash to the next Albuquerque exit and find a parts store. Cassy dried the fluid from me, grinning sardonically when I told her I didn't want to stain what was left of the *Rocket*'s front seat which contained a hole in the upright, courtesy of Killian's bionic leg. He probably hadn't meant to get us killed but damned near had, the stupid son of a bitch.

It was mid-afternoon and with any luck we could be on our way before dusk, allowing for everything. The eastbound traffic was light and I decided I could nurse the Nash to an auto parts store using the emergency brake if it worked, and wonder of wonders, it worked. Anyway, I didn't worry about getting shot until *after* I'd fixed the car.

The exit led to a frontage road and past a number of strip centers before I spotted the blue and yellow graphics of a Napa store in a detached building a quarter mile from the main group. I nosed up to a brick sidewall well out of any major line of sight so as to avoid being spotted working on the Nash in the parking lot, something generally forbidden yet done all the time. Getting out of the car was a lot harder than the last time and I silently vowed to pay Killian back the first chance I got past his Luger *and* his leg. Cassy helped me to the ground where I made one final reconnaissance of the rotten section of brake line. It was almost out in the open and easily accessed. Two-and-a-half feet of three-sixteenth steel line spliced in should have us on our way.

Inside the NAPA store, I bought twice the amount of steel line and double the number of brass compression unions I needed in case more rotten line was found. To this, I added flair nut wrenches, a small tubing cutter, a bleeder wrench, a light floor jack, four stands, a pair of disposable flashlights, and four quart bottles of brake fluid. It came to some sixty dollars that Killian paid with the cash Ralph had given us. He told us to wait outside while he made a phone call from the vestibule. "How long to fix this?" he demanded when he'd finished the call. I told him two hours including removing the wheels to bleed the system. Nodding, he smiled. He'd smiled before, but this was the first time I'd seen it void of belligerence.

"First," he said, "we're getting something to eat."

I protested that it meant likely finishing the job in the dark. "Let Cassy get the food," I argued. "We need to get started." Killian shook his head.

"If I let her loose I don't know what this little lady will come back with," he said, adding, "or put on what I eat. She thinks too much. I hate that in a bitch." He spat a brownish yellow blob on the ground. C'mon let's stow this shit in the car." We could, and as it turned out, and probably should have, driven the car to the restaurant—called the *Brutal Noodle*—using the emergency brake to stop. Killian had nixed that idea with a sarcastic comment about his ability to walk further and faster than 4F pussys like me on his faux leg. If there was some kind message in this for Cassy she was long past receiving it. Walking it was six hundred feet of pure hell.

The *Brutal Noodle* featured overpriced Italian fast food. I have always avoided Italian restaurants because they smell like vomit and so much of what they serve looks like it. We split a large burnt pizza with a topping that looked as if scraped off the interstate. Twice I tried to speed things along and twice Killian rebuffed my attempts. Now I was certain that the work on the *Mulholland Rocket* would stretch into the dark. Just after 4:30, as we walked out the vestibule, I was struck like a blow in the face by what I saw: in the first parking stall opposite the entrance was the Ford Mustang fastback with its huge areas of red oxide primer that covered the same half-done body repairs that had lured the police cruiser and its driver to destruction in Flagstaff. Its engine idled at the same angry growl I'd first heard on Yucca Parkway. And it was still impossible to see so much as a silhouette through the windows, which were, as I said, darkened long past the point where they could have been legal. I nudged Cassy and pointed to it. She shrugged.

We walked back to the Napa store. Turning the corner to where I'd parked, my eyes fell on a sight that made me forget the Mustang, and for that matter, everything else that came into view. The *Mulholland Rocket* sat lashed to the deck of a car hauler!

"Stop," I yelled. The flatbed's driver stood on the running board ready to step into the cab. His sunglasses didn't hide the fact that he was butt ugly and huge.

"That's my car," I shouted, "who the hell told you to take it?"

From within the cab I could hear a police radio crackling out dispatches. He smiled before speaking. It was clear that confrontations were among the things he relished and was good at. In a voice dripping with anticipation, he said: "there's twenty minute parking in this lot. You've been here over an hour."

"There's no sign that says that," I protested. "It's illegal to take that car." The man removed his glasses to reveal a face scared by what I guessed was skin cancer, acid, or having been shot. It reminded me of what Max had once said about there being no people as dangerous as the ones with nothing to lose. This guy would have doubtless relished the chance to disfigure someone else, and anyone handy would do.

"Well," said this ugliest of men, "suppose we just see what the police say about it." At that, he reached into the truck, produced a microphone, and depressed a button on the bottom of it.

"Suppose we don't," said Killian from about ten feet behind me. I turned around just enough to see the barrel of the Luger pointed at the driver. "Drop the mike and get off that truck." The man hesitated.

"Get down," demanded Killian.

The driver dropped the microphone and stepped first from the cab to the running board, and, from there, planted himself on the ground in front of me. From twenty feet away he was huge, now, standing directly in front of me, he was a school bus. I stepped aside to allow Killian a clear shot. After a brief hesitation, School Bus began walking toward him. Killian didn't fire for several seconds probably assuming as I did, that one shot would be all it took. He was wrong and fired twice, but too late. School Bus gave a slight shudder, and without breaking stride, delivered a kick to Killian's chest that brushed away the gun and sent it flying. I heard an anguished groan and would have gladly watched School Bus go to work, but my attention was riveted on the flight of the pistol that ended with it lodged under the flatbed's right front tire.

Five seconds later it was mine.

Killian lay prone while School Bus kick-smashed his torso, breaking here and there to stomp an arm or leg, but sparing him head blows lest his victim pass out and miss anything.

Seizing the gun was one thing; doing something with it was another. In a minute, Killian would be past saving…which should have been a good thing. There would be enough of a window in time for Cassy and me to jump into the truck and leave the two of them to cancel each other out.

With any serious luck, School Bus would finish off Killian and the slugs from the luger would finish the School Bus. Still, he'd yet to show a sign of slowing down from what Killian had pumped into him. I had beaten my wife's lover close to death by the account I got later through Max, but I was a rank amateur next to what I now watched and had taken almost as much as I'd dished out. With School Bus it was all one way. Killian threw me a pleading look that I tried not to acknowledge. I thought of what he said he'd done to his wife and told myself that what went around came around. I looked at Cassy who tried not to show me she was loving every second of it. I could have too, but was already cursing myself for what I knew I would do next.

"Alright enough! I've got the gun," I announced. The fact that I actually did made me croak out the words as if my larynx had imploded. I'd never before fired so much as an air pistol.

School Bus paused, and gave Killian a final kick before turning his attention to me. I looked straight at the ravaged face that surgery with a crow bar could only improve. He was about twenty feet, perhaps six steps from me, when he began to move. This left me with two choices, shoot or run. Running meant abandoning the *Rocket* and the money, something I'd come too far for now. I raised the Luger, gripping it with both hands. There was no point in giving warnings or making threats, which would have been ignored, and no time anyway. It was impossible to miss; School Bus was a wall. I knew that I couldn't wait like Killian had. School Bus had already closed the distance to me by half. I fired, expecting the kick to knock me flat against the truck, but it was far less than I expected. I tried not to look at the torso and the wound fearing that I would be struck sick at what I'd done. My eyes remained locked on his. He winced and opened his mouth affording me a view of the veiny underside of his tongue. He'd stopped, and now stood absolutely upright as if obeying some unspoken command. I fired again. The bullet must have struck him off center because he spun a complete turn before collapsing face down on the asphalt. Telling myself that he was dead, I didn't go near him to confirm it, neither did Killian, who stirred, and in defiance of all logic, stood up and staggered toward me.

"How does it feel, Dickhead?" I asked suppressing a sudden urge to laugh hard. I leveled the Luger at his chest. This brought a look of surprise to his face, as if I had somehow betrayed the alliance School Bus had forced on us.

"You saved my life," said Killian. He looked remarkably unbruised for the beating I'd just witnessed.

"Only because I want to kill you myself, you sorry piece of shit." Apparently this tripped a wire in him that called for a show of spine.

"So what's stopping you?

"No cool drawer in a morgue for you, Killian," I replied. "You're going to bake on the asphalt for the buzzards and the crows to enjoy. I hear they eat the eyes first. Get in the truck and lay on the floor," I turned to Cassy, "Baby…"

"Yes, Sonny?"

"You know how to use these things!"

She nodded.

"Get in after him and if you even think he's making a false move, shoot him as many times as it takes to kill him…but put the first round in his crotch."

Cassy and I then did a kind of ballet while climbing into the flatbed's cab, all the while, keeping the Luger pointed at our guest.

Once under way, I made as discreet an exit to the frontage road as I could. Not one person had come to investigate the gunshots, and I wasn't going to stop and inquire why. None of the afternoon traffic from the commercial strip appeared to have noticed our little drama.

We accelerated down the frontage road. It occurred to me that we should have taken the wallet from the man I'd killed. When he was found and identified, it would be no time before the stolen truck I was driving would become white hot.

School Bus had been considerate enough to equip his rig with a police radio that might give us some warning. We were on the ramp that would put us back on the Interstate when I saw the blue Mustang with the red-primer-over-half-done bodywork. I hadn't seen it tracking us until now, and I'd paid at least as much attention scanning the rear view mirrors as the road ahead. It was locked one hundred feet behind us and was staying there as if we were towing it with a cable. Whoever drove it though, couldn't be what I now feared most: the law. And I had more reason than ever before to fear the law: I had just killed a man.

The realization that I'd let loose two eight-ounce lead projectiles at two-thousand-feet-per-second into a system of organs veins, arteries, and nerves so very much like my own, struck me like one of those shot-filled mallets they call a dead blow hammer. I'd killed School Bus. I'd watched him whirl like a corkscrew from the eccentric momentum of the second bullet I'd fired into him while neurons flashed the news to his brain that he was hit and would die. And I'd done it almost without thinking. True, there was no time to consider what gross arrogance the act of taking another life really is. Since my confinement at Huntsville, I'd wanted a score of people dead for a hundred reasons that had included the theft of my wife, my home, and a dozen violations of my body. I wanted the ones who'd done these things to me dead by the slowest and grisliest means, but in the end, my mind's eye had never really cast myself as the executioner. Now I'd done it for real, and without hesitation. I'd crossed the line into the kingdom of Cain or far worse, that of Max Morgenstern. My eyes danced between the road, Killian, and the Mustang still running a hundred feet behind us.

Suddenly, it wasn't behind us. With a screech of tires and torque, it was alongside. I looked at the window opposite me, black I thought, like a shark's eye. I glanced at Killian, who seemed to be anticipating something I couldn't begin to guess. Then, three blasts of the Mustang's horn rang out and it charged the road ahead of us to become a speck in less than half a minute, and was gone. Killian looked up at me, having realized by now that I still lacked what it took to finish him off. "Where now?" he asked wearing a smirk. "Cairo," I said, "Cairo, Illinois." The answer didn't seem to surprise him one bit. "It's all I want," he replied, his dentures seemed suspended in the perennial froth that I'd come to associate with his mouth. It was as if they were treading sudsy water in one of those old clothes washers with an open top and ringers.

"Did you say your brother has a place there?" I asked.

He nodded.

"Well, when we get there, we unload the car, I need two hours to fix it. You and your brother take the truck somewhere and burn it. When we're gone, we never saw each other and we were never in Albuquerque, Flagstaff, or on this road, for that matter, agreed?"

"How about Barstow?" The smirk had returned to his face as if he'd drawn the card that made everything I'd said shrink to one tenth of its importance. As I had suspected, he'd known about Barstow all along. I should have left him for School Bus to finish off.

"Yeah," I said, "there too," telling myself that I didn't need to wonder anymore about who killed Frank Delmagio and Paul Phengston. But I didn't have the time or strength left to stop and beat the reason out of him, though I would have loved to.

More exits to Albuquerque flashed by us in three and five-minute intervals. I signaled for a right turn and eased the truck into the last, or second to the last, of them. This got me puzzled looks from both Cassy and Killian. We followed a frontage road until I spotted a strip center with a Pharmacy. I parked the flatbed where the least amount of maneuvering would be required for a hasty exit. "Give me the gun," I said to Cassy. When she did, I pointed it at Killian's head, still keeping it well below the window and anyone's line of sight that stood on the ground. I punched the power button on the transceiver, which lapsed into silence. It had long since begun to give me a headache. Cassy's expression was one of relief as well.

"Okay, Honey," I said, "go in there and buy a bottle of extra strength sleeping pills, a box of No Doze and a couple of cold six-packs of Pop. Make at least one of them a Dr. Pepper. Get a whole shopping bag of snacks, chips, chocolate bars, whatever looks good. Quick as you can Honey, quick as you can."

"Pretzels," added Killian. "Yeah pretzels," I repeated. When she was outside and had shut the door I said to him, "say another thing and I'm going to shoot off your pretzel, Pretzelputz," borrowing a word Max had invented. I was sounding like him now too, and I didn't mind the feeling, not at all.

I never stopped looking at my watch. Stopping here was a risk I hated taking and maybe shouldn't have. We were going to have to gas up several times before Cairo at stations with roadside marts, but I doubted they would carry the sleeping pills I needed to make sure Killian was down for the count. How long, I wondered, would it take for the cops to find the body of School Bus whereupon the flatbed I was driving would become a target?

Cassy was magnificent. In less than six minutes she was out the door of the pharmacy and headed back toward us toting a shopping bag with string handles, walking at just short of a trot, so as not to add any more attention to what her still sumptuous body would draw by itself. Only when she was about two hundred feet from us did I see the expression on her face that told me that something was very wrong. A second later I knew what.

There are few less welcome sensations in your stomach than the ones brought on by a pulsating flash of red lights in a rear view mirror.

I looked up at it, praying silently that they were atop any kind of vehicle except one driven by an arm of the law.

The prayer went unanswered.

It was a New Mexico State Police cruiser. I didn't know how long it had been parked behind the flatbed from where I assumed its driver had called in its license number. Possibly finding the flatbed hot, he'd switched on the cruiser's antlers. The driver's door swung open and that perennial State Trooper cavalry hat emerged. And beneath it, the mirrored sunglasses that hid most of what I guessed to be a thirty-year-old face. He was some inches short of six feet, had made considerable progress toward an elliptical paunch, and of course, he was chewing gum. I wondered if there was a brand called "State Trooper." If not, there should be.

That aside, he could have been a mannequin. He was abreast of the driver's window when I read the name on his identification bar: "Borg." I'd long associated the name with the ever-stale breath of one George Borg who'd sat next to me in a freshman English class at Willkie.

"Afternoon," said Borg. I nodded. Killian looked at me from the floor; neither of us needed this. The next things Trooper Borg would ask for: my driver's license and registration, they would end the game. I wondered how Texas and New Mexico were going to divide me up, what with murder, attempted murder, bail jumping, and child molestation all hanging over my head. It would make for a grand old tug-of-war.

"How are we this afternoon?" asked Trooper Borg giving me a twenty-second reprieve. "Been worse," I replied, "been better," then added, "been younger." The line was my own invention and had usually gotten me at least a laugh of resignation. Trooper Borg responded with a not very amused grunt.

"You're from California?" he asked. I remembered the borrowed plate on the back of the *Mulholland Rocket*, which was bad enough all by itself. I decided no lie in the world was going to get me out of this so it was a waste of time trying to invent one.

"Indiana," I replied, trying to remain visibly calm.

"Yeah?" said Trooper Borg, "me too, I'm from Elwood."

Elwood, Indiana was Wendell Willkie's hometown, which he did not carry when he ran for President. "I went to Willkie High in Michigan City," I said.

"Yeah," said the Trooper. "My father knew Wendell Willkie real good, he was a great man."

"A great man," I agreed. Killian started mouthing something to me. I planted a heel on his neck. And then it came like the storm you lulled yourself into thinking you'd somehow escaped, but knew in the end you hadn't: "I'll need to see your driver's license and vehicle registration," said Trooper Borg.

I now had exactly the same choice I'd faced just fifteen minutes before when I'd taken a man's life because I'd lose the game, a hundred thousand dollars, and my life if I didn't. Now the stakes were nearly identical. I had no idea how far I'd get from this parking lot once I'd killed Trooper Borg, but clearly the game was up if I didn't. And if I did? Could Cassy and I drive the truck to some remote place, burn it and make our way to say, Mexico, and disappear, the thing I'd considered doing in the first place, before even stopping in Michigan City? At this point, we might still not be connected with the stolen truck's dead owner, or the *Mulholland Rocket* for that matter. Were we to abandon them, we would take the rental car's plates with us and bury them in the sand somewhere.

The way out was clear: kill the trooper, burn the truck, and murder Killian by the way. When your right hand is in sudden possession of instantaneous lethal force, a whole new dimension is added to your powers of reason, not to mention your concept of what's right and what isn't. I stared into the twin mirrors of the Trooper's sunglasses to see the image of myself, the last thing the man wearing those glasses would see before I killed him. I gripped the door handle and began to push down listening for the click. When I heard it, I would shove the door open, swing the Luger into position, and pump slugs into the face that stared up at me through the sunglasses.

"Sir," repeated Trooper Borg, "your license and registration." The door latch disengaged with an all but a silent click.

"Right here," said Cassy as she rounded the left front corner of the flatbed. The Trooper's head jerked to face her and having done that, made an obvious appraisal of her obvious attributes.

"You're the driver?" he asked finally, "not him?"

"Not since they stopped licensing half-blind epileptics," Cassy replied, adding, "he's my brother; he used to drive semi's and can't get the asphalt out of his blood." She extended a driver's license, having withdrawn it from a wallet that she seemed to have produced out of thin air.

"I can understand that," said Trooper Borg as he studied Cassy's license.

"This is your truck?"

"My boyfriend's," Cassy replied. "Sonny," she called up to me: "the registration: it's in the glove compartment."

I opened the glove compartment and reached inside to find an envelope that looked like it just might contain it. I handed it down to Trooper Borg. He pulled back the flap and slid out the contents. After a cursory inspection, he looked at Cassy. She'd ignited a cigarette, and appeared as if there wasn't a thing about either of us that wasn't the truth, the whole truth, and nothing but the truth.

"Your boyfriend, Victor Hernandez?" he asked, "2721 Fremont Street, Needles, California?" Cassy took a deep pull on her cigarette and exhaled with a delicious kind of decadence I'd first seen in the cabin of *Yesterday's Rainbow*.

"Not exactly," she replied, "It's 2127. You wouldn't believe how many times he's tried to get that straightened out. Everything from the State of California gets delivered six blocks away."

The trooper nodded sympathetically. "It's the damn computers he said. If you'll wait right here I'll check this out and you can be on your way." He walked back to his cruiser. I prayed that Cassy's license wouldn't open up more questions—Monterey was a long way from Needles. Killian started to say something—I poked his neck with the toe of my shoe.

Cassy had been brilliant. Her performance had outdone the one she'd fooled Frank Delmagio with. Her invented glitch about the wrong address couldn't have been better had a playwright scripted it. I had myself believed that Victor Hernandez was not just her friend, but her lover who had loaned her the truck.

Now we knew that School Bus was likely one 'Victor Hernandez,' or at least had worked for him. If only they hadn't yet found the body. Cassy looked up at me and discreetly displayed crossed fingers. I blew her a kiss. Five minutes later Trooper Borg emerged from his cruiser with the envelope and Cassy's license in his right hand.

"Ma'am," he asked, "where are you headed?"

"Cairo, Illinois," she answered without hesitation. "That beast back there"—she motioned at the *Rocket*—"is a birthday present, believe it or not."

She didn't have to say the last part. Indeed it might have called the trooper's attention to the *Rocket's* "borrowed" plate that our Trooper had obviously not yet noticed. God! What a master bullshitress Cassy was turning out to be.

"Well, Ma'am," he said, "this vehicle is due for a safety inspection eight days from today, and it's had one extension at that. I'd advise you to get it done as soon as you get back to California. They've got a load of heavy fines waiting for you if you don't."

"I'll see to it," said Cassy, "and many thanks."

"And may I say, Ma'am, that you have a very lucky boyfriend."

Cassy's smile was one of trying to hide an embarrassment that both of us knew she didn't feel for a second.

The cruiser and Trooper Borg exited the lot heading for the westbound lanes of I-40. Cassy climbed into the driver's seat while I slipped sideways, then, passing the shopping bag to me, she hit the power button of the transceiver. It crackled to life.

"When they find that body," she said, "Trooper Borg will be after us with a vengeance."

"And probably the New Mexico Air National Guard," I added. "We've got to get out of this State." Neither of us needed to mention that Cassy had officially connected herself to the man I'd murdered. Compared to what had happened in the past half-hour, my fear of entering Texas had shrunk to non-existence. Going north through Raton Pass, the mountains, and possibly snow, had zero appeal anyway. Cassy twisted the ignition key to the start position. I reached into the shopping bag and found the sleeping pills.

"Shut it off for a minute," I said and handed her the Luger she pointed at Killian without being told.

"Something we've got to do." I twisted open the bottle and shook four pills into my right palm. "Open a can of pop."

Cassy did this without once pointing the gun's barrel away from Killian's face. I had the pills in a loose fist that formed a funnel I held over his mouth.

"Open Pretzelputz," I said, "open wide."

"Fuck You," said Killian.

I kicked his rib cage. "It's pills or bullets in your mouth Killian—your choice."

"That's too many," he protested, "I'll throw up on your shoes."

"And I'll wipe them on your face."

"You want to kill me?"

"Actually yes, but I'll settle for having you out cold between here and Cairo. That is where you wanted to go isn't it? Open up, Pretzelputz." Killian logged a final protest but obeyed. I managed to drop three of the four pills into him. "Keep it open," I said taking the pop can from Cassy. I poured what I guessed to be a third of it into his mouth and told him to swallow. He did, but not without a coughing fit that covered his face and much of the floor with Dr. Pepper. At one point he spat out a denture, but I was pretty sure three pills had gone down.

Once again, when Cassy had started the flatbed's engine, I told her to stop.

"I want to take that plate we borrowed off the *Rocket*."

Cassy sighed, an indication that she thought getting under way was more important." I told her it would take but a minute, handed her the Luger, and bolted from the truck's cab onto its bed. I retrieved a screwdriver and vice-grip pliers from inside the *Mulholland Rocket* and made my way to the car's rear bumper. The rental car's license plate hadn't been mentioned, and had the Trooper checked and found it came from a rental car, that could have been the game's end.

But it was gone! I'd put it on myself and knew it couldn't have fallen off. School Bus must have removed it, but why? The truck had a bold California commercial plate that I assumed matched its registration.

Back in the cab, I told Cassy this as she shrugged and once again started the engine. The time for contemplating this and any other issue was after we were back on I-40.

This time nothing stopped us. Cassy handled the flatbed with a deftness that amazed me. She'd learned how to handle large vehicles, she said, by having once driven a bus for an asylum. Her license entitled her to drive about anything.

Half an hour later Killian lapsed into what I hoped was a coma.

So when Cassy and I could talk freely for the first time since the day began in Flagstaff, a huge irregularity came to us both at the same time: What was Victor Hernandez from Needles, California doing picking up an "illegally parked" car in an Albuquerque Strip Center?

Then: "Cassy," I said, "Those tow away bastards that pick up cars and ransom them never use flatbeds at all, only wreckers."

"Wreckers?"

"Wreckers, you know, tow trucks, they never use flatbeds. So who the hell was Victor Hernandez anyway?"

34. THE CAIRO EXPRESS

The fact that the flatbed's gas tanks were full allowed us to make it into Texas without stopping. When we did, it was well after dark. At the state line there had been nothing but a well-worn sign that told us that we were crossing it and that Texas welcomed us. I'd forgotten about the cops and inspection stations in Arizona and having done so, I was spared considerable worry.

We gassed up in an enormous fuel stop with a small supermarket attached to it in Glenrio. I remember only the unbelievably clean restrooms, great coffee, and the cheapest gas we'd yet bought. Cassy said she could drive another two hundred miles, and farther than that, if she had to. I could see she was fading, but our brush with the law had scarred us both into keeping her at the wheel until exhaustion would force the switch. I had no driver's license and one with my name on it in Texas was probably worse than having none at all. I hoped Cassy could get us as far as Oklahoma still half believing that state lines offered some kind of sanctuary that they actually didn't. Overlapping jurisdictions plus federal statutes made that an illusion. Still, information about us need only lag an hour or so to make a huge difference in our fortunes.

Since leaving Albuquerque, I'd not stopped combing the channels on the truck's scanner for any kind of bulletin about a body, a stolen truck with an old car on it, or worse, Cassy's name and description. I'd tried conjuring up some sort of plan to enact if I heard anything like that, but none came to me. With the tanks topped off, I checked the tie straps that secured the *Rocket* and stowed the Luger inside it under the front seat. I didn't want a gun in the cab of the truck should another arm of the law stop us, and I surmised that if Killian did wake up, he wouldn't be in any condition to take me on. I almost welcomed that prospect, his bionic switchblade leg notwithstanding.

When we were again under way and rolling east toward Amarillo, the thought of the Luger began chewing on me. Keeping it at all might make me guilty of first-degree stupidity, a crime Max had once said he regarded as worse than most felonies. Several times I almost stopped the flatbed to retrieve it, and pitch it into one of several small lakes we passed over. But I didn't. I still wanted it.

About thirty miles east of Glenrio, I saw the thing that cinched my decision to keep it. "There it is," I said to Cassy who replied that she'd seen it too. In the downlights of a fuel station almost identical to the one we'd stopped at, the Mustang's dark red oxide primer was almost pink. The passenger door had only begun to open before the whole scene was behind us and swallowed up by the dark.

"He's got to be tracking us," I stated flatly. "If he wasn't, he'd be a couple of hundred miles east of us. He's been on and off our radar since he was parked on Yucca."

Nodding, Cassy took a sip of coffee, but fumbled trying to place the cup back in a holder that was attached to the dashboard. Several drops splashed on the top of the transceiver and made their way inside. There followed ten seconds of hiss and some static before internal heat cooked it into vapor and the clarity returned. Once and only once did we hear anything about a flatbed, and that one had already been stopped and it's driver questioned. I imagined he might have been mistaken for us. We rolled east.

Less than an hour later, the lights of Amarillo blazed up ahead of us. There was no reason to stop. We weren't particularly hungry and feared a meal would bring on sleep. A sign that advertised the big Texan Restaurant dared its readers to try consuming a 72-ounce steak in an hour so as to get it free.

We dined on No Doz instead. Amarillo came and went. So did Conway, Lark, Groom, Jericho, and Alanreed.

We did a pit stop at the fabulous Conoco station in Shamrock and topped off the Flatbed's tanks though they were practically full. That done, we emptied our own tanks with one of us always covering Killian with the Luger I'd finally retrieved from the *Rocket*…and still so wanted to be rid of. If we were caught, it would be found in the

Rocket anyway, so I might as well have it on hand.

"I can still drive," Cassy assured me when I'd finished. In the ten seconds it took to reach the passenger door and open it, she was slumped over the wheel and asleep. She stirred when I tapped her forearm.

"Slide over soldier," I said. As I walked around the front of the truck to enter by the driver's door, the Mustang cruised by on I-40 at considerably below the speed limit. I had no doubt we'd keep seeing it until whomever inside decided it was time to dispatch us.

We crossed into Oklahoma at just after eleven thirty. Over five hundred miles, and two state lines, were now between us and Albuquerque. Surely somebody had found School Bus and alerted the Khakis. If they hadn't, the crows and the coyotes were in for a night of gourmet dining. I never stopped watching for police cruisers. In the dark, it was almost impossible to detect their telltale head gear at any distance behind us. Three had passed us, as had three going the other way, by the time huge green signs and an epidemic of mercury vapor lights announced our approach to Oklahoma City. The sudden rush of lights caused Cassy to stir and awaken with a start. "Where is Oklahoma City?" she asked groggily, having spotted one of the signs. I replied that it was in Oklahoma, which got me a playful slap.

"There's still half a state to get through before we make Missouri," I said, when we'd gobbled up about half of the sixteen mile I-240 bypass around Oklahoma City that exits to I-44 and Tulsa.

"I can drive again," Cassy offered. I told her to save her strength and try to get some more sleep. Then an inspiration struck me that made me feel both brilliant and a fool for not having thought of it until then.

"There is something you can do."

Cassy turned to me. "What?"

I pointed to the bulge in the left rear pocket of Killian's trousers. "See if you can get his wallet. I might need a driver's license." By 1980, state driver's licenses all had portraits so there was no way I could pass myself off as Killian. God only knew what kind of arrest warrants carried his name, but I wanted to know who he really was, although there was no guarantee his license would tell me that.

I withdrew the Luger whose barrel I'd wedged between the upper and lower seat cushions. Steering with my left hand, and not slowing down, I pointed it half way between the top and bottom of Killian's torso. But his would place Cassy in the line of fire when she went to yank the wallet from him. I was going to tell her to wait while I thought of a different strategy, but she had the wallet out and opened before I could tell her to stop. Killian remained face down and motionless the whole time. After a brief probing excavation, Cassy produced a driver's license. She studied it and after a moment said: "Well, I would have guessed his name was an alias. Want to know his real one?"

"Yeah," I said, "or whatever name he was going by before it was Wilson Killian."

"Alright," said Cassy, "according to this it's Wright Kilbourn from Cairo, Illinois."

The words were icicles shoved up my nose. Not, for the smallest fraction of an instant did I connect Wilson Killian with the gorgeous youth I'd last seen when we were teenage comrades on a holy crusade to punish a world I'd believed had gone so wrong that it dared cheat me out of Alice.

Even "Killian's" prosthetic leg had failed to spark a connection to "Woody" Kilbourn, the heir to a fortune I'd once imagined was inexhaustible. *The* Woody, who'd loaned me the money I'd used to attend Colin Walker's funeral, and never repaid, was the passed out derelict on the floor of the flatbed, the one whose dentures flopped in frothy spit when he talked. I remembered Woody once saying how he was one of a tiny minority of people who liked their names when I'd told him that I liked my own.

Had Woody, like me, become one of Max's underground fraternity of fugitives? Or had he just been on board for a colossal joke Max decided to play on me when he sprung me from Huntsville? Or had Max just used Woody's name to amuse himself? I tried remembering Woody's height compared with the derelict's on the floor. It was Woody, it had to be. The prosthetic leg and certain voice inflections I was now remembering cinched it. I was glad to have seen him actually walk for the first time.

I began, and then arrested a laugh, while shoving the Luger's barrel back between the cushions.

"I guess this means something," Cassy said, "care to tell me what?"

I replied that I wouldn't know where to begin.

"Try twenty-five words or less," said Cassy.

After a moment's contemplation, I replied that I could in fact, do it in seven. Pointing down, I said simply: "His name is Woody, Max sent him." I could just hear Max telling me over and over again between his peculiar kind of belching laughter how I was the dumbest white man that ever lived, his most favorite description.

We rolled east toward Tulsa on I-44, that section of which is called the Turner Turnpike who's outstanding feature is that it's riddled with toll booths. The difference between turnpikes like the Turner and the great roads like Route 66, which it replaced, is that you paid to drive them. It's called progress. Once past Tulsa, where I-44 became the Will Rogers, the toll booths thinned out, and we saw the first signs that rattled off the mileage to Joplin and points inside Missouri, the last state between us, Illinois, and Cairo. The fact that "Killian" was no threat did nothing to make getting there in a single hop less pressing. At that point, I still believed that the man I'd shot in Albuquerque was just as dead and the truck I drove, just as stolen.

Pieces were falling into place. Since Woody had named Cairo, it meant Max had selected it, and driving there meant we were following a script Max had laid out for us. Had Max placed Woody in our company as a belligerent simply just to amuse himself? An oppressive realization fell over me that knowing this, I still was going to Cairo and that no matter how I resented it, Max Morgenstern was the only game in town and had been ever since he'd sprung me from Huntsville. But, there was no reason for him to know that I knew it, and was still playing the puppet.

"Cassy," I asked, "do you think you could get it back in his pocket?" I padded the wallet. Her look told me she regarded it a silly question and had it back there in less time than an answer would have taken her to give.

"Good girl," I said and then gave her a brief history of my career after leaving Willkie High. It included Max, Woody, *Velocity Jane*, the Legion, and the subsequent demise of our class President, Wally Motruska, a memory I'd often turned to when I needed an upper. Though I never knew the particulars, I'd heard from one source that Max had buried him alive.

The Will Rogers took us to the Missouri state line. It was just before three A.M.

"Missouri," I said to Cassy believing she was awake. She hadn't been, but the one word brought her up with a start. I cursed myself for breaking into her sleep. We stopped in Joplin, the first stop since Shamrock. Our gas gauge was well below the quarter point, and the cab of the flat bed contained a cornucopia of torn open snack bags; some of their contents spilled on the floor: candy bar wrappers, empty, and near empty pop cans. It amazed me what we'd consumed. I gathered and stowed it in a pump-side trash barrel already so overfilled that it regurgitated some of our debris as I walked away. The wind caught it and it was gone. I'd never taken my eyes off the highway the whole time we were stopped.

"It's here," said Cassy as I climbed back into the cab. She pointed to a trio of fuel pumps three lanes to the left where sat the Mustang. Now I was pissed. It was time for the unmasking. I grabbed the Luger.

"Sonny," Cassy proclaimed, "it's too bright here for that, they're going to see it right away and just might open fire."

She was right. I handed her the gun.

"Who do you think they are?" Cassy asked.

"I don't know," I replied exiting the cab and lowering myself to the ground. I marched across the lanes separating the Mustang from the flatbed with a self-righteous strut as if I were owed an explanation I had every right to expect. The Mustang thought otherwise. I'd only begun to cross in front of it when its engine revved to a roar and its right front fender dug into my thigh. I was spun two complete revolutions against the right side of the car as it hurled past me. The rear bumper clipped my shin and I was on the ground face down in smoking tire tracks. Cassy rushed over to me, "Sonny," she screamed.

"Help me, Baby," I croaked out, sure that something was broken. But apparently nothing was because I could walk back to the flatbed where I sat on the running board while Cassy knelt to face me.

"I'll drive," Cassy declared. I shook my head but would have allowed her to had she protested. I hurt too much to argue. But she didn't protest, and I drove. I wanted to be at the wheel the next time the Mustang showed up. We bought more coffee and rolled east.

Even in the dark it's not hard to tell how much prettier are the Ozark Highlands of Missouri than the plains of central Oklahoma or the Texas Panhandle. I wondered if any of I-44 contained sections of old 66, the road I had last driven at age 17 going the other way when I was then, just as now, on the lam. The more things changed, the more they'd remained the same. But we weren't long on I-44. I thought it a better than even chance that we'd lose the Mustang if we picked up US 60 just short of Springfield for the last leg of the run—if only we weren't spotted at the turnoff. I was sure we hadn't been, but I'd been too sure of too many things and wrong way too many times.

Cassy turned on the truck's interior light, studied the map, and began adding distances. "Just over 300 miles," she said before switching the cab back to darkness.

"That's five hours," I computed aloud, "right now I'm more than up to it." And I was. Massive caffeine doses, the pulsing of pistons, the staccato of yellow road dashes, squashed animals, and a sense of conquered distance had set off in me a road high. I'd felt it before, but it had been years since the last time. I was all fire, pain, and omnipotence now, and would remain so unless I stopped and found I couldn't restart because my fuel was exhausted long before I had any idea it was. Until then I was in zero danger of falling asleep. The blow to my thigh had left it a cauldron of pain stretching from my toes to my crotch. If I saw the Mustang, I wouldn't be sorry, but whoever drove it would.

And I told myself that Max had better have something in it for me having played his game of insanity. We rolled east ticking off the names of counties and towns along US 60. Periodically Cassy would total up and call out the remaining distance to Cairo. She too now was done sleeping for the duration. The pain in my left side rose to inferno proportions. Among the things I'd neglected to have her buy were painkillers, but I wouldn't stop now, even for those. A road sign that told us we were 95 miles from Cape Gerardo, Missouri coincided with traces of first light to fall on US 60.

We were just 150 miles from Cairo and there was no sign of the Mustang. Now one hundred thirty five miles to Cario, and still no sign of it. One twenty, one hundred, then ninety-two, and there it was. It must have been nested at a crossing because I'd been scanning the road behind us as well as ahead ever since we'd entered US 60 at Springfield. It was behind us and I was sure within inches of the exact measurement that separated us from it when we'd fled the parking lot at Albuquerque. Headlights appeared in the lane opposite us, followed by a second pair. Both shot by and we were alone again, the flatbed, the *Rocket*, the Mustang. It eased to the left lane and crept to a point abreast of us at a rate no faster than a man walks. I had the Luger in my right hand and my window cranked down.

The Mustang's window opened a crack and remained there for some seconds before proceeding downward much too slowly not to have been cranked by hand. It was half way down and I stared inside long enough to note that a jet-black form in the passenger seat so blended with the interior that only the vaguest definition was possible, and might still be that way even in daylight. I waited until it opened to the three-quarter point, swung the Luger across my chest, and opened fire. Every round, I thought, had made it inside because not one had hit the sheet metal or shattered the glass. Shell casings swarmed about the Flatbed's cab. I was, I believed, an incredible marksman. The Mustang didn't shudder, jerk or, break its stride. I fired two more rounds, and both, like the first, must have missed everything but the Mustang's black interior. And then, the realization struck.

"Cassy," I barked, "get down." She quickly obeyed. I aimed the gun at the passenger window opposite me and fired. A blast of flame and soot exited the barrel with an ear splitting crack and yet another shell casing ricocheted about the cab, but the blackened glass stood intact.

"Blanks," I roared incredulously, "this fucking gun is full of blanks!"

Why should that have been a surprise? Max had all but placed it in my hand. Our theft of the flatbed had been staged for the purpose of handing it to me, and Victor Hernandez, or "School Bus," like Woody, was just another actor. I wondered how they had managed to stage that fight as convincingly as they did. That Woody emerged from it almost un-bruised should have set off alarm bells.

"Goddamn you, Max," I said, looking at the Lugar. I could almost hear him laughing at me through the muzzle, howling about how I had given new meaning to the word stupid, and of course was, indeed, the dumbest white man to have ever drawn a breath. There remained the matter of the Mustang. Its passenger window was now fully open. In a gesture as automatic as it was futile, I hurled the pistol into the black void where it doubtless hit absolutely nothing except the Mustang's floor. I was convinced, as I ever would be, that the killers of Paul Phensgston and Frank Delmagio were about to add me to their list of missions accomplished.

I wasn't going to wait for the muzzle of an automatic weapon to appear and fill the side of the flatbed and my body with a storm of slugs. I had one chance at surviving: a flatbed is one hell of a lot bigger than a Ford Mustang. I punched the accelerator and at the same instant swerved hard left. It was something the Mustang didn't expect. The truck's rear tire caught the right front corner of the car, sucking it beneath and tearing the fender from its mooring along with the bumper and hurling both out behind us. But I'd swerved too hard and was all the way across the oncoming lane on a gravel shoulder bordered by a vertical drop that appeared bottomless. A tree branch struck the truck just above the windshield and smashed down the roof a couple of inches with a clang that could send my brain down my digestive tract. The Mustang was still coming on in the eastbound lane, minus half its nose. Something dropped from it and a rooster tail of sparks followed as it finally ground to a stop. I tried easing the flatbed back to the pavement and was greeted by a swarm of blazing headlights and blasting horns.

The shoulder had narrowed by a couple of feet. I tethered the brake to a halt as the flatbed tilted left toward the chasm and stopped. Had Cassy or Killian not been on the opposite side of the cab, I'm sure we'd have rolled over and into the abyss. The traffic I had to cross—almost non-existent in the previous hour—had become a torrent that wouldn't quit for a couple of minutes. I could hear the stones and cinders that supported us trickling down the drop. Finally, a window appeared in the traffic. I turned the wheel to the right and gunned the engine. Instantly, the trucks left rear tire skidded and swung over the edge and into the void spitting a storm of debris into the fresh April foliage. We began a sideward slide. I prayed that the truck didn't have one of those rear axles that allowed one wheel to spin full tilt while the other sat useless and dead. For a moment it seemed it did before a so-slight jolt told me the right wheel had bit deep into the gravel. I held the accelerator to the floor and the slide ceased. We inched forward and when the free tire ripped into the earth, we surged across the asphalt in a orgy of burnt rubber and sprayed gravel. Back in the eastbound lane, I held the accelerator to the floor until the speedometer read eighty-five. In the mirror, and far to the rear, I could make out the crumpled hulk of the Mustang, its one remaining headlight fixed straight ahead as if to say it was not yet done with us. We pressed on east. Cassy and I were yawning now and reeling, having been awake a whole twenty-four hours.

"Long way from Albuquerque," I said after a time. She reminded me that it was not Albuquerque but Flagstaff where we'd begun our day.

Woody had been grunting and moving in short bursts ever since the shot I'd fired inside the cab. Finally, he awoke and rolled over with quite an audible fart.

"Morning, Woody," I said abandoning my idea of not letting on that I knew who he was. He blinked, tried to focus on my face and gave up. The air was filled with ripe sulfuric flatulence. Cassy cranked down the sooted window, allowing a cross draft to sweep the cab.

"Looked in my wallet did you—Legionnaire?" asked Woody, rubbing his eyes. I felt an answer unnecessary, and merely nodded. Talk had become an expenditure of energy I felt I could ill afford. I wanted to pull over and ring answers to a thousand questions out of Woody while I pummeled him with the butt of the Luger before realizing I'd thrown it out the window. Also, I knew that the instant I pulled over, I would collapse on the seat.

"Where are we?" Woody wanted to know. I replied that we were about eighty-five miles from Cairo and asked what the plan was once we got there. I was snatching glances of his face, searching for flickers of familiarity, and trying to superimpose on it the once gorgeous features of the youth I'd known. It was no use. That would have to wait for daylight.

"The main drag," he replied, "Washington Street..."

I'd already forgotten my question.

"There's a place downtown called the *Powerglide Café* that never closes. Max will meet us there. Look for a blue Mustang with primer on it."

I turned to Cassy and, as if it were necessary, said: "That was Max back there?" Had it been anyone else I might have been convinced that I'd hurt or even killed him. Instead, I burst into a hoarse laugh. There was nothing I could do that was more appropriate. Cassy looked somewhat amazed.

"He's going to be pissed," she said.

"Max?" I laughed, "Trying to kill him is the first thing I've done that he'd approve of."

"What if you had succeeded?"

I shook my head. "He can't be killed by mortals, Cassy. I don't think God could do it on the first try."

35. EXIT THE ROCKET

When I told Woody we were eighty-five miles from Cairo, which computed to something like an hour and twenty-minute drive, I was wrong. Signs announcing the junction with I-57 sprang up just minutes later. Once past it, we gobbled up the remaining twenty-four miles in fewer than that many minutes, were on a bridge into Cairo, and a direct path to Washington Avenue. There wasn't a single turn off for me to screw up. Had there been one, I'm sure I would have.

The *Powerglide Café* stood aside a large parking lot among blocks of empty one- and two-story brick cadavers that were once a business district.

"This is it?" I asked as I pulled abreast of the entrance, though I was still on the street.

"What does the sign say?" Woody snapped, still on the floor since awakening. Judging from what was parked in a full lot and the number of Interstate trucks on the surrounding block, the *Powerglide* served a steady mix of traffic from at least four states. And at what I guessed was eight in the morning, there was one nice pull-into slot on the street for the flatbed which was providential since I was past negotiating the simplest maneuver. The *Powerglide* was an amazing counterpoint to surroundings that looked like they'd ceased breathing decades before. Besides it, and the two convenience marts we'd passed, downtown Cairo was a corpse that nobody had yet bothered to bury possibly because its traffic lights still blinked like the EKG of a brain dead patient.

Ignoring Woody, I switched off the ignition and promptly toppled to the seat. The last thing I remembered looking at was Cassy's face. She'd fallen asleep so that when I kissed her forehead, she was quite past acknowledging it. A minute later, I was out too.

The cab was empty when I stirred, probably a good thing too, because I'd had another Alice dream with details all plucked from others I'd had down through the years. How many times, I wondered, had Courtney heard me vow that I would love Alice forever before she resolved to destroy me? Cassy had heard it but once, and although Woody had never heard the slumberly vows, he'd certainly known about Alice Miranda Jones from our previous lives, those events on the far side of time. A dashboard clock, I'd never before noticed, read 8:32. I guessed this was Pacific Time since the truck was from California. This translated to 10:32 in Illinois were it correct. I lifted myself from the seat and peered out the passenger window to the *Powerglide's* parking lot.

It was there.

At first glance it seemed a miracle that it could have moved at all on what was left of its mangled front end, the right side of which was without fenders revealing an exposed wheel and half-inflated tire hanging from a suspension twisted from the encounter with the flatbed. But there stood the Mustang. Nobody could have beaten thirty more miles out of that carcass; but of course, Max had.

There was a pool of antifreeze beneath it and the entire front end was bathed in a boiling green cloud. A slight breeze pushed the ethylene glycol stench from it up my nose. I wondered if the Mustang would keep appearing every time I looked over my shoulder for the rest of my life. Max might have it in mind to arrange that.

I stepped from the flatbed never taking my eyes off the Mustang's half-primered carcass. With my first step on the ground, the forgotten pain in my left side bit to the bone and shot through the rest of me with an electric jolt that left me on the ground believing I smelled the ozone. Cassy rushed from the entrance doors and knelt beside me waiting for me to say something.

"It's all right," I said, almost laughing at the insanity of my own words. "Help me inside."

She carried at least half my weight through the entrance. I never took my eyes off the Mustang. Its twisted metal seemed to bare a grotesque expression of rage at what I'd done to it. I half expected its hood to fly open and a metal appendage to spring from beneath it to impale me.

"Max is inside," said Cassy as we passed through the vestibule.

"You've met him?"

She nodded making a face.

"Charming fellow," she replied, "the first thing he mentioned to me after he said his name was that he liked to hunt jocks and assorted human flotsam."

"You ain't seen noth'n, girl," I told her. She hadn't.

Because Max was seated inboard of Woody in a booth opposite School Bus, I saw him last. It had been just two weeks since Max sprung me from Huntsville and advised me to go on the lam. He was talking to Woody who was devouring an omelet and didn't appear to be listening. Max looked up at me, snatched a hard-to-miss-glance at Cassy's chest, and looked back down.

"Pull up a chair, Dillinger, I believe we are all acquainted," he said tonelessly. I did, making it a fivesome at the booth. Cassy sat outboard of School Bus on a small sliver of seat his enormous mass left for her. You couldn't really make out anything on the face of School Bus. He might have been smiling, but it was too easy to confuse expression lines with scars.

There was a half-minute of silence before Max began to speak following a sustained cough.

"Where do you want to begin?" he began, adding, "you must have some idea." I had the distinct feeling that he wanted me to explode into a hail of angry questions and accusations.

"What are we doing here, Max?" I asked in a tone as normal as I could make it.

"Having breakfast." He motioned to a menu, which sat on the table before me atop a sizable object. It was the first time I paid it any attention. I lifted the menu to reveal the Luger.

"I believe you lost that," he said.

I dropped the menu back over the gun. "Did you put in a fresh clip of blanks, Max?"

"No" he replied.

"It's not real anyway," he said finally. "A real Luger won't fire blanks."

"So Max, fake guns, fake rounds, fake bad guys," I said passing a glance to School Bus and Woody. "Nice choreography boys. What else was fake? Those stiffs back in Barstow?"

"What do you think?"

"They had to be real, Max."

"And who do you think killed them?"

"Are you telling me it wasn't you? You were there."

"I didn't say that," he replied, amused. I told myself Max had no motive. But at least he owed me a denial I could believe, and not more games.

"Why don't we let the beaver tell us?" He nodded to Cassy who I noticed had suddenly become red faced.

"Killers," Cassy said. "Ralph sent them."

I took a deep leisurely sigh of relief that I felt I'd earned. I desperately didn't want it to be Max, and his word that it wasn't him was good enough. But Max had to have at least seen the killers.

"Either they followed us," said Cassy, "or they went on ahead and waited for us at LAX. Ralph must have told them the flight we'd be on."

I couldn't imagine why Max deemed it safe to discuss murder and mayhem in a place so public unless it would be assumed that we were talking about a book or a movie had anyone picked up on it. It seemed an insane risk to me.

I looked at Cassy. "You knew all along?"

She nodded.

"Paul Phengston had already agreed to give up the damn car," I said, "What the hell did they want from him? Revenge for stealing that pile of junk twenty years ago?" If Cassy knew who'd killed Paul Phengston and Frank she must obviously know much more.

"No," she said, "but in a way, yes." I looked past her toward Woody, and then made a visual sweep around the table.

"She knew!" I exclaimed. Not one face at our table bore a trace of surprise.

"Were they supposed to kill me too?"

"Tell him, Beaver," said Max. "I would love to, but Dillinger here wouldn't want me to enjoy myself that much, so you do it."

"That was my job, Sonny," she said. "As soon as you and I were alone in the desert, I was supposed to kill you, burn the car with you inside, and drive away in the rental. They wanted you dead and as far from Paul Phenston's body as possible. I told them I would do it and they believed me."

"Even I didn't know you wouldn't kill him," Max added, so I sent in Woody here to see that you didn't. Dillinger, do you remember the phone call in Flagstaff you broke in on?"

I nodded having all but forgotten it. Max hadn't forgotten.

"Beaver," said Max nodding to Cassy.

"I had just told Ralph you were dead, Sonny," said Cassy, "and then your voice broke through loud and clear. From that point on we were both marked for hits."

"And this was to do what? Stiff me for my half of the two hundred thousand? Ralph couldn't collect it without the *Mulholland Rocket*. You said you were supposed to burn it."

At this point, Max erupted in one of his laughs that brought on another coughing fit complete with a belch of cigar smoke and spray of brown droplets, some of which landed on Woody's omelet. It didn't seem to bother him, he continued eating.

"Dumbest white man alive," roared Max again invoking what had to be his favorite phrase, at least his favorite of the month. Shaking his head, his expression was one of blissful satisfaction. I glared at him knowing how much he loved it. He seemed on the verge of a second eruption.

"You thought that bet was real?" exclaimed Max, "Incredible! It's about as real as that Luger and, by the way, I'd sooner give my ten-year-old niece, who hates me, a real gun than you, Dillinger. You belong in a home for the dangerously dumb." He stifled a laugh by blowing it through his fist.

I shook my head wondering if the next word out of my mouth should be "how" or "why" but could decide on neither. "Money Cassy? Was it for money?"

She replied without changing the red expression still on her face. "It was about the money we stole twenty years ago, Sonny."

What this meant still escaped me. "What the hell is that supposed to mean, Cassy?"

"You mean, why did I agree to kill you, and why did they trust me to do it?"

I looked at her without even nodding.

"Because I had the most to lose, I was in the deepest, and I'm the proven commodity. I killed Colin Walker."

This time the meaning sunk in. The children I'd sat next to in classes at Willkie had pulled off a six million dollar armored car heist and Cassy had put Colin Walker in the very coffin I'd flooded with urine two days later.

I had not noticed the waitress approach us until she deposited plates with identical orders in front of Max and School Bus. She tapped my shoulder and asked if I wanted anything.

"Working on it," I replied. Had I said 'no' she was liable to collect the menu and expose the gun beneath it. She turned away, walked several steps, and did an abrupt about face, "Is that your truck?" I nodded. "Sir, the manager has asked if you would move it. We're expecting a commissary shipment and that's where the driver usually parks."

"I'll do it," said School Bus and turning to me, adding: "You've already done enough damage." I gratefully surrendered the keys. If the truck was actually his, he had a right to be mad, but at Max, and Max alone. I could see the damage to its roof through the window from where I sat. I also noticed that the branch that had done it had likely smashed the windshield of the *Mulholland Rocket* and pealed back sheet metal above it. A few minutes before, I might have cared about that.

"When this is over, Sonny, I think you should buy him a new truck," said Max.

That really set me off: "How the hell do you expect me to do that?" I snapped angrily, though almost amused, "with what? You scripted this production, you can pay for the fucking thing."

"We'll get to that," he replied, amused. "I think we can buy him a new truck out of the six million." Max obviously planned to make the heist money his.

Through the window, I watched School Bus settle into the cab of the flatbed. The waitress stood two tables away taking an order. When done, she returned to us and said something she might just as well not have: "It's funny you know?"

"Funny?" Woody inquired looking up at her.

"The two men working on it before you," she said, indicating me, came in wearing coveralls; I could swear you weren't them, but that was you out there wasn't it?"

Outside, the truck's starter sounded and the engine caught with a slight roar. It might have taken me a minute, or maybe several minutes, to comprehend what this meant. It took Max Morgenstern about one second. I wasn't facing him and the next thing I felt was a hammer blow just inside my left shoulder that forced the whole upper half of me down to where my chin caught the edge of the table, slamming my jaw shut. What had struck me was the full weight of Max's body delivered by his foot as he'd leaped into the air. By the time I'd brought myself upright, Max had reached the doorway after stomping across three tables and several breakfasts. He stormed through the vestibule screaming something I couldn't make out, though it didn't matter. He was too late.

The force of the explosion hurled him back through the two doors and threw him against an inside wall where he'd landed in a pile of glass. A shock wave followed that sent tables, shelves, and stacks of plates airborne. A rush of heat shot through the smashed doors to bathe the interior of the *Powerglide* with a scorching slap on any uncovered skin. Instinctively, I shut my eyes and held them closed until I was convinced that they wouldn't be facing flames if I opened them. Then I looked through a still intact window to where the flatbed and the *Mulholland Rocket* had been. Remains of both lay fragmented about twenty feet from where they'd been a moment before. Part of the truck's cab where School Bus had been sitting might be the tangled metal rag about five feet from the glass I was looking through, or that might have been the *Rocket's* hood. I couldn't tell, not by the color, nor the shape for that matter. The rest of the car's body had been torn from the frame, though the floor, seats, and a pair of wheels remained peeking through the blaze. The *Rocket's* roof, still the discernable pillow shape with window cavities, was the piece farthest away. It was inverted, rocking like a cradle, while a massive flame soared from the wreck's main body sending a tower of black smoke into the morning sky above Cairo, so much like the ones in Barstow and Flagstaff.

Cassy was the first of us to reach Max. I was the last because I'd doubled back to retrieve the Luger. The rest of the *Powerglide's* patrons had themselves to worry about. Neither Cassy, Woody, nor I, had the slightest idea of how to assess Max's condition. His eyelids stood at half-mast, occasionally blinking. I'd so often seen my father pry back eyelids and examine something or other with a flashlight, but I'd never bothered to ask him what he was looking for. Max's skin was a pale red and his clothes were shreds. He was awash in cuts and abrasions; still no blood gushed from a shrapnel penetration so far as I could see. He lay just as he'd landed: amid a pile of shattered glass. Woody was the first to ask the question we all wanted answered but were afraid to ask: "Max, are you alright?"

He nodded. "Dillinger," he whispered, "go get his wallet." He raised his right arm and pointed at something beyond the vestibule. I looked…and narrowly arrested yet another impulse to vomit, now becoming so familiar.

Just past an outer set of doors lay an enormous torso. "We don't," said Max, "need to make it too easy for them."

I gathered he meant the law.

"Now Dillinger," he snapped, still whispering, "And I do mean now."

I got up and obeyed, walking through the twisted aluminum extrusions of the doorframes from which hung glittering crystals of smashed glass. The fact it was tempered glass and broke into obtuse fragments was the only reason Max had not been sliced to ribbons. Halfway between them and the corpse, my right foot hooked into something that remained attached to it. I looked down and the face of School Bus (Victor Hernandez, or whoever he was) stared at me; the front of my foot had plunged a considerable distance up his severed neck and I now wore his head on my shoe. I kicked it off with my other foot and it rolled away still looking at me once per revolution. I could have sworn it blinked. This was the second decimated human I'd been treated to in four days. The ranger under the train was the first. The others did not qualify; they were merely dead from holes shot in them.

It was amazing how quickly the nausea passed even when I stole a look down the black of School Bus's esophagus. When I tried tugging the wallet from his back pocket it wouldn't budge. The man's huge mass had wedged it tightly in place. Only by holding the torso by the belt still on it was I able to yank his wallet free. Done, I walked back to where Max was still lying in a heap.

Something that at first felt like a large lump of gum had adhered to my right shoe. I ignored it rather than look. I thought it was another piece of School Bus that would detach itself on its own, but it didn't, and by the time I reached Max, I forced myself to look. A small burnt green triangular wad peeked up at me from the sole of my shoe. Convinced that there were no human innards that color, I pealed it free. It was, or had been, currency. Nothing unusual about that, I first thought. It was part of the ten thousand Ralph had given me, and now, like the *Mulholland Rocket*, had been blown to bits. But Ralph's cash had been a loose pile we'd carried in a canvas satchel like a paper salad. These had been twenties, still tightly bound by a blue band with black print in a style that had long since fallen out of general use. "Rolland Goff Security Company," read the first line, and below that "Indianapolis, Indiana." On the third line were hyphenated numbers, "12-59." I stared at it for some seconds, the meaning of it pouring through me like liquid into an empty flask, when Cassy suddenly said to me, "So now you know, Sonny."

"Yeah," said Max, still the battered heap on the vestibule floor, but having recovered his voice complete with its full range of sarcastic tones. "Now the genius knows."

36. THE BANDS THAT BIND

Max tried to force himself erect, but collapsed on the smashed glass having raised his body only inches. A siren could be heard, then another. It wasn't hard to figure their destination. Woody signaled me, and each of us grabbed an armpit. Max's face was a contorted mask of pain, but he said nothing.

"Does it run, Max?" I asked, not even bothering to point at the Mustang. He nodded, adding, "maybe." Only once when we were loading him into the passenger seat did Max cry out. With Cassy and Woody in the back, I twisted the key in the ignition. The car started.

"Where to?" I asked, turning to Max.

"My place," Woody answered and followed with directions. "I live here now." I thought he might be kidding.

He wasn't.

Woody lived in a mobile home in a lot between two abandoned mansions. Alongside it was parked a faded Ford half-ton pickup with rusted-out doors. When I pulled up next to it, the Mustang, having run without coolant for God only knew how long, gave one final shudder and stopped. Its pistons must have become molten lumps fused into their cylinders. I turned to Woody and shrugged as if to ask how this onetime heir to what I'd always imagined inexhaustible wealth had come to live in a trailer in Cairo, Illinois. He read my unasked question and answered: "Later."

I would learn afterward that the answer was as simple as it was foreboding since it more than hinted at my own fate. Like me, Woody was wanted, though unlike me, he'd freely admit to committing two murders for which he harbored zero regret.

Max deemed Woody's case so hot that Cairo was among the few places that offered a reasonable chance at non-discovery. Besides the *Powerglide's* traffic, virtually no one had a reason to stop there.

Woody didn't really mind the two years he'd lived in Cairo. A sizable piece of his fortune remained intact and accessible. And he didn't use an alias; it seemed to me Max would have insisted on that.

Max had allowed Woody one weekend in Memphis per month—a less than three-hour drive—calculating that it fell within the range of acceptable risk. "The whores of Beale Street could stand comparison to any on earth at any price," Woody claimed, citing firsthand data from his days of wealth, freedom, and glorious decadence—a minor surprise. I had never imagined Woody paying for sex. He hadn't once mentioned my now ex-wife Courtney.

Two weeks before, Max had called him and offered the onetime head of "The Legion" a role in the maelstrom of events he expected my release would trigger. "It might be risky," Max had told him, or it might come to nothing at all, and it was, Max had stressed again and again, voluntary. Woody, who hadn't seen me since high school, leaped at the chance. He'd always wanted to try his hand at theater.

Max had the passenger door open by the time I'd gotten to the outside of it. Cassy, who'd followed me, took his arm, or tried to.

"Unless that's an offer for a blow job, Beaver," said Max, don't touch. If you do, I'll take it that you want to give me one." After two aborted tries, Max forced himself to a near upright stance and proceeded to the stairway of the mobile home. Woody dashed ahead of him to open the door through which Cassy and I followed. As we were passing through it, Max suddenly pointed at the car's carcass.

"That was a Shelby Mustang, Dillinger," he said, "in case you didn't notice. Thanks for nothing."

Inside, Max lowered himself into the nearest chair, something of a cone shaped pillow in a chrome plated frame. I imagined similar injuries would have left me screaming like an infant.

"I know a doctor," said Woody, "who can keep his mouth shut."

I expected Max to squelch the idea immediately, and perhaps to add a threat. He did neither, nor did he protest when the doctor turned out to be an enormous Negro whom Woody only referred to as "The Doc." Max did throw Woody a look hinting betrayal that the latter ignored while "The Doc" went to work examining him. Woody tapped my side and whispered: "he's very good."

After some very rudimentary tests, "The Doc" told Max to roll over and face down. When he did, Max's back was seen to be a vast expanse of old scars that hinted at a massive burn. I flinched, glanced at the Doctor's face for a reaction, and saw none. As far as I could tell, he was focused on the spine.

"Nam?" he asked presently, obviously referring to the scars.

"Yeah," Max replied, "same place you left the fingers?"

"Um hum," was the reply as if Max had asked if it were raining outside. It was only then that I noticed "The Doc's" left hand had but two whole fingers, half of a third, and a short stump for a thumb. From then on, I witnessed a comradery I'd never imagined Max capable of showing a man that wasn't white, or any man for that matter. Both he and the doctor seemed whisked back a dozen years to a place I'd moved heaven and earth to avoid. For a moment, I felt a touch of envy before reminding myself that no matter what kind of scars or medals I'd carried with me, they wouldn't have put me a millimeter closer to Alice. In my mind, Clifford Fitch had proven that.

After some twenty minutes, "The Doc" faced Max with an expression that told me the news would not be bad:

"You've definitely got a concussion," he said, "but I guess you know that. The burns are all first degree. There's a danger of cracked vertebrae, maybe several, which only X-Rays can tell for sure. I would recommend a real examination at a real hospital like Memphis General. Of course, you're not going to do that since there would be questions. I've got a pretty good idea of where you were this morning and, by the way, there are two dead bystanders, neither of them yet twenty years old."

It was the first time the subject of bystanders had occurred to me and I was pretty sure the same could be said of Woody and Cassy. From the beginning our concern had been with ourselves exclusively and we didn't remember seeing any other victims of the blast.

The Doc went on: "I'm going to give you a prescription for an antibiotic ointment and some fairly powerful painkillers. You'll have to get them filled in Paducah. The last drug store here closed two years ago. You're going to feel like you're on fire in a few hours, if you don't already."

Max looked at him as if he'd just been told he'd live a thousand years, "Would Jack Daniels substitute for those pain killers?"

The doctor broke into a half smile that displayed a huge set of very white teeth that made his face almost a caricature.

"Only if the dosage is sufficient," 'The Doc', replied.

Max pressed a thick folded wad of bills into the Doc's whole hand while they shared a laugh I thought might end sometime after dark.

With "The Doc" gone, we slept, all of us awaking roughly at the same time, which was well after nightfall, except for Woody who had arisen earlier and disappeared so as to procure a fabulous barbequed rib dinner. On the wrapping was the name *Powerglide Café.*

When we'd finished eating, and while Max uncorked the second fifth of Jack Daniels Woody'd procured. We'd shared the first, but Max had meant the second for his exclusive use. We seated ourselves in a rough circle.

After a long belt, he began: "I believe we were discussing burnt bills, the ones Dillinger found stuck to his shoe and the bands that bound them, 'them' being the heist money. Is that right, Dillinger?"

I nodded.

"Everybody else concur what that means?" He gestured for me to take it up from there.

"The *Mulholland Rocket* was the stick up car," I said, looking at Cassy. She nodded at this and all that it implied. Cassy, Bobby, Ralph, and Colin—the oldest of them barely twenty-two—had pulled off the armored car heist that had gone unsolved for over two decades. Five years later, the robbery of a British mail train by "professionals," which had netted less money, was cracked within weeks. Probably the Indiana investigators had never imagined anybody but professionals pulling that heist.

"And this was what you were after," I said producing the charred clump of bills from trousers I'd put on back in Flagstaff. It was not a question, but a statement Cassy also confirmed with a nod. "How much of that six million dollars went up this morning with the *Rocket?*"

"It couldn't have been much," she said. "I'd thought we'd completely unloaded the car before it was stolen." She shrugged. "We were so wired that we cleaned out the car in Ralph's driveway with the trunk facing the street and the car still running. Anybody could have spotted us carrying six million dollars into the house like groceries. Six million dollars! No one noticed. When we were done, and inside, nobody remembered that the trunk was still open and that Ralph hadn't shut the engine off. We were still wondering how we'd hide this huge pile of cash—now that we actually had it—when we heard the trunk slam shut. We looked out the window and saw the car being backed into the street. By the time we got outside it was gone. Only then did Ralph look for his keys and realize that they were in the car. We couldn't decide whether or not to report it stolen. We did finally, but we never worried about stray evidence; it just didn't occur to us."

"You probably got all but a few bundles," ventured Max. Cassy nodded, her eyes still closed.

The few bundles they'd missed had to have fallen into that steel pocket in the car's quarter panels behind the wheel wells that yield everything lost for years when excavated on any car. That evidence so damning, yet dormant for so long, was finally unleashed by the explosion that had killed School Bus and two others that morning twenty years later. But what was the rush to retrieve it now, and murder whoever had the *Rocket*? There was but one answer: blackmail.

"Blackmail," I blurted out.

"A cigar for Mr. Dillinger," exclaimed Max, "but nothing that cost more than a quarter."

"That would be the kind you smoke, Max," I shot back, hoping to at least elicit a giggle from somebody.

Nobody giggled.

Wordlessly, I recounted the story Paul Phengston had given us in the minutes before he was murdered. It was plain that he'd never seen any of the heist cash, nor had he connected the *Mulholland Rocket* with the heist. All Paul or Nell had known about the *Rocket* was that they'd taken something that wasn't theirs, and that had bothered them so that all they wanted was to give it back to its rightful owners.

Cassy, who'd produced and lighted a cigarette, pulled on it through the now familiar black holder. With her eyes closed, she appeared as if watching an old movie being screened on the inside of the lids.

"Blackmail," I repeated, this time speaking directly to Cassy. She opened her eyes and confirmed it with a nod. I wondered at what point in our odyssey Max had figured the blackmail angle. Was it when we were boarding the plane for Indianapolis, or before that? I started to say something before realizing I could go no farther and looked back to Max as if inviting him to take over. His face bore the expression of an orchestra conductor about to unleash the overture. But instead, he turned to Cassy. "Beaver?" said Max, "how did it all start?"

Cassy took a deep pull and began exhaling a blue contrail as she spoke: "The very beginning?"

"No," Max replied, "I'll want to hear about that too, but later. Let's just start with the blackmailing…"

"It was a letter," Cassy replied, "just an envelope that is, no letter in it at all. An envelope with a typed address to Ralph with a San Bernardino, California postmark and a band just like that one inside. She pointed to the band on the burnt bundle of bills. "The first one came to Ralph's office right after Thanksgiving. There were two more after that."

"Did Ralph let you know right away?" Max asked.

"No, he only did that after they'd gotten the third letter with a band in it," Cassy replied. "Bobby and he were sure that they had their blackmailer pegged well before getting the second envelope with the band. Charlie Novak was arrested in September. Bobby's firm has been preparing a defense for him."

"I assume for free," said Max, "since all he has to do is roll over on you guys if they refused."

It was the first mention I'd heard of Charlie Novak being in the mix.

"He has no money he can spend," Cassy concurred. "They caught Charlie in September during a traffic stop, and almost released him before they realized who he was and what he was wanted for."

"Which was?" asked Max somewhat amused.

"He'd killed his wife twenty years ago," said Cassy. "He's actually wanted in a lot of places for a lot of things he's done since, mainly bank robberies, a number of rapes too, mostly children. Anyway, when he was at Crown Point they ran him through a series of psychological tests. One involved hypnosis. The examiner was your cousin Harry Fisher, Sonny. Ralph and Bobby guessed that Charlie had leaked something to Harry while he was under since the first envelope came just three weeks later. They theorized that Harry had the bands sent to Ralph by some confederate in California. They never bothered with details like how Harry had gotten his hands on them, or why he hadn't sent them locally. The time line matched, and it came up, Harry."

Cassy stubbed out her half-smoked cigarette and began fitting another into the black holder. Her hands were trembling. Woody sprang to offer her a light.

"Did they ever show the bands to you?" Max asked, "And did they match the ones on the bundles?"

Cassy shook her head, "I never saw them, why?"

"Because they were probably copies," said Max. "If your sender had found even one of the bundles of cash in the car he'd have certainly cleaned the last of them out. But they were still there as of this morning. If nobody knew the money was in the car, where could the bands Ralph was sent have come from? Rolland Goff would never have kept any, being dated they were useless. What was sent had to be copies."

"What did it matter if they were copies anyway?" asked Cassy. "Somebody was on to us. Ralph and Bobby were in a panic and as I said, the time line came up 'Harry.' So they met and drugged Harry at *The Glass Dragonfly* and threw him under the train."

"Just like they did the Ranger," I interjected.

"I don't know about that. Harry wasn't big and he was an alcoholic. Ralph told me it was easy. Felix—that's the bartender—may have helped them with the Ranger."

I looked at Cassy recalling Felix as only a faded tattoo in the forest of forearm hair. The face was harder to conjure up. I remembered only the enormous nostrils. "I've met Felix," I said. "He's in on it?"

"He knows everything," replied Cassy. "He bugged the booths and confronted Ralph and Bobby with tapes of conversations about the heist. As of about a year ago, he's been our partner. They were so damn sloppy."

"It's a good bet he killed those two men back in Barstow," I offered, "and maybe School Bus too. Incidentally, was Victor Hernandez his real name?"

"That's something you don't need to know, genius," snapped Max, picking up the narrative and turning back to Cassy. "You never wondered if one of you sent the bands? There were three of you still at large."

"Three out of the original five of us that pulled the heist," Cassy concurred, "the fourth should have been Charlie Novak, the fifth was Colin Walker. He couldn't have sent them."

"Okay, Dillinger?" snapped Max. "Now are you clear on the cast of characters?"

"Charlie Novak could have had someone on the outside do it, but he had no reason to," Cassy offered. "And with Harry dead and the bands still being mailed, the likely suspect was Randy. Certainly Charlie could have told her about the robbery. And that we—I—had killed her husband. I don't know what they would have done about Randy, but then something happened that made Ralph and Bobby forget all about her."

"The *Mulholland Rocket*," Max mused, "I do like that name."

"Yes," Cassy agreed. "Ralph saw that magazine shot of the *Mulholland Rocket*, and determined it was taken in Barstow. The simplest explanation was that someone had found leftover money in the car, researched the robbery, and traced the *Rocket* to Ralph. The fact that the bands were being sent from Southern California cinched it. They expected the next envelope to contain a demand for money. The fact that it didn't made it worse. It was like a taunt. And for the last month and a half Bobby and Ralph spent every minute trying to figure out a way to get at whoever had the car. They were convinced it was them who sent Ralph the bands. And if they dared go to Barstow themselves, they were afraid they'd walk into a trap. They had no idea how much the blackmailer knew about them, but if they found him they expected him to be ready."

Cassy turned to me. "When you showed up in Michigan City last Wednesday, Ralph saw you as salvation. If anyone could find it, you could, and if you were killed by their blackmailer, so much the better. Then Ralph decided that you should die regardless. I'm sure Bobby was all for that."

"Like you told us, Beaver, that became your job," added Max.

Cassy nodded, pausing before she went on as I shook my head.

"As it turns out, the *Rocket* was in Paul Phengston's carport from the day that picture was taken up to the day we spotted it," I said. "On that day it just happened to be right out in the open. When we left Paul Phengston, the killers marched in on him and Frank Delmagio. I guess they were dead within seconds."

Max glanced absently about the room and then, looking directly at Cassy, said: "Nice little story, Beaver, I'm sure Dillinger here believes every word of it. Don't you Goyface?" (Goyface was a less used moniker Max had hung on me, referring to my un-Jewish features I knew he coveted.)

"That's right," I replied, "every word."

Cassy tried to throttle back a tremble.

"You believe it, Woody?" Max asked, turning to him.

Woody nodded.

His face was once the only one I'd once thought I would want for my next life if I couldn't have my own and I'd finally accepted that it was now the apparition attached to the top of the slouched figure five feet from me in the parlor of his mobile home in Cairo, Illinois. Time is indeed a lousy beautician. And I never believed it the great healer I'd always heard it was.

"Well," Max said finally, "it is the truth so far as it goes. The whole thing was an inside job. Colin and Charlie Novak were both drivers for Rolland Goff Security."

"But," I broke in, "if it was all theatrics, why did anybody have to die?"

"Because Charlie Novak was supposed to be the other driver, but he wasn't. It was a last minute change that nobody saw coming," said Max, puffing smoke furiously as he spoke. He broke a huge ember onto a paper plate that made the leftover Rib grease sizzle, then focusing intently on Cassy he said, "the Beaver will, of course, concur."

I turned to Cassy, but she'd covered her face with her hands, then, exploding into sobs, shook her head "yes."

"And the last minute substitute," said Max, "turned out to be someone you were a lot closer to than Charlie Novak, wasn't he, Beaver? And

Colin Walker wasn't going to let that detail spoil something that would allow him to live instead of just exist for the rest of his life as well as"—Max turned suddenly to me—"holding on to your beloved Alice. He might never carry so much as one million dollars again if ever. So they, Colin Walker, and Ari Kaufmann, your cousin from Israel, and Beaver, who was Colin's new partner, drove straight into a staged hold up that everybody but Ari knew was bogus. Did anyone get in touch at the last minute and let you know that?"

Cassy had uncovered her face to reveal an oval tangle of crimson mounds that seemed to be at war with each other for territory. Her voice broke twice, but she got it into gear on the third try. Shaking her head, she said: "There was no time."

"So," said Max reiterating, "little Ari walked into this pre-scripted drama and once it was underway, believed it to be real. How did he happen to wind up there anyway?"

"He was staying with us, but we had no idea he'd taken a security job," Cassy croaked out, her words weak and fragmented as if her larynx was hemorrhaging air. "I suppose he didn't want us to worry. He'd gotten his visa extended." Cassy covered her face again, shook silently, got up and left the room. Max signaled for a time out and held up five fingers to signify that many minutes.

We took twenty five.

Cassy amazed me. Her powers of recuperation were astounding. I'd never have guessed I was looking at the same swollen half hysterical mask she'd worn less than half an hour before. Instead, Cassy's face was one of the naked girl in the cabin of *Yesterday's Rainbow*, still young, lovely, and seductive.

"Suppose you tell us who came up with this whole enterprise," suggested Max, "the robbery I mean."

"Colin and Charlie picked out this particular payroll," said Cassy, "although the idea had to have been germinating since they found out that Rolland Goff carried huge sums every six weeks or so. It was a matter of waiting for the right one. Charlie had a pretty good fix on when that would be by paying bribes." Cassy paused to light a fresh cigarette. "Charle knew, and recruited Bobby, who recruited Ralph and me. The plan at that point was rough and full of kinks. Neither

Colin nor Charlie Novak could plan something that wouldn't unravel with an investigation. Ralph took it over and directed it like a play that, of course, it was. And Ralph, the perfectionist, insisted it be as real looking a holdup as possible from the start. That meant using real guns and live ammunition. We wore masks so if they polygraphed Colin and Charlie, they could say without lying that we wore masks and exactly what kind of masks. We had to tell ourselves that it was real, since an inside job was going to be the first thing they'd suspect."

"Right," agreed Max, "There were going to be a lot of questions later. You had to expect that. You did, didn't you?"

"We gave it some thought," said Cassy, but we were nothing but kids remember, Charlie was the oldest and he was twenty-five. I don't think anybody had any idea of what we would be in for; we were so high on the idea of pulling it off." She glanced briefly at the three of us. "Colin and Charlie were to tell how the truck stalled and we just appeared and robbed them. That would have been the story. Colin had complained how the truck kept stalling for about the week before that and the garage kept checking it out, finding nothing each time. I doubt that any story they told could have held together under five minutes of interrogation, but there never was one. Dead people are pretty hard to interrogate."

"It's easier when they're alive," concurred Max, pushing out a plume of smoke that added substantially to the choker already hanging over us. "So," said Max, "Colin stops the truck, gets out, opens the hood, and you three pounce on him. Ari is still inside. They have some kind of distress button don't they, one that sends out a Mayday or something like that?"

"Yes," Cassy agreed, "but Charlie had disabled it. He knew enough about it to make it look like it had burned out on its own. They're tested very infrequently. If Ari pushed it, nothing would have happened. Once Colin was outside, Bobby appeared, put a pistol to Colin's head, and ordered him to throw down his gun belt. Then Ralph ordered Ari out just as if he were Charlie Novak."

"So far, so good," said Max. "You were going to act the whole thing out just the way it was to be with Charlie, weren't you? You had to etch everything into Ari's head because Colin and he would both have to tell the exact same story, right down to the shoelace tips. Only Ari didn't know it was a play. And the minute he stepped out of the truck, he recognized you, didn't he?"

"We'd had breakfast together an hour earlier; I was wearing the same clothes."

"Your body is pretty hard to miss too, Beaver," said Max. "And then Ari said the one word that would end his life: your name."

Cassy shook, but her voice remained controlled.

"Colin had tossed away his own gun just as Bobby had ordered. When Ari recognized me, Colin walked over to Ralph and took his gun. Ralph had absolutely no idea what to do so he let him take it."

"But," said Max, "Colin knew what to do, didn't he?"

"He shot Ari," said Cassy, "just shot him, first in the chest, then the stomach, and again in the chest. Ari never stopped looking at me as he went down. There hasn't been a day since that one that I haven't seen that beautiful face, looking at that grotesque rubber mask, and knowing who was behind it. So I shot that bastard Colin, that filthy, fucking bastard. I emptied my gun into him and then I took Ralph's gun out of Colin's dead hand and emptied the rest of it into his corpse." Cassy took several deep gasps and then appeared to recover, "I seized Ari and shook him and screamed at him to say something. He died with me shaking him and demanding that he answer me. They had to tear me away from him. And they put me in the back of the Nash screaming, then, Ralph and Bobby loaded the money into the trunk of the car. I don't remember anything after that, anything about the rest of the day. The next thing I remember was being in Ralph's driveway and it had already been dark for hours."

Cassy shook her head as if trying to expunge the memory from it before continuing: "Bobby and Ralph were taking the money into the house right through the front door as if it were groceries. At first I screamed at them when they told me to help. But something took over. Ari was dead, and if I didn't get a grip, we would all wind up in the electric chair. So I helped unload the money." Cassy began to cough.

I got up, walked over and knelt by her, but she waived me off. Then, with her face again buried in her hands, she rushed to the sink and threw up. Max looked at me as he exhaled another blue plume. He reminded me of a car that needed a ring job. In ten minutes, he'd burnt through three-quarters of his fat cigar and now studied the tip. "I think it's time we took another five," he said. And with that he stood up. Again we took at least twenty-five.

Woody and I sat regarding each other without words while Cassy went to work rebuilding her face for the second time that evening, again amazing me with the results.

When she rejoined us, Max nodded, and we resumed. Believing that we had beaten the last detail out of the holdup, I seized the initiative: "Cassy," I asked, "if Ralph and Bobby meant to use me to find the *Rocket*, why did that asshole set off the fight at the reunion that nearly had me on the way back to Texas in irons?"

"Ralph had been trying to reach Bobby for two days so as to tell him he had the chump they needed to locate the *Rocket*. When Bobby finally showed up at the reunion, Ralph had only been talking to him maybe half a minute when you crashed in. Bobby had twenty years of rage against you boiling inside of him. There was no stopping him. Only after the fight did Ralph get to Bobby and lay out the trap the two of them set for you under the guise of a wager." Cassy paused…

"Remember when Ralph sent you to the supply shack in the harbor for batteries? That's when he laid out his plan to me along with telling me my job was to get rid of you once they'd gotten their blackmailer. I agreed to kill you believing I could talk you out of going to California in the first place. But you went for it anyway. I couldn't have told you anymore without telling you everything.

"You did try to stop me," I admitted. "Max," I said, suddenly turning to him, "Did you have to make me take the truck and 'shoot' Victor? Couldn't you have just had him hand it over to me and tell me who he was and that he worked for you? Or couldn't you have jumped in any time and told me everything you knew about Bobby, Ralph, and"—I looked at Cassy—"her?"

Max sat impassively contemplating the ash of his cigar.

"But you had to make me jump through hoops, didn't you, Max? This was all a big game for you from the time I told you I was going back to Michigan City. I almost opened fire on a trooper's face with blanks. He would have finished me then and there."

Max continued listening to me, though now casting a polite gaze around us, as if doing the kind of appraisal a puppeteer would of marionettes to which he'd assigned roles.

"You are correct Dillinger," said he, I could have handed it all to you."

"But…"

Max cut me off, "But you were never in the military, Dillinger, and that's too bad. You're likely going to have to save your own life by shooting somebody that stands between you and what you want before this is finished. And whoever that is, they will be more than ready to kill you. This is a long way from over, Dillinger, so I set up a boot camp for you. I had a bet with Victor Hernandez that you wouldn't shoot him and that we'd just have to give you the truck. You really surprised me, Dillinger. It was the best hundred dollars I ever lost. You can thank Victor Hernandez for a couple of other things too, like that ruckus at the Arizona border that got you past the Smokeys with no license plates."

"That was School Bus?" I exclaimed. "They never did catch up with him, did they?"

"School Bus? Is that what you call him?"

"Yeah," I replied, "he wore a yellow jacket and he was as big as a school bus."

"Victor was a professional," said Max, "the best wheelman on the West Coast. He was the driver in at least thirty bank jobs and jewelry heists. Nothing ever went wrong because of his work."

"Sounds like a great man alright," I said sarcastically. "By the way, what was his real name?"

"Don't get smart with me, Dillinger," Max snapped. "He died for your sins, the worst of which is the usual one: stupidity."

I let that one pass, it seemed to me that School Bus, and or Max, had not exactly acted like geniuses given what they'd known. And Max had no right to blame me for what happened to School Bus.

"Who was it that got rid of that cop in Flagstaff, the one that went under the semi?" This was a silly question. Who else could have been driving the Mustang?

Max blushed. "That was me, Dillinger," he said. "That was me, as if you didn't know. I was really only going for a distraction, just something to get Smoky out of your way, and I happened to wind up ahead of that semi. I kept about ten car lengths from it, and then nailed it passing the Motel. Smokey took the bait. As I said, I only meant to distract him. The fireworks were pure gravy." He paused reflectively, "pure gravy," he repeated. "It was a payback for a lot of traffic tickets too."

"So Max," I asked, "When was it you realized I was walking into a set up?"

"When I first talked to your friend Shrinko," he replied. "When we started out, he sounded normal enough, no strain in his voice whatever. When I pinned him down to specifics, it was like breaking open a piñata.

"He was that easy to read?"

Max gave me an exasperated sigh but did me the courtesy of not making a game of it like he had everything else.

"When he's lying," said Max, "he inserts syllables into words that don't belong there. "It's a common enough trait. If I've seen it once, I've seen it…oh never mind."

I had indeed noticed Ralph doing that. "I just imagined it was a nervous habit, like a tick."

"A tick," Max mused. "Shrinko is a lying sack of shit, Dillinger. I hate people like that they should be killed.

"You're right, Max," I said, "they should be killed." But Max knew that I didn't mean it, not when it came to Ralph. Despite all the treachery, Ralph had promised me a meeting with Alice, and on that he'd delivered.

Max signaled without a word that it was time to decide what we'd do now and any more discussion of the past be put to bed. We could have gone on for hours, but the details that remained were inconsequential drivel.

Max began by spiking it into my court: "Alright Dillinger, what are we going to do about this?"

I almost said that all I wanted was to retrieve my fifteen thousand from the storage locker in the Franklin Street Station and head for parts unknown. This would not do. The fifteen thousand might stake me for two years, or possibly three with every penny pinched, something I was never good at. And I needed Max's protection if I was to remain at large.

"We're going to get the six million, Max," I declared, sure that it was the answer he wanted.

Max clapped his hands in concurrence.

"Beaver," he asked, "how much of it is intact and in one place?"

Cassy said she had no idea.

"Any idea where they're keeping at least some it?"

"Not for sure," Cassy replied, "it's been in a dozen places."

"Has it been in any of them more than once?"

Cassy nodded.

"Good," said Max, "they're out of ideas, so they're rotating it. Tell me the ones you know about."

"From the beginning?"

"The beginning," insisted Max.

Cassy proceeded to do that: For the first few months it stayed in attics and crawl spaces or packaged in steamer trunks. Once they'd gone off to various colleges, Ralph bought a small enclosed utility trailer and parked it in a self-storage locker for which he was fanatical about paying the rent on time. It had been there about ten years, even after Ralph got married and bought his first home with an attached garage. His wife never knew about the robbery so he could hardly keep it there long before there would have been questions. For a while after that, Bobby was in charge of keeping it. For a couple of years it had actually been buried in the ground.

"None of you worried that another would grab the money and do a disappearing act," asked Max, "especially with it being in something so portable as a trailer?"

"We were worried Charlie Novak would try," Cassy said, "but as I told you before, he had to skip town to escape being charged with killing his wife. Just knowing about the heist kept us all in check. If anyone talked, the best he could expect was a five percent reward and immunity from prosecution instead of a fourth of six million dollars, so no one ever threatened to do that. Even when Charlie was on the run, he never worried about us trying to screw him out of his share."

I broke in, "You never tried to fence any of it?"

Max looked at Cassy as if my question was the next one he was going to ask.

"A few times," she replied, "and each time we came very close to getting caught. It's all silver certificates, fifties and hundreds. The bills I saw are nineteen fifty-three issue and the older they get, the more attention they draw. When's the last time you spent a hundred dollar bill? They're really scrutinized. They're looking for counterfeit bills of course, not hot ones, but pass more than say five of them within a hundred miles radius and you're running a risk. They take down license numbers just in case a bill turns out to be phony and if somebody discovers it's not counterfeit, but hot, they know who passed it. I'm sure the serial numbers are recorded."

"Yeah," interjected Max, "It's how they cracked the Lindbergh kidnapping."

"We once believed that Vegas would be the place to dump a big piece of it," Cassy continued. "Ralph and Bobby used assumed names, bought a car under one of them, and stayed at a two-star motel some distance from the strip. Using the hot bills, they gambled for several hours until they'd exchanged most of the money on them, and then went back to their motel, but there were men waiting for them. Ralph spotted them just in time to get out of there. They might have been anybody from Feds to casino dicks. It didn't matter. They came home on a bus. You don't have to give your name to ride a bus."

"No prints in the motel room?" asked Max.

"They wore gloves in the room," Cassy replied, "but couldn't anywhere else."

"When was this?" asked Max.

"That was four years ago. We haven't tried anything since. Then Felix, who, as I said, forced his way into our partnership, said he'd found some fences that could be trusted. But they'd set him up and he killed them. She passed Max a warning glance, "He's very dangerous, Max," she said, addressing him with his own name for the first time.

Max smiled, indicating he considered this a detail he looked forward to. "Where does Ralph store that boat of his during off seasons?" asked Max suddenly. It was no surprise to me that he knew about *Yesterday's Rainbow* as well as everything else.

"He stores it inside one of those metal prefabs behind his house that's alarmed to the nines," replied Cassy.

"Not in a boatyard?" mused Max, "he keeps it in a special building, hmm, interesting.”

He looked about the trailer.

“My guess,” he said, “is that the money is on the boat. Now that the boat’s in the water, Ralph or Bobby can sail off with it anytime things overheat and they want to try the new identity route. The Great Lakes are a big chunk of water. The glitch is that if the money is as radioactive as you say, it’s useless to them. So the boat’s the first place we’ll look. There are a lot of hiding places on a boat. We’ll probably have to do some demolition. Don’t expect it to be in the sail locker where a burglar could stumble onto it, but, of course, we’ll look there first. You did mention, Beaver, that they’re sloppy.”

Cassy nodded.

This sounded simple enough; we would break into *Yesterday’s Rainbow*, rip out its innards and take the money.

“But we’re going to offer them a deal first,” Max said, surprising me. “Dillinger, you’re going to put it to them.”

We all sat looking at Max wondering what he was ready to offer Ralph and Bobby who would be no match for him in a game of murder that they had already started playing.

“If they agree to turn over the haul from the robbery, we’ll split it six ways,” declared Max, “the four of us, and the two of them. Fencing the money will be no problem. I can get at least sixty-five percent on real currency. That’s six hundred fifty thousand each and no tax, of course. But, by the time you make the offer I want us to have our hands on the money. If they accept, we’ll honor it.

I shrugged.

“What about Felix and Charlie Novak?”

“Part of the deal,” Max replied. “Nobody will ever have to worry about those two again, nobody.”

Max turned to me. “I suppose you’re wondering why I want to let them keep anything seeing as how they tried to kill you, Dillinger.”

I nodded, offering Max an upturned hand.

“Call it professional courtesy,” said Max. “At seventeen years old, they pulled off a heist that some of the best people I know two or three times that age wouldn’t have dared try. In a way, we all earned our share. Beaver here certainly did. I've known a lot of people that once wanted me dead, Dillinger. But I considered the whole picture, gave them a pass when I could have killed them, and a few, not all, of course, became the best friends I ever had. I really hope this works out, but if not…"

37. HOMEWARD

I should have slept far better than I did considering my sack time since Flagstaff probably totaled less than five hours out of thirty-six. Cassy was apparently in the same mode lying alongside me except she cried a lot. We made no attempt to conceal from Max the sound of an aborted try at sex around one AM. A wafer-thin partition was all that separated us. It was half done to remind him I still had a few cards of my own including the one he'd probably trade all of his for. I had a great compulsion to rub his nose in something—anything—considering what he'd put me through.

Sometime during the night I heard him on the phone ordering the car that would take us to Michigan City. I couldn't imagine any place that rented cars being open at that hour, but remembered that Max almost always operated through third parties. I hoped he'd order one with a back seat big enough for me to pass out the minute we hit the road for Indiana. Max instead ordered two cars, both of them Cadillac Sevilles like the one I'd blown up in Barstow along with the remains of its owner Frank Delmagio, and those of Paul Phengston. He even had the color matched. Max had a thousand ways of letting you know just how much in control he was.

They were delivered before daybreak and a flatbed picked up the remains of the Mustang around the same time. At an amazingly good breakfast, which Woody cobbled together, Max told Cassy and me to confront Ralph with his proposition when we got to Michigan City, that he would get in touch with us there, without saying how, or if it could be the next day. Max said he ordered two cars because he had all of me and my blundering he could stand for the moment, and assumed that I was equally sick of his calling me on it, though an imbecile could see this wasn't his reason. He wanted time to find the money. We were to leave *no less* than four hours behind him.

Woody was offered the chance to quit or stay on for the finale. Max had a plan that he said could work with, or without him. Woody would get his share of the chips either way, but Max revealed nothing else. I was another matter. He wasn't done with me by a long shot.

Woody said he was in, and Max's final act before departing was to press into my palm a sharp edged metal rectangle with rounded corners: "Nash Motor Works," it read, "Kenosha Wisc." It was the body plate of the *Mulholland Rocket*. I didn't even try to figure how he'd gotten that. Cassy and I had no trouble sleeping with Max gone, and we left not four hours behind him, but six. Since Max had not imposed a time limit, we decided to take a whole day to reach Michigan City and confront Ralph on the following one. For some reason, Max had slackened the reigns, anticipating what we'd do even before we decided what that was, or maybe he just didn't care.

We left Cairo a few minutes after one that afternoon.

Cairo is very roughly triangular, its three borders being the levies of the Ohio and Mississippi Rivers and the wall that closes off the City from the north when high tides threaten. The only road north out of Cairo passes through a rectangular breach in the wall that can be guillotined shut by an immense steel door that looks as if lifted from some medieval castle, though I doubt any were ever that large. Bridges to Kentucky and Missouri both feed and drain the city's traffic from the south. The only other way out of Cairo is by boat or a long hard swim.

Crossing the bridge from Missouri the day before was but a vague memory. I had been too close then to passing out. Cassy told me that Woody's only real complaint about Cairo was that it was too easily sealed off should his whereabouts become known. They'd had quite a conversation while I slept after "The Doc" had left. I asked her if he'd mentioned how he'd gone from the heir to vast sums of old money to become part of Max Morgenstern's fraternity of fugitives, a fate that loomed before me should I survive the next forty-eight hours. He'd told her the same story that I'd heard along with the same scant details. It was nice that it checked.

After that we had only stillborn conversations for a hundred miles. Both of us avoided one topic: Alice.

Through the two decades that I'd never given up on winning over Alice, I took for granted that Alice had never given up on nailing her husband's killers along with a fury at me for the renal sendoff I'd given his corpse. How much Alice knew was the wild card. If she'd sent the currency bands to Ralph, she knew everything. It was not hard to imagine Charlie Novak spilling the whole story to her. And even if he hadn't, she was just too close to all of them not to have figured something out. Why Bobby's firm was defending Charlie for free was no mystery. If, as Max had reasoned, Bobby refused, there was no reason not to squeal. If Charlie did squeal, he could kiss his defense goodbye. The six million might be downright radioactive, but nobody that knew about it was about to give their share for a one percent reward and a plea bargain.

Why then, had Alice sent the bands? One answer sufficed. She wanted the heist money herself and had begun a game of cat and mouse with the hope that Ralph and Bobby would turn on each other, placing the money up for grabs to someone with knowledge and a little muscle.

Max planned to offer six equal shares along with eliminating Charlie Novak and Felix. He had not mentioned Alice in that calculation and I knew damn well that he hadn't forgotten her. I didn't like what it implied.

As it stood, Ralph, Bobby, and Felix had good reason to believe that I had died in the explosion of the *Mulholland Rocket* in Cairo. And finally, they probably still believed that they had disposed of their blackmailer in Barstow who was never a blackmailer in the first place.

Since we doubted we were being followed, there was no reason not to take the route to Michigan City that anyone would who looked at a map: I-57 to a point just South of Chicago, then a few miles of intermediate manipulations ending on 94-East. It was practically a straight line.

At a roadside complex north of Kankakee that included a restaurant called *The Undercarriage*. We ate the first normal meal alone since finding the *Rocket*. All the others since had been either bags of snack food or two meals shared with Max where normalcy was impossible.

A primary rule of life on the road is that where the trucks are, the food is either very cheap or very good but generally not both. *The Undercarriage* is one of those exceptions. Its food was neither cheap nor good. We ate it anyway. The only real conversation commenced when Cassy asked me if I'd meant what I'd said about my cousin Harry being a criminal.

"Harry was a criminal," I affirmed, adding that neither Harry, nor his mother, were actual relatives, biological or otherwise. Harry was a sick son of a bitch (literally) who after getting his ticket as a psychiatrist, graduated from torturing animals to taunting children to the point of suicide.

"The one redeeming thing about your enterprise so far," I said, mimicking a gun with my fingers to indicate I meant the holdup, "is that Harry was a casualty, and ironic too, since he was never one of the players."

"Ironic," Cassy agreed.

"Throwing Harry under a train may well be the thing that will keep Ralph and Bobby from burning in Hell," I mused.

"Well, now that you've granted them redemption, what must I do to keep from burning in Hell?" There wasn't a trace of mirth in her voice. I sat mute realizing how far I'd just shoved my foot into my own mouth.

"I killed Colin Walker you know," she said, fitting a cigarette into the now perennial black holder, and searching herself for a light that I finally provided.

"I'm working on that," I answered. She replied with a stare intense enough to make the tablecloth burst into flames were it directed that way.

"Do you believe in God?" she asked. This set me to groping for any way out. "I used to claim I didn't," I replied, hoping she would let it go at that.

"And now?" If anything her stare had intensified. I could have sworn the fork I held was getting warm.

"I don't believe," I said—hoping that this would end the topic— "that anyone or any group of anyones could have made this mess we call the universe without divine help…not even Max Morgenstern, and mess making is a mission with him."

At that Cassy's stare dissolved.

I stood up and put a tip on the table that reflected my assessment of the food. Perhaps the waitress, whose only crime was delivering it, deserved better, but I didn't care. Someone needed to take the fall. Cassy got up and we headed for the cashier. She was still shouldering the bag containing the bulk of Ralph's ten thousand dollars, the cash meant to buy the *Mulholland Rocket*. It hadn't blown up with the car as I'd first thought, Cassy had kept it with her.

It was Wednesday. The one week that had passed since I'd stepped off the train on Eleventh Street seemed a decade. The *Mulholland Rocket* had come, gone, and taken seven people to the grave with it in the three days since I'd found it and that didn't include the ranger.

"I got it," I said to Cassy fearing she was about to unzip a duffle bag and have an avalanche of bills tumble out. I dropped a twenty on the counter.

"How was everything?" the cashier asked, not even looking at me.

"Fine," I replied, just fine, but you could have included a milk bone for desert; dogs love that kind of thing after eating what you just served."

He took a minute to digest this. "Sir," he said, "would you like to speak with the manager?"

I didn't answer.

"Sir," he raised his voice a notch, "Would you…"

But I was past responding, held up a left palm, and preceded with a lunge at the newspaper rack. And there it stood, in the leftward most column in italicized lower case type:

"Accused killer at large after N. Indiana jailbreak."

I had no need to read any further for a name. I snatched two copies, which emptied the rack, and plopped them on the counter. The cashier dropped my change on top of them. "Take this out of it I said, tilting the newspapers. About two and a half dollars slid off the counter and spilled on the floor. We walked to the car and got in. I handed Cassy one of the papers and clicked on the overhead reading light, then each read our separate copies.

"Crown Point Indiana: Charles Darwin Novak, charged with the 1959 murder of his wife, a string of subsequent Bank Robberies, and juvenile rapes in eleven states over the last twenty years, broke out of the Lake County Jail Wednesday at about 1:30 AM local time and remains at large."

I'm a slow reader and Cassy reached the two critical lines ahead of me. She let out a slight gasp before I caught up with her.

"Novak made good his escape using a Luger automatic apparently smuggled into his cell. It was later recovered and found to be a replica capable of firing only blanks. By the time Novak abandoned it, he had seized several actual guns from prison personal. A massive manhunt involving law enfacement contingents from eight counties is under way. Novak is considered armed and extremely dangerous."

"Another player," I said, "joins the fray."

Cassy lit a cigarette, this time without the holder, and drew hard on it.

"Max?" she asked, exhaling smoke.

The details screamed it. Somehow Max had provided Novak with the exact kind of phony gun he'd given me. The front-page story was as if it were Max sending me a message in the personals—and it triggered a really ugly thought: Clifford Fitch was the obvious conduit for getting the Luger to Charlie Novak. Clifford and Max had known each other since 1959 thanks to me and what I'd done at Colin's funeral. They'd also known each other in Vietnam. I was furious at the idea of Max dragging my best friend into this.

Max was already moving and on ball bearings. Eliminating Charlie in a prison cell would have taken too long. At large, Charlie was a sitting duck for someone like Max. The phony Luger was perfect, and if he were shot dead using it to escape so much the better. That hadn't happened, but Max clearly was drawing a bead on Charlie Novak and loving every minute of it.

I inserted the key into the ignition and twisted it past the "on" notch to "start." There was no sound from the starter. Instead, three beeps from behind the dashboard told me that we were both probably dead. I sat still and said simply to Cassy, "Get out!" I didn't bother to reach for the door handle since I had in that split second decided that whoever had placed the bomb would never have given us a chance to escape.

Cassy had barely moved when the Seville's rear speakers crackled to life:

"Five," barked a recorded voice, "Four, three, two..." At "three" I recognized the owner of the voice and exhaled hard. What followed, a recording of a nuclear blast, aided by GM's latest of gizmos, the *Delco Bose* sound system split the interior of the Seville and everything within it, beginning with our ear drums! When it had not quite died away and our brains still hammered against the interior of our skulls, a voice I had once tagged as the "Max Morgenstern Taunt" began:

"Good evening, Dillinger. Now that you have been vaporized by yet one more act of incredible stupidity in an incredibly long list of incredibly stupid ones, may I acquaint you with the simple rules of starting a car when someone has demonstrated an intense desire to see you dead and has already tried the very same thing once already? Rule Number One..."

I punched the eject button on the dashboard's tape player and yanked the cassette from the slot.

"Cassy," I said, "get out of the car and stand at least a hundred feet away."

"You don't think."

"No, I don't," I replied, "but indulge me anyway."

When she did, I twisted the ignition key. This time the Seville's starter sounded for an instant before its engine caught and lapsed into a smooth idle. I stepped outside, leaving the driver's door open and walked toward her.

"What now?" she asked.

"Let's find a place to spend the night," I replied, "I'm fucking tired."

Half an hour later we were bedded down at a *Ramada Inn* nipping at bottles of PBR. I told Cassy how I intended to approach Ralph when we got to Michigan City.

"Are you sure that's what our fearless leader wants?" Cassy asked.

"I'm guessing it's why he handed me the body plate from the *Rocket*. If he had anything more specific in mind he'd have said so."

"Will he know what you're doing, Sonny, and when?"

"You haven't guessed?'

"No"

"It's very simple. Max had the same clown that rigged that bomb stunt bug the car. Open the trunk and I have no doubt there's a transmitter inside, a very powerful one that lets him hear us wherever he is. Try not to let on that you know it, and whatever you say don't let the word '*troll*' slip."

"I can do that," she replied, "and there's one more thing you should have from the *Rocket*." She reached into her duffle bag and produced Mother Mulligan's automatic. I'd completely forgotten about it.

"It's loaded," Cassy added, "and not with blanks. I bought three full clips for it in Flagstaff. Any reason anyone else has to know?"

"None I can think of, Cassy, nope, no reason at all."

38. IT SO HAPPENS
HE'S TELLING THE TRUTH

On Thursday afternoon just after four, I nosed the Cadillac Seville into a parking stall in the garage that made up the ground floor of the building where nested the practice of Ralph Falolnhurst, MD. There was an elevator to the two office floors above the garage which Cassy and I never considered taking, having seen enough movies to convince us they were death traps—as if stairways weren't.

The receptionist's desk in Ralph's office was empty. I motioned Cassy to a chair positioned at right angles to the one where I sat after surveying the contents of a magazine rack on the opposite wall. To my amazement, the rack now held another copy of the magazine where Ralph had spotted the *Mulholland Rocket*. I opened it to that page, sat down, and passed it to Cassy, who tossed it on the table between our chairs.

The intercom on the desk had been left on, and a prolonged moan from it bounced about the waiting room walls. It was followed by an equally prolonged, "Yessss." Cassy started to giggle and I motioned her to stifle it although I couldn't keep from grinning myself.

That intercom system must have been brand new because the sound quality was the equal of hi-fi systems then on the market.

The moans and "yesses" formed a cadence so regular that a drill team could have marched to it. Some two minutes later the breaks between the moans and "yesses" were filled in with a series of grunts. There wasn't a single crackle of static.

"Moan, grunt, yesss, moan, grunt, yesss." It was the most perfect (and only) verbal interpretation of a boat being rowed that I'd ever heard. I offered Cassy a mimic of the rowing with my arms timed to the beat emanating from the speaker.

That was too much.

Cassy doubled over in a silent convulsive laughter that took me over as well. We eased to the floor from our chairs, hands over our mouths to keep from howling. Finally, the cadence was broken by a low level shriek that I guessed signaled Ralph had detonated. His grunting melted into a moan and the pair moaned together in protracted harmony like a pair of coyotes until one of them ended it with a loud fart. Both Cassy and I remained on the floor, our hands still tightly clamped over our mouths, silent still, but unable to keep drool from making its way between our fingers. We managed to get back to the chairs only seconds before the door opened and we got a look at Ralph's secretary. It was obvious that, had Ralph not hired her on the spot, she would have had another job within the hour, and if she'd actually reached eighteen, it must have been on that very day.

At first she looked quizzically at us. Then a succession drawer clicks and a second flatulation from the speaker announced that we'd missed none of the performance. She swatted the intercom off and threw us the kind of angry glare that only enhanced the hilarity.

"Yes?" she said finally.

"Yessss," responded Cassy.

"Who are you?" snapped the girl. "And what are you doing here?"

"We have an appointment," I replied. She went to her desk and opened a leatherette bound book.

"There are no appointments this afternoon," said she, with another adolescent attempt at indignance.

"My name is Rocket Mulholland," I said, "and this is my co-pilot Betty Blastoff. Please give my card to the Doctor." I got up and tossed the *Rocket's* body plate onto her desk. It fell flat after a short clanky dance. The girl pushed a button on the phone's base unit.

"Yes, Jennifer," said Ralph through the speaker that had offered such a static free delivery of their performance.

"Yesss," hissed Cassy and we both broke out laughing all over again.

"There's a Mr. Mulholland here with a woman…an older woman," the girl replied. Her glare had regenerated into a much-improved version that actually transmitted the anger she felt.

After a ten second pause, Ralph's voice broke through the speaker,

"Show them in." Jennifer pointed to the door. I retrieved the body plate with the girl glaring at us all the while. As we passed through the doorway, Cassy smiled at her.

"Get someone to teach you how to fake an orgasm, Honey," she said. "That one wouldn't fool the village idiot."

"She's right," I concurred. "But it just might fool, Ralph." I winked at the girl who said: "fuck you," and turning to Cassy said: "fuck you both.

"Shall I see if the Doctor would like to make it a foursome?" I quipped.

"Nah," answered Cassy, "once a month is his limit. After that, he can only shoot a kind of bloody pus. Hope you didn't get any on your playground, Honey." Cassy made a face. "I'd recommend an industrial strength douche A.S.A.P. I think *Janitor in a Drum* makes one that they sell over the counter."

"You would, of course, know," the girl fired back. She was a fast learner.

"What lovely fangs you have, Grandma," I said to Cassy as we stepped into a short hallway."

"All the better to impale your cookies with my dear," said she.

The path to Ralph's office seemed to have shrunk from the last time I'd been there. His door was closed and we entered without knocking. Had it not been for the performance Ralph and his secretary had treated us to, I'd never have done this since it was fair enough to expect Bobby and him to be waiting for us locked and loaded. In the last analysis, for reasons I could never fathom, I half trusted Ralph.

He sat at his desk perspiring and toying with the cast aluminum model of the Nash. I tossed the body plate on his desk. He picked it up and read it.

"That's all that's left of it?" he asked finally.

"Oh no, Ralph," I said, "it's just all I could bring you. The rest is back in Cairo, and among the pieces left there are those of the man that died in the blast that destroyed it along with two others, which makes for a total of seven in the last few days. And Ralph, none of them had anything to do with blackmail. In fact, the man I bird-dogged for you, the one that stole the *Rocket* in the first place, was seriously considering returning it. It only bothered him that he'd stolen it. He knew absolutely nothing about the robbery."

"A man died along with him," Cassy interjected, "He was following us because I'd promised him sex for information, turns out we didn't need it; we'd already located the car."

"I'll give you this, Ralph," I said, "You really got your money's worth. You should have seen that bloodbath in Barstow. But your man, or was it 'men,' really delivered for you in Cairo. I counted five large pieces of the guy that was supposed to be me. Also there were two dead bystanders, kids really, victims of our silly games."

"And, Ralph," I continued, "need I mention that it would be a bad idea to make any move that might be construed as going for your gun? It's still in the second drawer, isn't it?"

As we refocused our stares at each other, Ralph pushed and pulled that cast aluminum model of the Nash back and forth in vigorous six-inch strokes. I had a thousand threats and curses saved up in me to unload on Ralph but now realized that they were all redundant. I'd just said everything.

"How are you going to get the money if you kill me?" he asked.

"First, Ralph, are we talking about the hundred thousand I'm supposed to get for bringing back the *Rocket* in that bogus bet you and Bobby staged, or are we talking about the six million dollars from the heist?"

Ralph looked toward Cassy who shook her head 'yes.' Ralph breathed a sigh of resignation, "The heist money, of course."

"Now you're talking, Ralph. It so happens this could be the best day of your life, certainly the best one since you pulled that heist, because there's a way out for all of you, Bobby, and Cassy here with the same, if not more of the money you figured on getting in the first place. The money will be divided six ways instead of the original five, but my man can fence it at sixty-five percent. That means six hundred and fifty thousand for everybody."

"This would be that lawyer you called, Max, the one that I talked to Saturday morning?"

"Right you are, Ralph, his name is Max Morgenstern…and get this Ralph: Max likes criminals, Ralph, he likes them. The fact that you pulled off a heist like that when you were in high school really endeared you to him. It's something he would love to have done himself. Trust me, I knew him then. He actually looks up to you."

Ralph turned to Cassy, "He knows everything I take it?"

"Everything," she replied. Hadn't I just revealed that?

"Well, he doesn't know everything," Ralph offered.

"No?" I exclaimed. "There's something you care to add?" I couldn't imagine what that might be.

"The man I sent never killed those people," declared Ralph, "or anybody else, at least in the last week."

"Uh huh," I snapped sarcastically expecting Ralph to start inserting syllables where they didn't belong.

"He was several flights ahead of you out of Indianapolis, Sonny. I dispatched him before you left. He was supposed to follow you from the LAX terminal. Instead, he was spotted and pinched on an old rap from when he lived in California. He was in the Los Angeles County lock up until yesterday. He's out on bail."

"And back here already?"

Ralph nodded.

"And, of course, you provided the bail, fearing he'd talk."

"Of course."

Ralph exhaled the words with a slight cough as if they were soot.

"It's Felix, isn't it, Ralph?"

Again Ralph nodded.

"One thing always leads to another doesn't it? So now the monster has one more head—really sloppy how you bums let him get on board. That's how you found out *The Glass Dragonfly* was bugged isn't it?"

Ralph looked down. I thought he was going to cry. He reminded me of the day he pulled into the gas lanes at Ray's service station with the *Mulholland Rocket*. I put my hand on his shoulder.

"Ralph," I said, you have no idea how lucky you are."

He looked up at me in anticipation.

"As part of the deal, Max says you'll never have to worry about Felix, or Charlie Novak, who is at the moment free in case you didn't know. But not to worry; they will be cut from the equation. Max guarantees it and he's a man of his word."

Ralph looked like I imagined a man does when he's just been told that he doesn't have the cancer that he was certain would kill him.

"But, Ralph," I added, "and don't fucking lie to me. What do you know about the killings in Barstow and Cairo?"

"Nothing, Addison, I swear to God, nothing."

"Nothing?"

Ralph shook his head emphatically.

"What about Bobby? Could he have hired back up that did it?"

"Impossible," answered Ralph. "Once I'd put Felix on you, Bobby figured it was a done deal. He could never have hired anybody on such short notice. He doesn't have the connections. He thinks Cassy bumped you off too. I told him she did," he said, turning to Cassy then to me, "I only knew about Cairo because of a story in the Chicago Tribune with a picture. I picked up the outline of the *Rocket's* roof in it. Only I could have known what I was looking at and there were any number of conclusions I could have drawn, but we hadn't done it, that I knew. There had to be other players. Somehow I figured you'd survived. If so, there was no point in trying to hide from you. It appears you're indestructible."

"Ralph," I said finally, "I have ten thousand reasons for calling you a lying sack of shit and to believe absolutely nothing you say but for some no good reason, I believe you."

It occurred to me that Cassy and I had yet to sit down and I was suddenly tired. I looked around for chairs, snatched two from along the far wall opposite Ralph's desk, and seated Cassy and myself facing him. So far, he had yet to insert extra syllables into words.

"Thank you, Addison, for believing me," he said flatly.

I might have expected a little more gratitude in his tone. Nor was there a trace of an apology for having set me up for the slaughter… there was a beep from the intercom. Ralph touched a button on it.

"There's a man on Line One who wants to talk to a Mr. Dillinger," came the voice of Jennifer.

"It's Max," I noted.

"Put him through, Jennifer," Ralph said. She did. Ralph handed me the receiver, "Hi, Max."

I didn't bother to ask him how he knew where I was. The car had to have been bugged. I almost told him that I was in Ralph's office but thankfully arrested the words. Max would have made the most of again calling me an idiot.

"Ralph," I said, and pointed at the intercom. "Shut that goddamn thing off."

"Oh yeah," said Max, "you might mention to Dr. Genius there, that the jail bait he's been fucking has yet to turn seventeen."

"She's sixteen, Ralph," I said pointing at the intercom with a laugh that inflated my cheeks.

Ralph sat red faced.

"Max," I added, still fighting off laughter, "I think he accepts your offer."

Ralph nodded his head vigorously mouthing the word "yes."

"What about his partner? The one you're so found of."

"What about, Bobby?" I said.

"I can guarantee he'll go for it," was the reply."

"He guarantees Bobby will…"

"I heard him," said Max, cutting me off.

"Max, Ralph says it wasn't his man that did Barstow or Cairo. I almost believe him."

"You would, Goyface, yeah, you would believe him. Is he inserting syllables?"

"No, Max, he hasn't done it, not once."

"You sure?"

"Yes, Max."

"Okay, Dilllinger, it so happens he's telling the truth."

I almost blurted out: "What now?" too late. They would have sounded like the abject surrender they were, a dog anticipating a command. Max had at least done me the favor of not making me ask.

"We all meet at the—what's the name of this place?"

There was a pause and some mumbled words in the background that I couldn't make out.

"*The Glass Dragonfly*," he relayed, "*The Glass Dragonfly* at 8:30."

Ralph's desk clock read 4:20.

"That's four hours and change from now, Max," I said, knowing I was going to regret saying even that much.

"Amazing," said Max, "the gentleman can count and tell time on top of it. Well, they're all yours to do with as you please, all of them. And

I have no doubt that you'll manage to fuck up every minute of them, and I know exactly how."

I hung up without saying goodbye and turned to Ralph.

"*The Dragonfly*," I said "at 8:30. Be there with Bobby. Max knows your man didn't do Barstow or Cairo."

He sighed, exhaling hard.

"I almost look forward to meeting this 'Max'."

"I can guarantee you'll eat those words."

"I don't see how I'm going to avoid it, see you at 8:30."

"Where are we going?" Cassy asked as we got up to go, "Oh."

I looked at her as if it weren't obvious. "Oh, what?"

"Oh, her," said Ralph smiling for the first time since we'd entered his office.

As we walked back to the car, a fresh and very bad thought struck me. If Ralph's hit man didn't commit the murders in Barstow, the spotlight fell right back on Max. I so desperately didn't want it to be him.

39. TOLL HOUSE COOKIES

How many times had it been that in anticipation of seeing Alice Miranda Jones that I would do so with the certainty that this time it would be different? Down through two decades I'd concocted an uncountable number of scenarios preparing for it. I had expected my marriage might have halted it, but should have known better. I would find myself in not always silent mock conversations, imagining Alice's retort to some stroke of brilliance I'd floated, and then my brilliant counter retort. Or would it be some little manufactured antidote that would prove once and for all to her that I was the cleverest, most interesting male on the face of the planet, as well as, if it weren't obvious, one of its best looking? They had all been as perfect as they were dead wrong. Alice had never read the scripts I'd written and couldn't recite her lines.

The only option open to me now was to wing it, just like I had on my first date with Alice, the only time when things had ever worked, the time when I'd almost kept my mouth shut.

Per the Michigan City white pages, Alice lived in a townhouse on Fairburn Avenue not far from the home where Ralph's family had when I decked his father. It was just before five when I nosed the Seville up to the curb. I actually hoped she wouldn't be home for another hour or so, but an open doorway could be seen through the screen.

"Good luck," said Cassy as I left the car. She didn't seem the least bit worried that I would tell Alice who had killed her husband.

I rang the bell.

Alice called out that she'd be right there. She was. Our eyes met and her expression halted somewhere just short of a scowl. "What?" she said, after almost no pause at all.

"I came here to finish our dance," I replied.

"My stereo is broken."

"There's the radio."

"It's broken too."

"I can sing if I have to."

"But you won't leave, will you?"

"Not till I've said my piece."

Alice snapped open the screen door lock.

I went in.

Her parlor had been decorated recently. I would have thought Alice, herself a work of art, might have shown better taste. The furniture looked as if made of orange crates and painted with a broom so as to hide that fact. It was new though. I'd seen it in showrooms that pedaled overpriced schlock. I knew there were suckers somewhere buying it, but I'd never imagined it turning up here. There was a sepia painting that looked like it had been produced by allowing monkeys to wallow in their own waste and sealing the result in lacquer.

Another painting was of a clown.

But the most amazing thing was that there wasn't one picture of the late Colin Walker. I'd expected a dozen of them to be glaring back at me. There was no explaining that.

"Are you renting this place?" I asked.

"My place, my stuff," was the reply. "You don't like it?"

"I didn't say that."

"You don't have to," Alice retorted. "What's that bulge in your pocket? Oh Jesus! Alright what do you want?"

"What? Oh that."

Mother Mulligan's .32 was in my pocket only because I'd forgotten about it. I pulled it out and set it on the coffee table, aimed a whole 90 degrees away from Alice and closer to her reach than to mine.

She bolted backward nonetheless. "What do you want?" she demanded. "Money? Is it loaded?"

"No Alice, not from you, and yes, it's loaded." I couldn't imagine Alice believing I'd come there to hurt her, but as I had once said, Alice had never read any of my scripts. She was eying the telephone. I reached in my other pocket and produced the burnt wad of money from the explosion in Cairo. I was sure there was no need to explain what it was. I dropped it on the table. We both stared at it.

I tried fighting off that now too familiar sense of non-reality, half of me refusing to believe that I was talking to the Alice I had promised myself I would make mine through every day of two long decades.

I shoved the burnt money across the table. Alice picked it up and read the name on the band. She gazed back at me. The puzzled look that momentarily replaced the angry one had set off a small, warm tidal wave through me. Was it possible I might yet strike a positive cord with her, undo all the old damage of twenty years before, and convince her of what I was already so convinced of: that there was absolutely nobody else for either of us but each other?

"Finally she said: "*Rolland Goff Security*. Colin worked for them." It hardly sounded like an admission.

I nodded. I wondered if, or how I should tell her that her husband had killed an innocent boy, a child really. Yet, to what lengths would I have gone in order to hold on to Alice? The answer was that I'd have done whatever it took.

"The robbery," she declared finally, giving me my opening.

"The robbery," I repeated, "was an inside job. Your husband and Charlie Novak planned it. Colin was killed when it didn't follow the script they'd worked out with the others."

"So you know who killed him?"

"No Alice, I don't," I said, wondering just how much it showed that I was lying.

"It was Cassy," said Alice, with a calm certainty as if she was telling me which way was up.

"You knew?"

"Yes."

"For how long?"

"Since October."

"Then Charlie Novak told you."

Alice nodded.

There was nothing else to tell her. If she knew that, Alice had known everything and had known it long before I'd set foot in Michigan City.

"And you didn't go to the police?"

She shook her head, "Why should I?"

"Your Husband..."

"After three and a half months of being married to Colin, I wanted him gone even more than I wanted you gone, and believe me, that's a lot of gone. Marrying him was the worst mistake I'd ever made in my life. Why would I want to put the one person who got him out of my life in jail for the rest of hers?"

It was the last thing I would ever have expected to hear. For twenty years I'd imagined Alice crying herself to sleep over her beloved Colin, vowing to bring his killer to justice. The axis of the earth had shifted. *Alice didn't want Colin!* I spat out the first thought that came to me: "There was another reason too, wasn't there Alice?"

She didn't answer.

I continued: "Another reason you never went to the police. It was the money. Rat on that gang and nobody would get the money except its rightful owners. Now that's a disgusting thought." I hesitated, not believing I'd just accused Alice of the kind of greed found in normal people.

She was silent for a moment, then: "I don't know what you're talking about, Addison July." Then: "I want you to leave." How could she say that she didn't know? She had to know everything.

"Alice, the little blue currency bands, the replicas of the ones on that burnt cash you're holding? You had somebody in California send them to Ralph. You imagined that Ralph, Cassy, and your cousin, and yes, I know he was in on it, would suspect each other and panic, maybe unearth the cash, and you, or rather your friends, would pounce on them, and seize the money. What I don't understand is how it took you twenty years to come up with the idea of sending the bands."

Her 'you are insane' look didn't fool me.

"And what were you going to do then?" I asked. "You would have to kill them wouldn't you? They'd already killed to get it, and had killed again to keep it. They threw my cousin under a train just because they suspected he'd sent the bands. What would stop them from doing the same thing to you? Why didn't you have somebody force one of them to tell you where the money was? Or couldn't you recruit the muscle to do it? That's it, isn't it? You needed the muscle and you didn't dare to bring in anyone else that didn't already know. And you sat there while Ralph and Bobby concocted that bet that I could find the *Mulholland Rocket*. You knew what their game was and that even they had no idea you did. How did you ever keep a straight face, Alice? I know I couldn't. Everybody knew it was a hoax, even Cassy. Everybody knew except stupid little me."

"I think I've heard about enough," Alice snapped. "Now I think you should leave."

"That's a shame Alice," I said. "I was just getting started."

For a moment, I didn't care how much more damage I was doing, or how angry Alice got. I had to let her know that I wasn't a fool—Alice would never love a fool.

"When you had those bands sent, Alice, did you have any idea of what you unleashed?"

"I told you I don't know anything about bands," she replied. "Now get out!"

"What are you going to do, Alice, are you going to call the police? Would you like to know how many people are dead because of those stupid pieces of paper?"

"Get…" The phone rang. Alice picked up the receiver, listened to it, and handed it to me looking somewhat dumbfounded. I didn't even bother to say "hello."

"Max," I said, "she knows everything. Charlie Novak told her."

"Yeah," Max replied, "everybody knows everything except you."

"What did I miss?"

"A minor detail," answered Max.

"What? That Charlie Novak…"

"Is in the doorway to the next room," said Max. "Don't look that way and for God's sake if you have a weapon don't go for it and don't make a break for the door; he'll cut you down before you get halfway there. His twelve-gauge is already leveled at you. If you're lucky, he'll want to play cat and mouse before he blows off your beautiful little face. Stall him and try to maneuver him to where you're standing right now. Squirm, say anything you have to, beg him not to kill you, he'll love it. I'll do the rest. Now, slam down the phone like you're angry and say something 'like fuck you, Fred.' It just might throw him off."

"That's it, Fred?" I snapped trying to put on an angry tone, remembering that I had just called him 'Max.'

"Yes, except he'll probably rape the girl when he finishes with you, but it won't matter if you're dead, will it?"

"Fuck you, Fred," I roared, sure I'd fooled nobody and slammed the receiver on its cradle. The impact made Mother Mulligan's gun tumble to the carpet. Now only its barrel projected from beneath the couch. I was sure I could have dived and gotten it in time, but decided to obey Max.

Alice looked at me, dumbfounded still the dominant expression on her face, then: "Who was that?"

"The choreographer," I replied. We both stood. Alice turned to walk away and put about ten feet between us before stopping in her tracks.

Charlie Novak walked into the room. Max was right about the artillery being pointed at my chest.

I was amazed how much Charlie resembled the image I had of him: a compact muscular assemblage of repulsive components that began with a balding dome and progressed downward through a face sculpted like a half-eaten apple. The apple sat on a neck that wasn't there at all. The torso was stacked tires, supported by a pair of tree trunks plugged into enormous shoes. From certain angles he might have made Max look attractive.

One look at him told you something else: that he was as dangerous as he was ugly. Charlie Novak was radium. The face fidgeted as if the flesh and tendons were themselves debating the expression to display, finally scttling on something teetering between a triumphant scowl and the kind associated with a perfectly timed orgasm. I wondered if he would climax when he blew out my chest, or if he could hold on until he was raping Alice. Maybe he was already discharging. He angled the 12-gauge so as to align its barrels with my neck. Staring at him, I computed the steps between Alice and myself. In a split-second dash, I made them and threw my arms around her without breaking stride.

For a moment, the man's expression lapsed into one of genuine curiosity before assuming the rage that went with the realization he'd been checked.

"What are you doing?" Alice demanded.

"I'm saving our lives. Want an explanation?"

She didn't answer. She might have figured it out. But I didn't wait for her to tell me that.

"You see Alice," I said, "besides killing me, he's here to rape you. But I'm in the way. He can't use that 12-gauge without turning you into blood and gore along with me. You're no good to him unless he likes fucking the dead. Maybe he wants to slit your throat while he's climaxing. Hell, you know more about him than I do. He's a very bad boy, Alice. But he can't kill us one at a time with that shotgun. In a way, it proves one thing at least for now: we can't live without each other."

I kissed Alice for the first time in twenty-one years. She didn't parry or try to deflect it because she hadn't seen it coming. I backed off and waited for a reaction. There wasn't one. Her face was one of neutrals, a meter connected to a long-dead battery. I would have preferred a slap, a groin kick, or anything to that.

I'd kissed a wall. I looked back at Charlie Novak. He had begun to advance on us, moving further still from the spot where Max told me he herd him. I could almost feel rising rage in him override that equilibrium that had kept him from pulling the trigger and making a bloody pulp of us both.

Certain I was going to die, I thrust my face at Alice. When the gun went off, a swarm of pellets would rip simultaneously through our flesh, bones, and organs. There would be a tidal wave of blood, hers and mine, gushing into each other as we died. And they would never be able to separate, absolutely, what had been hers and what was mine, never absolutely. We'd each go to our graves with fluid and pieces from each other in our corpses. If I had to pick a way to die, this might have been it. I pushed my face at Alice, my mouth aligned with hers, and sucked as if trying to inhale her. She tried fighting me off. I ignored it, drawing her still tighter to me. How much of the blast I wondered, would I hear before it all went black, or would it all go black?

I waited.

In an instant I would know. But the instant passed, as did another, and finally a third. Slowly I released Alice and turned back toward Charlie Novak wondering when the scorching swarm of buckshot would tear through us.

He had advanced no further. He had in fact backed off and was smiling. With his eyes, and with a quick nod, he told us that he'd found the solution to his problem, the way he would kill me without doing the same to Alice. Inclining his head, he made for that place on the floor where he'd spotted Mother Mulligan's .32. A crimson ripple radiating from mismatched nostrils spread across his face. He set the 12-gauge on the floor then lifted and aimed the .32 at my chest. He'd risen to perhaps three quarters of his erect height when the window behind him exploded. I don't remember any sound of shot at all, nothing but a shower of glass filling the room. Impulsively, I turned away just as the oncoming shards sliced into my shirt and left forearm. I was fairly sure I had shielded Alice from all of them. We stared at each other for some seconds, me not wanting to turn away, until the realization broke that it was all over. Alice wrenched herself free and we both took in what remained of Charles Darwin Novak.

The bulk of him was half on the coffee table that threatened to overturn from the oblique load his torso had imposed on it. A leg extended down to where its knee dug into the carpet. The left arm was beneath him and the right hung at an impossible angle, its hand still gripping the .32.

There was a long furrow torn through the center of his back like one made by a plow on virgin soil. His coat, shirt, and flesh were neatly parted so as to reveal smashed vertebrae some of which still hung on a severed spinal cord. Others were scattered on the floor as if beads removed from a string. Blood, and what I guessed was bile, trickled from the end of his neck where his head had once been attached. I spotted that several feet away. I could swear a smile was still half-frozen on the intact face that bore an inch-wide hole on the forehead just below the hairline from which brain tissue had formed a reddish-grey conical shape at the exit wound. It occurred to me that Charlie Novak had not said one word to me and never would. I looked back toward Alice, but she was gone. Just then I could hear that particular clanking sound toilet seats make when they're hoisted against the porcelain tank. A retching noise followed. I could not for the life of me imagine the sight of Alice hurling vomit.

The doorbell rang.

I dashed for it determined that nobody must be allowed to see the interior of the townhouse. But it was Max.

We walked back into the parlor. I closed and bolted the front door behind us. Alice stood in the middle of the room wiping off her mouth with a towel. It was the first time I could recall not wanting to seize and kiss her. After pulling down the window shades, Max went over to inspect the headless corpse. It was as if he were trying to determine whether or not it was dead.

"Did you check his pulse?" I asked playfully. Max flashed me the kind of glare a renowned surgeon might give an impertinent intern.

After a brief survey of the torso, Max found and placed its former head on an unoccupied corner of the table. He gathered vertebrae from the floor and restrung them on remains of the spinal cord that was not long enough now to accept the last three of them. Max placed them in his jacket pocket as if they were change. He'd yet to say a word. Then he stepped back so as to take in the scene of the entire room, as an artist might survey a canvas he'd just completed. It was clear Max considered it exactly that, and I wouldn't have argued the point.

"Max," I said, "I had no idea he was coming here."

"No, Goyface, you wouldn't have. For the record, he came in the back door just as you were coming through the front. Actually my idea was for him to die trying to escape prison, but…." He smiled, picked up the head of Charlie Novak as if addressing it. "All's well that ends well, right?" He set it down on the table with a delicate deftness one might use to handle a valuable artifact. It was obvious he was savoring every nanosecond.

"Where's the telephone?" he asked finally.

"I think it's under him," I answered.

Max hooked the toe of his right foot under the edge of the table and with one heave lifted it. Charlie Novak and his head spilled to the floor. A chartreuse stream belched from his neck and puddled on the carpet. Mother Mullingan's automatic tumbled to the carpet. Max picked it up. "Yours?" he asked.

I nodded.

"Interesting," he mused, "a chrome automatic, the kind old women carry in their purse. You would keep the one thing to tie you to Barstow if it's registered. If you wanted a gun why didn't you ask me for one?"

"I've already had one of yours, Max," I said. So did that poor bastard (meaning Charlie Novak). But I wanted one that actually worked." The fact that I'd kept Mother Mulligan's stung me afresh as the kind of stupidity Max never stopped accusing me of.

He sighed. "Point well taken," he said. "The next one you get will be real. You'll need it too." Just great! It meant that this was a long way from over.

Max found the phone, allowed blood to drip from the handset, and dialed a number. I heard it answered after two rings.

"Morgenstern," he said. I couldn't make out anything from the other end.

"Forty-Three-Forty-Three Fairburn, Michigan City. What? One!" he snapped. "New orange carpet, about 400 square feet, ocher paint for the same size room and glass for a window, a casement; about two feet on each side. Clear out everything else. I'll get the furnishings. What? Incinerated! What do you think I want done with it? A rush job, four hours max, a bonus if I hear it was done in less, and I'll know. Any problems? I didn't think so. Goodbye."

"One what?" I asked.

"Body, of course," said Max. He looked over at Alice.

"Her?" he asked.

"Yes, Max," I said, "it's her."

"He's told you about me?" asked Alice as if somewhat surprised.

He's never stopped," Max replied. "Amazing, for once, Goyface, I can't say I blame you."

I arrested the impulse to ask him what next. I didn't have to.

"And uh, Alice is it?" asked Max.

She nodded.

"Alice, a disposal crew will be here in about thirty minutes. In a few hours, there won't be any trace of this. But it's best if you don't see them, there's always a possibility you might know each other. Come with us if you like. Oh, Goyface, you have ten minutes to shower and change. He'll need to use your shower, Beautiful."

I expected Alice to protest. She didn't.

"How about later, Max?"

"Take a look at yourself, Goyface."

There was a full-height mirror in a hallway niche. When I looked at it, I knew better than to argue. I was covered with blood and pink tissue. Glass shards glistened in my shirt, hair, and on my forearms.

"I think I still have a fresh set of clothes in the Caddy," I mentioned.

"The Caddy's gone," said Max. Beaver took off with it as soon as you walked in here. But never mind, I have fresh threads for you." He would have. Why the Hell had Cassy left?

I never needed a shower more than the one I took that afternoon. Standing in a large red puddle for several minutes until the water that hosed Charlie Novak off me ran clear, I found myself in the middle of an Alice dream for real in the very shower where Alice had stood naked perhaps hours before. I suddenly wanted to touch every surface in that room and breathe in every residual molecule that Alice had exhaled.

Presently the door opened and Max walked in with a folded stack of fresh clothes. He knocked my keys and change off the counter and groped about the floor retrieving them. It surprised me that he would bother.

"There's a locker key in that, Max," I called out to him over the fan and shower noise. "It's not attached to the others. There's fifteen thousand dollars in that locker that I'm going to need."

"Got it," he replied setting keys and coins back on the counter.

When I'd finished showering, I picked up the larger pieces of Charlie Novak that had been sprayed off me, had gathered at the drain, and wouldn't go down. Those I flushed down the toilet.

In addition to my coins, keys, and clothes, Max had left something else on the sink counter: a cobalt blue .32-revolver in a holster woven into a wide belt.

"Where are you going?" Alice asked as I reentered the parlor. I could not know whether she'd meant Max or me.

"*The Glass Dragonfly*, Max?" I offered. He gave me the exasperated look teachers give doltish second graders, the one that I've come to know so well.

"We're a little past that, Goyface, it's the boat now," said Max, "the money's there."

I didn't ask how he knew this, but it had to be more than a guess.

"What's a Goyface?" Alice asked.

Max smiled ruefully. "A Jew that looks like he isn't one, something I want for my next life."

I would never have imagined an admission like that from the man that never admitted anything. Alice and I took last looks at the headless corpse, and then at each other.

"I guess he's done raping little girls," I said finally, remembering his career synopsis from the newspaper."

"And you?" she asked.

It was an icicle thrust into my liver. If anyone ever earned a crack across the face, Alice had for that. Nobody could have delivered a harder one with greater pleasure than me, had it not been Alice Miranda Jones. It was the one thing I wasn't up to.

"You'd believe anything about me wouldn't you, Alice?" I said, "Anything so long as it's something like that."

"I've seen you in action," she replied obviously meaning the funeral.

There was no trying to take it any farther. I could deny everything until hell froze over and Alice would believe it so long as it was something like that. I stared at her wishing by some divine stroke she would become so repulsive that I would have to look away. But Alice was as lovely as ever. I turned to Max.

"Is it alright if I meet you at the harbor? I think I'd rather ride with Cassy." It was the only retort I could come up with and it impacted Alice like a ping-pong ball might impact cement.

"I already told you," said Max, "she lit out of here right after she dropped you off."

I'd completely forgotten. "She's gone Max? Where?"

Max answered with the same look he'd given me a moment before. "Come on," he said finally, "with any luck you can head them off at the pass. I assume the lady will be on board for this."

Alice nodded. I'd hardly have expected that.

It was no surprise at all that Max had again switched cars; the Seville from Cairo had been replaced by a Chrysler Fifth Avenue. I believe that Max rented every car he ever drove, and never drove the same one for more than a week, fearing that any behavior pattern would leave him vulnerable. What did surprise me was that in the car's rear seat sat Clifford Fitch. There was a large rifle with a scope standing butt down on the floor next to him. It was not hard to guess who had made the shot that killed Charlie Novak…and saved me along with Alice.

I opted for the front seat to the right of the driver (Max). Had I picked the rear seat, Alice would likely have selected the front and for once I was close to not caring. The rape comment had really drawn blood. But it would pass. In a few minutes, I'd want her as much as ever.

"I do believe all of you know each other," Max offered as he yanked the door shut. There was a collective clack of latches as Alice and I did the same.

I expected Max to start the car right away, but he just sat there. Finally, Clifford Fitch spoke: "How did I do?"

Max's reply was one of those rare smiles devoid of his usual cynicism: "Like I once told you, Sergeant, you've got a gift few can match and nobody can ever take away."

Only then did I remember Cassy telling me that Max had served with Clifford in Vietnam. His smile was one of comradery he probably reserved for fellow veterans, one that abruptly dissolved as he turned back to me, the draft dodger.

"You can thank the Sergeant for this," Max said, reaching into his pocket and producing a vertebrae. He wiped it on the fresh shirt he'd just provided me and grinned. "Sergeant," he said, blowing through it like a whistle and then offering it to Clifford, "Souvenir?"

"No thanks," replied Clifford, "seen enough of them already."

"Sorry," Max said smiling. "You're right of course. I would have loved to have made that shot," he said, turning back to me. "Would have given anything for a chance like that, but it had to be done right on the first try, or both of you would be dead now. And there was only one way to make sure of that. Would you like to know what his nickname was in Nam?" He obviously meant Clifford.

"Uh, Max," interrupted Clifford, gesturing to Alice.

"It was PH," said Max ignoring him, "PH, as in pubic hair. It denotes precision. They said he could shoot a pubic hair off a sleeping Gook's pussy at thirty feet without waking her up. We never got around to trying it, but I'm sure he could. Let's see, you would have to stand her on her head, spread her legs and paint one of her pubs with nail polish to make sure he got what he was aiming at, and then he'd have to aim close enough to the flesh to make sure the folicle was ripped out by the transverse force of the shot. Hmm, thirty feet, has anybody got a calculator? You see, if it's long enough, any marksman can shoot off the top of a pubic hair, don't you agree, Sergeant?"

Clifford sat red faced.

"I'm guessing there's some point to this, Max," I said trying to mask my anger.

"I'm getting to that," Max snapped at my impertinence. "Your friend here just saved your pathetic life in case you've forgotten, Goyface, just like he once did mine a long time ago, so indulge me."

It was obvious that Max had a fresh clip of taunts yet to fire off at me. It was also plain that they were at least partly for Alice's consumption. There was no reason in the world that she should listen to this kind of crap and no reason for her not to bolt from the car except one: like everybody else, it was about the money. And Max had to prove it to me, once again, the thing he'd never stopped preaching since I'd known him: that all women, and now Alice in particular, were for sale and henceforth whores. It was the pure, undiluted Max bellowing his dictum that if you couldn't raise the bar, you could always lower it and make anybody you wanted to grovel beneath it, and push their faces into shit so long as the incentive was right. And I'd known Max long enough that, from his intonations alone, he'd only begun to pour it on. I glanced at Clifford who offered me only an upturned hand. We were about to once again witness the true depth of Max's rage at his creator for making him among the ugliest of men.

Max paused like he so often did as if to rewind his mainspring before letting fly a fresh swarm of taunts. There was no more stopping him than stopping a natural disaster.

He stared almost straight ahead as if at the speedometer, and then tilted his head back as if to take in the ceiling of the Chrysler before letting go. I braced myself. I was wrong again.

"This is where I get off," he said abruptly.

"What?"

"This is where I get off."

"Uh Max, what about the money?"

"Your problem," Max replied. "I told you it's on the boat. Go earn it Goyface before your dear classmates sail off with it. While you're at it, tell your friend the shrink, what's his name?"

"Ralph," I replied.

"Yeah, tell him I said that the deal is off."

"And Sergeant," he said, turning only half way toward Clifford so as to face me.

"Yes sir," Clifford replied.

"Try to keep these two nit wits from getting themselves killed, but don't die saving them. You're worth more than ten of them both added up."

Clifford sighed.

I could not but agree.

"Yes sir," my friend replied.

Max spun another half turn to face Alice. "You're right, Goyface," he said, then turning to me, "she is one gorgeous bag of organs. But I'll bet her toll house cookies are terrible." He broke into yet another kind of peculiar smile I'd seen him wear but a few times in the decades I'd known him.

40. WE'LL ALWAYS HAVE BARSTOW

In the ten-mile drive up US-12 from Michigan City to Snug Harbor you cross the state line between Indiana and Michigan. I had to stifle any compulsion to drive it flat out on the near empty road knowing that a traffic stop now would be as big a catastrophe as during the Odyssey of the *Mulholland Rocket*, the details of which were dissolving into a blur of gore, explosions, and the ever present meddling of Max. Another compulsion was impossible to control: stealing glimpses into the rear view mirror. Though Alice sat as far from me as the car's interior would permit, she was but four feet away.

When she realized what I was doing, Alice offered me a glare cold as a sewer cover in winter. It was the Alice stare from my dreams that had me swearing aloud from my sleep that I would love Alice forever—the dreams that destroyed my marriage and put me in Huntsville. This was the girl who said all she wanted from me was to be left alone. I knew otherwise, had sworn that I would win over Alice or die trying, was a long way from dead and a longer way still from giving up. And she was just as far away from admitting her feelings for me.

We exited US-12, at Water Street, and were blocked from the harbor by a slow moving freight train. I tried to make out Ralph's sloop through the voids between the boxcars that flashed by. It was impossible. Finally, with the road clear, we coasted down an incline to the parking lot. The cars were there. Ralph's Citroën parked far away from the main throng of cars as owners of such machines will do to avoid door dings. Next to it stood the Seville Max had rented which made me think of Frank, of his bullet-ridden corpse and the car that I'd turned into a bomb trying to wipe out traces of my having been at the murder scene. That had been a Seville—the same color of the one now in the Snug Harbor parking lot. There were perhaps ten more boats in the harbor than the eight it had contained one week before, but Ralph's sloop was still by itself, its closest neighbor some five slips away. Dim light glowed through the cabin windows. We walked a labyrinth of narrow piers in single file to where *Yesterday's Rainbow* was moored, stopping at a point directly ahead of the bow. None of us had the slightest idea of what to do next. To attempt stealth was pointless. Though her inboard diesel throbbed in the dark, it took a huge leap in logic to imagine it masking the clatter of our approach because the piers and walkways were aluminum and we'd made no less noise walking them than a platoon might. I walked alongside the sloop's length and eased myself aboard. The boat rocked none too gently under my weight. I imagined somebody would have to have been dead to not know I'd boarded her. I knelt and peered into the cabin.

The belt with a holster that harbored the .32 Max had given me was wide and chewed on my sides. Leading with the pistol, I stepped through the hatchway and down into the cabin. What I first saw was almost exactly what I'd seen one week before.

Cassy's quite lovely left calf hung down from the built-in seat, her toes not quite reaching the carpet. Her other leg was draped diagonally across a cushion. The nakedness of a week before ended this time at a black bikini bottom. My eyes marched up Cassy's exquisite torso to her bare breasts. Only then did I see that her arms were firmly bound behind her. A fat strip of duct tape covering her mouth was wrapped completely around her head. I had but a second or two to take it all in when a hand seized my left wrist and hurled me at the floor of the cabin. In midflight, I saw the USMC tattoo on the arm and remembered that Felix was now part of the equation.

Boat carpeting is a nasty place for bare skin to land. Tiny plastic blades bit into my arms and face. The .32 had broken free of my hand and landed someplace God himself might not find in the dark. I looked up at Felix and realized it might be a good thing. I was staring straight at a pistol twice the size of the one I'd just lost. Probably not having the gun to point back at Felix would prolong my life by a few seconds. His downward stare at me broke into a broad grin on a pock-marked face with knotty cheeks, stub covered jowls, and flaring nostrils from which thick hairs and dried snot hung like filthy icicles. He was butt ugly right down to his molecules.

"I remember you," said Felix, "you don't give tips. We call your kind 'shitheals.'" He pointed the barrel just over the bridge of my nose facing downward. The pistol's hammer rose. The grin on his face broadened.

"Any last words, Mr. Shitheal?" he asked.

"Uh huh," I replied trembling. "When that bullet finishes going through me, it's not going to stop until it puts a hole in the bottom of this boat, so if you're thinking about taking it someplace, think again." My trembling made the words come out so garbled that I couldn't believe Felix actually understood them, but he apparently did: his grin dissolved while he considered this.

"All right," he said finally, "not a problem." The grin returned. He grabbed my shirt with his left hand, hoisted me from the floor like a derrick might, and realigned the gun's barrel. I could feel a cold ring-like shape pushed hard in the soft flesh just inboard of my jaw. I guessed a hole in the cabin's roof ringed with my brains wasn't going to bother him. I readied myself for it.

The sharp blow that grazed my neck was the last sensation I thought I'd ever feel. But it wasn't a bullet. Cassy's lovely foot had kicked the enormous revolver from its nest under my chin. A second later, it discharged searing my face slightly and wrenching itself from Felix's grasp. It flew straight out the sloop's hatchway to land in the cockpit with blunted clunks. Felix threw me at the floor and bolted toward the hatchway. Cassy's foot poked at my face. Puzzled, I looked at her and saw she was pointing at a nook in the boat's cabinets where my .32 lay. A second later, I had aimed at the middle of Felix's immense back. He was climbing the steps to the outside so as to retrieve his artillery. Warning him to stop would have been a waste of time, and probably my life. I fired twice. It was impossible to miss; he was enormous. Felix staggered but remained upright. His left arm thrashed about in wild jerks searching for something to grab onto.

He was still teetering when an explosion of bone, brains, flesh, and hair replaced what had been his head. He toppled backwards to the floor and landed in a heap, now headless, save for a section of jaw. The rest had been sprayed everywhere inside the cabin. Gold teeth lodged in the teak cabinetry glistened through the gore. Clifford Fitch, holding that enormous gun that landed outside, ambled almost casually down the steps to face me grinning.

"Exploding bullets," said my friend, "we used them for taking out a vehicle when the VC had them." He raised the pistol and blew a wreath of smoke from the tip of the barrel. "They're quite illegal too. An idiot like that," said Clifford gesturing to the corpse, "*would* have them."

We both broke into a glorious laugh.

Cassy delivered a kick into my buttocks. I'd forgotten she was still bound up. When I undid the tape she hugged and kissed me though a puddle of goo sprayed from Felix that kept dripping down from my scalp.

"Where's Ralph," I asked almost as an afterthought.

"The back cabin," Cassy replied.

I found Ralph there and had him unbound a minute later. He had obviously taken a real thrashing from Felix. Dried blood could be seen in abundance all over the cushions, though the bleeding had apparently stopped by itself. Ralph was quite conscious. When we walked through the passageway back into the main cabin, Alice was there too. The scattered remains of Felix's head didn't seem to bother anyone. Ralph, who'd said nothing, walked past a teak divider toward the bow, emerging a short time later with an ice chest that held a dozen now ever familiar bottles of PBR. We each took one, passed the opener around, and waited until the last of the bottles was uncapped before raising them in silent to toast the demise of *The Glass Dragonfly's* proprietor.

Clifford poured a few ounces on Felix—that brought on a collective laugh—then swallowed the remaining contents of his bottle. Ralph quickly passed him another and offered me a second one too, though I was less than one third way through my first. I held it upright, between my thighs, like an erection which cracked Cassy up. When her laughter died away I asked abruptly:

"Alright, kids, who tied you up? Felix couldn't have done it all by himself. It does take two." They looked at each other as if they'd never expected the question to come up. "Bobby," said Cassy, turning to Ralph as if for confirmation.

"When did Felix cut himself in by the way?" I asked Ralph.

"About six months ago," replied Ralph. "He played us a tape he'd made of our discussing the heist and demanded half the take. Since then we found out he had a terrific little information sideline going and has had for years."

Except for calling Ralph's "six months" a year, Cassy had told an identical story. It was nice that it checked.

"A lot of people will owe you two," said Cassy, meaning Clifford and me, "and they'll never thank you because they can never know."

I motioned at the corpse.

"But for you baby," I said, "that would be me."

About then, I realized that Bobby and Ralph never could have dragged two men from the *Dragonfly* and pitched them under a train without Felix knowing. In fact, that one of the two, the ape, who'd thrown Jerret Traff on the tracks, had to have been Felix himself.

"So he was on board since long before Harry Fisher went under the train," I surmised the all to obvious.

"Sonny," Ralph said, I didn't know about your cousin until Felix and Bobby had done it."

I arrested a laugh.

"Ralph, Harry wasn't my cousin. Anyway, getting rid of him was strictly trash disposal. Don't give it another thought."

I then remembered mentioning to Alice an hour before that Harry was my cousin. "Ralph," I continued, "you know your deal with Max is off. You know that?"

"I kept up my part," Ralph protested. "Bobby was so enraged at the idea of cutting you in on the action that he turned to Felix. Instead of splitting it four ways, they settled on two. Cassy and I were the odd ones out. When I called Bobby and told him about Max's offer, he said to meet him on the boat. Felix collected Cassy from in front of Alice's place. He was waiting for Bobby to come back when you arrived. They meant to deep six us alive."

"I doubt that, Ralph."

Ralph gave me a worried look as if I thought he was once again caught in a lie. "You don't believe me?"

"No, Ralph. *They* wouldn't have done it. Felix would have deep-sixed Bobby along with the both of you. And Bobby's just dumb enough to walk into it." I gestured to the corpse.

"Right, Felix?" I said. "Nod your head if you agree. Oops sorry. By the way, Ralph, what was Bobby supposed to be doing just now?"

"Disposing of you," replied Ralph, "and your friend at *The Glass Dragonfly*. He wanted that job for himself."

"So you told him I'd be there?"

"Yes, isn't that what your friend said to do?"

"You told Felix where to pick up Cassy," I said, "and bring her here to get deep-sixed."

Ralph pointed at his injuries. "I didn't exactly give Felix that information," he protested.

"I just saved your rotten life, Ralph." I reminded him before he'd gone any further toward making himself the victim.

"I know that, Sonny," said Ralph, "and Cassy saved yours. And Cassy was with me so it's a wash, anyway, what are you going to do now, shoot me?"

"No, Ralph, I owe you for the reunion ticket, remember?"

Alice, who had yet to say a word burst into a short laugh. "Yes, Ralph," said Alice, "thanks for that, thanks loads, heaps, and gobs. You're a real gem."

I remembered her use of the "gem" phrase, hearing it at the reunion and so often twenty years before. There are some things that stick with you, and apparently even with Alice.

After a short silence Ralph said, "I suppose you'll want to wait here and settle with Bobbie after he deals with your friend Max."

It was the one thing he could have said that could crack me up.

"It will be a long wait, Ralph," I said laughing. "If he was headed for the *Dragonfly* and meant to cross Max, he won't be coming back any time soon." I wondered what kind of end Bobby would meet at the hands of Max but dismissed that delicious thought.

"Why don't we go out on deck?" Ralph suggested, "I'm getting a little queasy down here. Anyway, we're going on a short excursion to get rid of him," pointing to Felix, "and we need to clean up this tub, at least enough that it doesn't scream murder scene."

"Not bad, Ralph," I nodded in agreement. Ralph was the first of us to think about anything like a next step. I was dripping blood and gore for the second time that evening. The sloop had a shower, and I hoped

Ralph kept fresh clothes on board. We might tie Felix to the boat's anchor and hope it would keep him underwater long enough for his corpse to fall apart.

"Try not to track any of Felix onto the deck if you can," Ralph suggested.

With Alice leading, we climbed the short ladder to the hatchway, and outside, where it had gone a long way toward becoming night since we'd boarded *Yesterday's Rainbow*.

The sloop's engine, still running, and now thoroughly warmed, had gone from rough pulsations to an almost melodic drone of an electric fan. The other boats must have been empty because the gunfire had apparently alerted no one. We'd seated ourselves on the fiberglass benches built over storage lockers on each side of the cockpit. Both Clifford and I had left our pistols on a fold-down table inside the cabin figuring them as among the first things to be jettisoned once we were out in the lake.

I didn't think anything of it until Ralph emerged at last carrying the .32 I'd shot Felix with—and pointed it at me.

"All ashore that's going ashore," he announced, "and I believe that means the three of you."

"Ralph, you're kidding."

He pulled back the hammer while fine tuning his aim to the center of my chest.

"Okay, Ralph, so you're not kidding."

As I stepped over the gunnel and onto the dock, Ralph said: "Your money's in the Citroën in the backseat foot well. It's your hundred thousand for finding the *Rockelet*. And you can keep the car, consider it a bonucus. And tell your 'Max friend' he shouldn't have gone back on his word and cut me out." He gave the keys an underhand toss that I caught. I held out my hand to assist Alice onto the aluminum dock. To my amazement she took it.

"Thank you, Addison," she said. Could this be the same Alice? Clifford followed Alice. Cassy was last. She'd gotten up and was about to make a short leap to the dock.

"Not you Cass, snapped Ralph. "I'll need somebody who can take this damn thing where we're going."

"Burn in Hell, Ralph," she shot back. "I'm done with you. You'll have to shoot me and I'm no good to you that way." She prepared for a leap to the dock.

Ralph's face hardened, "You're coming Cassy, because if you don't, I'll shoot Sonny, and he's no good to you that way either." She looked at me for an inkling of what to do.

"Go with him Cassy," I said. "If he meant to take you out, he'd have done it by now. You can get in touch with me through Max. He's in the Houston directory." I turned back to Ralph. "If I don't hear from her, Ralph," I said, "I'll track you down like the low live varmint you are." I knew that Max would likely track down Ralph and kill him anyway just to show me he could do it, not to mention the money. I reached over to the gunnel, seized Cassy, and kissed her hard.

"Goodbye, Sonny," she said, "and if I never see you again..." She paused.

"We'll always have Barstow," I replied. I prayed that Clifford wouldn't try any last-minute heroics to rescue Cassy. If he did, Ralph couldn't miss him at that range. Thankfully, my friend didn't. Still at gunpoint, I cast off the lines tying *Yesterday's Rainbow* to the dock.

Cassy stepped back into the cockpit, took the helm, and without a word, engaged the sloop's propellers so as to back it from the slip. She never stopped grabbing glances of me until they entered the channel.

Clifford, Alice, and I walked single file up the aluminum walkways to the shore where we paused to give each other the kind of look that said something like "Okay, we're alive and the money's gone, what now?"

"You two will need rides back," I said finally, expecting Alice to say that she'd rather hitchhike to Chicago than ride back to Michigan City with me. To my amazement, Alice nodded. Together we walked toward the Chrysler when I fished a ring of keys from my pocket, held them up, and rattled them. "Give me a minute."

I reversed course and headed toward Ralph's coupe.

There was the hundred thousand and the car Ralph said was mine. I'd loved to have kept that stunning machine as well, though it hardly seemed feasible for someone entering life as a fugitive. But the money was something I could take with me.

I was still thinking of how I didn't want to trash the upholstery with any wet remnants of Felix still stuck to me, when I froze and replayed Ralph's words: *It's your hundred thousand for finding the Rockellet and you can keep the car, consider it a bonicus."*

They were there: the extra syllables Ralph inserted into words that flashed like neon that he was lying or up to far worse. I reached the Citroën and peered inside. There was a large attaché case in the foot well behind the driver's seat just as Ralph said there would be. And there was something else. I almost doubled over laughing. Once again, Ralph had proven himself a study in incompetence.

"Clifford," I called out motioning him to come over, "do you have a flashlight? You've got to see this." He found one in the Chrysler and we surveyed the coupe's interior from outside.

Both doors were rigged with white magnetic switches that visually screamed against the Citroën's tan upholstery. Both were spliced to red wires that ran in plain sight to the case in the rear foot well. Were either door opened, the circuit that kept the detonator in check would be broken and the "hundred thousand" would go off a few seconds later were there a time delay that allowed me to get inside, or it just might go off immediately. Had Ralph made any attempt at concealment it might well have worked. Clifford and I looked at each other.

"Good old Ralph," I said grinning, "a novice to the last."

Alice joined us and Clifford pointed out the bobby trap to her.

"Clifford," I said, "I really hate to destroy this car. Is there any way we can disarm it?"

He thought for a minute.

"We could slip in through the rear hatch, and shunt the wires to the case. That would defeat the door switches. With luck we might drive it somewhere, remove the explosive, and set it off with a slug to break the shunt." Then he shook his head, "Sonny, it's not worth it. Jarring alone could set it off. We've got to blow it here. If we just leave it like it is somebody's going to die."

"There's the police," Alice interjected. "You could just phone in that there's a car with a bomb in it, but that would spoil your fun wouldn't it?"

"This is between Ralph and us," I snapped. "And I do mean *us*, Alice; he meant to take you out too if he could. Right now he's watching the sky above the Marina for a fireball. If he doesn't see one he'll know we're alive. If he does he'll still have to wonder. If I know Ralph, that alone could drive him crazy."

"What do you say, Clifford?" I asked. "Unlock the door with a key, back off, and put a slug on the latch button?" I held up the keys.

"I'll do that," said my friend reaching for them.

"Like hell you will," I snapped, "You've put your life on the line for my sorry ass enough times already. Back off you two, a hundred feet at least." When they did, I inserted the key and twisted it. The lock button popped up. I turned and ran without withdrawing the key. "By the way," I said, when I'd reached Clifford and Alice, "do we have any small-bore artillery with us?" I remembered only then that our guns were still on the boat.

Clifford pointed to the Chrysler. "That's Max's car isn't it? What do you think?" He walked over to it, opened the trunk, and after picking through the contents, he returned holding a pistol with a long slender barrel.

We backed away from the Citroën yet another hundred feet. Clifford took aim.

"Is that thing noisy?" I asked, realizing in mid-sentence how idiotic the question was since I expected an explosion.

"It's an air pistol," he replied without pausing. He took aim and fired in a smooth single action. There was a ping in the night air when the pellet struck the car. With a slight click, the driver's door popped ajar.

A blinding white/orange eruption lifted the Citroën two feet into the air and blew it into components that were hurled in every direction. A section of door landed two feet from me. The hood, spinning like a disc, flew ten feet above and beyond us while debris of every type rained down like hot hail. Every piece of glass in the Cadillac Cassy had parked next to was gone and its interior blazed. The Citroën's engine and transaxle landed atop the Cadillac's hood. A pool of white fire was all that remained where the gorgeous French coupe had been. We looked at each other jaws agape. Ralph had taken no chances. He meant to get the three of us if he could, while sparing Cassy. At least he couldn't bring himself to kill her. And he needed Cassy to sail the boat.

Suddenly, lights were going on from a dozen different sources, from overhead pole lamps in the parking lot that had been off, from what I guessed was the harbormaster's office, and from a half-dozen boat cabins in the harbor. They hadn't been empty when the shots were fired. Figures began running up the docks toward us. Now was definitely the time to depart. We made for the Chrysler. To my amazement Alice seated herself next to me in the front.

I gave silent thanks when no train blocked our escape up Water Street to Route 12. Within the first mile we drove, half a dozen police cruisers shot by, sirens and lights at full tilt, heading opposite us for the harbor. It was all becoming much too familiar.

In spite of two wrong turns I made, we were in front of the townhouse on Fairburn twenty minutes later. We had been gone less than two hours and I wondered if Max's men had finished purging it of Charlie Novak. That seemed impossible. I expected Alice to bolt from the car, make for her front door without a word, and slam it behind her. Instead, she turned to me:

"One for the road?"

That nearly struck me mute. I'd expected anything but an invite. I furrowed my brow; sure I hadn't heard her right. She repeated herself through a slightly amused expression that fell just short of a smile.

It wasn't clear whether she'd meant to include Clifford. With all he'd done for me I still wanted to be alone with Alice. My ever-faithful friend rose to the occasion:

"You kids go ahead," he said. "I usually don't get oiled twice in the same night, but I'm not going to work tomorrow. Take your time."

Alice turned to him amazed. "You were drunk when you made that shot?" She pointed incredulously at the death window.

"With obvious pride he nodded, "Well, on the way you could say." Clifford then reached into the foot well and produced a half-full fifth of Crown Royal. "I find that the right amount really helps my aim. As I said children, take your time. I've got all I need and all night to enjoy it."

41. ONE FOR THE ROAD

Any traces of Charlie Novak were gone. Only remaining was the solvent-rich scent of fast drying paint that could probably have killed birds and small mammals. The wall hangings had been replaced with modern abstracts including two prints of works I'd done in college with my signature removed. About half the furnishings were pieces I'd designed as well, including two end tables that had won awards. That Max could lay his hands on them on such short notice didn't amaze me, nor could anything else about him, not any more.

He'd seen to it that Alice would be living with creations of mine at least until she found this out. It didn't end there. Atop a Styrofoam chiller sat a serving tray on which rested four fat bottles of P B R. Max Morgenstern was the consummate puppeteer. Max the incredible.

Alice set the tray on the table, then seated herself opposite me while fluids, once those of Fleix, still dripped off me onto the new furniture and carpet. Two hours before, the headless corpse of Charlie Novak had occupied the very space between us.

"Tell your friend that his taste in furniture leaves something to be desired," Alice offered.

That Alice would disapprove of the furniture figured, though I doubted she knew it was mine.

"It might grow on you," I replied, adding silently, *"as might I if you'd give me half a fighting chance."*

One fact was front and center. The moment, that apex of a thousand scenarios—the one I'd spent the previous two decades planning—had arrived for a second time, and this time there would be no Charlie Novak or Bobby Dardanelle to come crashing in. I had once envisioned myself seizing Alice, tying her to a chair, and then screaming at the top of my lungs how I loved her, would always love her, and furthermore, that I wasn't a lunatic.

As it turned out, no chair or rope would be necessary. All I had to do was to penetrate that wall of cold surrounding her with one hot blast of brilliance: some magic combination of words I'd had twenty years to compose for delivery at that very instant.

"Do you have a bottle opener?" I asked.

"They're already open," Alice replied, almost amused.

They *were* open, so much for Max omitting anything.

Looking straight at Alice I thought of the first time I'd seen her at the Franklin Street Station from the back, standing in that maroon corduroy jumper, and of the pink blouse which was at first hidden by that sculpture of blonde hair that she'd yet to change and never should. I remembered the surfaces of her face rotating into my view because I had approached Alice from the side that time, had walked beyond her, and executed the two left turns that placed me opposite her just as now, from about the same distance. Nothing had really prepared me for the first time I saw Alice, or for any time since, including this one, maybe especially this one. The twenty years since I'd last seen her had done nothing to dull that glorious assembly of planes, curves, and prisms composing the face that made perfection irrelevant.

"I wonder," I said, "if the four o'clock train stops here?" Those were my first words to Alice on that afternoon in 1959. I'd never meant to say them now, but they'd broken out of some file cabinet in my brain and forced their way past every checkpoint that should have stopped them. And now they were out there no less a matter of record than had they been etched into the glass of the table I'd designed—that Alice disliked.

"What?" asked Alice.

"I wonder if the four o'clock train stops here." Her quizzical look bore a hint of irritation.

"It was the first thing I said to you in the South Shore Station twenty-one years ago last month. I never stopped beating myself up for not being able to do better. But here we are twenty-one years later and it's still the best I can do. I didn't know your name then and I was already swearing that I would win you over or die trying. Well, I've been swearing it for the twenty-one years since I saw you and I've yet to do either. I wonder if the four o'clock train stops here," I mused. "Do you remember what we talked about after that?" I couldn't believe her answer:

"I remember something about brain tumors."

"Yes!" I said, astounded, "Yes! I told you my name and how people called me 'Sonny July,' and although it was a cold March afternoon there were worse things than cold March afternoons, like brain tumors, and you asked me if I'd ever had one. Do you remember what I told you then?"

Alice shook her head.

"I told you that you were talking to one, and how my brain tumor was what I used to pass math tests. It took me about twenty seconds to paint myself into a corner. I was amazed, Alice, that I could get sentences out, but I'd already run out of words. I couldn't have come up with another syllable. I don't know, maybe I could have done a grunt or two or accidentally spit on your sleeve a second time like I'd already done once. But somebody rescued me, Alice, and that somebody was your Colin. He marched in like the two-minute bell that ended a boxing round. Of course, he saw immediately what I was about and wanted to kill me right then and there, but in fact he'd saved me. I would have thanked him for that if I could have. Another guy, even one that wanted to kill me, was something I could deal with."

Alice winced when I mentioned her late husband. Both of us were wondering where I could be going with this. I was going to run through the history of the two days that followed, how I'd gotten her name from the buffoons running her school, and how I'd found out that "Randy Jones" was in fact Alice Miranda Jones.

"You see Alice, I…"

"Yes?"

"You see Alice, I was already in love with you. Nothing like it had ever happened to me, much less so fast. I'd become a power station with all my circuit breakers frozen shut and my dynamos rigged for full output. It's like my brain has been shorting out for the past twenty years. Sometimes, when I woke up from dreaming about you, I could swear I smelled ozone." And then I fell silent, replaying my last sentences to myself. They sounded like a physics lecture. Alice did that to me, she'd unleashed that repressed talent men like me have for jamming both feet in our mouths and going off on some skewed tangent like the charge of the light brigade. I wondered if I'd done more damage than the sum total I'd done up to now. But I had no choice but to forge on:

"Alice," I said, "nobody will ever love you as I do. I suppose I should hate myself for making such a botch of my campaign to win you over, but I don't regret anything Alice, not one single act. I did the best I could at the time, just like I am now..."

I paused.

For an instant she seemed to being weighing the words.

"Give it a chance, Alice," I coaxed. "Give it a chance."

She sighed. It was the first time I'd ever seen the taint of age on her features. Then she spoke: "You're a fugitive, aren't you? Where are you going, and what are you going to live on?"

I'd completely forgotten since being at the harbor that I was wanted, and but for Lola's cash, broke. Being that close to Alice had overpowered everything.

"I'm not sure about where, Alice," I said, and I'm innocent by the way."

She smiled, although it was a long way from the kind of smile I would have wanted, but a smile nonetheless.

"I believe you," Alice affirmed. "You're a lot of things Addison July, but I doubt you're a diaper dipper." An hour before, Alice had more than implied I was one.

"How about someone you could love back?" I asked.

Her empty stare left no doubt what her answer to that would be so I moved in to head it off while there was still time. Like the man holds off checking the numbers on a lottery ticket, I wanted my hope alive for the longest time possible.

Then: "I'll have money Alice, my share of the six million dollars."

"Your share?" she snapped, her anger instantaneous, "what gives you the right to any of it? And how are you going to get the money away? Ralph just sailed off with it."

I took my first sip of beer. "Yes, Alice, Ralph sailed off, he was supposed to do that, but I can guarantee you it wasn't with the money. Max would never have allowed it."

"Max? You mean that horrible little troll?"

"Yes him, Alice. And he's the most dangerous man alive, by the way, especially when he's called that. Don't ever do it again. Your place is probably bugged."

"Troll!" Alice shouted. "*Troll! Troll! Troll! Troll!*"

"Dammit Alice, don't do that."

"How the hell did you get involved in this anyway?" she demanded.

"I thought you knew, Alice." She had to know but must have wanted to know just how much more I did. Well, with Felix and Charlie Novak dead, and Ralph and Bobby no threat either, if they were alive at all, what did it matter what I told her? So I gave it to her from the beginning:

"Alice," I began, "I came to Michigan City to get money from my stepmother a week ago and met Ralph by accident at *The Glass Dragonfly*. He told me about the reunion and that you'd be there, and that he had a job for me that would pay big money. You know what the job was: to find the *Mulholland Rocket*. Somebody in California was sending him currency bands from the heist. Of course he didn't tell me that part.

"Ralph found out that the car that he'd used for the holdup—which was stolen from him right after the heist—was now also in California. He assumed that whoever had the car was sending the bands. Turns out that wasn't true. His name was Paul Phengston, and he did steal the car. It was probably the only thing he ever stole, but it would cost him his life twenty years later. Other people are dead too, Alice, people that got sucked into this little production one way or another. Some deserved it, others just got in the way."

"This little production?" Alice asked, "you mean like a play?"

"Or a chess game, or a puppet show, or a mathematical equation with only one outcome. That's what it is now. When they dragged me into it they got Max Morgenstern in the bargain. When Max heard from me about the two-hundred-thousand-dollar bet Ralph made that I could find the *Mulholland Rocket*, he knew what it was, and he couldn't have been happier. From then on it was Max against Ralph, Bobby, Felix, and Charlie Novak. They never had a chance against Max. No one ever does. It's amazing what those bands you had sent unleashed."

I stared down at the coffee table I'd designed and had been so proud of until Alice's assessment of it a few moments before. Why couldn't she like even that?

"Why do you keep accusing me of sending those goddamn bands?" she shouted.

"You didn't?" I replied, not believing that for a moment. "You had to have."

"No, Addison July, no I didn't, she said, adding angrily, "Why would I?"

"The money, of course, Alice, to make Ralph, Bobby, and Cassy suspect, and then turn on each other, what else? And until tonight I thought it was to avenge Colin too."

"Colin!" She almost spat out the name. It was the tiniest comfort that there was someone Alice might show more contempt for than me. "And as for the money, I don't need that either, not anymore. There was a time when I had a use for it, but now—no, I have all I need."

Then Alice fell silent, having realized she'd unraveled more than she'd ever intended to.

"So why did you go with us to the boat if not for the money?" I asked. "We could have all been killed."

"I didn't think it would happen, and it didn't, did it?" she replied. "I guess I just got caught up in this play your Max friend wrote. I had to be out of here a couple of hours anyway. Is that what we're doing now, reciting lines from a script? Is it ever going to end?"

I wasn't clear on whether Alice meant the drama at hand or my intrusions on her life, or had she meant both?

I tried to make it appear that I was staring over her shoulder at someplace beyond, but in fact, I had never taken my eyes off her face, studying how her making words altered its composition before it snapped back into gorgeous default.

And just as I'd done every time I'd seen Alice, I was committing updated details to memory that might have to last me a very long time. Finally, I couldn't hold one last roll of the dice any longer:

"Alice," I said, "when this is over, do you think you might be there for me?"

She hesitated maybe a second or two, maybe three, but no more than five.

"No, Addison," she said in a flat monotone, adding another "no" a few seconds later like a hammer blow delivered to a nail that's already as far down as it can be driven.

So that was what Alice had meant by "one for the road."

I sat the half full P B R on the table, got up to leave, pausing at the door without knowing why, until the words tumbled out of me as if spoken by someone else altogether:

"What did you once want the money for, Alice? You said you wanted it once for something." I expected enraged words about it being none of my business. Her wistful smile came as a medium grade shock.

"Did it ever occur to you, Mr. Addison July, that you're not the only person that ever wanted someone they couldn't have?"

Of course it did. I didn't have to look any further than Clifford Fitch, and what wanting Cassy had cost him, to know and feel very ashamed, but Alice?

"*You Alice?*" I said incredulously, "there was someone you wanted and couldn't have?" That was impossible!

She nodded first and then said: "Yes there was."

"He must have really been something," I offered.

"You have no idea."

"I don't suppose I knew him."

"No, you never knew him at all. Goodbye, Addison July."

"That's funny, Alice, funny, because you never knew me at all either, you never began to…"

She looked away.

My voice was breaking up and my last words to Alice crumbled like dried clods of dirt hurled against a brick wall.

"You could at least have tried, Alice," I said, gripping the doorknob. "You could have at least done that."

I was outside and half way to the Chrysler before a convulsive spasm doubled me over. I staggered the rest of the way to the car, collapsed beside one of the tires, and began pounding at the sidewall. I was a formless lump of flesh, sobs, tears, and snot, half wishing that I'd blown up with the Citroën as Ralph had intended.

Presently Clifford stood over me, extending his arm and hoisting me erect. He amazed me with the strength he could muster.

"You might want to ride in the back," he said, releasing me so he could open the door.

"It's over, Cliff," I bawled and wept.

This time it really was over, and it was all for nothing.

42. IN THE BRAIN OF YOUR BELOVED

"You might want to ride in the back," he repeated.

I didn't need to be offered that a third time. I wanted to lie down and continue crying myself sick. The fact that Clifford smelled like a distillery and drove with one arm didn't bother me. Were we to crash and burn, so much the better.

I lied flat in the back seat of the Chrysler bawling like the same adolescent I'd been twenty years before for the very same reason. My late mentor, Ray, had predicted it all so well. There were things I would never get over. Finally, I sat slouched.

We drove about Michigan City in aimless loops for what seemed like well over an hour. I remember passing a number of sights twice and others more times than that. One of them, Willkie High School, must easily have been the worst public building in all of Indiana. When Clifford thought that I was about cried out, he headed south on Franklin and picked up 94 East, turning off at the exit ramp for Crown Point. Just outside the downtown, I was treated to the visual assault of a sign barrage that turned night into day for the better part of a block. Besides flashing incandescent bulbs, there was an orgy of moving arrows directing potential buyers to the office of Jessip & Sons of Crown Point. It was a shack flying three enormous American flags. The Jessips had obviously found more than a few chumps like Ralph since he'd bought the *Mulholland Rocket*.

Clifford must have glanced at the rear-view mirror and sensed my question as to what we were doing there, "It's still early, Addison. You should get some sleep, I live here now and it would be a bad idea for you to spend any more time in LaPorte County than you have to. We're in Lake County. Technically, I'm not supposed to live here with my job and all, but they're known to bend the rules." He made a final left turn onto a block of Victorian homes and parked the Chrysler abreast of one whose proportions dwarfed anything in sight of where we stood. Then he answered another of my yet to be asked questions:

"My grandparents," said my friend, "left it to me among other things, like a lot of money. I took it over two years ago."

"Must be worth a fortune," I offered inanely.

"I suppose it is," he replied. "I never had it appraised. But a time comes for everything. Now it has for this too."

Clifford might have still hoped to raise a family in the great house. And it was more than obvious with whom. Now it seemed unlikely that he ever would.

We crossed an enormous front porch with opposing swings, entering through a doorway inlayed with rosewood and decked out with brass hardware that gleamed from a recent polishing.

The parlor was the equal of, and appropriate to the building's exterior. The ceiling vaulted a dozen feet above a floor full of Victorian furniture. When Clifford snapped some switches on, an explosion of patterned light from an immense prismatic chandelier filled the great room. Though a trained architectural modernist, I couldn't help but be bowled over by this composition of everything I'd been programmed to scorn but had never actually seen in such a three dimensional display. I guessed that much of what I was looking at were pricey antiques. Some of it might have been reproduction, but it would be impossible to tell had I known exactly what I was looking at, and I certainly didn't.

Clifford gestured me to a chair which I was afraid to sit on wondering if there might be wet remnants of Felix left on me that could leave stains, something I hadn't worried about at Alice's place. Her furniture, which I designed, was stain resistant.

"It's okay," said my friend. "He's dried up enough. I can get you a robe if you want."

"Yes, please," I replied as Clifford walked out of the room. I was getting a little sick with the realization that much of what I wore was brain tissue. I desperately needed another shower, but I was exhausted. The urge to sit down trumped everything.

He returned a moment later with the promised robe. I dropped the rags I was wearing into a bloody heap, and slipped into it.

"This is all so so..." I gestured with large sweeps of my arms.

"Unexpected?" he offered.

"Yes."

"Yes," said my friend. "My grandfather owned half of Whiting and sold it all just before the fire in '55. I didn't know how filthy rich he was until I was somewhere in my teens. I remember visiting this place once or twice as a kid with my mother. The grand folks never approved of dear old Dad so we were cut off from the family fortune while he was alive. I never imagined any of this coming my way until three years ago when I got a letter from the executors of their estate telling me that all this was mine."

"Are both your parents gone?"

Clifford replied by nodding. I had imagined that, both were serious drinkers.

"Clifford Fitch, rich son of a bitch," I mussed, "do you live here all by yourself?"

"Cousins come from time to time for long stays," he replied. "They're always welcome, even when they get drunk and wonder aloud why I got all this and they got zip."

"That doesn't bother you?"

"Bother me? It amuses me. There's a simple enough explanation and everybody knows it. Of all my cousins, I'm the only veteran and the only other one in the family besides dear old Granddad. He fought in World War One and believed everybody should serve."

Clifford didn't need to mention what "dear old Granddad" had thought of draft dodgers like me.

"With all this you kept your job?"

"I did," said my friend. "I like my job, and I love knowing I could buy and sell any of my so called superiors with what's now pocket change. And I love knowing how they would freak if they knew it, but they don't. I was going to break it to them one day when the moment was right. It just never came. Maybe I should throw a retirement party here before I sell the place."

I smiled at this wonderful revelation. "Then I guess I should be flattered to be admitted to the land of them what knows."

"It's not why I brought you here, Sonny. Like I said, you should get some sleep and…"

"And?"

Clifford's expression suggested he was reconsidering some decision he'd made that wasn't as clear-cut as it had first seemed. He turned away momentarily, focused on lighting a cigar before fixing his gaze back at me and exhaling a long blue plume. Even in the soft light and smoky haze, his pocked face still seemed to mimic the surface of the moon. I thought about what I'd once been told about looks: how they were only unimportant to the dead, the blind, and those whose heads are so far up their asses that everything is dark. Clifford had deserved so much better.

"And," added Clifford, "There are things you should know, things that not even the illustrious Max has told you."

"No surprise there; Max rarely told anyone everything, though I doubted there was anything he didn't know.

"Okay, Cliff," I said, "I'm listening."

"Would you agree," asked my friend, "that we're living the last act of a drama that began over twenty years ago?"

"Are you sure this is the last act or could it go on another twenty years?" I replied, though that seemed unlikely. Of the original five players, three were still alive as far as I knew. "Okay, Clifford, let's for argument's sake say that tonight is the last act."

"Alright," he went on, "where would you say it started? Give me a point in timc."

I had once grappled with the same question about other matters, but had yet to apply it to the kaleidoscope of people and events that had us all in our places the morning of the heist, the crucible which fused an ongoing attachment between all the players for over twenty years, though it had only recently dragged me in. It had killed others and spewed flames we were stamping out just two hours before.

"If a starting point has to be fixed," I said, "it was the morning of the holdup."

"How about when somebody first thought it up?" my friend offered.

"Okay," I allowed. "When Colin Walker and or Charlie Novak decided that they would be sitting on a fortune and would be crazy not to try taking it, let's call that the starting point."

"I suppose it would be logical to conclude that, but anybody that does is dead wrong," declared my friend.

"So I'm dead wrong, Clifford?"

"You are," he affirmed. "It was hatched in the brain of your beloved Alice. Charlie and Colin may have toyed with the idea of disappearing with the cash one day, but a staged holdup was something they could never have concocted."

Had this been a movie, the words might have tripped a crash of piano keys.

Clifford studied me for a reaction, fairy sure, but not one-hundred percent, so that I wouldn't be thrust into a rage and demand he recant this blasphemy.

"Where the hell did you get that idea?" I snapped, trying to sound angrier than I was. Actually, I didn't care what Alice had done.

"Charlie Novak," my friend replied with no hesitation, "Charlie Novak told me."

As he spoke, it seemed that the words themselves were composed of the smoke he exhaled.

"And you believed him?"

Clifford only nodded, again. Drawing hard on his cigar, he blew another enormous plume, this one directed at Chandelier's glass prisms so as to make patterned shadows on the walls of the room.

"I believed him," he said. "There was no reason for him to lie about it."

He processed more smoke and continued:

"They give me a lot of guard duty, believe it or not. I'm well liked, if not feared among the inmates because of this," he said, nodding toward the stump attached to his left shoulder, "there's more vets among them than you might imagine; also they assume that my first reaction to anything would be to shoot. Charlie Novak was one of my principal wards so to speak. I have a pretty good feel for the truth. We talked a lot and I have no doubt that he spoke it. He told me how Alice—your precious Alice—masterminded the whole thing. It wasn't very hard for someone like her to sell a scheme like that to the dolt she married, and Charlie of course, especially when she promised herself to Charlie in the bargain. She also told him who else to recruit: her cousin—your friend Bobby—whom he already knew slightly. Bobby was dating Cassy—sleeping with her anyway—and Cassy signed Ralph on, but the three of them were never to know that Alice had hatched the whole thing, and I don't think they do to this day. Ralph was itching to commit some new act of defiance against his old man at least once a week. He was looking—and get this—for some way to ape the decking you'd given this old man. Cassy was a lot like Ralph. Her father had just taken her car away. And—get this too, Sonny—he took it away partly because he'd been told she was making plays for you. And you never had the slightest idea. It's fair to say you inspired them both."

"A couple of nice Jewish kids," I mused, "like Loeb and Leopold. By the way Cliff, I supposed you related this to Max?"

"He called me as soon as he knew you were headed to Michigan City. He knew everything before you stepped off the train. And everything after that too. Ralph's office was bugged and his telephone tapped. I hope you're okay with that."

I was. As far as I was concerned Clifford had betrayed nobody. And it explained away so much of the uncanny genius I'd attributed to Max.

It occurred to me too, what it must have taken from Clifford having to speak this way about the Cassy whom he'd wanted so badly, the Cassy that was mine for the taking while he'd fought a war and lost an arm trying to prove he was worthy of her. And all of this was because of his bad skin. And he'd yet to cry foul about it while he watched the same kind of thing turn me into a hysterical infant. I had never felt quite as ashamed as I did at that moment. But there wasn't a thing I could do to change any of it.

"I guess that about rounds it out, I said finally.

"Actually," said my friend, "it doesn't."

"There's more?"

"There's more."

"Colin," said Clifford.

"Yes I know," I said. "Charlie Novak was replaced at the last minute by Casey's cousin who recognized her. When he did, Colin panicked and shot him, and Cassy shot Colin. Nobody was supposed to get hurt, but that last minute substitution left Colin and Ari dead, right? And there's more you say?"

"Yes."

"What?"

"Just this: Somebody was supposed to get hurt, to die in fact. Charlie Novak was to kill Colin Walker in the course of the robbery. If anybody was fated to die that day Colin was. When Charlie couldn't kill Colin, fate decreed Cassy be the unwitting executioner, she just never knew it." Clifford paused to let it all sink in while he drew several short puffs of smoke through which I could see flickers of satisfaction on his face. Then he went on:

"It placed Charlie Novak in a terrific position you see; he had the goods on everybody and could still deny having ever been involved. Of course, that had its limits. He could threaten to turn them in, but if he did, the money would be recovered and the reward might be a thousand or so, and worthless to a wanted man like Charlie would become. Ralph, Bobby, and Cassy were kids that could never stand up to two minutes of interrogation."

"The money," said Clifford, "was supposed to be divided five ways: between Colin, Charlie, Bobby, Cassy, and Ralph. With Colin dead, five shares became four. And finally, when it was over, and the money divided up, Charlie, and your beloved Alice, were to go away together. You saw Charlie Novak. It's hard to imagine him turning that kind of offer down. I doubt if he was going to divvy up the money anyway. He'd have done whatever it took to get it all."

The vision of Charlie Novak and Alice seemed as laughable as it was nauseating, but it more than explained him turning up at her place once he'd broken out.

"You're telling me he believed that he could have Alice?" That human flotsam Clifford's magnificent rifle shot had obliterated right in front of me, believed he (it) could have Alice?

"He believed it," said my friend, "because he wanted to believe it. What do you think the two of us have been doing for the last twenty years if not believing we could have what we never could because we refused to believe otherwise?"

I looked away from him trying to focus on something in the room that might dull the sharpness of what he had just said. I had never heard the thing I'd refused to consider put better than that terrible assembly of words that cut through brain tissue like a circular saw. Nobody could tell me that I couldn't have Alice, not even Alice herself, maybe especially not Alice.

My friend went on: "When Charlie sought to collect on the bargain, that is for Alice to run away with him, she refused on the grounds of something she'd known all along, namely that he was married. Also, what would they live on? The money, as it turns out, was too hot to spend, and the serial numbers had been recorded."

Smiling, Clifford shook his head. "The first problem, Charlie's wife, was no problem. He promptly murdered her. It was his first murder, a sloppy one with tons of evidence. At the time, he refused to believe that it was Alice who leaked it to the police and forced him to make a hasty exit. He might have died tonight still trying to convince himself that Alice hadn't ratted on him." My friend shook his head.

"Charlie told me that he now believed that Alice must have had a lover waiting in the wings, and that she meant to have him done away with, maybe by the unnamed lover. But not even a killer like the one Charlie would become could bring himself to hurt Alice even if he were sure, which he wasn't. Once on the lam, he launched the career that made him famous, never fearing for a minute that he could be screwed out of his share of the money knowing what he knew. The money was too hot to be disposed of then, and it's even hotter today than it was when they took it. Seeing that it's all silver certificates, it's fucking radioactive. Of course, Max could have easily fenced the money for them, but he wasn't in the picture until a week ago."

"What about Felix?" I asked.

"Yeah, Felix," said Clifford, "There's a piece of work for you. Ralph and Charlie had been in constant communication for the whole twenty years, both face to face and by telephone. Remember, Ralph was never under suspicion for anything so there was little danger that his phone was tapped. When Charlie heard how Felix had forced himself in, he was so angry with Ralph and Bobby that he took matters into his own hands and came to Michigan City to silence Felix. He got pinched for running a red light by a sharp-eyed cop who realized who he was. That was in September.

A silence lasting what seemed a block of minutes followed. Clifford's cigar had long burned past mid length, and he drew on it in short puffs a few seconds apart.

"Now," he said finally, "tell me about Barstow."

"Barstow?"

"Remember telling Cassy how you two would always have Barstow? I want to hear about Barstow."

I never expected that coming home to roost, but, of course, Cliff had been right there when I said, "we'll always have Barstow."

"Do you have any beer?" I asked trying to forestall the subject.

Clifford rose and vanished through a dark doorway. A light went briefly two rooms away. He returned with a twelve-bottle carton cradled under his one arm that he set in front of my feet. He ripped it open, handed me one, took one for himself, and opened it with a one handed trick that I didn't quite catch.

Seating himself, and again facing me, he said simply, "Barstow."

"There's not much to tell," I said.

"Whatever there is to it," Clifford snapped, half smiling, "I want to hear about it."

So I told my friend about Barstow, about Frank DelMagio, about Paul Phengston's odyssey, the bloodbath we'd found there, and finally how I'd rigged the house on Yucca to blow up, and finally about how the Mulligans had become the late Mulligans.

Clifford listened intently. Stubbing out one cigar, he unwrapped a fresh one, ignited it, and drew continuously until a huge smokey drum enveloped him. When it finally melted into the carpet he said, "I knew Paul Phengston. He was a little older than us, and a very good man."

"So he seemed," I agreed, "from the little I could gather. I would hardly call him a thief anyway for stealing that car from Ralph. As a matter of fact, I don't think there can be such a thing as a crime against Ralph Falonhurst," and adding obtusely, "I don't suppose you ever met Phengston's wife?"

"He shook his head. "I didn't know he was married," said Clifford, "much less to a colored girl."

I was trying to get angry at Alice for having unleashed this maelstrom. It was true that most of the people who had died in it were of little value, and some were a definite liability to the planet. But clearly, Paul Phengston had not deserved to die. Still, anger at Alice was an exercise in futility. I couldn't have cared less what she'd done, were it hatching up the heist, or having the currency bands sent. I wanted Alice as much or more than ever.

And had there been no heist, the *Mulholland Rocket* would not have been where it was for the Phengstons to steal. And had it not been, they might not have survived that night twenty years before. The heist Alice dreamed up had placed it there. Subtract one piece of the equation and the whole thing, like life, becomes an orgy of wild cards.

I was suddenly tired, already slipping into a half sleep, when I said something I thought hardly worth the air it took to make the words:

"Funny," I said. "The whole mess had festered in a kind of equilibrium for twenty years until Alice had those bands sent to Ralph from California. That's what really set it all in motion."

"What?" exclaimed Clifford.

"For some reason," I went on, "Alice had some bands made just like the ones the stolen money was bound in. She had them sent to Ralph from California. The first of them arrived last October, about a month after Charlie Novak was taken into custody. I thought she'd first learned about the hold up from Charlie then." I exhaled a short laugh through my nose. "Alice denies doing it, but it had to have been her. For some reason, she decided to stir the pot, maybe to amuse herself. A few months later, Ralph saw a shot of the *Mulholland Rocket* in a car magazine, knew from the context of the picture that it was taken in California, and connected the bands with the car and a blackmail scheme formed up in his imagination. Actually there was no scheme and no connection between the bands and the car at all.

"Alice still denies sending them," I added yawning. "Funny, I never figured her for a liar." I said this sitting with my head already tilted forward and my eyes closed. I'd surrendered any hope of staying awake when seven words crashed through the fog:

"She's not lying," insisted my friend. "I had them sent."

"You what?"

"I had them sent, Sonny. It was me."

"What the fuck for, Cliff?" There wasn't a trace of sleep in me now. I almost said "What the fuck for, Cliff?" a second time when my friend gave me the answer that should have been all too obvious:

"I was reaching out to Cassy," he said, "or at least trying to. I'd been looking for her since I came into Granddad's money. No luck. I didn't know her married name or that she was living in California or anything at all about the *Mulholland Rocket*. Ironic, isn't it? You can't believe how many dead ends and cold trails I followed. For a time I thought she might be dead or living abroad. Only when I got the job of guarding Charlie Novak did I find out what we all know now, although he didn't know where Cassy was either. So I had the bands made up and sent to Ralph. A good friend of mine tapped his telephone for me. I thought that the bands would make him get in touch with Cassy, and it did work on the third try. That's when I heard her voice for the first time in more than sixteen years. I don't have to tell you what that was like, do I?"

No, he didn't. Nor did I have to wonder why he didn't just ask Ralph if he knew where Cassy was. I knew the answer. He was just too embarrassed to make the inquiry, having once placed Cassy so far above himself—and that had been before he was maimed—that he probably feared Ralph would laugh at him. The bands and the taped telephone were the kind of things I would have come up with.

Clifford set his cigar in the free standing ash tray alongside his chair and took a long hit off a freshly opened bottle of beer only to hurl it back in a convulsive coughing shower that covered him. He tried to set his beer on the floor. It toppled off the edge of a rug and its contents spilled.

"Oh God, Sonny," he said, trying to cover his face with one hand, "I killed those people. If I hadn't sent the bands none of this would have happened!"

I tried putting together a denial, something that would prove that what Clifford said wasn't true. But it was no use. It was true, at least as far as it went. The mailing of the bands had set it all in motion. And Clifford had sent them. In accusing Alice of touching off the mayhem, I had in fact accused my friend, and there was no undoing it. But I had to try. I got up and began walking toward him, but he waived me off, buried his face in his one hand, and began to shake and sob. I was suddenly furious. I'd really had enough. I advanced to Clifford's chair, stood over him, and all but shouted:

"Listen here, Cliff. You didn't kill anybody. And nobody died, that is, that didn't need to, and some of them needed it very badly, I might add. You saved my life not once, but twice tonight, and once more last week when you sprung me from jail. You put your life on the line for this fat, dumb country of ours when I moved heaven and earth to avoid it. I'm ready to kick the living shit out of anybody that doesn't call you a hero."

"Paul Pfengston," he sobbed.

"I have no idea who killed Paul Phengston or Frank Delmagio," I was shouting now. "Nobody does. It may not have been connected to us or the bands or to anything at all." I tried to tell myself that it was true.

"The Mulligan bitch took a shot at me and nailed her husband instead," I went on. "If I'd sent those bands I wouldn't lose a minute of sleep over it. And if Max had sent them he'd be laughing himself sick right now."

None of it registered.

Clifford Fitch was a man gripped by a conscience reserved for the rarest of tortured souls.

Finally, I said: "You would make a great Nun, Cliff. They never stop accusing themselves of all kinds of shit."

He looked up at me. "You're Jewish aren't you, Addison? What's that like?"

"It's the greatest thing in the world, Clifford; we're the crown Jewel of the white race." I actually believe I'd said that line I'd stolen from Max with a straight face.

"Could I become one?" he asked. Now this worried me. Clifford's question might mean that he had really lost it. I wondered if he was now constructing a new scenario with an oblique path to Cassy at its core. Cassy's first husband had been a Baptist.

"Sure, Cliff," I said. "All you have to do is study the Old Testament for about eight years and then take a battery of tests and have your cock clipped…if it hasn't been done yet."

"It hasn't," he said.

"It hasn't? Then you're in for a rare treat. Okay," I said, beginning to laugh. "We go to plan B; it's a little simpler."

"Plan B?"

"Plan B," I affirmed. "I'll convert you tonight for $29.50, cash only though, and no receipt. You have to trust me. You'll get a certificate in the mail in ten days along with a deluxe yarmulke, the kind with a propeller. The Israeli Air Force cadets wear them. Next week the price goes back to $33.95."

We stared at each other and then he burst into a wild wonderful laugh. I felt like I'd done my first useful thing in years. Cracking open fresh bottles, we drank them down and were soon asleep. The shower would have to wait for the morning.

We awoke to ringing blasts of a large black telephone on a table directly opposite us on the far side of the parlor. Clifford answered it on the forth ring.

"Yes he is," said Clifford, listening intently, and finally saying "Okay." He hung up.

"Max?" I asked. It was a silly question. Cliff nodded while walking back toward me. "He didn't want to talk to me?'

"No."

"What did he say?"

"That it would be a good idea for you to be on the 5:34 Eastbound out of Eleventh Street. Leave the Chrysler in the parking lot and dispose of the keys later when you're miles away. Max says they're copies."

"What time is it, Cliff?" He looked at his watch: "4:37."

I gave off a groan. "Did the son-of-a-bitch happen to say why he had to cut it so close?"

My friend nodded again. "He said if he gave you anymore time than that, you'd be back groveling before that bucktoothed baroness of Fairburn Avenue, the one that called him a 'troll.'" Max *had* bugged Alice's place.

We broke into wonderful laughter for the second time that morning. That was our goodbye; there wasn't time for a shower, or anything more than a change of clothes. When I dropped the robe in a heap, its inside was blood soaked. Clifford tossed me the keys and pointed at the door. I stepped outside into the dark, damp chill of an April morning and turned about to face the one true friend I had for what I was sure to be the last time.

"Thanks Cliff," I said, "for everything."

"You're welcome, and cheer up. You'll always have Barstow."

I had the Chrysler's door open and one foot inside it when I heard the single crack of gunfire coming from the parlor.

I shut the door and was half way back to the great house before realizing that there wasn't a thing I could do for my friend. He couldn't have botched that. Not Clifford.

43. THE MORNING EASTBOUND

In the spring of 1980, the South Shore Station at Eleventh and Franklin still opened at 5:00 AM, one hour after the first train—a Westbound from South Bend to Chicago—stopped in front of it. It was to the wheels of that Westbound that Jerret Traff had been fed a week before. An hour and a half later, the first Eastbound—a train never more than three cars long—rolled out of the South Shore Yard headed west for a short trip to Eleventh and Franklin, picked up passengers, and reversed course for the Amtrak station at South Bend. The full-length trains from Chicago came through later.

I left the Chrysler in the lot where—and maybe exactly where—Cassy and I had been parked in her rental a week before. There were three cars in the lot besides mine. One of them was a blue Cadillac Seville, this one with blacked-out windows. It reminded me of the Mustang. I had no doubt that it was supposed to.

I slipped the Chrysler's keys into my pocket, and walked a wide arc around the Southeast corner of the station so as to avoid the possibility of a blind corner ambush. It was another of Max Morgenstern's habits I'd picked up from observing him. It was raining when I entered the waiting room, and a clock on north wall read 5:27.

At the bank of lockers, I reached into my trousers and retrieved the key to number 44 that held the cash Lola had given me. I had no trouble slipping it into the lock, but when I tried twisting it, I found I couldn't. It took everything I had to fight off a panic. After several brute-force attempts at turning the key, I yanked my pockets inside out and a storm of change scattered on the floor. A second key was not among the coins.

In a desperate flashback, I remembered that the keys had been knocked from the counter in Alice's bathroom, then picked up and replaced where they had been by Max. I pulled the key from the lock and looked for the number 44 on it. It wasn't there. In an instant, I was hemorrhaging sweat. Could there have been a similar key on the floor that Max had mistaken for the one to the locker? That might have been possible with anyone else, but with Max it wasn't. What the hell had he intended with this stunt? I could hear the muffled hoots from an approaching train.

The way out was as simple as it was obvious. The Chrysler's trunk probably contained a small arsenal. It was Max's car after all, wasn't it? This Clifford had reminded me in the parking lot of the marina.

I would shoot off the lock, grab the cash—it was mine anyway— dash out with my money, and escape in the Chrysler. Forget being on the 5:34 and, for once, forget obeying Max. He might have intended this anyway. I didn't bother asking myself why.

Seconds later I unlocked and lifted the trunk lid only to be struck dumb at the sight inside: there were guns all right: two rifles, a pair of automatics, a revolver, and the long barreled air pistol that Clifford had used to detonate the bomb in the *Citroën*. So too was there money, a lot of it. It was grouped in fifteen bundles wrapped in deteriorated paper, sufficiently gone from enough of them to leave no doubt what I was looking at. Each bundle contained twenty bricks of cash five rows wide and five high. It was the bricks that were bound by the infamous blue bands…the real ones.

Max had to rub my nose in it one more time. The mission to Snug Harbor to "keep Ralph from escaping with the cash" was either for his personal amusement or Max could have known Felix was going to deep-six Ralph and Cassy, and actually decided to send Clifford and me to rescue them and dispose of Felix. He'd reached Michigan City the day before Cassy and I which gave him more than enough time to snatch the money from the boat and set up whatever else he'd planned. No wonder he wanted us to leave hours behind him and not arrive until the next day.

With Clifford dead, I'd never know the answer. He was the one person that wouldn't lie to me. But he hadn't told me everything either.

Clifford had known that the money was in the Chrysler the whole time. He'd seen what I was now looking at when he'd opened the trunk at the harbor and hadn't as much as flinched. He may have helped Max put it there.

I selected one of the automatics from the arsenal to shoot my way into the locker.

"Maybe," a voice from behind me said, "you would like to try this one instead—just a thought."

Max, probably watching from the Seville, had meant for me to jump a couple of inches at the sound of Woody Kilbourn's voice, but I didn't.

A hand extended a key with "44" stamped on it. I spun about, and the gorgeous face of Woody Kilbourn looked back at me. It was the Woody I remembered, that with Max, had run the crusade to right all things wrong with the world of our youth, the world that had cheated me out of Alice.

Gone were the broken teeth bathed in frothy saliva. Gone too, the scars I'd thought forever etched by slashes and burns on the once beautiful cripple that was beautiful still and a cripple no more. That science, too late to save Woody Kilbourn thirty years before, had come back to make amends. Seeing that alone almost made up for everything—almost. What had it taken to produce the apparition that had presented itself to us at Flagstaff and forced us to take it along? That had been a pure Max production and Max had never done anything other than at full tilt.

"Is the son-of-a-bitch in there?" I said, pointing at the blue Seville. Its blackened windows made it impossible to see anyone inside. Woody shrugged. I flipped a one-finger salute at the Seville anyway, sure that the son-of-a-bitch was in it, once again laughing himself sick.

"Uh," said Woody, "these are advised as well," he said, handing over a pair of acrylic gloves. There was no point in demanding answers nor was there time. I put them on.

Back in the Station, I opened the locker and reached for the contents. It was not what I'd put in there one week before. The case containing the fifteen thousand had been replaced with one with twice the dimensions of the one I'd left. It lay sideways. I pulled it out and was almost dragged to the floor by the unexpected weight. I turned to Woody.

"What's in it?"

"Payment on a debt," he replied. "And remember to keep the gloves on. "You'll need this too." He extended an envelope to me. In it was a one-way ticket from Michigan City to South Bend.

"Get off at Hudson Lake, there's a red '68 Ford Wagon in the parking lot, south side of the tracks. Keys are under the mat. By the way, ride in the last coach."

Max was obviously not done with me. A three-coach train set had eased to a halt in front of the station, its air horns still offering muffled hoots in the dark. There was nothing to do but get aboard.

"So long, General," I said.

"So long Legionnaire," he replied, his tone a pleasant blend of wit, sarcasm, and perhaps irony, "it was nice to see you again after all these years."

I thought of saying something about getting together again sometime, but didn't. It would never happen unless Max ordained it.

The coaches had already begun moving when I bolted aboard the last and longest of them: an ancient Pullman that bore the number "14" in gold leaf on the vestibule door. But for me, number "14" was empty, and that had probably been intended since it had been west of Franklin when the train was stopped. No lights were on inside.

It was too late for a last look at *The Glass Dragonfly* when I crash-landed into a window seat. I did just barely manage a decent glimpse of the house where we once lived thanks to someone's forgetting to turn off the porch light.

An irritated conductor punched my ticket, while mumbling that I was not supposed to have been on this coach.

"Why? I snapped. "Where's it going the rest of the train isn't?" He tossed the punched ticket on the seat beside me and left the car mumbling a little louder.

It's a short roll Eastward from Eleventh and Franklin to the stop at Carrol Avenue. With the suitcase on my lap tilted to support my chin, I was nodding off in dots and dashes.

Carrol Avenue had come and gone when I was awakened by the scent of *Eternal*, the cologne that mimicked secretions of the deceased. I'd smelled it on but one person before now.

"Good morning, Ralph," I said, my eyes still shut, "fancy meeting you here."

"Yes," he replied, "Fancy."

"How was your trip?"

"Short," the reply came. "And don't, worry Cassy is fine. I'd never hurt her."

Knowing that he wouldn't, I hadn't worried.

"Nice of you not to try to kill her along with the rest of us, Ralph," I said.

I opened my eyes and turned to him. Ralph hadn't changed his clothes; they were in tatters. With the beginning of daylight, he looked far worse than he had on the boat. There were cuts on his face that had yet to be dressed or even washed. His arms were a gallery of abrasions. It was obvious he hadn't slept, washed, or rinsed his mouth since the beating the late Felix had given him.

"Where's the boat?" I asked.

"We sank it and came ashore in the inflatable."

That was a good idea. The boat carried enough evidence to put us all away.

"Was Felix in it?" I asked, genuinely curious.

"No," Ralph replied, "we put him overboard miles from there. Give me a little credit."

I didn't ask whether they weighted him down or just set him adrift. "And that was after you found the money was gone?"

He nodded, "Your friend did a great job, leaving dummy bundles that made it look like the cash had never been touched. Incidentally, what happened to Bobby?"

I didn't know and said so, but remembered that, among other things, Bobby was once a jock and how much Max had really hated jocks, declaring uncountable times that they were "animal puke." That Max would know this about Bobby was something I could take to the bank.

"Ralph," I said, go home and forget the whole thing, nobody is going to talk; after twenty years you're a free man."

"Randy will talk," he said, "she knows everything now."

"Ralph, she always knew. She planned the robbery in the first place. Clifford told me that an hour ago. He's dead incidentally. Ralph, you're out of your league, go home and quit while you're ahead."

I expected some kind of reaction to the news of Clifford, but it seemed that Ralph was either incapable of digesting it, or more likely didn't give a shit.

"Incidentally, Ralph, how did you know I'd be on this train?"

"Cassy told me."

"She what?" Until an hour before, I hadn't known myself. Then I smiled. There was but one explanation. By some means that I couldn't imagine, Max had managed to feed Ralph that information through Cassy. The poor son-of-a-bitch still had no idea who he was up against.

Just then I felt a small cold circular impression in my left side just below the rib cage.

"I'll be taking that, Addison," he said matter-of-factly. I had momentarily forgotten that just eight hours before, and after I'd saved his life, Ralph had reciprocated by trying to blow me to bits.

"It's all yours, Ralph," I replied, fearful that in his condition, a quick motion might cause him to fire, "so please put the artillery away before somebody gets hurt, namely me." It was quite plain now that Max had meant whatever was in the suitcase to be for Ralph. I'd been demoted to delivery boy.

Ralph reached for the handle and in doing so dropped the .32 to the floor. It was the one Max had given me. When he reached for it, I stomped down hard on his hand hoping to break something. He recoiled with a yelp.

"Get the fuck out of here, Ralph," I said.

With both hands, Ralph ripped the case from me and made for a seat several rows toward the rear of the car. He had apparently not noticed I was wearing gloves. We were well out of Michigan City now, having accelerated to a considerable clip, when I was suddenly aware that my lap and legs were wet. I looked at them. They were covered with fresh blood. I could hear the latches to the case being snapped open far behind me in the empty coach. I waited and wondered.

It was a short wait.

A howl of horror went up, followed by a thumping splash that had to be the case and its contents spilling on the floor. I waited for Ralph's reaction to whatever he'd seen to subside. It never did. It only jumped a few octaves to become a wail that went on long enough to exhaust every last trace of air he could have had in him. Only then did Ralph draw in long gasps, gag, and begin to puke.

I picked up the gun, stood, spun about, and walked towards him.

Max's piece de résistance lay in the aisle of the coach floor: the case was split open in the middle laying face down, and sitting half atop the upper third of Bobby Dardinelle, which had obviously been inside it. The head was intact, the face still easily identified, though bathed in blood, and the hair caked by hardened scab-like clots that formed something resembling irregular cornrows. The arms were outstretched as if still reaching for some means of escape. A torn sleeve covered one of them and a Rolex watch was still on the other.

Max might have left the Rolex for me as a souvenir. The rest of Bobby ended just below his nipples where he'd been sawn from his lower two thirds. Part of a large organ—probably his liver—swelled just below the cut line. Half a heart, some arteries, and other pipes still oozing fluids hung among entrails framed by portions of a rib cage. All of it rested in a pool that I guessed by its color to be mostly blood, but couldn't have been one hundred percent of any one thing. Bobby had become the Texas Ranger from a week before that he'd helped throw under a train.

Ralph was crouched on the floor hurling successive waves of vomit mixed with blood from the beating he'd taken from Felix. Suddenly, feeling irrationally sorry for him, I put my hand on his shoulder and patted it gently. He continued to wretch, unaware of me. I wondered why the sight should so spook him. I had thought they routinely took people apart in medical schools.

"C'mon, Ralph," I said finally. "It's not as bad as all that." They were the exact words I'd said to him twenty-two years before when he'd come to me with the *Mulholland Rocket* and its destroyed engine.

"C'mon, Ralph," I said, grabbing Bobby's left hand, "we'll just throw him out the back door. "You take the case, and I'll drag him. You can pick up any pieces that fall out of him, put those in the case, and out he goes. When they find him, they'll think trains did it, especially if a few roll over him."

Ralph crouched almost into a fetal ball. Having thrown up the last loose morsel in him, he'd lapsed into a convulsive continuum of groans and belches. I shrugged and dragged Bobby to the rear door of coach number 14 using his Rolex arm. I found the door to the outside unlocked and pulled it open and watched the gleaming rails being pumped out behind us. The light rain had become torrential. For a couple of seconds, I considered taking Bobby's watch but heaved him overboard still wearing it. In seconds, he vanished into sheets of rain. Then I hurled the .32 I'd retrieved from the floor as far as I could into the underbrush, hoping the first to find it would be archeologists.

I walked back to Ralph who was still crouched, gratefully noting that Bobby hadn't left much solid debris in the aisle, just fluids and goo. I retrieved the case, threw it out the back of the train and returned once again to Ralph. Once more, I tapped his shoulder and waited for a reaction.

This time there was one. He lifted his head to face me. Its colors varied from pale orchid on his forehead to chartreuse around his mouth with a dark and clearly defined band the color of a blood blister that divided his face horizontally in line with his nostrils. There was no describing the expression on it. Terror, horror, or fear wouldn't begin to. Neither the face nor words could do each other justice.

He grabbed my shirt, wiped his face in it, and began to bawl hysterically. It was the one thing I could understand since I'd done it six hours before when I knew for certain that I could never have Alice. But his cry differed. It was a grinding wail that must have ripped at his throat like a rotary rasp. Finally, he looked up at me.

"I'm sorry, Addison," he balled. "I'm so fucking sorry." His grip on my shirt bit at the back of my neck. "I'm so fucking sorry," he repeated, still bleeding from his mouth. "It was their idea to wire the Citroën."

Yeah, right, and he'd tossed me the keys. He'd tried to kill me at least three times in the previous week, had failed each time, and minutes before was ready to kill me over what was in the suitcase, the loser. I almost pitied him for his incompetence and wondered if I wasn't losing it myself. Finally, I slapped him.

"Forget it, Ralph," I said.

"Don't let them hurt me," he wailed.

"Who Ralph? Nobody's going to hurt you. I told you, it's over."

He shook his head, "Don't let them do that to me Sonny, please, Sonny."

"Don't let who do what?"

"Your friends," he balled, and pointed to a pool of goo on the floor.

"Listen to me, Ralph," I said, "it's over; we're done with you. Go home, get drunk, take a shower and get some sleep. You're never going to hear from us again."

Ralph just shook his head. Either he hadn't heard me or didn't believe me. He was convinced he was next in line for what Bobby had gotten.

I tried to pat his shoulder—a mistake. He recoiled as if my hand was connected to a magneto. Then, looking wide eyed at me, he began to shake like a paint mixer. Finally, he shot straight into the air above the seat, landed standing on it, and with one quick bolt, leaped over me and ran down the aisle to the back door. The impact of his shoes on the floor made the fluids—all that was left of Bobby—splash on the seat cushions of coach number 14. Ralph tugged at the door, that for some reason, refused to give for several seconds. I raced after him and reached him just as it gave. He turned, and we faced each other. He was unrecognizable. Behind us, the rain had diminished only slightly. For a moment, I thought that Ralph was going to leap into an eighty-mile-an-hour death roll in the train's wake.

But he didn't.

Ralph seemed almost suspended in space until I realized he was holding an outside grab bar. His shoes clawed and skidded on the wet riveted steel end of coach number fourteen. After calling out his name four times I gave up.

Ralph's feet had found a perch on the outside window ledge. I wondered where he'd go from there and had my answer before I could form a guess. Ralph had seized on something above us that I could neither see nor imagine, but something must have been there because he continued to climb. I stepped onto the ledge of the car holding the same bar Ralph had hung from. Except for the quick glimpse of a shoe above me, Ralph was gone. He'd made it to the roof of the train, still trying to get away from me. I pictured him staggering across the rain-soaked top of the coach knowing what would happen when he grabbed on the only thing that could keep him from sliding off: a steel pantograph with fifteen-hundred volts surging through it, each of them looking for the shortest path through the wet to the rails below. There was a muffled crack and a fireball with writhing arms still attached, that danced in space above me before tumbling end over end to the tracks. Other pieces of him followed it, the largest of them, the burnt lower half of a leg; the shoe still in place landed on my shoulder, only to topple off and join the rest of Ralph on the tracks. Then a brief cascade of hot fluids splashed on me through which I could still make out the scent of that God-awful cologne.

Gripping the bar, I hung as far as I could into the downpour, and only when I was sure I'd been douched as clean as I thought possible, did I step back into the coach and shut the door. We were slowing down. I headed for the forward vestibule. A conductor, his back facing me, stood there having announced the stop at Hudson Lake. I turned away hoping to avoid his catching a full image of my face. He walked behind and past me, surveyed the interior of coach number 14, then turned around.

"Well, Dillinger," he said, "it looks like that for once you got something right. Congratulations."

44. IN THE DAMNDEST OF PLACES

The red Ford station wagon was exactly what I'd expected Max to serve up for my departure.

Its hood and roof were a massive tangle of dents that defined a dozen pools of captured water. The fenders hung like tattered rusted metal rags ending in jagged lines at the bottom from which water ran like streams of clear urine. The doors behind them, and the quarter panels behind the doors, were variations on this theme, and the chrome trim where it still existed was smashed flat as if crushed over an anvil. There were no hubcaps, and I doubted that any one tire had much in common with the others with the exception of being somewhat round.

The lead edge of the driver's door bound against the fender when I tried opening it, and took several heavy heal kicks on the latter to break it free. I plopped into the seat and flinched at the realization that I wasn't alone. Beside me, Cassy sat groomed to perfection and smiling, the now familiar cigarette in its black holder between the fingers of her right hand. If anything, she looked younger than she had a week before. As Max would say, "a beautiful bag of organs, if ever there was one." At least Ralph hadn't lied about not hurting her. Had he, I would have been surprised. Probably he'd only forced her to stay aboard so as to save her from what he'd planned for Clifford, Alice, and me.

Her eyebrows rose into gentle arcs. Exhaling smoke, she asked: "Can a lady get a lift to the airport? I'm going home."

"I envy you," I replied.

"Do you know where you're going?"

"I haven't the slightest idea, do you?"

She nodded.

"So you've spoken to Max?"

Another nod.

"Well?"

"Tonopah."

"Where?"

"Tonopah, Nevada. Max said to check in at the Mizapah Hotel. There's a reservation there for George Harry Taylor, your new name."

"Such originality."

She shrugged. "Your new ID," Cassy added, opening the glove compartment. She withdrew a worn three-leaf wallet and handed it to me. I slipped it into a trouser pocket. Besides being my new identity, it was my official membership in the Stern Gang.

"You're not going to look at it?"

I shook my head. If Max had made it, there would be no reason to.

"Then shall we go?"

I reached under the mat and found the keys just ahead of a sizable hole rusted through the floor. Were this car to remain parked another week, it would never move again. Besides, the one key needed to start it, there were ten others with no purpose at all on the ring, another Max barb.

I found one that looked like it fit the ignition, and did, though there was hardly a need for it. The lock was so worn that a screwdriver could have started that car.

The engine rumbled to life and settled to a coarse idle. I shifted the transmission into Drive. The car didn't move. I hit the gas and ten seconds later it suddenly lurched forward amid a chorus of clunks and mechanical groans.

When I stepped on the brake pedal, it nearly went to the floor. I turned to Cassy. "Aren't you going to ask me about Clifford?"

"Actually I was," she replied.

"No you weren't."

"Well, are you going to tell me or aren't you?"

"He's dead," I snapped. "We killed him."

"What?"

"We killed him," I repeated.

"How the Hell did *we* do that?"

"You started it by sleeping with him back in 1963."

"I've slept with men before him, and many more since," she freely acknowledged, her voice in full anger mode. "One died of a heart attack two hours later, but that's it. Are you telling me I killed every man I ever slept with?"

"No, but between us, we killed Clifford."

"You're out of your mind."

"You slept with him and gave him a taste of something he never imagined could exist for him and then you pulled the plug the next day. After that, he went to Vietnam trying to prove himself worthy of you and we know what happened there. And after he saves my precious ass once last week and twice tonight, I had to show him I could have you just for the asking. *We'll always have Barstow*," I mused in disgust. "I really rubbed his nose in that one: *Barstow*." He was the best friend I ever had and I killed him."

"No," Cassy said, "you were right the first time, we killed him. What about Bobby and Ralph?"

I drew in a deep breath and exhaled hard. "Most of what's left of them will be fertilizing whatever grows between the crossties of those tracks about five miles from here," I said pointing west. "The local flies and maggots are in for a real treat too, once the rain stops." I gestured to my well-stained shirt. "The rest of them I'm wearing."

"Well," said a familiar voice, "now that that's settled, I guess I can curse you both from the grave once I really am dead, which I hope won't be for some time." The pock-scarred face of my best friend rising above the seat back was the most beautiful sight I'd ever seen. I shook my head in joyous disbelief and said finally: "The gunshot, another blank?"

"No," Clifford replied, "there is a hole in the ceiling where he fired it. I'm not exactly thrilled about that. That plaster was about a hundred years old."

"He?" I asked, realizing before the word was out that by "he" Clifford could only have meant Max. "Was he in the next room while we spoke?"

"Two rooms away."

"He was there the whole time?"

Clifford nodded. There was nothing left to be said. I eased the car onto the highway and aimed it east for the South Bend airport.

But if there was nothing left to say, we said a lot of it nonstop in the forty-odd-minute drive on Route 20 to the airport. I suppose it had more to do with none of us having slept more than maybe three hours in the past twenty four as we rambled through a score of topics, the only one of which I can remember being how I'd stuck Lila Coincap with the "Pila Cowcrap" moniker that I'd been told had clung to her for two decades and still counting.

Though we meant to separate at the parking lot, I decided at the last minute to see Cassy all the way to the boarding gate. My clothes were nearly dry and the blood-stains might have passed for some really bizarre attempt at graphic design.

Only when both of them bought tickets for the same flight to San Francisco, did Cassy tell me that they meant to travel together for a while and see what happened.

The tickets purchased, Clifford conveniently made a side trip to the men's room. Alone for a moment with Cassy, I said: "Whatever you do baby, handle with care."

"I mean to," she replied, "for more reasons than you think, and don't imagine any of them are charity. He's better in bed than any man I've ever met." She paused smiling and added, "including you, Sonny."

"Really?" I said, trying to seem non-pulsed.

"Really," she affirmed. "He's got perfect TDM, and he won't be pining away in his sleep for the buck-toothed Baroness of Fairburn Avenue."

She had talked to Max, well of course she had. Cassy lit a cigarette, still smiling.

I'd heard women mention TDM before and had yet to ask what it meant. Now I had to know. "What's TDM?"

"You don't know?

"I'm asking, aren't I?"

"It's an index for measuring a man's performance in bed. TDM means Timing, Dimensional Attributes, and Muzzle Velocity. Need I explain any further?"

I shook my head.

"My God, you're crying," Cassy said, exhaling a deep draft of blue smoke. "Is that what finding out there's better lovers out there does to men?"

"I guess so."

"And hey! What the Hell are you staring at now? My crotch? Oh Jesus. You're staring at my crotch, Goddamn you!"

"I am not!" I protested, but I was, still remembering one of the first things Max had said to me almost twenty-one years before: *"when you thought there was no justice left in the world you will find it alive and well in the damnedest of places!"*

Clifford rejoined us looking at Cassy the way I was sure I'd looked at Alice.

"I'm parched," he announced. "There's a coffee bar on the far side of that wall, can I get anyone anything?

"Only if you'll let me buy," I replied producing a ten.

"You're on," said Clifford, and reaching for it he turned to Cassy. "What'll ya have?" asked my friend.

I shot Cassy a glance expecting the kind ironic smile born of inside jokes, but there wasn't a trace of one on her face. She was over me. And I couldn't have envied her more.

A short while later, I walked them to the boarding gate where Cassy offered me one final parting shot: "You know something, Sonny?" she said, "I really do hope you win her over. You two deserve each other."

At that, Cassy turned and walked away arm-in-arm with Clifford, a ray of daylight bouncing off the nearly horizontal line that defined the top of her glorious afterburners.

"When was the last time you saw Max?"

"Two days ago, but it was on my birthday, a month ago, that I told him I wanted to see you. I thought he would argue with me, but he just said he would need some time to make the arrangements. He called me two days ago, and had it all set up, even the rental car which I could never have gotten myself, being a minor."

"How is Max?"

"Well, now that you mention it, he looks terrible, I thought he looked bad a month ago, but now," she paused, "he might be dying…do you mind if I smoke?"

I said "no" in a resigned tone of disapproval.

She lit up, inhaled deeply, and blew out a dense blue cloud in one smooth practiced motion that suggested she'd been doing it a while.

"*Just great,*" I thought, "*thank you for nothing, Courtney—Courtney the wonder mom.*"

"And he gave me this for you," she said, producing an envelope from her purse that was about one size larger than the standard kind. I opened it with a quick ripping action and read:

"*Dillinger,*" it began. Max would never stop calling me the name he was so proud of sticking me with.

By the time you read this, I will likely be dead. Life has best been described as a train ride and all of us pathetic creatures mere passengers that get on and off at different stops. I haven't decided exactly when I'll get off, but it will be long before I have to wait writhing in my own muck for some uppity racial anomaly to change my bed sheets. Shiloh has probably told you what I looked like when she left to find you. There will be no record of my dying; I shall just disappear. I want certain people to think I'm alive and still about to strike at them from the shadows rather than them having any peace in knowing that I no longer can.

Soo…this is your official notice that the Stern Gang is dissolved and with it your need for any more masquerades. All records and charges relating to Addison July in the various criminal justice systems have been expunged right down to your fingerprints. You can take up your old name, and life, any time you like. This will be true for the rest of the "Gang," none of whom you know besides Woody.

In your case, it's the least I can do for somebody that gave me the best week of my life back in that April of 1980. I hadn't laughed so hard since they fried the Rosenbergs. Now…

There has been a trust set up that will pump funds into an account for 'Addison July' in the Bank of Houston. You will have to pay taxes on it, no getting around that.

I can't begin to think you will understand the reasons for the things I've done, but if you can, imagine me as someone that tried to purge this planet of liars, traitors, cowards, communists, sex deviates, exchange students, and legions of other flotsam that are passed off for human. I'm sorry I won't be around to see you screw up the rest of your life, but I've got a pretty good idea how that will go. Anyway, it would have been great entertainment.

A few final items, the first of them the carnage in Barstow:

If you thought I'd done it, you are half right. I killed Frank Delmagio. When I saw him outside the house on Yucca, it took me a minute to realize that he was a man I once defended on a manslaughter charge. I freed him easily of course, a minor challenge, though he was guilty as sin. Only after the acquittal did he confide in me things he'd done that made me tag him as 'Frank the Ripper.' He was one of those before-and-after types that rape women before and after he's killed them so as to make comparisons. He confided to me that he generally preferred a warm corpse.

Believe me when I tell you I looked for evidence for years to leak to the police but I never found a scrap. I cannot begin to imagine his body count. I knew he would kill whoever was inside the house and wait for you two to return. Had I recognized him half a minute before, I might have saved Paul Phengston, and not just the Beaver and you.

I don't know who blew up Victor Hernandez and his truck in Cairo, and that has driven me slightly crazy for the last decade. It's the one unresolved episode in that glorious week you gave me. I doubt it was Felix, Bobby, Ralph, or any combination of them. They were simply too incompetent, although they did manage to throw Jerret Traff under a train. Maybe he wasn't up to his reputation either. Victor did have enemies who might have tracked him to Cairo, in which case he died in